BLEARY EYES

A YA PARANORMAL HORROR

THE EYES
BOOK ONE

SUMMER RAIN

To Kate,
Thanks for being
an amazingly supportive friend!
I'm so glad to have met you
& the rest of the English club.

Summer Rain

For information about this title or to order other books and/or electronic media, contact the publisher:

Copyright © 2022 Summer Rain.

All rights reserved.

ISBN 979-8-88722-346-9

***

Summer Rain

writingbleary@authorsummerrain.com

www.authorsummerrain.com

Cover image and inner artworks by Miha Brumec.

Advertisements and title page design by Summer Rain.

Map image by Andrea Dalla Bona.

Symbol art by Makhiyo Trish Sy.

Interior Formatting by AB Book Services

To the four people, without whom this novel would not have been written.

To Robert K. McLean— for instilling in me a wonder of books and writing that never left. For making me believe in authors as supremely magical beings.

To Mollie R. Nicholson— for waking me up and reminding me that life doesn't wait, and neither should I. For leaving me to find myself.

To Xenøn H. Light— for being my Axel and Winter when Bleary loomed, the light in the dark corners of my mind. For saving me. For giving me purpose.

To Joleen S. Jones— for reminding me to breathe instead of suffocate, and seeing this through to the end. For continuing the journey by my side. For not leaving me alone.

Thank you all for being what I needed when I needed it most.

TRIGGER WARNING

RECOMMENDED PLAYLIST

Fairly Local - Twenty-One Pilots
PMA - All Time Low ft. Pale Waves
Forever Fifteen - Mothica
Redecorate - Twenty-One Pilots
Mind is a Prison - Alec Benjamin
One More Light - Linkin Park (Recommended: Amber Liu &
Gen Neo Cover)
The Anonymous Ones - Evan Hansen Soundtrack (Amandla
Stenberg)
The Hard Way - Pale Waves
The Devil Doesn't Bargain - Alec Benjamin
Darkside - Neoni
Running Up That Hill - Loveless
Hate Me - Layto
Don't Feel Quite Alright - Palaye Royale
Popular Monster - Falling in Reverse

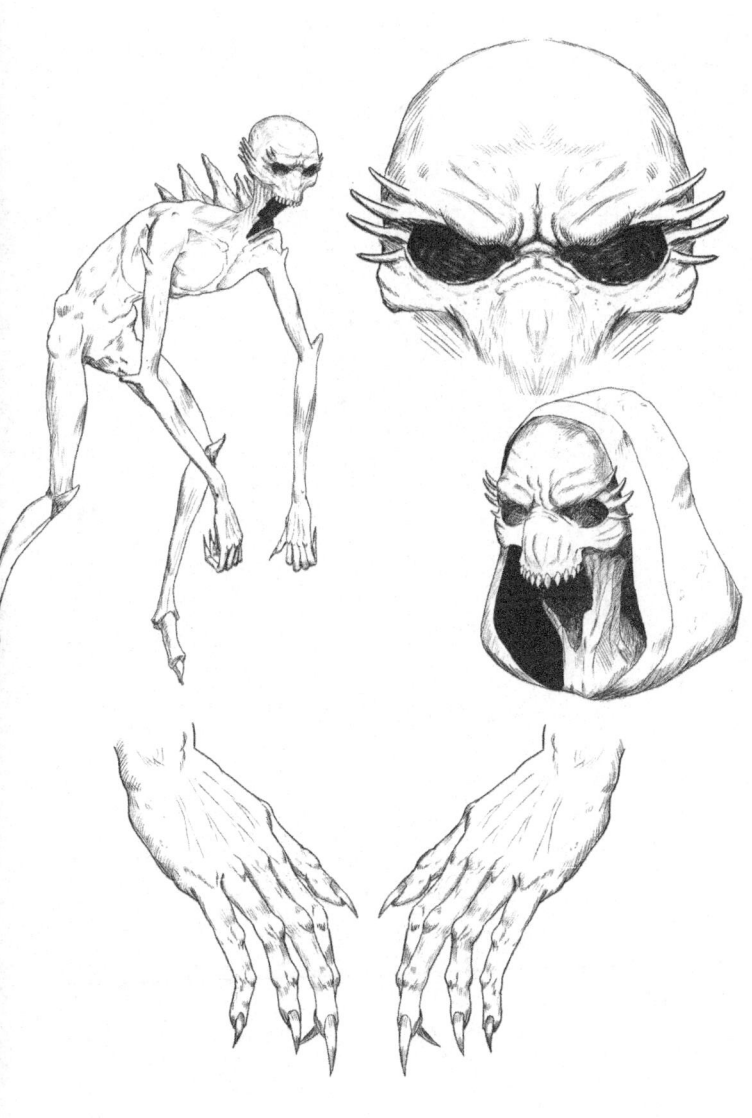

Blind anger hit Axel, his blood pumping as he grabbed a rock from the ground and chucked it at the monster, only to watch it bounce off the thing's back like an insignificant pebble. It didn't even turn its head, Axel staring daggers into its rounded gray skull.

Fight it, Winter, Axel thought desperately, turning his attention to his friend. *Don't believe whatever shit that thing is telling you, it's not true.*

As the seconds passed, he could see Winter's face growing paler, her body relaxing. She was losing.

That was it. Axel couldn't stand by anymore. If he did, he'd lose her— and if he lost her, he'd lose everything bright in the world. *His* monster would win. He'd spent the last few years of his life forcing himself to keep fighting it, he sure as hell wasn't going to let it win now. It had taken so much from him already. So many people… He wouldn't let it take anymore. True to form, he cared more about saving others than saving himself.

Looking down at the broken ground between them, he started to back up, several feet for a running start.

Oh hell, am I really doing this? He thought, swallowing his nerves.

Looking up, his eyes focused on Winter. She was the one he was taking the leap for...

So he started running.

UNWELCOME ATTENTION

Just another ordinary Monday at Clamare High. That was what Winter thought, anyway. It was the start of her junior year of high school, the cool air of September 1999 bringing with it a new start. Sliding out of her grandfather's truck, she bid him goodbye and joined the stream of students flooding into the school, walking past the statue of their school patron. Winter had never liked school, but not in the way most people would assume. It wasn't that she disliked the classwork, or the act of learning. She didn't even dislike tests and got above average grades.

Rather, it was the actual act of being there that got under her skin. The loud personalities, the constant feeling of being surrounded in halls full of people, suffocating crowds of students and peer pressure hanging overhead. Winter had never enjoyed this environment, exhausted each day by the time she left. She wasn't one for club activities, or after school parties, though she hung around for a few, preferring smaller groups or even just being on her own. School, for her, was a place where she didn't quite fit in anywhere. She merely floated like a butterfly, flitting from clique to clique but never truly tied to any single identity. It was anxiety inducing, even if she managed to act calm on the outside. It was safe to say that in the halls of this school, she was never truly herself.

Luckily, her locker that year happened to be right next to the locker of her best friend. Kaya Morito was a girl that could be compared to a pixie. Half Japanese, half Hawaiian, she was a tiny little thing with the smallest hips Winter had ever seen, and the skinniest arms. More than once, she'd longed to be like her best friend, who was a full seven inches shorter than Winter was.

"Hey, you've gone green. My favorite," Winter remarked, referencing Kaya's hair as she stopped beside her friend, pulling open her locker. Kaya had short, sleek black hair, but she often had several strands of color woven into it at any one time, the brighter the better. Today, it was a neon green, matching bright green contacts she had on behind black lined lids. Kaya was the queen of makeup— the most Winter ever managed was a bit of lipstick.

"You know it. New year, new color!" Kaya declared, looping an arm around Winter's waist to pull her into a one-armed hug. She wore bell bottom jeans and a denim jacket, pursuing the look of a fashion icon. "What do we have first?"

"Don't you have your schedule?" Winter asked, though she already knew the answer.

"Uh... Maybe?" Kaya fixed her with a sheepish smile. "I don't know... Might have left it at home." It never failed. Every year, they were given their school schedules at orientation in the summer, and every year, Kaya managed to not have hers by the time school started.

Fishing her own out of a stack of papers in her locker, Winter held it out to Kaya. "History first. Mrs. Dunn."

Kaya immediately made a face of disgust. "Oh, yikes. The

dragon lady. I hear if you get her infamous pop quizzes wrong, she eats you alive." She stuck her tongue out, earning a laugh from Winter.

"Come on, she's not that bad. She lives across from me. Definitely not a dragon lady, just another teacher." Winter defended her neighbor. Looking down the hall, her eyes scanned the lockers for a familiar head of black hair.

The Dunn family across the street was not one Winter knew particularly well. She knew Mrs. Dunn only by recognizing her as a teacher. Mr. Dunn was rarely home, though sometimes his car would come and leave from the house late at night, something Winter noticed when she couldn't sleep. The Dunns' had three sons, however, and they were the ones Winter saw the most. The older two, not so much anymore, but the youngest son was close in age to Winter. Only a year younger, if she was right, a sophomore.

Though she didn't know his name, he had started at the same high school as her last year. They shared a few classes, and his locker was a row down and across the way, within sight. He stood there now, wearing his signature black jeans and a black hoodie over a dark blue shirt. A small pair of Walkman headphones were tucked over pierced ears, bobbing his head to some type of music as he stood by his locker. Winter could see the resemblance to Mrs. Dunn— it wasn't hard to see her Japanese heritage in him, with his long angular face, large nose, plump lips, and monolid eyes. Though he certainly had unique irises; the brightest blues Winter had ever seen, framed with impossibly long lashes. They were beautiful. If she remembered right, the youngest of the Dunn boys was the only one to inherit the blue eyes from his father.

"You're staring at her son again," Kaya's voice dragged Winter from her thoughts.

"I draw him a lot," Winter mumbled the truth. She wasn't

thinking about how weird that sounded, until she pulled her gaze back to Kaya and saw her friend smirking. "Not that way! I just... He lives right across the street. Sits in the window a lot. His face is... angular."

"Righttt... Well, while you become a stalker..." Kaya teased her. They had been friends since they were eight years old, so all Winter did was roll her eyes in response.

Just then, a hand slammed Winter's open locker shut with a loud metallic clang, making both the girls jump as a taller figure loomed over them.

"Winter." It was Ian Bryars. Ian was one of the infamous jock stereotypes that roamed their small-town school. Captain of the football team, he prided himself on his car, his hair, and the fact he'd been held back a year and was an eighteen-year-old junior. He was over six feet tall, with slicked up brown hair that had frosted tips, and blue eyes. His eyes, Winter thought, weren't beautiful. They were eyes that made Winter wary, an icy gray blue, not meeting the smile he wore.

"Ian. Morning," Winter mumbled, offering up a tight smile.

"Kaya. Also here," Kaya interjected, waving a hand when Ian spared her a glance.

His attention almost immediately was back on Winter. "I gave you my number, you never called."

His eyes looked her up and down, taking her in. Winter wasn't the most fashionable person, but she liked dresses, so that was what she wore: a mid-sleeve brown turtleneck dress that clung to her form with a small golden belt around her waist. Her brown hair was loose and fell in long waves over her shoulders, blonde highlights running through it that she had put in for the new school year. Her necklace, unlike her belt, was in silver, not gold. It was a single silver pendant, a flat disk with snakes curling around a Celtic pattern, hanging on a black cord. Winter was never seen without that necklace; she never took it off. It had once belonged to her mother.

Winter would never have called herself pretty but that didn't mean she wasn't. The truth of it was that she had pretty features, but she was different. Average. She was tall and curvy, with a larger bust than she would have liked—something that drove her crazy because of attention she didn't want. She felt broad and awkward, and overly noticeable in the wrong sort of way, as if she were clumsy and in a room full of fragile glass ornaments. She certainly didn't associate herself with the word pretty, and she was certain it wasn't her heart-shaped face, or her hazel-green eyes, that Ian Bryars was interested in.

When his eyes rose back to her face, she finally answered him.

"We finished your tutoring sessions. Why would I have called?" She said it as politely as she could, feigning a sweet smile.

"You know why," Ian answered, giving her a big, toothy grin. He glanced at Kaya again, who was staring him down, and sighed. "Hey, Kaya, do you mind giving us a minute?"

"Yeah, actually, I do mind—" Kaya started to step forward, until Winter set a hand on her shoulder, looking her best friend in the eyes.

"It's fine. Save me a seat in class, I won't be long," Winter implored her, giving a nod to let her know it was okay.

It took a very long look from her friend to make sure, but then Kaya pointed a finger right at Ian, fixing her stare on him.

"You behave." She warned him.

Ian gave her a little salute.

"Scout's honor, sweetheart," he remarked with a cheeky wink.

Kaya looked less than impressed, but with a final glance towards Winter, she grabbed the rest of her books from her locker, slammed it shut, and set off down the hall. She briefly stopped by the youngest Dunn boy, saying something to him that made him lower his headphones, blue eyes flashing Winter's way.

Ian, however, was determined to hold her attention. He set a hand on her shoulder, giving her another grin.

"Now that we're alone... Didn't you enjoy the summer? There's nothing keeping me from helping you enjoy the fall, too."

Winter was sure that she was remembering the summer far differently than Ian Bryars was. She was remembering uncomfortable afternoons of his arm creeping over the back of a couch, aiming lower than her shoulder as he leaned in close. Every time she brought up the literature they were supposed to be studying, he would try to change the subject — aggravating her to no end until the hour was up, and she could usher him out the door.

Honestly, she didn't know where the sudden interest came from. Ian had gone to the same school as her ever since she enrolled in the first grade at seven years old. She had known him even longer than she had Kaya. He had once been her most ardent bully, calling her piggy and tugging her hair in class, making pig snorting noises when she walked past him. Now, he seemed to have changed his tune, and considering he was well known for going after a variety of girls with no good intentions in mind, Winter didn't trust him one bit. Her papa liked to say that he was, "A boy with too much time on his hands", and that was a dangerous thing.

"I... am glad that you are going to get a better grade in our English class, Ian," Winter carefully chose her words, trying to let him down easy, "But I have a lot on my plate, so, you know... if you need any more *tutoring*, you're going to have to find someone else."

The smile on his face faded a little bit, and Ian reached out to take a lock of Winter's hair, curling it around his finger. Winter's heartbeat increased, though out of anxiety, not attraction. Swallowing, she held as still as she could, contemplating slapping his hand away. She would have, if she hadn't been worried about causing a scene.

"How about we just get together without tutoring? You're not such a little piggy anymore, huh?" Ian spoke in a coy, low voice that caused Winter to shiver, "Come on. It'll be a hella good time."

She might have found the flirting flattering, if she wasn't so uninterested.

At that moment, the school bell rang.

Thank God. The one time class has good timing, Winter thought, releasing a breath.

"Sorry... Got to get to class," Winter said, as Ian dropped her hair and she used the excuse to get away, jogging down the hall in a hurry, hugging her books to her chest. By the time she slid into a seat beside Kaya in their history class, she was out of breath and sporting flushed cheeks. Moments later, she saw Ian slink in and take a seat up front with a couple of the other junior jocks— Matthew Thorne and Daniel Gold.

"You okay? Need me to whoop Bryar's ass? Because I will," Her friend asked, holding up two tiny fists as a show of strength.

That earned a laugh, at least, Winter shaking her head, "No, no. It's fine. I tutored Ian this summer and he just... expects more. It's weird, I don't know... It's Ian. Not sure why he's bothering with me, you know?" Tucking a lock of hair behind her ear, Winter avoided Kaya's eyes, aware she wasn't telling her everything.

"Be careful with that one, Win. Ian Bryars is always up to no good." Kaya warned her.

Sighing, Winter flipped open a blue notebook she used for taking class notes. She flipped to a new page, setting it beside her history textbook. At the front of the classroom, Mrs. Dunn had come in, wearing her dark hair in the same tight bun as always and sporting a deep red turtleneck with a black skirt. She would be a very pretty woman, Winter thought, if not for her lack of ever smiling.

"I can handle Ian, Kaya," Winter reassured her friend, waving off her concerns as she settled in for their class.

"Can you believe him? Goes after every girl in the school. Freaking shark." Those had been the words Kaya had remarked to Axel Dunn as she walked past him, causing his attention to go towards Ian and the girl who lived across the street from him, drawing his headphones down to hang around his neck. He knew Ian, everyone did— he was the type of infamous that Axel didn't need to be his friend to know everything about him.

Hanging by his locker, Axel pretended to busy himself with his books, every so often glancing over his shoulder at his neighbor and Ian. Kaya was right; it was best to keep a close eye on guys like Ian Bryars. The last girl he'd pursued had been written about on the bathroom stalls, and if even half of it was true... Well, he'd hate to see the same debauchery happen to the Jozefson girl. Not that she didn't have a choice in associating with Ian, but the Jock did tend to be on the pushy side. It wouldn't hurt for Axel to be a little more aware of them, keeping an eye out while Ian was on the prowl.

It was a lucky thing that they had class. Axel watched his neighbor make a quick get-away. Lingering, he watched as Ian came down the hall, high fiving Matthew, the two marching on past together, heading towards the same class Winter had gone to.

"...I'm telling you, I'll have my hands on those jugs by the end of the week. She's sweet, she'll give in." Those words made Axel pause in what he was doing, watching the back of Ian's head as he walked further away, spouting filth about her to his friend.

Disgusting piece of... Axel scowled, slamming his locker shut and heading in the direction of his first class. He couldn't understand people like Ian Bryars.

"Good afternoon, younglings. For those of you who are new, my name is Goddard Poe. You may call me God if you wish— or Mr. Poe." The teacher of Axel's first class after lunch was clearly snarky. He was a tall man with long brown hair pulled back into a low hanging ponytail, and brown eyes behind small, round glasses that sat on the very tip of his nose. Axel thought he looked a lot like the type to go to coffee places and spew obscure poetry like Sylvia Plath, while wearing a turtleneck and smoking a pipe.

"The first project of the year! You'll be teaming up in groups of three for this one. I'll wait, go and find your partners and sit together," Mr. Poe continued as the students streamed into the class, repeating himself a few times for those that were lagging behind.

Axel found himself slumping into a chair in the back, hoping he wouldn't be seen or joined by anyone. Sure enough, by the time everyone had clustered with their partners, he was left sitting alone. A few minutes passed, Mr. Poe taking notes of the groups— until he came to Axel.

"Mr. Dunn..." Mr. Poe frowned, seeing Axel sitting alone, his eyes scanning the room. Everyone was paired in perfect groups of three, Axel the only one on his own. "That can't be right..." Axel heard the teacher mumble, rubbing the back of his neck with one hand while he scanned the attendance list, "Ah... it seems Mr. Dibattista and Miss Dorsey are both out today..." He took a second to think, glancing up from the list, "Okay then. I suppose we'll have to have a few groups of two. Do I have any volunteers to split from their groups and join Mr. Dunn?"

That's just great. Axel thought. There was something incredibly awkward about waiting in the silence, all eyes going towards him in a way that made him sink a little lower in his seat, tapping his fingers on his desk. Fidgeting was a habit his mother hated and had tried to stop, but Axel moved when he was nervous. Waiting like this, with all the focus on him, definitely made him nervous.

"I'll join him," A female voice spoke up, causing Axel to look up. It was the girl from across the street. She had been sitting in the very front of the class, with the spunky Kaya Morito and another girl Axel didn't know. When their eyes met, his new partner offered him a small smile.

Why she would offer to join him, Axel didn't know. But the teacher nodded in acceptance, setting the list on his desk.

"Good! Miss Morito, Miss Cohen, you'll be a team. Miss Jozefson, Mr. Dunn, you'll be a team. Then Mr. Dibattista and Miss Dorsey may be a team when they return." With a scuffle of movement, the Jozefson girl made her way to the back, taking the seat beside Axel and setting her things on the desk. As she sat, she tossed her hair over her shoulder, and Axel got a vague hint of her shampoo. He couldn't pinpoint what it was, but it smelled familiar, unconsciously shifting in his seat and inhaling deeply, glancing sideways at her as the teacher continued. After a few minutes, it dawned on him that it was a fruity scent.

"This will be a lesson in getting to know one another, kicking off the new year with the spilling of some secrets. Your assignment: Pick something you don't typically tell people and tell each other. Then write an essay on each other's secrets. At least two pages, due at the end of the month. Now, onto our lesson for today…"

What the heck kind of assignment is that? Axel thought, glowering at Mr. Poe as he droned on, the English teacher not seeming to care how absurd this homework was for them. All Axel could think was that not only would this girl, whose first name he didn't even know, know something personal about him— but so would Mr. Poe when he graded the essay. *Forget it. I'm making something up.* Axel thought, shaking his head.

"I'm Winter."

Her voice drew his gaze to her once more, finding brilliant hazel-green eyes staring at him, and that small, shy smile. Blinking at her, Axel didn't immediately understand what she had said to him.

"Sorry?" He asked.

"Winter. My name. We've never met, technically." Winter told him.

"Oh. Right." Axel answered, giving a nod of his head.

"And your name is…?" Winter prompted him.

Shit. I haven't said. Feeling slow, and clumsy at talking, Axel looked away from her, fixating his gaze at the front of the class as he answered her.

"Axel." After a pause, he added, "Sorry."

"For what?" She asked, so innocently that he almost believed she really didn't know what he was sorry for.

Sighing, he obliged her, "For getting stuck with me."

There was another pause between them, and then Winter said, "Well, don't be. I volunteered, didn't I?"

He hadn't taken her as being snarky, not in the same way as their teacher, and he was right. There was nothing sarcastic about her response, and when he looked back at her, she had opened a book with a red cover, and was sketching something, her hair falling like a curtain and hiding her face and the drawing from him.

They didn't talk for the rest of their English class, until Axel was leaving, and heard a distinct, "Hey, Axel!"

Slowing his walk down the hall, he glanced over his shoulder to find Winter jogging after him, nearly tripping over herself to catch up. For a tall girl, she walked with small, quick steps instead of long strides, and Axel noted her feet pointed outwards, like a duck.

No wonder she seemed clumsy, he thought.

"Yeah?" He asked, hands stuck in the pockets of his hoodie as he eyed the girl in front of him. He had seen her so often growing up, a familiar face, but it was different when she was standing right in front of him and not at a distance, looking up at him with the smile that never seemed to leave her face.

"When should we get together to talk about our essays? I've got some errands after school, but I can stop by your house after. Or, if you don't mind coming along, we could go to the library or something. I've got a few ideas for what I can tell you, for your essay, and—"

"Don't bother." Axel interrupted her, his voice cutting through her chatter, making her smile shift into surprise.

"I'm going to make something up, so… Just do that. Make it a good story."

"B-But…" Her mouth flapped like a fish, seeming not to know how to respond at first, until she finally found her voice, stammering, "D-Don't you want any say in what I write? I mean, even something made up… Do you have a phone, or a pager? Maybe AOL, I could send you some ideas?"

"Yeah, listen, uh…" He hadn't forgotten her name, but his hesitant pause must have made Winter assume he had, because she spoke up,

"Winter."

"Right, Winter. I don't really care all that much what you write. I don't really do group projects, I work better alone, so… I'll see you around, yeah?" He gave her a nod and a two-finger wave as he turned on his heel.

"…Yeah, see you." He heard her say behind him, her voice a lot less chipper than it had been.

As the day carried on, Axel had pushed his new English partner from his mind. The final bell of the day rang, and he made his way out of his daily prison, contemplating stopping by Torva's— a local coffee shop— on the way home.

Jogging down the steps of the school, Axel immediately headed west, planning on following Cinis Street to Timor Street, which was the main road of the town. *Maybe I'll even stop by the record shop.* He thought idly, pulling his headphones on and turning up the volume of his Walkman, letting music drown out the sounds of his surroundings.

Reaching the corner, Axel was about to duck into Sonus

Records, when his gaze caught on a familiar head of flowing brown hair. He paused, watching Winter walking up the sidewalk, across the street from him. She was alone, he thought at first, until he heard the loud revving engine of an approaching car in serious need of a better muffler. A familiar red Supra pulled up to the curb, obnoxiously gleaming in the sun. It looked like a little coffee bean, but the girls in their school went crazy when a guy had a car, it didn't matter what it looked like.

Ian got out, a grin that said he was up to no good curling on his face. He slicked back his hair and started up the sidewalk after Winter, like a shark going after the scent of blood.

What the hell does he think he's doing, stalking her like that... Axel thought, immediately annoyed. He shook his head, reaching for the door of the record shop, pulling it open.

Yet he couldn't help glancing back at the pair, watching his naive neighbor hurrying down an alley behind a cluster of shops. Ian picked up pace after her, both of them disappearing from sight.

"Hey! Dunn, you coming in? Katatonia's new album just came in!" Charlie McLain, the clerk of the shop called after him, eyeing the frozen teenager standing in the doorway.

"Uhh…" Axel's mouth hung open for a second, glancing between his freckled, music-loving friend and the alley that his two classmates had gone down.

Shit... I have a really bad feeling about this.

Spotting an ukulele hanging on the wall by the door he was holding open, Axel grabbed it with a short, "Let me borrow this, I'll be right back!"

"Hey! You gonna buy that?! Axel!" Charlie hollered after him, but he was already booking it across the street, heading straight for the alley he'd seen the shark chase his prey down.

2

UNLIKELY HERO

Winter knew she was being followed even before Ian's Supra pulled up behind her on Timor street. She had felt Ian's looming presence all day, from staring at her during gym to sitting near her at lunch. She had even caught some of the vulgar remarks he made to his buddies.

Turning her head, she saw him as he left his car, following her. *Seriously? Can't he take no for an answer?* Anger filled her, biting down on the insides of her cheeks. As she made her way quickly up the street, she could see the pharmacy from where she stood, where her prescription was waiting.

No. I have to ditch him first. She thought, setting a new path. As she turned down an alleyway, she made her way for the small parking space behind a row of shops. If she was lucky, she could do a loop through another alley and lose him.

But she wasn't lucky. When she turned the corner, into the backlot of the shops, she found a large supply truck at the end, blocking the other side. Winter's eyes scanned the chain-link fence and wooden walls, finding herself trapped at a dead end as she faced the way she had come.

Ian appeared only a few seconds later, sporting a too-sweet smile that made her take a step back. The way he approached her was predatory, sending off warning bells in her head as he grew closer.

"There you are, Winter. I've been waiting for a moment alone with you all day, to talk about getting together again." He said, eyeing her with interest.

"I… Um… T-Thank you, Ian, but I'm really not interested in… I don't really have time to be uh…" Winter stumbled over her words, distracted by Ian's growing proximity to her, balling her fists up at her side. "I d-don't see us spending time together like that. This summer was just tutoring, I'm sorry if you got the wrong impression." She had felt a lot more comfortable, a lot braver, in a hallway full of students. Alone, her voice shook, eyes darting from either side of Ian to try and find a way around him.

"Why? You seeing someone already? From what I hear, you've never been asked out before. Why is that? You're pretty enough. Rockin' body, if you know what I mean." Ian smirked and a chill went down Winter's spine. He had always been a bully, but peeking up into his face, she saw a new kind of determination. "There's something special about you, Winter. Let me take you out. We'll go for a ride in my Supra. I'll have you home by ten, baby."

Baby? Winter made a face at the nickname he'd given her. "I said no. I'm not interested, Ian, find someone else." Her tone came out sharp and firm, hoping to discourage him entirely.

She moved to shuffle past him, hoping he would just step aside and let her by, but his hand curled around her elbow, gripping her tightly and forcing her to stop beside him.

Winter's heart started racing, swallowing as she gazed at

Ian, who looked rather annoyed, glaring down at her with icy blue eyes.

"Don't be so rude, Winter. You're making me angry now — I'm being nice here, giving you some attention. I don't see what the big deal is." He said, his grip causing her arm to ache. "Come on. I'm bored, and you're probably lonely, huh? Let me keep you company tonight."

Yeah, right. I know what the girls you keep company think of you! Winter thought sourly.

"Let go of me, Ian." Winter fought to keep her voice steady, fear turning into adrenaline, her body shaking, "I'm not lonely, and I don't want any company of yours." She drew in a breath, snapping at him, "You were a bully when we were kids and you're being a bully now."

She yanked her arm, but when she took another step past him in an attempt to pull away Ian's expression changed. He went from a cold annoyance to pure fury, his face contorting into an enraged scowl. Ian Bryars wasn't used to not getting what he wanted, and he was prone to being hot-headed. As she tried to get away from him, his other hand reached out and grabbed a fistful of her hair, fingers digging into her scalp.

Winter let out a sound between a gasp and a cry of pain, her head being pulled back by his tight grasp as he glared down at her. She lashed out immediately towards his head, trying to smack him. The hand gripping her arm moved to her wrist instead, stopping her. Panicked, Winter felt a wave of nausea as she tried to think of how to get free.

"You ungrateful little bi—" Ian growled at her.

"Hey, Bryars. Didn't anyone ever tell you not to swear at a lady?" A voice loudly interjected. Musical notes filled the air as strings were strummed. A short, humorless laugh came, and the voice called out again, dripping with sarcasm, "Oh, wait. My bad. I forgot you're a piece of trash."

Their heads both turned to see Axel standing at the end of the alley, glaring with his blue eyes shifting between Ian and Winter. Dressed in entirely black clothing and holding a black ukulele, he looked like a fallen angel, his piercings glinting in the afternoon sun. Winter wasn't sure what was more bizarre— seeing him strumming an instrument so casually while looking so intense, or the fact he was here at all. Of all the people to come to her rescue, Winter would not have picked Axel Dunn.

Ian scoffed at him, already turning his gaze back towards Winter, who was unmoving as she waited to see what Axel would do. Maybe he would give her just enough of a distraction to get free— she just had to wait for the right moment.

"Buzz off, Dunn. This is none of your damn business." Ian retorted, irritation filling his voice. "Winter and I were just planning a date, that's all." His hand on her hair somewhat tightened, pulling her head back further so she was forced to look at him as he smiled down at her. Pain radiated across her scalp and down the back of her neck, Winter winced, gritting her teeth.

"Ian..." She spoke his name with a warning tone.

"Funny, I thought dates were agreed on. She doesn't look like she wants to go anywhere with you." Axel answered Ian, playing what sounded suspiciously like the opening tune of *No Rain* by Blind Melon. "Why don't you just let her go, man? No harm done."

He looked so calm, and Winter couldn't help but wonder if this was who Axel Dunn was— the cool, suave hero that swept in to save the day. She had seen him around for years, but he always seemed to stick to himself, never seemed to have any close friends or be a part of anything that involved people. What was he? Some kind of neighborhood vigilante? A superhero of Caligo?

It was clear from the look on his face that Ian didn't feel

very threatened by Axel. Why should he? A 5'6" goth kid holding a ukulele versus a 6'2" football captain was not exactly a fair fight.

As a result, Ian turned his back on Axel, giving a roll of his eyes. "Who invited this punk, huh? I'd rather make this a one-on-one date. Not into three's company, if you know what I mean." Ian spoke directly to Winter, giving her a smug little smirk. He began to dip his head down, eyes drifting shut. Winter, realizing where his pouty lips were headed, felt a squelch of nauseated horror.

Is he going to... Oh no! Think, Winter, think! She certainly didn't want her first kiss to be with Ian Bryars. Preparing herself, Winter envisioned her knee coming up, willing herself to put all her power into taking Ian's ability to father children away.

Only, she never had to go that far.

It happened in the blink of an eye— she heard the loud thud before she saw the ukulele slamming into the back of Ian's head. His entire body jolted, knees buckling as his hand let go of Winter's hair, the ukulele clattering to the ground with a discordant final note. As soon as he released her, Winter took several stumbling steps away from Ian, out of his reach.

Which turned out to be smart; when Ian straightened up again, his face was the shade of a tomato, twisted into a look of pure fury, and he whirled around so fast he might have knocked into her if she had been any closer. Winter could feel cold dread go through her, looking from Ian to Axel— who, to her surprise, now looked scared as well. His eyes were wide, face holding that expression one got when they knew they had just screwed up. With his instrumental weapon gone, Axel had nothing he could do but raise his hands in self defense as Ian charged him, grabbing onto the front of Axel's hoodie.

The first punch he threw connected hard with the side of Axel's face, Winter gasped as she saw his head get thrown back by the sheer force. Ian shoved him onto the ground, preparing to pummel him some more.

"Ian, stop!" Winter shrieked, her voice going shrill at the sound of the second punch, averting her gaze so she didn't have to see Axel's face.

At the third punch, she knew there was no stopping him. Ian was pissed, and he wasn't afraid to hurt either one of them at this point.

Winter, however, was not defenseless. She had a gift, and now was a good time to use it. Normally, she needed time to think, time to draw, time to envision— but she was running on pure adrenaline, her fingers twitching. She needed something to stop this, and the first thing that came to mind was a bottle. One of those old, green glass bottles, the image forming in her mind. One second, her hand was empty at her side, the next her fingers were curling around the neck of a bottle that had appeared out of nowhere. It was lucky the two boys were too occupied to notice her tiny bit of magic.

As Ian stood over Axel, cocking back his arm to throw yet another punch, Winter rushed forward. She lifted the bottle over her head and brought it down fast, smashing it over Ian's head. The glass broke, shattering over the two boys, Axel lifting an arm to shield his eyes as it rained over the back of Ian's head. The ukulele hadn't done the trick, but a bottle directly to the head certainly did. Ian let out a groan, falling to his knees onto the asphalt, releasing Axel— who quickly scrambled backwards away from him.

As Ian sat there, dazed and bent over on the ground, Winter stared at him with wide eyes. She dropped the bottle-neck that was left in her hand, a little horrified at what she had done to stop Ian from destroying Axel's face.

She hadn't realized Axel had gotten up, until she felt his

hand on her arm. Turning, she looked up into his face— and saw the bruise starting to form under his left eye, along his cheekbone. A long curved cut had split beneath his eye in the middle of the bruise, probably from Ian's football championship ring. It was already nasty looking, blood dripping down Axel's cheek. Winter's stomach churned just looking at it before she forced herself to focus on his bright eyes— which were still wide, looking as frantic as she felt.

"Let's get out of here before he gets up." Axel urged her.

Nodding, Winter let him drag her to the end of the alley. Ian started to shout after them just as they turned the corner, but they were gone by the time he got to his feet.

Breathlessly, the two teenagers ran at least three blocks down Timor st. At some point, Axel had let go of her, but with her long legs, Winter had no trouble keeping up with him. Reaching the corner with Damara's Diner— a quiet little place with a green thatched roof and mustard yellow walls— Winter lunged for the door and instructed Axel,

"In here." Slowing down and taking deep breaths to try and hide the fact that her heart was still racing, Winter glanced back at Axel. At least she didn't look as bad as he did, with his shiner growing darker by the minute. Not to mention his bloody cheek— though Axel had lifted a hand to cover it as they entered the restaurant.

At the hostess table stood Noelle Ritter— a girl that went to school with them. She was a year older than Winter, and a few inches shorter. With shoulder-length brown hair and big, round orange-rimmed glasses over brown eyes, Noelle was quite pretty, with one of those faces that could have been in a magazine, all high cheekbones and wide lips. She looked almost intelligent, although— as one of the school's resident potheads along with her boyfriend Nathan Silva— she could be accused of being spacey.

True to that, she glanced them over, popped a piece of gum, and looked absolutely unfazed.

"Yo. Table for two?" She asked, as if she saw scruffy kids from school all the time.

"Uh…" Winter glanced at Axel, who merely shrugged at her, "Yeah, sure. How're you doing, Noelle?"

"Oh, you know, so so. Could be worse." She remarked, grabbing two menus and leading them back to a booth, her sneakers squeaking on the linoleum floors. "You want anything to start with?"

Winter slid into the booth, sitting across from Axel. From the looks of it, they were the only customers in Damara's that day, besides Officer Chi, the local law, who sat at the counter talking to Damara herself, laughing over some coffee and apple fritters. Officer Chi was a middle-aged Korean man with a donut belly and a few tinges of gray in his hair. His sons, Jae-Hwa and Tae-Won, went to Clamare High as well. Meanwhile, Damara was a darker skinned woman in her mid-thirties, who made the best baked goods in Caligo. Sure, Damara's Diner served good meals, but the pastries were its real moneymaker. Upon seeing Officer Chi, Winter's heart leapt into her throat, worried he would spot them and come to question Axel about his bleeding face. Instead, he barely glanced their way, too busy with Damara. Or perhaps, he simply was turning a blind eye to Axel's state. Either way, the two students didn't seem to garner any attention at all.

Winter tore her gaze away from the pair to look at Noelle, who had pulled out her notepad.

"Just water for me. With lemon. And uh, do you mind getting us a cup of ice? And a towel?" Winter asked, Axel's face in mind.

"Uh-huh. Got it. And you, Dunn?" To her credit, Noelle asked no questions.

"The usual." Axel responded cooly, like he came here all the time. Noelle merely bobbed her head, and spun on her heel to go get their order.

Eyeing the injured boy across from her, Winter raised an eyebrow, "You know Noelle?"

"Not well."

It seemed being punched three times by an angry jock had done nothing to make Axel more talkative. A silence fell between them, Winter gazing out the window to watch for Ian's car. Within a few minutes, Noelle came back, setting down three glasses on the table and a baby blue towel. Winter expected her to ask if they wanted anything else, but she just wandered off again. Moments later, the door chimed, and in walked Nathan— Noelle's boyfriend; a tall, handsome senior with slicked black hair and forest green eyes. He leaned across the hostess counter to give Noelle a kiss, the two chattering idly and not paying attention to anyone else.

Turning her attention back to Axel, Winter's gaze dropped to the drink in front of him.

"What's that?" She asked, curious at the light brown liquid with ice cubes. "Iced coffee?"

Axel snorted in response, "Iced cocoa. Coffee is disgusting."

Finally, something they had in common.

"Tea is better." Winter answered, smiling at him. She had hoped he'd smile back, but he merely stared at her a moment before looking away again, lifting his cocoa to take a sip.

A familiar sense of awkwardness hit Winter, as she reached for the towel. Unfolding it, she scooped up some ice cubes, rolling them into a homemade ice pack.

Holding it out to Axel, Winter finally found her voice as he pressed it gently to his face.

"Why did you do that?"

"Do what?" Axel was playing dumb, she could tell by the way he spoke so bluntly, not looking at her but instead staring down at the table as he nursed his bruise.

"Come to my rescue." Winter clarified.

"You know, instead of questioning it most people would just say thank you." He answered with a heavy sigh.

"Isn't a thank you implied? I mean… You saved me from Ian Bryars— that's a pretty big deal. So, yes, thank you."

The only sign Axel gave of accepting that was a soft snort into his glass, taking a gulp of cocoa to avoid talking. Winter glared at him, waiting for her question to be answered. Finally, after a few minutes, Axel sighed and set down his glass.

"I don't like Bryars. Do I need any more reason to bash his head in?"

"It looked more like it was the other way around." Winter remarked, eyeing the bruises once more. The bleeding had stopped, staining the towel red. "Besides, lots of people don't like him, but they don't show up with an ukulele ready to throw down." Pausing, she took a sip of her water before asking, "Where'd you get the ukulele, anyway? Do you play?"

That got a reaction— Axel's expression turning even more grim than it had been before. Had she hit a nerve? Finally, he let out a soft groan into his cup of cocoa, answering,

"I… might have commandeered that from Sonus Records…" *That did not sound like a good thing,* Winter thought, as Axel rubbed the back of his neck. He looked uncomfortable as he continued, "I need to head back there, Charlie's probably having a fit."

Jezebel McLain was Charlie's little sister. Their family went to the same church that Winter and her grandpa had always attended— New Avalon, one of the only churches in

Caligo— and they always sat together. Usually, the McLain family invited a bunch of people over for Sunday brunch after the services. Come to think of it, Winter always saw Axel at church too, but he never sat anywhere near her, usually being one of the first ones to leave after the service.

Axel opened his mouth, ready to respond, when something caught his eye out the window.

"Duck!" He ordered, as his own head went down to hide from view. Winter immediately followed suit, and when she glanced up, she saw the taillights of a red Supra.

She watched it go down the street, making a wobbly turn. Was it even safe for Ian to drive with a head injury? Probably not, but that didn't make her any less relieved to see him go. Axel was the first to sit up again, swearing under his breath as he stared down the street.

"Well... at least we know we won't run into Ian again... until school tomorrow." Winter cautiously commented, hoping the smile she wore wasn't as nervous as she felt.

Gulping down the rest of his cocoa, Axel set his glass down with a loud thump as he stood.

"Come on then, let's go see Charlie." He remarked, agreeing to Winter's request to tag along, and tossing some money from his pocket down onto the table to cover their drinks. He was already stomping off to the door as Winter hurried after him.

It wasn't a long walk to Sonus Records, but boy, did Charlie McLain look steamed when Winter and Axel strolled through the door.

"Axel! What the hell, man?! Can't just go running off with

my merchandise like that!" He shouted at them, smacking a hand on the clerk's counter.

It was hard to take him seriously, though. To Winter, Charlie was about as threatening as a baby goat. He was incredibly tall, sure, towering over the two of them at 6'4" or so. But he was skinny as a pole, gangly and awkward. He wore an oversized band t-shirt that hung on his frame and hid his butt from the sagging of his jeans, and had a big, blocky pair of headphones hanging from his neck. Charlie's freckled face was as red as his wild ginger hair, which exploded from his head in curls, and his brown eyes peered at them behind heavy, rounded glasses.

"About that..." Axel began, looking like he would rather be anywhere else, the guilt of smashing the ukulele all over his face. As he approached him, Winter hung back, eyeing the ukulele display near the door.

Before he could finish, Charlie spoke again, his eyes flickering to the wall where there should have been an empty hook. "At least you brought it back in one piece."

Axel turned, and there it was— a perfect, undamaged ukulele, hanging off the wall. His eyes dropped to Winter, who stood beside it with her hands innocently clasped behind her back.

Giving him a big smile, Winter's heart was thudding in her ears, hoping they couldn't tell how nervous she was. The replaced ukulele was her doing, a quick bit of magic that, to her relief, didn't go noticed. Her fingers felt like she'd been rubbing a balloon, electrical tingling going up and down each digit— but the ukulele must have looked similar enough to fool Charlie, who just waved his hand at them.

"Don't pull that stunt again, Dunn. Next time you get dared to take something from my shop, at least run it by me first, okay? We can fool them together, work something out, you know?" He was shaking his head as he turned away.

Axel, still stunned, stammered,

"Y-Yeah. Sorry about that... Won't happen again."

His hands clumsily reached for the door, and Winter followed at his heels as he fled, suppressing a smile.

The walk home had been a relaxed silence, until Axel broke it by speaking.

"I don't get what just happened. We both saw that uke get totally destroyed." He was perplexed, giving her a sideways glance. They had never spoken before today, despite living across from each other nearly all their lives.

"Oh, I uh... Well, I knew where to get a replacement. You can thank me by paying me back." Winter responded with a smile, her voice coy and teasing, making him even more suspicious of her.

"...What do you want?" He asked, apprehension all over his face.

Bouncing in front of him, Winter turned to walk backwards down the sidewalk, facing him.

"Your phone number." She declared, as if it was already hers, "We're doing that school project together. My gift to you for helping me with Bryars is that I'll help you get a good grade for English. And your payment for me, for helping save you from Charlie's wrath, is that you're going to do the project with me and help me get a good grade."

He thought he might have seen a glimpse of uncertainty in her eyes as she looked at him, but her smile didn't waver.

They had come to a stop in front of Winter's house, and Axel stared at her for a long moment, but she didn't say another word, waiting for him to answer. Apparently, she wasn't about to back down under his intense blue gaze.

"Fine. Give me your phone," Axel sighed at last.

Happily, Winter handed it over, and Axel entered his number into her contacts before handing it back. As soon as he did, he set off across the street, Winter waved at his retreating form and called out,

"I'll text you!"

Great. What had he gotten himself into?

3

UNUSUAL PARTNER

"That's wild. Who knew Dunn had it in him, huh?" Kaya said with a laugh, shaking her head. She sat cross legged on the brown carpet of Winter's bedroom, going through a shelf full of records. "Shame he didn't get a few punches in with Bryars, though. I would pay to see him with a shiner." Her laughter had almost turned into maniacal cackling at the thought, short hair swishing as she shook her head.

"I still don't know what possessed him, but it all worked out. I got Ian off my back— at least, for a little while— and I forced Axel into being my English partner. That's good, right? I mean... it's beneficial to us both, he can't be that mad about it." Winter sighed. She sat at her desk, chin resting in the palm of her hand as she stared out the window. Across the way, sat the Dunn house.

Winter's room was... well, the term "plant explosion" fit pretty well. She had little potted plants all over, dark floppy green leaves bringing jungle vibes to her room. There were a few small ones on her desk; a large, cherry wood desk that had all her drawing equipment scattered on top of it. There was a stack of about ten sketchbooks in one corner, and a pile of large drawing papers in the middle, along with several cups of various pens, pencils, markers— you name it, she had it. The drawers were even frightfully full of paints and brushes. Her bed, which was usually the center of any bedroom, was woefully shoved into the corner, a small twin with green knit blankets and a currently-sleeping cat. Peeking out from beneath the bed was a large, antique wooden trunk.

Sitting in her oversized office chair, Winter idly wondered if it was weird that she had such a good view of Axel's bedroom window from here. Sure, his blinds were currently closed, but still... It felt even more stalker-like than drawing his face. Not that she had ever seen any inappropriate glimpses of him since living there.

"Speaking of, when is the goth lord going to grace you with his presence? You haven't seen him since fighting Bryars, right?" Kaya asked as she eyed a Beatles album from a shelf near Winter's bed.

It had been about three days. Winter had been worried about going to school— but Ian had left her and Axel alone. Other than a few nasty looks in the hallways, and under-his-breath insults towards them, it seemed he didn't want to let anyone at school know that they had taken him down with a bottle and an ukulele.

In those three days, Axel had been happy to ignore Winter. They walked by each other in the halls, sat apart in classes, and generally stayed away from each other. Every time she thought about it, she got nervous. How was she supposed to talk to him? He was about as approachable as a Komodo Dragon, and she thought he might have preferred it that way.

"Uh, probably never." Winter sighed, spinning in her chair to face her friend, "He hasn't called or messaged me, I haven't called or messaged him. He seemed pretty reluctant to do the project with me to begin with. I'm starting to think it was a bad idea to tell him he owed me."

"You always do that, Winter! You get a brilliant idea, take advantage of it, and then the next day think you're the devil for doing it." Kaya complained, tipping her head back with a dramatic groan, "Guys like a girl who takes charge! You're going to have to learn that if you ever want to get a date."

"I'm not trying to date Axel Dunn. I'm trying to get an A in English." Winter answered stubbornly. "Isn't it also one of your rules that guys should text girls first?"

Kaya was always getting silly gender rules from Cosmo. She called it her way of the world— wherever there was a problem, a magazine had the answer.

"Not this guy. You stand a better chance of surviving a shark attack than getting Mr. Gloom over there to text you first." Kaya remarked.

"Well, actually…" Winter started, about to correct her logic with the fact shark attacks weren't actually that common or that deadly.

"Shhhhh." Kaya interrupted, holding up a finger. Standing, she reached out with her hand to grab Winter's phone off the desk.

"W-What are you doing?"

"Texting Dunn, obviously."

"What?! No!" Winter immediately swiped for her phone, only for her agile friend to leap back, hurrying to type out a message. "Kaya! Give it back! Don't text him— are you insane?!"

She continued trying to grab her phone back, only for Kaya to sidestep her. The two of them danced around Winter's room, with Kaya giggling maniacally and Winter screeching at her. Books were shuffled, plants were disturbed, even Winter's cat lifted her head in confusion at the two girls.

Throwing open the bedroom door, Kaya dashed out, cackling as she held the phone close to her chest. The two stomped down the landing, as Kaya fled for the guest bathroom, Winter running after her. She passed her grandfather as he stuck his head out his bedroom door, disturbed by the commotion.

Winter was simply too slow. Kaya threw herself into the bathroom and slammed the door shut, locking it by the time Winter started to desperately pull on the handle. Her heart felt like it was beating out of her chest, panic setting in as waves of anxiety-induced nausea hit.

"Kaya, no! Please, don't text him! I wasn't going to bother him, I was going to let him off the hook! KAYA!" Winter pleaded, hammering her fist on the door.

A minute later, and the door unlocked. As it was pulled back, Winter caught sight of her friend's mischievous face, brown eyes— contactless— shining. She smirked, dangling the phone in front of her. "All done!"

Horrified, Winter finally snatched her phone back, flipping it open to check her messages.

W: Hey, Axel. Do you think you could come over tomorrow afternoon, around four? For our project? 😊

"Oh. My. God. Kaya, seriously?!" Winter asked her friend, distressed. Kaya only giggled in return, throwing her arms around Winter's neck in a hug.

"It'll be good! You'll get what you want. Just wait—"

At that moment, the phone chimed, and both girls fell silent. Huddled together in the doorway of the bathroom, they opened the reply text.

A: Sure.

"Told you."

"...Thank you, Kaya." Winter sighed, closing her phone. Sometimes, her wild best friend actually did know what was best.

It was strange to walk across the street to a house he had seen all his life but never gone near. The house across the street was a bright contradiction to Axel's own. Tall and narrow, it was painted a cheerful shade of spearmint green, the trim a lighter honeydew. The roof was slate gray, scalloped tiles. It was Victorian in design, two stories and an attic, with too many tall, white windows for Axel to count. The windows on the left side of the house seemed to pop out, like bay windows, giving the house an unusual shape. He walked down the gray tile walkway, past the white picket fence. Where the porch steps began, there was a small garden stone path that branched off from the walkway to the left, heading to the backyard— through a gray brick wall with a small, swirly wrought-iron gate. To the right, there was a small stone driveway and a carport.

Pausing, Axel took in the rose bushes that curled around the front, and the large tree filled with apples, just about ready to harvest. There was a metal loveseat sitting in the front of the yard. How many times had he seen Winter sitting there, sketching away in a book? This was a well-taken-care-of, beloved house. Different in the way his own was perfectly in place— you could tell that this house wasn't kept tidy out of perfect standards, but out of love.

He jogged up the porch steps, trailing his hand up the

white banister, stepping in front of the ornate door. A small sign to the side read, "729 Altum Ct."

When Axel rang the doorbell of the Jozefson residence, he heard a familiar female voice holler, "I'll get it, papa!"

Yet, she didn't seem to reach it in time. The door swung open, revealing an older gentleman glaring down at Axel. Tage Jozefson was an intimidating man even now, pushing eighty. Axel couldn't imagine how he was in his prime. The former Air Force Senior Master Sergeant still held an air of authority, even while standing before Axel in a pair of sweats and a white tank top that showed the belly he'd gotten in his old age. He was a tall, broad man, with neatly styled gray hair and deep set, dull blue eyes. Keeping one hand on the door, he huffed down at Axel— who must have looked like a real scoundrel in comparison, with his piercings and battered black clothing. The cut Ian had given him was still under his eye, healing slowly into a faded scar. Behind Mr. Jozefson, Axel spotted Winter on the stairwell, with flushed cheeks, wearing a blue sun dress. Winter remained quiet as her grandfather addressed Axel,

"You're the Dunn kid." It wasn't a question.

"Yepppp." Axel popped the p of the word, leaning back as he added a somewhat sarcastic, "Sir."

Mr. Jozefson gave him a reproachful, stern look.

"You will mind yourself in my house. Boots off, hands off my granddaughter. No doors closed, and you won't stay a minute after seven o'clock. Do we understand each other?"

"Uh-huh."

Axel wasn't sure who this intimidation tactic worked on, but he was unimpressed.

"Papa… We're just going to be working in the kitchen." Winter finally interjected. Jogging the rest of the way down the staircase, she appeared behind her grandfather, placing her hand on his arm.

"Just making sure he knows the rules of the house, Pumpkin." Mr. Jozefson told her, offering a smile. He stepped back, giving Axel one last wary look as the goth kid entered the house. "Your parents know you're here, Mr. Dunn?"

"I think so. Saw me leave the house." Axel answered, sure his mother wouldn't care when he came home. That answer seemed good enough for Mr. Jozefson, who grunted in response. He pulled Winter close to kiss the top of her head, telling her he would be in his room if she 'had anything that needed handling', and stomped up the stairs.

Winter, looking a little embarrassed, gestured for Axel to follow her after he took off his boots. "This way."

Winter's kitchen is so warm, Axel thought as she led him through the house. He thought the talk with her grandfather had been a bit uncomfortable, sure, but there was an unbelievably comforting feeling that washed over him the second he stepped foot into the back half of Winter's house. It almost felt like the oven was on, though it wasn't— and the lingering smell of sugar and spice in the air was intoxicating.

"Do you want something to drink? Tea? Milk?" Winter asked as she rushed around him, clearing things off a cluttered dining room table. In fact, every table was cluttered. From the counters, which had fresh fruit and cook books, knick-knacks and cooking appliances, to the table— which appeared to be a haven of newspapers, sudoku, and old coffee cups that Winter hurried to pile into the sink.

"Uh..." Axel stuttered, not wanting to be rude as he awkwardly asked, "Got any cocoa?"

For whatever reason, that brought a smile to Winter's face. "Iced, like at the diner. You got it."

As she busied herself making them both glasses of cocoa with ice cubes, Axel slid into a seat at the end of the table, pulling his bag into his lap. He couldn't help but take a moment to adjust to the kitchen, which was so different from his own. This kitchen was lived in. Peeling pale yellow paint on the walls, retro blue and silver on many of the appliances and even on the fridge. The stove and oven looked a bit worse for wear, as if used often— the grates on the stove top crusted black, the knobs on the front a little wonky. The tiles on the floor were a Spanish-styled ceramic, made up of colorful— but somewhat faded from age— green, yellow, blue, and white patterns. There was a sign hanging on the back door that went from the kitchen to the yard, which said "This kitchen is for dancing".

Tapping his foot nervously on a bar of the seat, Axel turned his attention to Winter as she finished their drinks, setting two tall glasses of cold cocoa on the table.

"Not as good as what Damara's can do, but it's edible." Winter remarked, watching him with a small smile.

Taking a sip, Axel nodded his head. It wasn't bad— she had even stirred in some cinnamon. "It's good. Thanks."

Before he could suggest they start their project, a rapid movement in front of him made Axel jerk backwards— as a large ginger *thing* hopped onto the table.

"Pesca!" Winter exclaimed, jumping forward to grab the rather fluffy... cat? It looked too big to be a cat— surely a Maine Coon of some kind, with the longest tail and greenest eyes Axel had ever seen on a house cat. It had been just about to dunk its face into Winter's glass before she lifted it off the table, ignoring its meows of protest as she cuddled the creature to her chest.

"Pesca?" Axel questioned. He had become frozen upon the presence of the cat— his parents had never allowed pets, and honestly, weren't cats supposed to be rather disagreeable? He didn't think they would like him much, although the one Winter now held had already started to purr.

"Yeah, uh... Axel, meet Pesca. Her name means peach in Italian. She's my baby." Winter introduced them, nuzzling a kiss onto the top of the furry thing's head.

"Peach, for the ginger fur?" Axel asked.

"No, actually..." Winter paused, hesitating. For a second, watching as uncertainty— or was it sadness?— crossed her face, Axel thought she would change the subject. But after a minute, she merely said, "My dad used to call me Pesca."

Axel knew that Winter had been raised by her grandpa, and that her grandpa's daughter was Winter's mom— he knew the Jozefson family only had girls in it, something his mom had mentioned on more than one occasion when cursing the fact she had three sons. He hazily remembered seeing her mom the day Winter got dropped off, but Winter had been six and Axel had been five, and honestly he hadn't been paying that close attention to what was going on across the street. But her dad, Axel had always assumed, had never been in the picture. The way Winter looked now, however, said otherwise.

Questions sprang to mind, but Axel held his tongue as Winter ushered her cat into another room. When she came back, she was bright and smiling vibrantly again, grabbing a notebook and a pencil from her bag and settling beside him.

"So... Where should we start?" She asked, as she wrote "SECRET" in big bold letters at the top of a page.

"With you." Axel answered.

"Why?"

His instant response had made her pout— a genuine, lower lip popping pout that made Axel sigh. Looking away from her, he crossed his arms and leaned back in his chair, as it gave a creak of protest.

"Maybe I just don't trust you with my secrets." It was a

blunt answer, but an honest one. Axel didn't trust anyone—least of all the girl across the street. Sure, she had one of those trustworthy faces, with her full cheeks and big, bright eyes, but Axel knew for a fact that a face said nothing about a person. The most beautiful people could be the most rotten, and he had nothing substantial to judge Winter on... yet.

"Well... what if I don't trust you, either? It doesn't mean I want to lie for our school project." Winter protested, eyeing him.

Something about her response, and the petulant tone she used, made Axel snort.

"Because you're that type."

"What type?"

"The naive, trusting type."

"I am not!" She immediately interjected, like he knew she would. Even though they hadn't talked before that week, Axel had a pretty good read on Winter. She was one of those girls that saw the world through a positive filter, and he hadn't seen any other side to her. "You don't even know me."

"So?" Axel sighed.

"So, get to know me." Winter remarked.

The stubborn suggestion made Axel scoff. He leaned forward on the kitchen table, propping his head up with his hand, eyeing her for a long moment. Her eyes, hazel-green, challenged him.

"It's that simple, huh?"

"Yes. It is. That is typically how people work. Start with their name, age, general facts. Then get into the likes, dislikes, hobbies. Eventually you'll learn some stories— and secrets, which is the purpose of this project. You just have to make an effort to care. People take effort."

This way of thinking made Axel want to laugh in her face.

An effort to care? To him, that was such a stupid thing to say. Caring came easy to people like Winter Jozefson. To

Axel, most of the time he couldn't care less. Why bother? No one cared about him, after all— most people went through life with the most selfish things to care about, but didn't really give a damn about anything that didn't benefit them. People do take effort, but in Axel's experience, it was remarkably lucky to have them give even half the effort back.

Incredulously, he looked away from Winter, wondering if she had been hit in the head harder than he had the other day. Axel almost immediately rejected the idea, but...

I owe her. He reminded himself.

"Alright, Winter. We'll do it your way. Still, I'll only tell you what I want you to know."

That seemed to be enough of an agreement for her. Winter nodded her head and focused on the task at hand. She started talking idly about herself, occasionally inter-jecting with questions towards Axel, and before he knew it, they were just sitting there talking. It had been a long time since he'd had conversations about much more than shared interests like music, but Winter seemed to have no issue steering them in new directions, bringing up new things, keeping it from getting boring. The hours passed with ease, hanging in her kitchen as she worked on getting Axel to admit little bits of information about himself.

Axel knew a lot of the things Winter told him about herself. Artistic? He had seen the way she carried her sketchbook around everywhere, that wasn't a surprise. Friends with a good handful of their classmates? Also unsurprising, considering how she had gotten him here. He learned things like that she liked plants— explained why she was always sitting in her yard— and that she spoke French pretty well, getting good grades in their French class at school. Axel happened to be one of the worst students in that class.

Still, the afternoon hadn't been a total waste. For the first time, Axel actually got to talk to her instead of seeing her from afar.

The sun had just set when Winter's grandfather came to start dinner, shooing them out of the kitchen.

Winter laughed as she led Axel to the door, hugging her notebook full of notes she had made on him to her chest.

"Guess that's it for today." She remarked as they stepped out onto the porch.

"Mhm." Axel merely made a noise of confirmation, jogging down the steps.

"Hey, Axel?" Her voice calling out made him stop, looking over his shoulder at her.

Winter leaned on the railing of the porch, hair fluttering slightly from the evening breeze, gazing down at him. She looked… nervous. Hesitant.

"What?" He asked bluntly. He wanted her to spit out whatever it was that was written all over her face.

"Would you mind if I called you, sometime… we don't always have to meet up to talk, you know? And I could learn a bit more, for the project." Her voice was timid all of a sudden, the confidence and charm she had been giving all afternoon nowhere to be seen. Was this one of those manipulative girl tricks? Act all shy, so he'd say yes?

Axel didn't trust it. But…

Worst case scenario, I'll hang up on her.

"Yeah, sure. We can call sometimes." Axel agreed, lifting a hand in a wave as he trudged back to his house.

Laughter erupted over the phone, followed by muffled snorting. It wasn't hard for Axel to picture Winter covering her mouth with her hand.

"No! Really? I can't believe that!" She exclaimed. They had been talking about middle school, and having gone to different schools, there were plenty of funny stories for them to swap.

"I swear. Blood shot like ten feet, it was great." Axel had thought Winter would have been squeamish or unhappy with his gross story. She, herself, admitted she wasn't a fan of blood when they began their call. But she seemed enthralled with the story. It was possible, Axel was willing to admit after two hours on the phone that evening, that there were more sides to Winter than he originally thought.

It was nearly eleven, Axel using up minutes on his cell since his father was using the landline to work.

As Winter's laughter subsided, their conversation lulled into a relaxed state. The next thing she asked surprised him. "Hey, why don't you ask me a question?"

"What?"

"Well... I've asked the majority of the questions today. Come on, throw one at me. I'll answer anything!" Winter chirped over the phone.

Silence followed, Axel staring at his ceiling. Mouth opening, he tried to find the words. It was a good thing Winter seemed to be patient— she didn't say anything, giving him time to figure out a question.

"O-Oh...kay then..." Axel mumbled, "...What are you afraid of, Win?"

He heard a clatter on the other end, as if something had been knocked into, and then a pause.

"...Winter?" Axel echoed her name, checking on her. She hadn't taken this long to answer him all night. Nerves were fluttering up his throat, his grip on the phone tightening as he switched from one ear to the other.

"Uh... Well... I don't like moths. And blood, but you knew

that one." She had this tone of voice that she used, Axel noted, when she wasn't saying everything.

"You know that isn't what I meant. I won't put it in the English essay, if that's what you're worried about." Axel told her. As more silence followed, other than a soft sigh over the line, he began to rethink his question. "You don't have to answer if—"

"N-No. I just… No, I'll answer. I guess my biggest fear… This is going to sound so stupid…"

"Try me." Now, Axel was truly curious. What could the warm, energetic Winter Jozefson fear?

"I uh… I guess I'm scared of being d-dropped. Abandoned. I try so hard to be a part of someone's life, to be important to them, to be… Well, to be loved back by the people I love. I- I try not to do anything wrong, but… sometimes you don't have to do anything wrong, and it still happens, you know? When you don't expect it, and you think they care about you too. People you see in your future, they vanish so easily. I guess… It's my fear that people I want around, won't want me around in return. Like…" Her voice had gone quiet, as Axel sat up in his bed, running a hand through his hair.

"Like?"

"…" She didn't want to finish the sentence, that much was obvious. Instead, she said quietly, "Your turn."

Axel let out a breath he hadn't known he'd been holding, followed by a humorless laugh. It wasn't all that shocking to him that Winter, a people pleaser that lived for others, would have a fear of not mattering and being abandoned. But his fear?

"That's a talk for another night. My fear would scare the crap out of you."

"Hey, that's not fair!" Winter wasn't angry. If anything, her voice sounded amused now.

"Okay, I'll give you a hint. You can't fight being abandoned, it's out of your hands. My fear? I can't fight it either." That could be a multitude of things, but that made the riddle all the more fun to Axel. Smirking, he finished, "Goodnight, Winter."

"...Fine. Goodnight, Axel." She told him as they hung up.

If voices could smile, hers was smiling, there was no doubt about it.

4

UNAPOLOGETIC PUNK

"**B**onjour! Comment allez-vous? Today we will be working on our basic conversation skills as a refresher course. C'est facile, oui?" Miss Popelin clapped her hands together, smiling at them as her voice rolled over them like silk. This was one of Winter's favorite classes. She studied pretty hard and got decent grades; the year before she had been among the top three students in the class.

Winter had just sat down, pulling out her notebook, when a familiar boy in black plopped down beside her. Axel had a sour expression, brooding as he leaned over the desk, laying his head down on his arms and giving a half-hearted, "Bonjour…"

"Well, aren't you in a good mood." Winter said, eyeing him. They had been talking daily ever since he had studied at her house, often on the phone for long hours at night, texting and calling. The cut Ian had given him, along with any bruising, had cleared up by now. Things had pretty much gone back to normal, only with Winter having gained a newfound friend.

"Oui." Axel sighed. Lifting his head, he added, "I freaking hate French."

"Je déteste le français." Winter echoed his sentiment, giggling.

Before long, however much he disliked it, the two of them were engaged in conversation in French. Winter wasn't afraid to correct Axel— which led to a lot of repeating his words and having him roll his eyes at her. She had never seen him quite this moody, and if she was honest... It was kind of cute.

Having been wandering through the class, Miss Popelin finally came to a stop at their desks. She was one of the youngest teachers on staff at Clamare high, and one of the prettiest. A petite woman, she had long, sun-kissed blonde hair pulled into a loose bun that had silver chopsticks stuck through it. Her honey-hazel eyes sat behind large glasses, a tiny mole underneath the left one. Her face was long, with large ears, a small nose, and plump lips molded into one of the kindest smiles Winter had ever seen.

"Bonjour, Mademoiselle Winter, Monsieur Axel." She greeted them, before asking Axel, "I have never seen you two sit together. Êtes-vous amis?"

Are you friends? The question was so simple that Winter laughed.

Thinking this was an easy answer, she went to interject,

"Oui!"

"Non."

What? Her head turned to Axel as the denial slipped out of his mouth. His eyes met hers, mouth opening in a silent, awkward expression. Clearly, he hadn't expected her answer either.

"Oh, dear... It seems you both still have talking to do, hm?" Miss Popelin remarked, giving an uncomfortable laugh as she moved on.

The silence was suffocating as she left, Winter looking down at her notebook.

"Winter…"

"No, no." She interrupted him. A knot formed in her stomach, upon hearing the regretful tone of Axel's voice. "It's fine." Lifting her head, she offered him a smile that she didn't feel. "Don't worry about it."

She couldn't meet his eyes. It was impossible to hide her disappointment that he didn't consider them friends. They hadn't been talking long, but… She couldn't lie to herself-not being valued as a friend stung a little bit.

The moment the bell rang, Winter couldn't gather her stuff fast enough.

"Winter, wait—" Axel tried again, sighing.

"I'll catch you later, Axe." Was all she said, slipping out of class amongst the other students. Luckily for her, he wasn't in any of her other classes that day.

The next day, a knock on her bedroom door made Winter look up from her sketchbook, spotting her grandpa in the doorway.

"Hi, papa." She greeted him, tucking a lock of hair behind her ear, "Did you need help with dinner?"

"No, no, dinner is fine, Pumpkin. I'll be starting it soon. No, uh… you've got a visitor. That punk from across the street's here to see you." Her grandpa answered her, looking a little disgruntled at the thought. Winter suppressed a smile, setting her sketchbook aside.

"Axel? Oh, um… He probably wants to work on our English project." Winter told him. At the scowl her grandfather gave, she added, "He's a good guy."

"Good guys don't dress like that and put metal through their face. Don't wear so many rings and bracelets neither. Sure is a queer thing to do." Her grandfather grunted.

Don't. Winter mentally stopped herself from responding defensively for her new school partner. She was glad her grandfather hadn't seen what she had been sketching— he wouldn't have liked seeing Axel's angular face etched among the pages.

Giving a tight smile, she stood up and softly answered, "Be nice, papa. We're just working on school stuff together. I'm sure that's all he wants." *We're not friends, after all.* She couldn't help but bitterly think, remembering Axel's denial in French.

Her grandfather ambled after her as she went downstairs. Winter glanced back at him before she opened the front door, and he mumbled, "I'll be in the kitchen if you need me. I can still knock a few heads, if called to, you know."

All Winter did was snort and shake her head, waiting until he was well out of earshot before she pulled open the door. She only opened it enough to lean between the frame and the door, pressing her cheek to the wood as she peered out at Axel.

He stood at the top of the porch steps, arms crossed as he leaned against the white corner post. It was the first time Winter had seen him that day, avoiding him at school in an attempt to collect her feelings before facing him again. Last night, he had called her, and texted her— both of which she had left unanswered.

"Your old man doesn't like me." Was the first thing Axel said when he saw Winter's face, "I thought he was about to grab something to beat me off the porch."

"Oh, he wouldn't do that." Winter told him, giving a somewhat nervous laugh. *Would he?* "You're not entirely wrong about him not liking you, though. He does think you're a punk." She added, an amusing afterthought.

It earned a small smile from her neighbor.

"A punk? No. I'm goth. Punk is an entirely different style." Axel returned, rolling his eyes.

"I think he was more concerned with the attitude, not the style."

"Do you think I'm a punk?" The question Axel posed managed to make Winter pause, gazing at him.

"...No." She answered, offering up a smile of her own. Her opinion of him had never really changed. Many at school had always seen Axel Dunn as the weird loner type, but Winter just took it as being quiet. Sure enough, a silence fell between the two, for just a few seconds until Winter pointedly asked, "Did you need something? For uh… the English project, or…?"

Pushing off the porch post like he had remembered why he was there, Axel shoved his hands into his hoodie pockets.

"No, actually. Do you have some time? There's something I want to show you." He sounded nervous, until he added a snarky, "If your pops won't mind me stealing you away. You know, to join the punk life and all."

That earned another laugh from Winter. Giving it only a second of thought, she stepped back to grab her boots from a small rack by the door, calling into the kitchen,

"I'm going out for a bit, Papa! I'll be back by dinner!"

"Not with that Dunn boy, are you? Winter?" He called back, but Winter had already slipped out the front door and closed it behind her, yanking on her boots as fast as she could.

"Come on, punk, before you have to sit through an interrogation." Winter remarked, jogging down the front steps of her porch with Axel at her heels.

Winter let Axel lead the way, walking beside him in relative silence, glancing at him every few seconds. It was the first time that they had hung out, in person, outside of school. Unless she counted the fight with Ian, but that wasn't really hanging out so much as it was running for their lives, or their project studies, but Winter didn't really count that either. As they were walking down Aurum Lane, in the direction of Timor Street, she finally spoke up.

"So, where are you taking me?" Winter's question was met with silence, and when she slid her gaze to Axel once more, he was smirking. "Am I allowed to know?"

"Do you like cars?" Axel answered her with a new question.

"Uh... I mean... They're okay? I guess?" Winter shrugged her shoulders, giving him a curious look. "I don't know much about them, other than they look pretty. My papa likes classic muscle cars."

Axel snorted, but didn't actually answer, as they continued walking. As they turned right to head up Timor street, it finally clicked for Winter.

He's taking me to the junkyard? The junkyard on Timor was less of a junkyard and more of an abandoned car lot. It was a large piece of land, fenced in and not far from Caligo's cemetery. Growing up, kids in school used to like to tell horror stories about corpses wandering through the junkyard at night, past the old cars.

In the middle of the day, however, it was almost serene to wander through. Axel took her all the way to the back of the lot, walking down a line of old cars until he stopped in front of one in particular, waving his hands at it.

"Check it out."

"Um…" Winter glanced from the covered car, back to Axel in confusion.

Grinning, he grabbed the cover and began to yank it off, unveiling it to her.

"It's a 1979 Camaro Z28. Thing of beauty, isn't she?"

She was not the worst car in the lot, but definitely needed a bit of work. The Camaro was most likely once a stunning car. It had the classic, strong exterior, the worn metal was a radiant of purple and blue, with only the trunk lid showing any sign of rust, and even then, barely at all. Camaros had distinctive grills and rounded headlights, with large front bumpers. It looked like it had been treated to new Goodyear tires, still clean and undriven. The windshield and windows were also surprisingly clean, as if they had been washed and polished.

"It's a she?"

"Hell yeah." Axel responded, prying open the passenger door with a metallic creak, gesturing for Winter to sit. She did so, and he shut the door behind her, jogging around to the driver's side.

The interior of the Camaro was not in good condition, but it wasn't terrible either. Where many of the cars of the junkyard had leaves and trash inside, the Camaro was clean enough, the dashboard clear. All the dials were easily viewed, the radio and gears didn't look too dingy. The steering wheel was a bit rusty looking, however, and the seat fabric was torn up and discolored from sunlight. Winter noticed her door was missing the lock piece that should have been poking up.

"Wait, this is yours?" Winter asked, running her hand along the dash.

"Yep. You know Jovanni, from school?"

"Jovanni Brooks?" Winter only vaguely knew him. He was an edgy goth kid, a lot like Axel, who tended to stay by himself. But unlike Axel, Winter had gone to the same middle and elementary school as him. She had known Jovanni before he let his hair grow out, and before he'd gotten multiple piercings.

"Yeah. His dad owns this yard. Total ass, but he told me I could keep the Camaro if I could get it running. I've been fixing it up for months now. Got everything except for a new spark plug. I thought the old one was alright but it keeps misfiring and I've checked everything else." Axel placed his hands on the wheel, sighing wistfully, "It's okay though. I'll get a new one next month. I help go through the recycling here, get a bit of cash to save up. Spark plugs aren't expensive, won't be long now."

Winter really didn't know a thing about mechanical issues. She had no clue what a spark club— plug?— chub— whatever did. Yet, Axel had her full, enraptured attention, staring at him as he spoke. This was the most excited, the most unguarded, he had ever been with her.

"If you got this thing running, and you know, painted it, and everything, it would blow Ian's Supra out of the water." Winter commented, leaning back in her seat.

"That's the plan. A Camaro versus a Supra? Not even in the same class." Axel beamed from ear to ear, truly delighting in the idea of making Ian put his money where his mouth was. He reached up to pull down the visor, revealing a photo taped to it. It was a photo of a pristine conditioned blue Camaro, so pretty it could have been a show car. Tapping his finger on the photo, Axel added, "When I'm done, this will be my baby."

"So... who knows about your, uh... baby?" Winter asked curiously, a theory forming.

"No one. Just you." He didn't even hesitate, answering her.

"Wait... Axel... is this... Are you apologizing?"

"What? What do I have to apologize for?"

"For saying we're not friends. This is a friend thing, showing me your car."

"No, I'm not apologizing. I just wanted to show you, don't make it weird." Axel looked away from her as he said this. Were his cheeks burning?

"You… You unapologetic punk!" Winter couldn't help but laugh, not truly upset at all. She was beginning to understand Axel. He was a complicated person, and he didn't always say what he meant. To her, he had some pretty heavy defense mechanisms. Maybe if she was lucky, someday she'd find out why. But for now… they were on the path of becoming friends, and she was set on earning his trust.

"Goth." Axel corrected her.

"Punk."

"Goth."

"…Ass."

That earned a laugh, Axel unable to stop himself as Winter bluntly swore to break up their tiny feud over the title. She wasn't the type to swear, but perhaps Axel's own mouth was rubbing off on her a bit. Besides, it was clearly harder to insult him than that. Clapping his hands on the wheel of his car, Axel shook his head at her. Pride at making him laugh swelled through Winter as she smiled at him.

"There are other cars on this lot— little dune buggies and things— that actually do drive. You wanna go for a ride? I'll race ya." Axel offered, as he threw the visor back up and kicked his door open.

"O-Oh no. I'm not much of a driver." Winter stammered as she climbed out of the Camaro, unable to hide her sudden nerves. She didn't have a license, for good reason.

"What, you've never driven? Or you don't like driving?"

"Um… well… a bit of both. I've driven a little, and I really don't like it."

"Seriously?"

"Mhm."

Axel looked at her as if she had grown a second head. As a car lover, it was surely a mystery how anyone could dislike being behind a wheel. Winter shrunk a little under his gaze, tucking a lock of hair behind her ear.

"Well... guess I'm the designated driver then. Come on, Win." Axel finally decided, gesturing for her to follow him.

The rest of the evening was spent with Axel driving clunkers around the junkyard, letting him tell her about the wonderful world of why Camaros were superior cars and the various parts that made it so. He really seemed to know his stuff, talking about Nascar and racers that Winter had never heard of. At last, she had the chance to just listen to him, unlike previous times they had talked.

Axel might have been a loner, but he had interests like anyone else— and Winter was eager to hear about them.

"Winter? What in the devil are you doing rummaging around out here?" Her grandfather asked, as he wandered out into the yard.

It was the next day— a Saturday morning. Dressed in flared jeans and a green blouse with flowy sleeves, Winter was standing under her house's carport, beside her grandfather's car. It was an old muscle car, not unlike Axel's Camaro— but her grandfather had a 1965 Plymouth Barracuda. Like Axel, he took extraordinary care of it, and had just gotten it repainted last year into a sweet cherry red, only slightly darker than Ian's bright red Supra.

In front of his parked car was a red tool stand, beside a metal workbench— which is what Winter was searching through. Glancing up, her hands still digging through the drawers, she answered,

"Hey Papa, do you have any spare spark plugs?"

"Spark plugs?" He asked, shuffling across the stone driveway towards her. "I have a spare for the 'cuda, somewhere…"

"Would that work for a 1979 Camaro?" Winter tilted her head, watching as her grandfather scratched at the five o'clock shadow on his chin.

"'Course not, Pumpkin. Cars take different parts, spark plugs are different. Why are you asking about a '79 Camaro?"

"Oh, uh… it's a school project, for shop class. We're working on a Camaro." Winter wasn't used to lying, and she wasn't a particularly good liar. But she didn't want to tell her grandfather it was for Axel— if she did, he might not help her. He certainly didn't like Axel enough to assist with his car, and Winter wasn't entirely sure Axel would want his car talked about anyway.

Joining her at the tool box, her grandfather pulled open a drawer that seemed stuffed with pamphlets and car manuals.

"Can't help you with the spark plug but I think I have a manual for an old camaro your aunt Joan had once." After a minute of searching, he pulled out a bent, little manual, yellowed with age, and held it out to Winter. "Here you go."

Taking it, Winter flipped through the manual, looking for parts. To her surprise, there it was— the name of the spark plug, followed by a grainy manual photo of it.

"Thanks, papa." She said, smiling at him.

"Winter?"

"Hm?"

"No funny business, you hear me?" These words made Winter's blood run cold, her smile dropping away as her grandfather fixed her with a stern gray-eyed stare.

"Nothing abnormal at school. No cheating, do you understand?"

She knew exactly what he was talking about, without needing to ask. Preparing herself to lie again, to promise him, she opened her mouth—

"Winter!"

Axel's voice interrupted the two Jozefsons. Hurriedly, Winter tucked the manual in the back of her jeans, throwing her blouse over it and fixing her smile back onto her face as she watched Axel strolling across the street towards them. As he reached them, he gave her grandfather a terse nod.

"Mr. Jozefson."

"Mr. Dunn. What reason do you have for being on my lawn?"

"Papa!" Winter whined, as the two men glared at each other.

"I'm not on your lawn, sir. I'm on your driveway." Axel cheekily answered, smirking shamelessly at the older gentleman.

Winter's grandfather gave a grunt, choosing not to respond and instead ambling into the house without saying goodbye.

As the side door to the house shut, Winter gave a sigh and turned to look at Axel.

"There is such a thing as being polite. Or, you know, at least respectful." She lectured him, frowning.

"What exactly has he done to earn my respect?" Axel retorted, crossing his arms.

She could have argued with him— but he wasn't wrong. Her grandfather always said something similar, actually— respect was earned, not freely given. Maybe they were more alike than they knew.

"What are you doing here?" Winter asked instead.

"Figured we could go to the theater. That new movie,

Chill Factor, came out a few weeks ago. You want to go see it?" Axel asked nonchalantly. Surely, he wasn't typically the movie theater going type— unlike Winter, who went at least once a month with Kaya. The last time she had been to a movie had been with Oliver Blaikwood, a childhood friend, to see a movie called The Sixth Sense; which had been incredible.

"I haven't heard good things about that one. Kaya went to see it after school Wednesday with Matthew, Korin, and Maya." Winter told Axel. Matthew and Korin were both on the football team at school, and Maya, Korin's girlfriend, was on the school paper with Kaya. Their similar names were often an amusing joke amongst the school paper crew.

"Well, I like to judge movies for myself. Besides, I got nothing better to do today." Axel peered at her, his blue eyes indiscernible, waiting for her to agree to go.

But I do have better things to do... Winter thought, thinking of the spark plug mission she had. Still, she didn't want to spoil the surprise, and if she gave an excuse, Axel was sure to know something was up. So, instead, she smiled.

"Alright then. I suppose I can come out for a few hours— but I have homework to finish tonight, so I'm coming right back after, okay?"

"It's a matinee, Win, it won't keep you out until midnight."

His sarcasm earned a laugh, Winter following Axel as they headed off to the theater.

It was nearing dinner time by the time Winter got back— she had let Axel rope her into going to the mall after the movie, where they discussed how bad Chill Factor really had been, and movies they both actually liked— such as Hellraiser and Jurassic Park. As they wandered through a Hot Topic, Axel had been surprised to learn Winter loved horror movies, giving them a whole new topic to talk endlessly about.

After returning home, she had dinner with her grandfather— and at long last, managed to slip away into her room. Flopping down onto her bed, she pulled out the car manual that she had kept stowed away from Axel's view all day long.

Grabbing a sketchbook off her desk, along with a pencil, Winter got to work copying the photo from the manual. A spark plug looked a little bit like a rifle bullet— but made out of nuts and bolts. Over the years, Winter had gotten good at sketching items she saw, and before long she had a decent drawing in front of her.

"Sorry, papa. I can't promise anything." She sighed to herself as she stared down at the drawing.

For as long as she could remember, Winter had a gift. The same gift that had let her form a glass bottle out of thin air to knock out Ian Bryars. The same gift that made her grandfather wary of her 'funny business'.

Stretching a hand out over the drawing after a good minute of studying it, she closed her eyes. She could see it, a strong image forming behind her eyelids of the spark plug.

I want to make this for Axel, for the Camaro. She reminded herself of why she was doing this. It wasn't often that she tried to make something of this nature, hiding away her powers out of habit.

It felt like static energy between her fingers and the page, a strange vibration, her skin growing tingly— almost like her hand had fallen asleep. The air near her hand turned warmer, the harder she focused on envisioning the spark plug.

Come on... I know what I need, so give it to me. She silently pleaded, as if asking an unknown force.

A good minute passed of concentration, until she heard

the soft thump of an object. Peeking open her eyes, the energetic aura against her hand faded as she pulled it away.

There it was. Laying on her notebook, atop the sketch she had drawn— a perfectly replicated spark plug for a 1979 Camaro Z28.

5

UNKNOWN ABILITIES

"**A**xel Octavius Dunn, take that monstrosity out of your lip right now. If we're late because you're dragging your feet—" Alessandra Dunn's sharp voice cut through the house from where she stood in the entryway, fixing her pearl earrings in a mirror by the front door.

Axel turned from her, so she wouldn't see the nasty scowl that had overcome his face, as he stomped back upstairs. Unkind words for his mother drifted through his head as he ducked into the hall bathroom, flicking on the light and wincing when he saw his face in the mirror. There he was— his own greatest enemy. Axel saw all the things he hated, things he assumed other people also hated. He was dressed up for church, his usual hoodie ditched for a white dress shirt that made him feel even more pale than usual, washing out his skin tone. His face was particularly hard to look at. There, glinting in the light, was his lip ring.

Honestly, if he could have, his face would have been much more full of metal. He had plans for snake bites and nostril piercings, even eyebrow piercings, as well as wanting several more in his ears. The only way his mother tolerated him having a single lip piercing was due to him having not asked — he had gone out with his brother Kaius one day at the tender age of fourteen, and come back with an unprofessionally done lip ring that one of Kaius' sketchy friends had given him. That day there had been hell to pay in his house, but now, it was begrudgingly accepted.

Except on Sundays.

Taking it out, Axel set the metal piece on the sink shelf with a soft clink. He turned on the water to rinse his face, lifting his head to scowl at himself once more in the mirror. Bright blue eyes stared back, the circles underneath painfully obvious.

"Axel! Get down here! Your father is already in the car!"

"Coming!" Axel hollered back, rolling his eyes as he went trudging down the stairs, ready to get the morning over with.

Sundays were his least favorite day of the week, and they always went the same. His mother and father bickering (or as Axel liked to put it, bitching) during the car ride about this or that, his mother correcting both of their appearances and postures. Kaius always met them at church, but Lisden had stopped going the second he turned eighteen— something Axel envied.

New Avalon Catholic Church was the oldest church in Caligo, more than half of the town's population belonged to its congregation. It was a long, brick building with stained glass windows and four saint statues on each corner, along with a large bronze cross over the front double doors. Streams of people were still heading in, as Axel dragged his feet, following along.

They found Kaius easily enough. He fit the proper look that Axel hated, wearing a sleek suit and tie, his black hair gelled back and his dark eyes as sharp as their mother's. He was the middle son of the Dunn family, four years older than Axel, and lived a few towns over, working for some kind of financial stock market company.

"Axel."

"Kai."

The two brothers greeted each other, both tersely polite as Axel flopped down onto the bench beside him. They had once been close, but... well, growing up tore everyone apart, didn't it? At least, that was how Axel thought it had to be. He had stopped having anything in common with perfect Kaius a long time ago.

The Priest, Reverend Callahan, was a short man with spectacles and salt and pepper hair. His daughter Grace, who went to Clamare High, sat in the front pews with her nearly identical mother. Both of the women sported long brown hair, baby blue eyes, and sweet salmon pink dresses. Grace was in the same grade as Axel, though they rarely spoke.

The cathedral hall was made up of high ceilings and banisters, a large bronze Jesus crucifixion statue at the head of the room, right behind the podium the reverend stood at. To the right of the room were a series of confessional booths — Axel's personal hell.

Another long, bland sermon was told, all about the dangers of the mind— *tell me something I don't know,* Axel thought.

Normally, he would have rushed out of church as soon as things finished up, but today, a familiar hand tapped his shoulder.

"Morning, Axel! Did you enjoy today's service?" Winter's warm voice washed over him, her smile ever present on her face. She wore a peachy sundress, with translucent sleeves, her hair flowing over one shoulder in a long ponytail. A pearl necklace hung at the apex of her collarbone, while her other necklace — the wrought iron disk that never left her neck— was tucked under her dress. She had slipped into the pew behind them, leaning against the back as Axel turned around to face her. Around them was a heavy buzz of chatter as everyone began to gather themselves to leave, talking over the morning service.

"Not particularly. Organized religion isn't really my thing." Axel answered her, attempting a tired smile.

"You got a girlfriend, little brother?" Axel had almost forgotten Kaius had been next to him until his voice cut into the conversation. His brother leaned over their pew, sticking out a hand to take Winter's and gave it a firm shake, smiling at her. "Kaius Dunn. You're... Mr. Jozefson's granddaughter, aren't you?"

"Yes! Winter. Nice to meet you. Although, I'm not Axel's girlfriend. We're just friends." Winter chirped, beaming back at Kaius as Axel glared at him. Their parents had stood and moved to talk to Mrs. Bryars'— Ian's mother— in the next pew over, leaving the three alone.

This time at the mention of being friends, Axel didn't argue. Though the way Winter addressed Kaius was unusual to him. Her voice had shifted to an overly friendly tone, her posture stiff and polite. Like snapping a mask up, every familiarity she had formed with Axel was gone. Perfect Winter met perfect Kaius, and suddenly Axel hated her a little. Fake didn't suit Winter. Maybe it just felt fake to him, though.

"I didn't know he had any. Moving up in the world at last, huh? Finally got some luck." Kaius laughed, as if the very thought was hilarious.

Axel kept his mouth shut, gritting his teeth. Winter's smile twitched, as if she wanted to respond to that, but instead she looked at him. Her hazel-green eyes met Axel's, and her smile seemed to soften.

"Well, I'm the lucky one." She softly answered, before

asking Axel directly, "I had something for you. Do you think we could go to Evadere? I packed lunches for both of us. I figured we could have a picnic or something, enjoy the afternoon."

"Sounds like a date to me." Kaius interjected as Axel opened his mouth to answer her.

"Oh eff off, Kai." Axel barely avoided swearing in the church, turning a pointed glare to his brother. Winter's cheeks burned red at Kaius' words, leaning back uncomfortably.

"N-No, I..." She started, stammering.

"Don't listen to him, Win." Axel interrupted her, before standing. "Let's get out of here."

"You're too touchy, Axel. Maybe having a girlfriend will do you some good." Kaius teased him, shrugging as Axel marched down to the aisle. When Winter caught up with him, he placed a hand on her back and steered her away as quickly as he could.

"Always starting shit... What a—" Axel grumbled as they left the church together. To his relief, the second they were out the doors, Winter allowed her shoulders to sag and her mask to fall away.

"I've got to grab something at my house, do you mind if we stop by? Besides, I want to get out of this." Axel asked, as they stepped into the sunlight, gesturing to his Sunday clothes.

"Sure, I don't mind." Winter answered, her cheeks still flushed from Kaius' teasing. She was a bit anxious, avoiding looking him in the eye as they walked. Did he think her asking him to the park was a date? But... he had asked her to the movies yesterday— that wasn't a date, was it?

"Seriously, Winter. Don't listen to Kaius, he's just being a prick. He's one of those 'guys and girls can't be friends' shitheads. He messed with at least a dozen girls in high school and didn't give a damn about any of them. He's the last person you should let talk shit about us going out to Evadere." Axel's voice cut into her thoughts.

Nodding, Winter took a deep breath. "I'm glad you're not like your brother, at least. He's..." She trailed off, not wanting to speak badly about the man, though he made her uncomfortable. Kaius reminded her slightly of Ian. Outwardly put together, but his eyes showed an inner instability that she didn't want to be around.

"Yeah, I know. I agree."

It wasn't too far from the church to the house. There was something fascinating to Winter about the Dunn residence. She had stepped inside once or twice before, when delivering something to Mr. or Mrs. Dunn from her grandfather, but never had spent more than a second inside, nor gone further than the entryway. Back then, she had always wondered about Axel, but the troubled youngest child had always been tucked away in his room somewhere, not eager to run into any guests.

The outside of it was magnificent. A large home, with a wrap around porch framed by black banisters and neatly trimmed hedges. The plot of land was larger than Winter's own across the street, and they had a full two car garage and a long driveway. The house itself was Victorian in style; it was slate gray, with black shutters to frame the windows of the second floor. There was a tall rotunda on the left side of the house, with an intimidating pointed top. The roof was made of dark blue, scalloped tiles, a red brick fireplace poking out towards the middle of the house.

In a hurry to grab his things so they could head out again, Axel remarked to Winter, "You can come in to wait for me, if you want."

So she did, jogging up the porch steps after him and stepping into the foyer of the house, closing the front door behind her as she watched Axel head noisily up the stairs to his room. While she waited, she wandered into the large, open living room. It was very neat, compared to her own home— where her grandfather's magazine pile and cigar dish were on the coffee table, this one was spotless and bare. A small wet bar in the corner looked untouched but didn't have a single spot of dust on it, glass shelves with intricate drinking glasses all lined up in a row above it. There was a small white brick fireplace that looked like it had never held a fire in it, and a mantle full of photographs.

Stepping closer, Winter eyed the photos. She could spot Axel easily in each and every one of them, his eyes brighter than either of his brother's, who took after their mother's darker eyes. They also had easier smiles than Axel, better at acting. She could pick out Kaius easily in the photos— he had a clean way of dressing and a stern posture in most of them, posing perfectly. The third boy was blonde and long haired, taking after their father— Mr. Dunn's blonde and blue eyed Danish appearance was unmistakable, and his eldest son was an almost identical copy, except for his dark eyes.

One photo in particular caught her eye— a young Axel, perhaps nine years old, sitting at a grand piano. Turning her head, Winter's eyes went to the piano in the corner of the room, the very same from the photo.

"Ready to go?" Axel's voice startled her from her thoughts, as he appeared in the doorway of the living room. He had changed into a dark blue knitted sweater, his hair all messed up from having yanked it over his head. His lip ring was back where it belonged.

"You play?" Winter asked, pointing at the piano. Axel followed her gaze, immediately frowning.

"Guess so. Is that important?" He asked with a sigh, watching her walk over to the piano. Her hands lifted the cover, a smile lighting up her face as she traced the keys with her fingers, idly pushing down on one and delighting in the melodic chime it made. It was a Steinway and Sons piano, certainly no older than ten years, in beautiful condition.

"Are you kidding? It's incredible." She said, her tone full of wonder and admiration, sitting down on the piano bench. "I've always wanted to learn. Piano music is beautiful. My grandpa had a sister who played, that he lost. I don't think he could stand the sound of it after that, so he never wanted me to take lessons." Her smile fell away at the thought, looking down at the keys. Her hand drifted over them once more, almost as if she were afraid to play on them, dusting them with the barest touch of her fingertips.

Axel watched her, his eyes trained on her face— their eyes met when Winter looked up again.

"Will you play for me?" The question came with an innocent, hopeful tone that Axel hadn't been expecting. His mouth opened, his face contorting into a grimace, and Winter expected him to reject her request. Instead, he sighed again, used to being asked.

"Scoot over." He mumbled as he walked over, sitting down onto the bench beside her. "My mom made me take lessons. She made all of us pick a classical instrument. Lisden plays violin, Kaius plays piano like me— and he's better at it. He likes the fast, jaunty tunes. I wanted to learn guitar, but that wasn't an option for mom."

From what Winter knew of Axel's mother, she could understand. There was her way of doing things— the right way— and that was the only way. Like most parents, she supposed.

Glancing sideways at her, Axel hovered his hands over the keys. "What do you want me to play? I know most of the slower classics. Beethoven, Chopin, Debussy."

"Anything!" Winter exclaimed immediately. Her cheeks burned, and she looked down at the keys to avoid Axel's stare. "Whatever you want. Your, uh… favorite, if you have one. Do you need sheet music?"

"No. I know a few well enough to play without." Axel answered her, taking a deep breath.

He paused, before beginning his chosen piece. The melody was slow at first, but his hands moved elegantly, fingers stretching over the keys beautifully. Winter's eyes never left his hands as the song began— not one she recognized. As the sound danced through the living room of the Dunn residence, she was left enchanted, watching the steady rise and fall of Axel's hands, the curl of his knuckles.

Halfway through the song, she couldn't resist leaning into him, laying her head on his shoulder. To her relief, it didn't stop Axel, his hands not missing a single note. The melody he played was almost sleepy, making Winter want to close her eyes— but she didn't want to miss watching the performance.

As the song drew to an end with a heavy final touch from both of Axel's hands, Winter lifted her head again.

"It's called Träumerei." Axel spoke first, before Winter could. "Which translates to 'Dreaming'."

"It's… wonderful." Winter whispered, unable to speak louder. Dramatically, in the back of her mind, she felt like if she spoke too loudly, it would break the feeling the song had put into the air. Her eyes were wet and glossy, staring at Axel as she softly asked, "You really hate playing?"

How could anyone hate anything so beautiful? She thought.

But to her disappointment, Axel nodded. "I do."

Silence fell between them, Winter looking back down at

the piano. Lips parting, she wanted to ask him to keep playing— to play anything more for her. Instead, she said,

"Thank you for playing for me."

"You're welcome." Axel answered her. She thought for a second he might have said something else, but instead he reached to close the piano lid, the beautiful keys hidden away from Winter's view once more.

She could have sat there and listened all day, if Axel had let her. Instead, he rose from his seat and grabbed the bag he had dropped on the floor, hiking it up over one shoulder.

"Are you coming or do you want me to leave you alone with the piano?" He sassed her gently as he made his way towards the front door.

"Is that a serious offer?" Winter joked back, getting up and pushing the piano bench in. She spared the grand piano one last, wistful look before she followed Axel out of the house.

Evadere Park was one of Winter's favorite places in Caligo. It was on the west side, south of the junkyard and the cemetary. It wasn't really a true park, more like a rolling hilly stretch of land with a few walking paths, gazebos, and picnic benches. It was a sunny day out, the last bit of warmth from the summer being soaked up before everything turned cold.

There was one gazebo in particular that Winter favored, at the far end of the park on a little hill, with a beautiful view of Timor st. in the distance. That was where she led Axel, trekking up the hill with the little basket she had packed with lunch— two cold cut sandwiches, a box of grapes, a box of carrots, and two bags of chips.

"Thanks, Winter." Axel remarked as he ripped open a bag

of chips, starving. "I never have time to eat before church—God forbid eating a bowl of cereal makes us late."

"You're welcome." Winter was unable to look at him, nervously starting to pick at her grapes. How was she going to broach the real reason she asked him to spend the afternoon here with her? She had gotten lucky that the park was empty today— they were the only two within sight. Most that had been at the church were likely at Damara's or heading home around now.

"You said you had something for me, right? Was this it?" Axel hadn't forgotten, it seemed, picking up on her nerves.

"Yeah, uh…" Winter reached for her bag, taking a deep breath. She had wrapped the spark plug in some brown paper, setting it on their table in front of him. "Here you go. I hope it's… I hope it'll help."

Axel gave her an odd, confused look, taking the package. "Let me guess— a rifle bullet to hunt down Ian Bryars?" He joked darkly, judging the shape of the package. Winter didn't say a word as he unwrapped it, watching his jaw drop when he saw what it really was. "No freaking way. Winter what— why did you…"

"I-I thought, you know… it's the last thing you need to get the Camaro running, so… I-Is it the right one? I wasn't sure…"

"Yes! It is, but… You didn't have to." He seemed stunned, turning the car part around in his hand, his food forgotten about.

"That's what friends do." Winter insisted, smiling at the title. To her surprise, Axel smiled back at her, ducking his head to hide the fact his cheeks were tinged pink.

"How did you get this? Did you buy it?"

That question made Winter squirm. She had been thinking about what to tell him if he asked her that. The truth? Only two people knew the secret of her powers; her grandfather, who had always known as long as she could remember; and Kaya, who had witnessed it accidentally when Winter was twelve. Kaya would protect her secret with her life, Winter had never doubted that— and other than the occasional joke or request to bring something into being, she didn't treat Winter differently.

Axel was a hard person to gauge the reaction of. He wasn't like anyone else she knew— they had talked about a lot, but they hadn't talked about deep secrets. For it being their English project, they had spent most of their time sharing more common things, like their interests, likes, dislikes. Of which, they had a surprising amount of things in common, along with some extremely obvious differences. They, on rare occasions, talked about deeper subjects like how they saw the world. Those conversations were her favorite.

Winter wanted to be Axel's friend.

Friends trusted each other.

"I'll tell you but… promise me you won't tell anyone." The air between them had grown serious. Was the fear all over her face?

Axel stared at her, giving a solemn nod. "I promise."

"I… made it. Created it. There's um… Well, I don't really know what to call it, but… This is going to sound insane so I'm just going to say it. I imagine things, o-or draw things, and they… come to life. Like, out of thin air."

For a long moment, they just stared at each other, Axel's brows drawing together in an intense expression, scrutinizing her. Did he not believe her? He looked like he was trying to see if she was pulling his leg, and all Winter could do was hold her breath. The silence was suffocating, so she began to ramble,

"I've been able to do it since I was little. Kaya calls it magic. My papa and her are the only ones that know. I've never done anything large scale. Mostly just small stuff. Like... moving an object from one location to another, or creating something new." She paused, eyeing him. Her hands, in her lap, were shaking, "When we were dealing with Ian... the bottle I used to hit him, it was something I made in the spur of the moment."

"Okay." Finally, he said something. Too bad it did nothing to ease her nerves.

"You don't believe me."

"No, I do, I just... I'm sorry— you just told me you have magic, I'm finding it a bit hard to... uh... process." Axel answered, running a hand through his curly black hair.

Biting her lip, Winter asked, "W-Would you like me to show you?"

"Sureeee." Axel drew out the word, leaning back. He reached for a carrot, taking a cautious bite. She could see it written on his face— he thought she was crazy.

"What's your favorite candy?" She needed something to make, after all.

"Uh... M&M's."

"Pick a color."

"Blue." His face had turned from skeptical to unamused, ready to be let down.

Winter took a glance around to make sure they were still alone.

Lifting a hand over the picnic table, she closed her eyes briefly. She loved M&M's as well, picturing them clearly, small, curved candies, faded white stamped "M" in the middle. Hard shell, soft chocolate interior. Envisioning them, she focused on the color, the shape, trying to get it as vivid in her mind as she could. Opening her eyes, the familiar vibration began to make her palm tingle.

The next thing she knew, M&Ms were appearing right from her underneath her hand. She could see them pop into existence, falling as dozens of them scattered over the table. Axel jumped back in his seat, swearing as M&Ms went everywhere, the half carrot he had been holding falling out of his hand.

Closing her hand, the creation of the little candies came to a halt. Instantly, she could feel the vibration of her powers stop, like a door being shut against wind. Pulling her hand back into her lap, Winter itched at her palm before reaching for an M&M, popping it into her mouth.

"Believe me now?"

"Y-Yeah. Holy crap, Winter, that's… You're a freaking…"

"Witch?"

"Um…" Guilt flashed over Axel's face, aware of what he had been about to call her. Witchcraft seemed rather negative— for good reason. Just the other day, witch trials of Salem had been brought up in their history class. Winter had to wonder if any of those women had powers like hers.

"It's okay, it doesn't offend me. Kaya and I have talked about it a lot. I don't know what I am, honestly. Papa doesn't like to talk about it, and he doesn't approve of me using it, so I try not to." Winter explained.

"Can you make anything? Like… big things?" Axel asked, as he cautiously picked up an M&M, rolling it in his hand. As he popped it into his mouth, his eyes went wide. "It even tastes real…"

"It is real. Everything I make is real." Winter told him. "I can make big things but it… it takes a lot more to do. Usually I have to sketch things out before I make them. Little things that are familiar are fine, like the M&M's. Or the glass bottle I made— that was pure adrenaline, going off of memory. The spark plug, I had to draw."

Reaching for her bag, she pulled out her red notebook, flicking to the page with the spark plug— an exact replica of the one that sat in front of Axel.

"See?"

"That's insane. I mean, it's…" He looked like he was deep in thought, hesitating. Before he could finish speaking, Winter interjected,

"I understand if you… if you don't want to hang out with me anymore. I just hope you keep my secret." She had a horrible feeling that this was it; that he couldn't accept it. That he couldn't accept her or her freaky powers. Winter's stomach was in knots, heart racing as she stared at him.

"No. I… I think it's incredible, Winter. I want to see more." Axel's words were genuine, she could tell, as he smiled at her. She was sure he still didn't know exactly what to think of it, but the idea of showing him what she could do was enough to ease her anxiety.

"I can definitely show you more!"

The rest of the afternoon was spent eating their lunch, and Winter drawing and making little things for Axel. She didn't know the limits of her own gift, but she told him what she could— what she did know. It was very much a mystery to her, however. To her surprise, Axel could feel the warmth and strange electrical vibrations coming off her hand when she created stuff. By the end of the afternoon, they had enjoyed two sodas, and she had given herself a new notebook, as well as Axel a lip ring— steel, not gold or silver, which Winter found herself incapable of making.

There was a certain relief in revealing her gift, but he didn't seem to want to abuse the magic Winter possessed. In fact, Axel was the one who suggested they stop, eager to get to the junkyard with his new spark plug.

Winter, of course, happily joined him to see her created car part in action.

6

UNDERSTANDING DEPRESSION

"I should let you go, we've got Ms. Noble's class first thing in the morning." Winter sighed heavily over the phone.

Axel lay on his back in bed, but he could still glance over out the window and see Winter's bedroom light on. His own room was pitch black, the soft glow of his phone screen against his face being the only light as he held it to his ear. To Axel, there was comfort in the dark. It was a little after midnight, and he had spent the evening listening to Winter talk. He more or less responded to her, for the most part just letting her ramble on. She was calming to listen to, distracting. It at least helped him not listen to the dark parts of his mind, which were far less comforting right now.

"Let's skip it." Axel responded, lips twitching into a half smile at the sound of Winter's laugh.

"I wish." A shadow passed over her window. Once, twice, three times. Was she pacing as they talked? "We should run away. Just hop in the Camaro and go until it gives out. How far do you think it would get? New York city?"

Now it was Axel's turn to chuckle, sitting up with a groan,

"In its current state, we'd be lucky if it went over the bridge without sputtering." The aforementioned bridge being at the end of Timor st. It went over the Effogere river, heading south out of Caligo.

More chuckles across the line, the figure in the lit window stopping. He saw her shadow widen, as if she had turned to face the window. A pause came over the phone, silence growing between the two, until—

"Axel… Can I ask you something?" Her voice was timid, but determined. Axel could almost envision her expression— the way her brows furrowed in class when she had something on her mind. They had only been closely talking for about three weeks, but it was easy to learn all of Winter's quirks. Easier now that he was able to see her close up on a daily basis. So far, she was unlike any girl he'd ever met— and he didn't even think of her unique abilities, saying that.

It had been around a week since she had revealed her gifts, and it felt like it had skyrocketed them into a true friendship. How could he not feel comfortable around her when she had shared something that huge? He had spent every day that week working on the Camaro, getting it running and taking it for small drives around Caligo. The spark plug worked like a charm, a marvel of a creation.

"Shoot." He remarked, making a little finger pistol and pretending to shoot upwards at the ceiling, dropping his arm back onto the bed with a small thump.

"Why is it you have no friends?" Her question disarmed him, his mouth dropping open, unsure at first how to respond. But she continued, "I mean… besides me, I haven't seen you hang out with anyone, ever. You usually sit alone in class, I never see you in the cafeteria at lunch… No one paired up with you for the English project, until I volunteered. But we've been talking every day since, and I don't see any reason why you're alone all the time."

She wasn't wrong. Sure, Axel talked to people here and there— like Jovanni Brooks, or Charlie McLain, who both shared his love of music. But could idle conversations about the latest bands, and not knowing a single personal thing about each other, count as friendship? Winter had certainly invaded his life far more in three weeks than they had in years, with her constant questions and storytelling. He wouldn't say he trusted the kids at school nearly as much as he had come to— cautiously— trust Winter.

Trying to stall for time, and maybe even avoid the question entirely, Axel turned it around on her, "What about you? You only hang with Kaya. Aren't you supposed to be... I don't know, a social butterfly or something?"

"I mean... I have other friends. There's Oliver Blaikwood."

"Oliver is friends with anyone who gets within five feet of him."

"Okay, what about the Chi twins?"

"Don't you share like... every class with them? It doesn't count if you never hang with them outside of school."

He had her there, making Winter pause as she tried to think of how to counter his words.

"I'm different, though. I mean, you're..." She trailed off, and Axel interjected,

"A freak?"

"No! T-That's not what I—"

"But I am, though." He bluntly answered her. "I'm different, and people don't like different. So screw 'em. I don't like people, anyway." His responses were harsh and he knew it.

"Why? I mean... I don't think you're that different." The innocent response earned a half smile as Axel glanced out his window. Winter's silhouette was gone— she must have finally stopped pacing.

He took a long pause. Was it crazy to want to tell her his

own secret? Unlike her, he had never breathed a word of it to a single person. Not his family, not his childhood friends, not even a complete stranger. His first thought was that he'd be shunned or judged for even admitting to his problems, tossed away and discarded, written off. But...

She has a secret, too. Maybe she'll understand. Maybe...

Who are you kidding? No one likes a depressed freak like you.

But Winter hasn't reacted badly to any part of me, yet...

Yet being the key word.

"Axel?" He had taken too long, Winter breaking the silence. He could hear the nervous energy in her voice.

"I have scars." The words came out as a whisper. Clearing his throat, Axel fought the urge to hang up on her, his hand shaking as he gripped the phone tighter. "On my arms."

"Oh."

Yeah, oh. Shame and embarrassment struck through him like lightning, rolling over to curl up on his side, eyes sliding shut.

"Having issues doesn't make other people real friendly. Pretty easy for them to judge you when you're fucked up in the head." He mumbled, sounding numb to the fact.

"...Can I ask a question?" Winter's voice poked through the static going through his head.

"Go ahead."

A dozen questions, actually. She asked about how long he had been cutting, if anyone knew, if he was using it to cope, and if he had plans to stop. They talked about tattooing over scars, about suicide, all the questions one generally had about depression. Axel couldn't answer all of them, anxiety rising from some— but finding immense comfort in others. Winter wasn't only curious, but rather, she was trying to understand him— something no one had ever attempted before.

"One more question." She said, about an hour later, after a

dozen other questions. "You never really answered me. About having no friends."

This question in particular, earned a sigh. He took a second, trying to formulate an answer. As was becoming increasingly easy to do with Winter, he spoke without a filter.

"People suck, Win. The majority. They're selfish, greedy, cruel. Most people go through life only giving a damn about themselves, ostracizing anyone that is different. The whole 'alternative culture'— we have our own freaking category, because no one likes people like me. Any time I've ever tried to be myself with someone, ultimately they don't end up being my friend. I could be fake, sure— but screw that. It shouldn't be this hard to like what I like, be who I want to be." He shook his head, despite her not being able to see it. "I have no friends because I don't want to put up with people."

"You put up with me." Winter reminded him.

"Yeah, well… You're not like anyone I've met before, so you're a special case. Most people really… I don't know. I just know I don't want to waste my time on people who wouldn't waste their time on me. You have to trust your friends— and anytime I've trusted someone, it hasn't been good."

"Do you trust me?"

Another pause followed as he thought about it. Did he? He had just told her his biggest secret, but…

"It's not easy for me to trust people… but I'm trying."

"Yeah… I know. I can tell." She answered, sighing. Glancing at the clock, it was already nearing two in the morning. As Axel opened his mouth to end their call, Winter's quiet voice echoed, "One more question?"

He couldn't resist, giving a genuine smile in the darkness of his room.

"Fine."

"Do I help? I mean… What causes it, for you? And… we're

friends so... does it help at all? Or... is it more like something that never goes away?"

Oh jeez... Winter sure did want to dissect what made him tick, didn't she? It almost felt like a betrayal of his own mind, but...

Careful to word it right, Axel answered her.

"You help. But... it never goes away, either. Someone like me... it helps not to be alone. When you're alone, you think, and then... It's like having a friend that treats you like crap. Telling you you're worthless, whispering in your ear. I'm the best self-sabotager I know. Good days, bad days, doesn't matter— those thoughts are always there. And it's when I'm alone with my thoughts that I end up taking actions I'll regret in the morning. It's... a cycle I can't break. A nightly game of waiting to see when I'll cave and give in. But you... I mean, you're the first person I've even told, so... it helps."

He felt vulnerable, talking about this. Winter had never been depressed before— she couldn't know what he went through each day. But... she cared enough to ask, to try to understand it— not from her side, but from his.

"...Thank you for telling me." Winter said softly. "If... if it doesn't bother you too much to talk with me about it, can I ask you about it some more, sometime?"

"Yeah. Not tonight though, okay? I'll see you in class tomorrow. And Winter?"

"Yeah?"

"This doesn't go in our essay." Fear struck him at the thought, placing trust in the girl across the street.

"Of course not. Your secrets are safe with me, Axe. I promise."

He really wanted to believe that.

Axel was usually comfortable with silence, but as he stared up at the ceiling of his room, anxiety pulled at his heart as he listened to the soft sound of Winter breathing over the phone line. It was a few days later. The conversation about depression had led to all sorts of deeper conversations. Winter was relentlessly curious, eager to learn more about him. Not everything she asked was comfortable to answer, but most of their conversations were interesting and unique. It wasn't the normal way to speak to someone— it almost felt like nightly phone interviews, one question bouncing off another. He even got to ask a few questions of his own during their nightly conversations, learning more about Winter with time.

Should I say something? He thought, the air uncomfortably heavy between them, his mind churning over tonight's serious conversation. Winter must have been thinking along the same lines, as she broke the silence.

"Hey, Axe?"

"Yeah?"

"When was the last time you told your mom that you love her? Or… she said it to you?"

The question was so innocently asked, and yet, along with being surprised, Axel felt a dagger sliding into his chest. He had to think about that, wracking his brain. His family wasn't… overly emotional. His mother was more likely to rag on why she ever chose to have children than she was to tell her sons she loved them. She would admit to being proud if they did something notable— but frankly, the only Dunn who had ever done anything notable was Lisden, the favorite son. Even perfect Kaius couldn't catch up to Lisden's reputation as the heir of the Dunn family.

To her credit, Winter didn't interrupt the silence this time, waiting until Axel hesitantly spoke.

"I... uh, don't know." It felt like a lame answer, but it was honest.

"...Do you love her?" This question gently prodded for him to say more, and Axel sighed.

"Of course I do. She's my mom. It's just..."

"Not easy to say when she's... the way she is."

"Right. Hit the nail on the head." Axel confirmed.

There was some shuffling on the other line, and when Axel glanced out his window, he could see Winter— sitting in view of her window. She was at her desk, her head down, hunched over what he could safely guess was her sketchbook as he heard the scrabble of a pen. Staring at the top of her head, with her long brown hair, he listened as she began to speak.

"I can't remember the last time my mom said it. I don't know if she was the type to say it a lot, or... Well, I really don't know my mom at all. I only remember certain things." It was the first time Winter had brought up her mom in the three weeks they had been talking.

"Do you mind if I ask about your mom? She dropped you off here, right? You don't have to talk about it, if it's a sore subject."

"No, it's fine. I don't mind." She took a shaky breath, pausing, "My mom and I... we lived north, in Washington, with my dad. I don't know what happened, really. One day we just got in the car, and came here. I had never met my papa before then. But... She left me here. I haven't seen her since. Or my dad. Papa doesn't know where they went— or if he does, he doesn't tell me. I was five, so... I have some memories but I can't say I know much about my mom. I don't even know what kind of mom she was— just that I was happy, as a kid. I love my papa too, though. He's never made me feel abandoned, I can't say I didn't have a good time growing up.

"But I do wonder… what it's like. You grew up with both your parents, and your brothers. Kaya has both her parents, and her little brother. It's… I mean, I'm not jealous but…" She sounded wistful.

"I get it." Axel answered. "I don't think you're missing out on much, though. I mean… My dad is never around— he lives for his work. Kaius is the same way, that's why we only see him on Sundays. My mom… She has an impossible standard. If you're not living up to her expectations, you're just not worth her time. I mean— she bad mouths everyone, she never has a positive thing to say. If I were to tell her about my… my issues, she would just tell me it's all in my head and I need to grow up. The word 'help' doesn't exist in her world. Every man for themselves, you know. No complaining, no crying, complete independence. She doesn't give a shit if I'm struggling, she just thinks I need to work harder. It's… how she was raised, it's how she raised us," he scoffed at the thought, "Look how that turned out."

Looking out his window, he saw that Winter had stopped sketching and now stared back at him, listening intently.

"What about Lisden?" She asked. "That's your oldest brother, right?"

"I think Lisden is as sick of it as I am. He left home at sixteen and hasn't been back except for holidays. He values his independence— doesn't need us. Got that from mom too, I guess."

A silence lulled between the two of them, until Axel said softly,

"I don't know if she loves me. I mean… I disappoint her enough, that's for sure. You've seen how she treats her students that fail her expectations— it's not that much different for her sons."

"I'm sure she does, Axel. It's like they say. A mother always loves her kids, right? Maybe she just… doesn't know how to show it." Winter's voice was soft, frowning in the window of her room.

"Do you think yours did? After she left you?" It was bluntly asked, but luckily Winter didn't seem to take offense. Instead, her answer came immediately.

"Yes. I have to think that way. I... choose to believe she left me for a reason. I could have been put in the system or something— my mom hadn't had contact with my grandparents for years by the time she brought me to Caligo, that much I do know. She could have dumped me anywhere, she chose to bring me here, where I'd be safe. That was an act of love. I... I have a lot of mixed feelings about my mom, but I've never doubted she loves me."

That evening, after getting off the phone with Winter, Axel wandered downstairs. His house was stone cold silent, not a sound besides his creaking footsteps as he stepped down into the entryway. It was nearly midnight, but his father wasn't home yet.

His mother, however, sat by candlelight at the desk in their living room. She had a stack of papers in front of her, along with a cup of tea. Already in her nightgown and house robe, she seemed to be doing some late night grading. Her long black hair was loose, her reading glasses slid to the tip of her nose. For a second, Axel studied her, looking for a resemblance. Her hair was straight, his was curly. Her expression was pinched, his was blank. *Am I even her son?* He wondered, knowing that he unfortunately was.

"What are you doing?" She asked as Axel moved to walk past her.

"Just getting a drink, mom."

"Stayed up late again, I see." Her comment bit, but Axel didn't bother responding.

Shuffling into the kitchen, he got the glass of water he always grabbed before bed, making his way back into the entryway. As he put his foot on the first step of the stairs, he hesitated, glancing back through the archway into the living room. His mother was unmoving, reading a paper with a red pen balanced in one hand, poised to mark the page.

"Love you." Axel called, holding his breath.

Nothing. Silence.

"...Night." He tried again, gripping the banister of the stairs.

"Mhm." His mother hummed back in response. He couldn't tell if she was merely distracted or not.

Stupid. Axel's mind echoed, shaking his head as he continued on back to his room, taking a sip of his water. If she didn't say it, that was an easy way to feel like she simply didn't feel it. *Don't be so stupid, you don't need her to say she loves you. What are you, a baby?* He berated himself as he flopped down on his bed once more.

Still… it would have been nice to hear.

"Axel?" Winter's voice came out in a wispy, frightened tone. She was standing in front of an old prison cell. Dark, dank stone floors and walls, barely any light in the room behind the wrought iron bars. She could hear the squeaking and scratching of rats, but her attention was on the boy within the cell.

Axel was sitting on a black chair with a tall back, almost like a throne. He certainly didn't look like a king though— he was a prisoner, hands chained to the arms of the chair. His hair was dirty, the strands sticking together like tough straw, framing a pale face covered in bruises. His lip was split, and it looked like his lip ring had been torn out, dried blood caking his chin, his clothes ragged and torn.

When he lifted his head at the sound of her voice, his eyes were startling, like bright blue car coolant, a shiver running through Winter as their gazes met. He coughed, air rattling through his chest, grimacing as he narrowed his eyes at her as she gripped the bars of the cell.

"Win... What are you doing here? You need to leave before it comes back." Axel croaked at her, watching as she pushed her way through the cell door— which, to her surprise, was unlocked. She made her way to him, hands reaching for the chains along his wrists. They weren't locked, merely looped over him, as if their weight alone kept him in place.

"Before who comes back? I'm not leaving you, Axel. Hang on, let me get these off you." She answered him, focused on the task at hand. As she peeled off the chains, however, she noticed long burns on his wrists, like the chains had been placed on burning hot and had cooled against his flesh. Horrified, she almost dropped it back onto him. "Who did this to you?"

He didn't get a chance to answer, as a creaking door opened at the end of the hall. Heavy footsteps followed, until a new person stopped outside the prison cell. Only, it wasn't a new person at all. Looking up, Winter found herself face-to-face with a second Axel.

This Axel was in pristine condition. Clean, curled hair that looked fresh from a shower, impeccably dressed in deep black robes made of velvet. He had a smile on his face; this wide, bright smile that Winter had never seen on Axel before. He looked stronger, more buffed-up than Axel's gangly limbs usually were, and maybe even a little taller. The biggest difference was his eyes. Instead of bright blue irises— his were pitch black, empty and unnerving. Alien, foreign, wrong.

Moving in front of the seated Axel, Winter protectively positioned herself between the two, eyeing his black-eyed counterpart.

"Well, well. Axel never gets visitors here, besides me." The intruder said, giving Winter a sickly sweet smile. "You must be Winter. He thinks about you a lot."

"W-Who are you?" Winter stammered, taking an unconscious step back as the inhuman imitation stepped through the cell door, the backs of her legs bumped into Axel's knees.

"I'm him. He's me." The answer came smoothly, like it really was that simple. "We're about to start the game again. I caught him, you see, I won. We've spent the last few nights here, waiting for daybreak together. But I'm going to let go of him again— for a little while. It won't last."

Looking back at Axel, Winter could see his head hanging, a shameful expression of regret on his face.

This sounds familiar.

Winter flinched as Axel lifted his head to look up at her— there were red tears dripping from his eyes. He was crying blood.

Turning back to the black-eyed version, Winter spoke, "Why don't you just leave him alone? Haven't you done enough to him?"

"No. He doesn't deserve to be left alone. This is punishment. For being worthless. For being ugly. For not being enough. For being a burden. For being—" The monster in Axel's form would have went on, if not for Winter shouting,

"Stop it! Just shut up!" It made her angry— no— furious to hear those things said. Did he really think about himself like this? Wasn't there anything she could do to block those words from harming him anymore?

Bending down, Winter worked on the chains again, eager to free Axel. His counterpart didn't stop her, crossing his arms and watching with a smirk. Winter pulled Axel out of the chair, whispering soft encouragements for him to move, wrapping her arms around his waist to support his weight and letting him lean on her. He felt like bones in her arms, malnourished and wasting away in this prison of his mind. Yes, Winter realized, that's where we are. The dark parts of Axel Dunn.

"I'll let you into the labyrinth, let you lock all the doors. But I promise you, I will find my way in." The dark Axel hummed as Winter started pulling the real Axel out of the cell. As she walked past him, he leaned closer to whisper to her, *"Better yet... He's going to let me in, willingly. That's the best part. He does it to himself, and he hates himself for it."*

Winter stubbornly stared into the creature's black eyes. She wanted to say it wasn't true, that it was all a nasty lie. But... this was the truth of depression. The disease that plagued Axel was a cruel one. It was an endless cycle— pain, relief, guilt, pain, relief, guilt. Over and over again, that was what Winter knew from the past month of talking to her friend, of glimpsing his darkest moments. Leaning closer to the demon in Axel's head, their noses almost brushed. She didn't want to show how afraid she was, her eyes filled with defiance as she responded in a steady voice. *"The day will come where he doesn't need to let you in anymore. When that day comes... I'll pity you."*

One second the black eyed man was smiling at her— the next, reality shifted, like dreams often do, and Axel and Winter were running. Axel was no longer bruised, no longer bloody. He didn't even look unhealthily thin anymore. He was holding her hand, pulling her through a maze of rooms. Every room they entered, they stopped to lock the door behind them— barring it until there was no way anyone could get through. Each room had photos on the walls, memories that Axel wouldn't let Winter stop to look at. Instead, they continued going further and further into his mind— and as they went, he seemed happier. It was like the more he closed himself off, the less chance there was to be harmed. Maybe this time it would work.

When they reached the last room, it didn't take more than a minute to hear it. At first, Winter thought it was a wolf howling, but that wasn't right. It was more like a distorted screeching sound.

"Axel... what is that?" Winter asked in a hushed voice, staring at the final door they had locked— a large, black iron door.

When she didn't get a response, she turned around— and saw her friend kneeling in the middle of the room. He was calm, but he was holding his head, bent over.

"Axe?" She called for him again, but he shook his head, not saying a word. Moving over to him, she knelt by his side, studying his expression. He looked like he was in pain, his eyebrows drawn together, his mouth tightly clamped, rubbing his fingers into his scalp.

"It's only a matter of time... I have no defenses left." Axel mumbled, occasionally glancing up at the door, growing more agitated.

The screeching grew louder and louder, a pounding soon accompanied it. Now, Winter understood. It was coming for them. Each minute, growing closer, until Winter reached to grip Axel's hand, lacing their fingers tightly. When the creature reached the final door, the pounding shook it by the frame, making Winter jump. She couldn't look away, watching each thump the door made, the locks breaking away like they were made of glass instead of metal.

When the door was thrown open, one final ear-aching shriek came as a tall, robed creature with large clear black eyes and a blurred gray face came in.

All Winter could do was scream as it lunged towards Axel.

7

UNBOUND DEMON

I t was with a sharp gasp that Winter woke, her body twisting against the sheets of her bed as she fought to sit up, breathing heavily. Her blanket and nightgown were all twisted around her body, as if she had been tossing and turning in her sleep, and the extra pillow she often had tucked between her knees had been kicked to the floor. Skin beaded with sweat, the cold air left her feeling clammy. Her room was pitch black, and the red glow of her alarm clock's numbers told her it was just after four in the morning. It was the last week of September, a Wednesday.

Tears immediately began to prick at her eyes as she recalled the vivid dream. *It felt so real. It came for Axel.* Turning her body roughly to reach for her nightstand, her hand groped for her phone in the dark, frantic until she found it and could open her texts.

W: Axel? You awake?

Every second her message went unread, her anxiety grew. Her chest tightened as tears rolled down her cheeks. The dream wouldn't stop flashing through her mind. That horrible beast... its screeching voice... its dead eyes. It held none of Axel's light, and Winter couldn't think of anything that scared her more.

> W: Please be awake.
> W: I had a nightmare.

Her breathing was short and tight, clutching her phone with an iron grip in the dark of the room, her eyes locked on the log of messages. *Answer. Come on, Axel, answer, please.* She knew if he didn't, she had no chance of falling back asleep. As the minutes passed, her breathing successfully began to slow, hand wiping tears from her eyes. *It was just a dream, Win. It wasn't real.*

But the thought of what Axel did *was* real. She couldn't help but close her eyes and picture his arms, with those cuts he had told her about. She hadn't seen them— but somehow, that only made her imagination worse. In a month, she had seen more of his darkness than anyone. She knew his secrets, and he knew hers. Was that where he was right now? Causing more harm to his body? She highly doubted he would be asleep.

Winter had all but given up hope of hearing from Axel, about to turn off her phone, when it chimed. Eyes opening, she read his response.

> A: I'm here, I'm here. You okay?

Releasing a shaky breath, Winter paused with her thumbs over the keys, hesitating. She remembered her own promises, and as much as she wanted to reassure him, or explain away the fearful awakening, she texted him back honestly.

W: No. Are you?

Heartbeats. Winter's anxiety was skyrocketing, her fingers tingling. Three minutes. Five minutes. *Why isn't he responding? Serious, Axel, this is not the right time to go silent on me.*

When the first stone smacked into her window, Winter swore her soul briefly left her body. Throwing herself off the bed, she ran over just before a second stone tapped against the glass. Unlocking and easing up the window, Winter leaned out to look down. Two blue eyes peered at her from the dark yard below.

Winter almost started crying again, just out of pure relief not to be alone— and to see him alive and well, no monsters in sight.

"You coming down or am I going to have to scale your house and climb in the window?" Axel called up in a hushed whisper. It was a good thing he knew to be quiet— if her grandfather caught him lurking around her house, gunshots would be heard in their neighborhood that night.

"I'll be right down." Winter whispered back, sliding her window shut. She was wearing a long dark blue nightgown, so she grabbed a sweater and some shoes before she crept downstairs and slipped out the back door. She didn't want to risk alerting her grandfather with the sound of the front door— it had bells hanging from the handle.

Axel was waiting for her at the gate to her backyard, hands stuffed in his pockets. He looked like he had just haphazardly thrown on his clothing— a pair of jeans and a white top with dark blue palm trees on it, a gray hoodie thrown on over it and left unzipped. His curls were more unmanageable than ever, clearly bed-head. Although from how tired he looked, Winter quickly realized he hadn't slept at all yet.

"Palm trees?" Winter questioned his shirt, raising an eyebrow at him in the moonlit night.

"I grabbed the first thing I could reach in the dark." He mumbled, reaching up to rub the back of his neck awkwardly.

They walked over to the little bench in Winter's front yard, sitting together. Winter laid her hands in her lap, bending her head down. Axel was staring at her face, and she was sure he could see that she had been crying.

"You didn't have to come over. I just… needed to know you were okay." Winter broke the silence.

"Well, here I am. Alive and breathing, that's as okay as I get." Axel answered nonchalantly, shrugging his shoulders as he leaned back on the bench. "Your nightmare had something to do with me, then?"

That was a question Winter didn't entirely want to answer. She had nightmares and even just dreams with Axel in them before, but this one…

"It felt different. Real." Winter mumbled. She licked at dry lips, her throat suddenly feeling uncomfortably tight. She expected Axel to push her for information, but he just kept his eyes on her, clear and steady as he gave her time to speak. She got the feeling he would have sat there all night in silence, even if she ultimately didn't say anything at all. Winter always spoke, though, she just needed to figure out how to explain it.

Leaning back on the bench to mimic Axel's comfortable stance, Winter nervously ran a hand through her hair, taking deep breaths until finally, she started to explain.

"It was a torture scene. I… We were in your mind, I think, and there were two of you. But the second you… wasn't you. I knew that. It was something different. His eyes were…" A chill ran through her, lifting her gaze to meet Axel's own, trailing off from her words. Axel didn't interrupt her, merely waited until she finished, "...scary." She could have told him the truth— how empty they were, how soulless, but she couldn't bring herself to put the image in Axel's head.

Taking another deep breath, she sniffled and said softly, "It felt like... I mean, some of it was like some of the things you've told me. But put into a real scene, like in a movie. The worst movie, Axel. I... I don't like seeing you like that."

"It was just a dream, Win." He answered, quietly reaching to take her hand. Lacing their fingers together, he gave her a half smile. The gesture, rare for him, was comforting.

"But it wasn't. It was... exactly how it is, isn't it?" The more she remembered the dream, the more her stomach churned. "Just a dramaticized version, but that's exactly what you go through— what you've told me about. Taking actions—"

A soft shushing noise came from Axel. Winter had started to raise her voice, frantic feelings scratching at her own heart. Quieting herself, she pulled her hand away from his to cover her face, taking a shuddering breath.

"It's horrible, Axel. It's..."

"I know. I never told you it was pretty. It's pretty damn ugly. But don't get so worked up, Winter. I'm used to it." He sounded so calm.

How? How could you get used to being that helpless? How could you not be angry? You're hurting, Axel. She wanted to yell at him.

Over the last month, he had told her a lot over their phone calls, even occasionally in person. He had a deeply metaphoric way of describing his depression, his cutting, his feelings. When she managed to get him to talk about it, it was... beautiful and sad, and made her want to protect him.

Looking over at him, their eyes met. Winter had fanciful thoughts running through her head. Ideas of connecting in a dream, of glimpsing something real, of having a bond with a depressed boy. Whatever that monster had been was still looking back at her now, the heaviness of it all a thick shroud over her friend.

"It was so real, though, Axel." Winter sighed.

"I promise you, it was just a bad dream. There aren't two of me. And what I do at night… the only monster responsible for that is myself, Win." He sounded so sure of it that Winter almost believed him.

Still, she couldn't shake the black eyes of the demon of Axel's mind.

"Ba-da-ba-da-ba-da~ I don't know about you guys but I, for one, am looking forward to hearing some secrets!" Mr. Poe declared, drumming his hands on his desk before leaning back in his chair with a heavy creak. "Hope you wrote some good, juicy ones, kiddos. I have a lunch date after this and I want something to talk about!"

What a piece of… Axel rolled his eyes, taking his seat beside Winter. It was the moment of truth. The first English class of October, where they had to present their essays written on each other's secrets. Axel had wanted to read the one Winter wrote beforehand, but she requested they surprise each other. He was worried about what she had written, but… it couldn't be that bad, could it? A month of talking every day to one person gave a lot of insight into their lives.

Winter, beside him, seemed a little too calm. Her hair was in pigtails with little green ribbons that accented her eyes, and she had her essay in a sleek manilla folder covered in doodles— his own was face down on the desk.

With their teacher choosing students at random, class got underway. Most of the secret essays were half-assed, some clearly faked, and some about secrets that weren't really secret. As the halfway point of the class came along, they finished listening to Lucas Lokken's essay about Jovanni's crush on Miss Popelin. That wasn't a secret at all— Jovi practically stalked the woman, flirting heavily in her class; not that she gave him the time of day, although he did manage to make her laugh at some of the stuff that came out of his mouth. Pierre Popelin, her brother, glared daggers at Jovanni the whole time. Jovanni's essay, however, was just as amusing, claiming that Lucas' twin sister, Lacey, was pregnant with Hayden Grant's baby, one of Lucas' fellow members of the football team.

"That's not true! You take that back, goth freak!" Lucas hollered, standing up at his table.

"Nothing to take back, I'm not the one spreading my legs." Jovi droned in a nonchalant tone, smirking at Lucas. He glanced back with a sway of his long black hair, dark eyes catching where Lacey was sitting beside Kaya, both looking disgusted. "*Oh, Hayden! Not in the grass, I don't want a stain~*" He put on a falsetto tone, one hand to his chest, pouting his bottom lip.

This was a major difference between Jovanni and Axel. Jovanni liked picking fights— Axel usually just ignored situations like these, couldn't be bothered. It was lucky that Hayden wasn't in this class— he would have murdered Jovi right then and there.

Lucas looked like he was seeing red as well, but if he got in trouble for fighting, his parents would surely take him off the football team for the season.

Mr. Poe's voice cut in,

"Okay, okay, that's enough of that. Let's move on. Miss... Jozefson, why don't you get up here and start you and Mr. Dunn off?"

Giving Axel a smile, Winter stood and made her way to

the front of class. As she walked by, Ian Bryars shamelessly whistled at her, grinning from ear to ear as she glanced his way, frowning. He had gotten over their scuffle, reverting back to his daily antics of harassing all the girls in school.

Glaring at the back of the jock's head, Axel crossed his arms and leaned back, focusing on Winter as she cleared her throat and began to read her essay.

"The secret of Axel Dunn... In the last month, as I have gotten to know Axel, I've come to realize he is a compli-cated person. An iceberg in human form, there is more to him than meets the eye. Most surprising of which, I consider to be his mastery of cars. An experienced driver and mechanic, Axel knows cars better than he knows people. His love of cars has even led him to some extraordinary experiences. Just three years ago, in 1996, a new Nascar speedway was built in Las Vegas, Nevada. The Las Vegas Motor Speedway, to celebrate, let a number of kids come to drive with professional Nascar drivers. Our very own Axel Dunn was one of these kids— at the age of thirteen, he drove passenger side to Dale Jarrett, a renowned racer."

She went on to describe this so-called event in great detail, as if it were a story that Axel had told her.

The entire thing was a lie.

Staring at her incredulously, Axel felt the eyes of almost every guy in class on him. He gripped the edge of his desk, stunned. For someone who didn't like lying, here Winter was with everyone clinging to her every word. She smiled as she read from her essay, looking as sweet as could be, not stam-mering once. As she finished, Mr. Poe— as well as a few classmates— clapped for the story.

"Well, well. We have a future Nascar driver in our midst! An interesting side to a rather mysterious student— reads like a good novel! Okay then, Dunn, it's your turn."

As they passed each other, Axel briefly caught Winter by the arm, leaning to whisper in her ear,

"Why?"

"You don't like sharing your secrets." Was all she whispered back, smiling at him.

Releasing her, Axel turned his head to watch her go back to their desks, before he continued to the front of the class.

Now, staring down at the page of his essay, his mouth went dry.

"Winter Jozefson." He started with her name. Axel found himself unable to look at her, so all he could do was focus on reading the piece of shit— at least in his view— that he had written. "We see her as the most likable girl in school. A girl with many friends, who always seems to be around and involved in everything. What people don't know about her is that she isn't shallow."

Peeking up, he saw her face had fallen, staring at him as though he was about to insult her. Steeling his resolve, Axel continued,

"Many people think of the likable girl as a pushover. As naive, or gullible. They know that if they ask her for anything, she would likely do what was asked. That's just the kind of person she is. I had the same opinion of her, to begin with. I thought Winter was too nice to be anything more than a doormat, to be walked over. She isn't a cheerleader, or a geek. But she fell into her own category of being... unforgettable, simplistic. A Mary Sue, with no interesting qualities that I could see. I stereotyped her, by thinking what you see is what you get, and she wasn't worth talking to. I thought... that she was like everyone else— surface level, basic.

"Instead, over the last month, I have learned the secret side of Winter Jozefson. I have learned what makes her magical. The purpose of this assignment was to learn each other's secrets, as a way of getting to know each other. Winter is not someone I would have ever thought would enter my life, or that I would enter hers. We were, I thought, as different as night and day. She was a secret I hadn't learned yet— and now I know her. To me, the secret of Winter is Winter herself."

Once he finished, Axel looked back at Mr. Poe, making sure he was free to go. His teacher gave a nod of approval.

"Well written. Not what I had in mind, but… fitting enough. Serves the purpose of the assignment, at least." He said, before calling on another student.

Sitting down beside Winter, Axel peeked at her as he laid his essay down on the table. She was looking down, her hair providing a curtain so he couldn't see her face.

"Winter?"

Finally, she lifted her head— and he saw why she had avoided looking at him. Her eyes were wet with tears, the green looking even brighter than usual as a stray tear dripped off her eyelash.

Did I hurt her feelings with how I first saw her? Shit.

Instead of telling him off, however, Winter met him with a smile, wiping her eyes on the back of her hand.

"T-That's a beautiful way to see our friendship, Axe. I wasn't expecting that at all."

With his cheeks burning, Axel awkwardly rubbed the back of his neck with his hand. "Uh… Yeah, well… Don't mention it."

The class was just finishing up their essays when the bell rang, signaling the end of class.

"Excellent work today, buckaroos. Leave your essays on

my desk for a proper grading, I'll get them back to you next week." Mr. Poe called.

Standing, Winter and Axel began to gather their things, when Winter's hand knocked into her red sketchbook. It fell to the ground, flopping open. Reaching to pick it up for her, Axel suddenly froze.

Etched on the pages were pencil drawings of a monster. There was no other way to see it— even though it had a humanoid body in a long cloak, its face was hideous. Winter had shaded in the area of its jawline and mouth to be faded and indistinct, but it had a clearly drawn skull, with two harsh black eyes that looked like empty pits. In one of the drawings, its claw-like hand was lifted as if to wave. Others had it in various poses, while others still had portraits of its face. It covered a whole page, parallel to some sketches of Axel himself. Flipping to the page before, Axel's heart dropped into his stomach when he saw his face staring back — but his eyes had been drawn in to be pure black, as if mixing himself with the monster.

"What's this?" He asked Winter, holding out the sketchbook.

Guilt crossed her face, quick to take the book from him. "Just… something I've had on my mind."

"Still having nightmares?" Axel pressed.

"I don't want to talk about it—"

"Oi! You two, class is dismissed, get going."

They had been standing there long enough to be the last two in class. Mr. Poe was staring at them, waiting and gesturing to the door.

Axel had no choice but to let it go, following Winter out of the room.

Study hall was easily Axel's favorite time of the day, for the simple reason that he could listen to music. Sitting in the library with a stack of history books, however, he wasn't studying alone for once. Winter, Kaya, and Oliver had joined him. Winter and Kaya were a given— however they had run into Oliver Blaikwood in the hall and he seemed to invite himself. He was an alright kid, Axel supposed, one of the super friendly types like Winter. He was of average height and build, neither too pale nor too tan, with a flop of messy chestnut brown hair and big brown eyes. The guy never seemed to stop grinning and cracking jokes— he wasn't exactly Axel's type of person— but he chatted more with Kaya and Winter and let Axel sit back in silence, listening to his music.

Of course, that meant he didn't hear a thing when Winter spoke to him. Not until she lifted one side of his headphones from his ear.

"Hey. Earth to Axel."

"W-What?" He sputtered, zoning back into reality.

"What are you listening to?" Winter asked.

"Oh, uh… Foo Fighters. Song of theirs from a few years back— 'Everlong.'"

"They're a rock band, right?"

"Yeah. I mostly listen to rock. Bit of metal, too. Sometimes a few good indie artists."

Winter seemed to hesitate before she said,

"Last spring must have sucked for fans of rock. They blamed rock music for those school shootings."

Just last April had been the tragedy of the Columbine shootings, a school shooting in Colorado. Twelve students and one teacher had been murdered by two twelfth grade students— who were ultimately also killed. It had been insane for highschoolers all around the country. Even Clamare High had been all shook up by it. A few idiots still made horrific jokes over it, but most saw it for what it was—a terrible thing that should never have happened.

The media had blamed the likes of heavy rock, like Marilyn Manson, and treated his fans with suspicion. Instantly well aware of why Winter mentioned it, Axel pulled a sour face.

"Well, I don't listen to Marilyn Manson, but music didn't cause that shooting. The only thing that caused that shooting was the actions of two guys who were screwed in the head." Axel responded.

He must have sounded a little defensive, as Winter quickly added,

"I agree with you." He believed her, though she wasn't wrong that people who liked rock music had been bullied and looked down on after the shooting.

Unfortunately, their conversation was interrupted by the last person Axel wanted to see. The next thing he knew, his headphones were yanked off his head so hard that they disconnected from his music player. Ian Bryars, who stood behind Axel, held them up high over their heads.

"Listening to boy bands?" Ian said with a humorless laugh. A table not far from them held a group of jocks—Bryce Dibattista, Daniel Gold, Lucas Lokken, Hayden Grant, and Matthew Thorne. Ian seemed to have left his buddies just to antagonize them.

Great.

"Give it back, Bryars." Winter sneered beside Axel, who was silently glaring up at Ian.

"Got your girl fighting for you, Dunn?"

Not bothering to correct him calling Winter his girl, Axel shrugged his shoulders. "Not really. I don't control her. I just don't feel like wasting my time on you."

"We still have a score to settle, one of these days. I haven't forgotten. Maybe I'll just keep these as payment for what you did."

That wasn't going to happen. Axel stood to face Ian, pushing back his chair with a loud clatter. He held out a hand for his headphones, staring down the jock.

"What I did was a result of what you were doing. I'd say we're even. I'll take my headphones back now." He was really tired of dealing with Ian's shit. He seemed to pick on every little situation he could, just because he could. Axel really couldn't stand people like Ian Bryars. It was exhausting just to have him around.

Kaya, Oliver, and Winter were watching from behind him, letting Ian and Axel have their little standoff in the library.

Ian paused and seemed to think it over, holding the headphones out.

"Sure thing, buddy." He said, smirking at Axel.

Axel knew something was up, but he reached for them anyway. Unsurprisingly, Ian dropped them to the ground and stomped on them heavily. A sickening crunch sounded as one of the sides snapped right off the flimsy headset.

"What the—" Axel's voice rose, anger finally cutting through his cool exterior.

"Mad, Dunn?" Ian taunted him, seemingly amused by Axel's anger. "Go on, attack. You're just like a mad dog, aren't you? A real mangy mutt!" To provoke him, Ian began to bark — loud, wild barks.

Winter only had to blink, and suddenly Axel had lunged — his hand closing around Ian's shirt collar.

"Axel Dunn!"

Oh no.

His mother's voice called out. As soon as it did, Axel let go of Ian and stepped back in a hurry. All the students turned their heads to see her marching through the library with a stern look on her face. Coming to a stop, she fixed him with a look,

"What is going on here? Up to no good, looks like it."

"It's not like that, Mrs. Dunn! Ian broke Axel's headphones!" Kaya's voice rose up in protest, coming to Axel's defense. His continued grip on Ian's shirt was far more damning, though.

"It was an accident. I was just giving Axel his headphones back and they fell." Ian was a good liar, putting on an offended expression as he looked from Kaya to Axel. "He's the one attacking me!"

"Bullshit!" Axel snapped at Ian, releasing him at last and bending to pick up his broken headphones.

"Axel!" His mother glared at him. "Detention Saturday— I won't tolerate disrupting study hall, nor will I tolerate picking fights. Mr. Bryars, back to your table."

"Wha—" Winter began to speak, her face contorting in shock, but Axel shook his head at her as his mother turned on her heel to walk away. After she left, Winter's big hazel-green eyes turned to him.

"It wasn't your fault, Axel. You shouldn't be the one getting detention!"

"Seriously. Ian could use some detention time, it might bring him down a peg." Oliver agreed, leaning back in his chair.

Even some of the jocks seemed surprised— high fiving Ian as he returned. Only one, Bryce, looked their way with any degree of sympathy on his face.

Throwing his broken headphones down on the table, Axel scoffed.

"That's just how it is. I'm the troublemaker, Ian is golden. I'm used to it." That didn't mean it wasn't unfair, though. He was pissed, seething, but there was no use arguing with his mother.

Kaya smiled awkwardly, suggesting,

"Well, let's finish up this homework, alright? At least Mrs. Dunn can't be mad if we get decent scores in her class. Her infamous pop quizzes scare the living daylights out of me."

As they resumed their studying, Winter reached out to gently touch Axel's arm. Meeting Axel's gaze, she smiled at him.

"I'll make you new ones." She whispered, nodding towards the headphones.

"Thanks, Win." He mumbled, attempting a smile in return.

Luckily, the jock table soon left, and the rest of the study hall went peacefully enough. Though, now Axel had detention to look forward to…

8

UNBORN OF INSANITY

W: I can't believe you're stuck there while the twins and I go for tea at Torva's.

A: Me neither. Mommy loves me, right? DX

W: At least it shouldn't be too long. Want to come over for dinner when you get out? Making meatloaf tonight, I think.

A: Meatloaf? Man, I love that dude. I'll bring my BOoH2 vinyl for him to sign.

W: Haha, very funny. Is that a yes or a no?

A: Sure. Cya.

Axel sighed as he snuck his cellphone back into his pocket, glancing up at the teacher in charge of his detention. Sun-Hi Chi was the original dragon lady before his mother took over the role of the most fearsome teacher at Clamare High. Mrs. Chi was the grandmother to Axel's classmates Jae-Hwa and Tae-Won, with whom Winter was out with at this very moment. She was a seventy-something year old woman; a tiny, frail thing that stood at 5' nothin' and had steel gray hair kept in a short bob. She always wore pearls, was never seen without her reading glasses, and was almost always at school on the weekends.

Detention was usually held on weekdays, but they were a small town. The school was the heart of Caligo, and even on weekends, teams and clubs met up at school— which is why, with Mrs. Chi willing to sit for detention, most teachers stuck their students here on Saturday instead of having to stay late at school.

At that moment, she had her nose in a book with Hangul-Korean text on the front, ignoring Axel's blatant use of his phone. There were a handful of other students. Notably, Noelle Ritter was present for smoking weed on school grounds, and Jovanni was present with a bloody nose after getting his ass handed to him by Hayden Grant due to the comments he'd made in English. Jovi and Axel would have been talking, if it was allowed.

Mrs. Chi let students get away with a lot— but she did demand silence in her detentions.

Silence, for Axel, was a dangerous thing. His mind wandered from the distractions of the day— to the dark. The air seemed particularly heavy that afternoon. Tugging at his sleeves, he tried to ignore the uneasy feelings snarling within him. Sometimes, he couldn't explain it. It just was present, and even he didn't understand.

Something about today was different, though. The longer he sat there, the more uncomfortable he felt, itching to get out of the room. It was more than just the natural urge not to be in detention. Mouth running dry, he started to raise a hand to ask Mrs. Chi if he could go to the restroom, when—

SKREEEEEEECHHHHHHHH~!!!

The most nauseating sound hit him. Doubling over, Axel grabbed his head as his brain rang out with white noise, like nails on a chalkboard mixed with a scream in a microphone.

He let out a yelp of his own, nearly falling out of his chair as his nails dug into his scalp.

"Mr. Dunn?" As soon as his teacher spoke, the sound came to an abrupt stop.

Sweating bullets, Axel looked up, breathing ragged as he focused back in on the classroom. Noelle, Jovanni, Mrs. Chi, and the few other students present all had their eyes on him.

"What, exactly, was the meaning of making noise like that?" Mrs. Chi prompted him, setting her book down as she fixed him with a glare.

Did no one else hear that? He wondered. His head was pounding, but there was no more of the screeching white noise, to his relief. Still looking around, no one else seemed to be in the same state he was. Even Jovanni was giving him a weird look, mouthing, *'You good?'*

No, no he wasn't. But Axel wasn't eager to look like a headcase.

"S-Sorry, Mrs. Chi. Bad headache." His answer was lame, coming out in a weak voice.

The Korean woman looked even more annoyed by his response, opening her book again with a pointed remark of,

"Perhaps next time you should suffer in silence."

Yeah, right. Axel thought, sinking into his chair, his hands falling into his lap. As everyone seemed to get back to their various detention activities, however, his mind seemed to be acting up again.

"Axel…" *Something* whispered his name. He could tell it hadn't come from a voice— but rather, like a second thought popping into his mind, other than himself.

What the...

"Axel…" The whisper came again, slithering across his mind in a way that made him want to scratch at his forehead.

"Jesus… I'm losing it." Axel mumbled.

That was when it caught his eye. In the small window of

the classroom door, a tall figure walked past. Axel caught sight of gaunt, spiky shoulders and the back of a gray, bald skull as it walked by. Blinking, Axel thought he was imagining things. For several seconds, gripping the edge of his desk, the only thing he could hear was the steady ticking of the clock over Mrs. Chi's desk. He kept waiting, on edge, certain he would hear or see something else. The feeling of dread never left, but the voice didn't come again, and neither did that terrible screech.

A: Meet me under the west bleachers. ASAP.

Never before had a text from Axel— aloof, quiet Axel— come so urgently. Winter had been sipping on a tall cup of jasmine tea, listening to Jae-Hwa and Tae-Won bicker over whether poppyseed muffins were good or not. After getting tea and muffins with the Chi twins at Torva's, a beloved coffee shop on Timor st, the three of them were heading back towards the school. Having plans to meet up with Axel, the twins willingly became her guides back to campus, joining her. A chilling breeze clawed at them as they walked, and Winter gratefully clutched her warm travel cup a little tighter, letting it heat her cold palms. Having come back to the school campus, they had just crossed by the statue in the front courtyard when Winter's phone buzzed.

"Everything okay?" Tae-Won asked upon seeing her face. Both twins had come to a stop, Tae studying Winter curiously while Jae-Hwa watched a group of jocks walk by with their girlfriends.

Distracted, Winter took a second to type out a quick response to Axel, before looking back up at the twins.

"Yeah, uh… Everything is fine. I have to go, though.

Detention's already let out, I guess Axel wants me to meet him at the field. I'll see you Monday." She told them. Waving them off, she watched Tae drag Jae off into the school.

Winter changed course, heading south to where the Clamare High Stadium was. It took her a good ten minutes before she reached it. The stadium was really just a large field, surrounded by bleachers and a chain link fence. Letting herself through the unlocked gate, Winter started marching her way to the west bleachers. She tossed her now— nearly empty cup into a trash can along the way.

The field was empty, the grass still damp underfoot from rain the night before, smelling of dew. Looking around for Axel, Winter wasn't paying much attention, glancing off towards the field as she stepped underneath the bleachers.

She walked right into something hard, and turned her head to find herself face to chest with...

Oh God. Horror filled her as she looked up into the pale face of a classmate. Bryce Dibattista's lifeless body was swaying from a rope in front of her. His lips were tinged purple, dark circles under his eyes. Eyes that, instead of his normal bright green irises, were pitch black— the whole of them, even the whites, looked like they had been injected with black ink. His usually tan skin had gone pale and ashen, Winter realized, like a dry eraser clapped along his face. Where the rope was tied around his neck, Winter saw deep, dark bruises, the other end of the rope wrapped around one of the bleacher's seats several times. His feet were dangling a few inches off the ground, just barely grazing the grass. He was wearing his football uniform, as if he had just gotten ready for afternoon practice.

"B-B-Bryce!" Winter's voice came out in a high pitched squeak, stumbling backwards. It wasn't until a hand grabbed her wrist, however, that she let out a scream.

"Shh! It's just me!" Finally, her gaze had been drawn away

from Bryce's face, and onto Axel's instead, her friend looking back at her with intense blue eyes.

It took two seconds of looking at him, before a horrible feeling overcame Winter. Turning away, she doubled over and hurled her tea onto the grass. Suddenly, she was glad she had chosen not to eat muffins with the boys. If she had ever wondered how she would react to seeing a corpse, she now knew.

Axel reached down to grab her hair, pulling it back for her, one hand rubbing up and down her back as she recovered. He waited until she was just breathing heavily, before he spoke.

"You alright?"

"Do I look alright?" Winter couldn't help her exasperated retort, giving Axel an incredulous look. Slowly, she straightened up, hesitantly glancing at their classmate. Bryce Dibattista, the football star of Clamare High. He was a senior, already had a full college scholarship laid out for him. Winter didn't know him that well, only enough to know of him as a fellow student. She knew his mother was Brazilian, and she had heard him speak Portuguese from time to time in the halls. She knew he had better grades than most of the dummies on the football team. But she couldn't say he would have even known her name.

Bryce was usually so vibrant, but now he hung before them with dead eyes, making Winter shiver.

"Is this what you wanted me to come see? Bryce's... s-suicide?" Winter asked Axel, as she drew her eyes away from Bryce again. She couldn't look at him anymore. It was horrific.

"Yeah. I found this at his feet." Axel said, looking solemn as he held out a crumpled note to Winter.

I'm sorry, I can't do it anymore.

As Winter read the short suicide note, Axel kept speaking, "Wouldn't have expected this from him. We were... sort of friends, back in elementary. Used to go over to his house a bit, before he decided he liked sports and girls over having friends." He sounded so nonchalant about it, so monotone and blank. Was he just numb? In shock, like she was?

"I'm so sorry, Axel." Winter said, looking up at him. To her surprise, his face didn't have grief on it like hers did. Instead, he looked... angry?

"Don't be. He didn't do this."

"What?" Winter was shocked by Axel's certainty, the bite of his words made her nauseous once more.

"It's been awhile, but I knew Bryce. He would care too much to kill himself. He'd be worried about his family finding him, how they'd handle it, what they would do with his stuff, how his siblings would grow up without him. All the things a depressed person considers before they go this far. I don't think he would have done it."

What he said made sense. Bryce, if Winter remembered right, had four younger siblings. Still... The facts were right in front of their faces.

"Well, he did, Axe. I mean..." She peeked at Bryce once more, swallowing the sour taste in her mouth.

"Maybe he was high as a kite or something. Maybe he was uh... into choking and didn't intend to die. Look how close he is to the ground." Axel answered her.

It was true— his toes could have grazed the gravel under the bleachers. Not enough to support his weight and prevent his death, however.

At that moment, Winter felt ready to cry. Her eyes

implored Axel as she said, "If this was an accident... that makes it even more tragic than if it was on purpose."

Axel stared at her for a second, before sighing and looking away. "Listen. If it makes you feel any better... It was painless. People don't feel strangulation— he passed out, and just drifted to sleep as he died."

"How do you know that?"

"That's what the survivors say. You lose oxygen and like... fall to sleep, and then, if the choking stops fast enough, they wake up. Bryce... He died peacefully, Win."

His explanation was enough to console her, Winter choosing to believe him rather than imagine the ugly truth of Bryce's death. Taking a deep breath, she nodded.

"Okay... Well, that's good to know at least." Winter sighed, sniffling. The air around them smelled *horrible*, between her vomit and the slowly decomposing body. Looking back at Axel to avoid looking at Bryce, she studied him in silence, before something clicked. "H-How... How did you find him?"

Axel's expression morphed from anger to a peculiar, almost fearful look. He shivered, lowering his head and taking a deep breath. "I don't uh... I don't want to talk about it. Trust me, it's..." He trailed off, frowning. "It's a long story."

Suspicious, Winter wanted to push him for answers. But... honestly, she couldn't stand another second by Bryce's still-hanging body. Deciding to let it go for now, she told Axel,

"Alright, then... We should go tell someone. I... I want to get him down from there, Axel."

So they went to find a teacher, and twenty minutes later, Winter found herself standing back and watching as they cut Bryce down from the bleachers, lowering him gently to the ground. Crossing her arms, Winter couldn't hide her discomfort, squirming beside Axel. By now, the area had been roped off, so they were the only two students present as Mr. Alvarez, the Headmaster, and Mr. Kelp, the school nurse, started to respectfully cover up Bryce's body. There had been an afternoon practice scheduled for the football team. Winter could only imagine the horror when they were told of what had happened to Bryce.

"Axel?"

"Yeah?"

"I never want to see you like that."

"...Yeah."

School wasn't quite the same during the aftermath of Bryce Dibattista's death. On Saturday evening, parents called their kids home to watch the nightly news. On Sunday, Reverend Callahan gave a sermon on the Catholic view of suicide— which Axel did his very best to drown out. That evening, Axel had confessed to Winter that he had heard something strange in detention. He couldn't bring himself to tell her everything, but he told her enough to convince her that something strange was going on.

First thing on Monday morning, an assembly was held at Clamare High to discuss Bryce's death. A tragic suicide, their principal Mr Alvarez declared, that would forever change their school. It was the first death Caligo High had ever had amongst their students, since opening in 1912. Over the weeping of Ruby Stout— Bryce's girlfriend, a pretty, blonde senior— the staff recounted some of Bryce's football accomplishments, his dream of going pro, his Brazilian-American heritage. They talked about the eulogy that would be run in the paper, and that eventually, he would be buried right here in Caligo, in the local cemetery.

Axel had been as jittery and anxious as Winter, for once his ability to produce a poker face failed him. He was unable to quiet his mind as he rocked uncomfortably in his seat during the assembly. About halfway through the assembly, Winter's hand snaked into his own, gripping it tightly. He couldn't look at her, and instead chose to squeeze her hand in return, not letting go as their principal droned on about Bryce.

Still, he couldn't get his mind off the heaviness he felt, as he sat in a chem class, listening to Mr. Perelli drone on about the elements. Winter had been dragged off to sit with Kaya, near the front of class, leaving Axel to sit with Jovanni Brooks in the back.

Jovanni wasn't a bad looking dude, as long as you could accept his sense of style— which most people couldn't. People liked to call Axel goth— but compared to Jovanni, he was tame. Jovanni was six feet of pure death energy. He was so skinny and pale that he resembled a walking skeleton in the halls. He had pitch black hair, which he had grown so long that it fell down to the middle of his back in straight, luxurious strands. He had a narrow face with a pointed chin, thin lips and thinner eyebrows. His eyes were so dark they were nearly black. Peeking out of his nose, which was the only large part of his face, was a silver septum piercing. It was his ears that held the majority of his metal— countless hoops clinging to them, flashes of silver peeking out from behind his hair, the most impressive being an industrial piercing.

"Axe. Hey. Yo. Ass." Jovi's deep voice cut through Axel's thoughts.

"Hm?"

"You're spaced out today. More than usual." Jovanni remarked, eyeing him with those intensely dark irises. "This about Bryce? Everyone's freaked out that he bit it, but you knew him, right?"

"Uh... knew, yeah. Past tense." Axel answered, feeling awkward under Jovanni's gaze. *Maybe it couldn't hurt to ask...* He thought, chewing on the inside of his lip for a second before speaking again. His voice came out hesitantly,

"Say, Jovi... Does anything seem... off, to you? Around school?"

"You mean besides the boo-hooing?" Jovanni was blunt as ever, looking disinterested as he drew funny-shaped S's in his notebook.

"No. Well, yes, but..." *How in the hell do I say this?* "I was thinking more like... a heaviness. A... uh... presence. Like the school feels a bit..."

Jovanni was frowning at him already, quirking an eyebrow.

Confidence fading, Axel deflated, shoulders sinking as he shook his head.

"You know what? Nevermind."

As Jovanni went back to his notebook, Axel sighed. He didn't feel anxious, so much that he felt... well... like how he usually felt late at night, in the darkness of his room. That heaviness, that way his mind wandered to the thoughts better left alone— he had always found distraction in school. Now, it seemed harder to ignore, a fog that he couldn't shake, an unwavering presence. Tongue tied, he glanced towards his dark haired classmate for a moment, wishing he could find the words to describe it. Why, he thought, it was so easy to talk to Winter and not as easy to describe it to Jovanni, he would never know.

Soon, the bell rang and signaled the end of class. As students flooded into the hall, Axel broke into a jog to catch up with Winter and Kaya.

"Hey!" He called, watching them stop to wait for him.

Kaya had foregone her contacts, wearing a big pair of glasses with spearmint green frames, and an outfit that made her look like an acrobat in the way it clung to her lithe body. She looked prepared to do somersaults any minute, giving Axel a two fingered wave as he approached.

"Yo, Lord Goth. We were just talking 'bout you." She said, winking as Axel gave her a strange look.

"N-No we weren't!" Winter stammered, giving Kaya a horrified glance. Gulping, she hugged her red sketchbook tighter to her chest.

"Don't care." Axel said bluntly, focusing on Winter, "Are you free tonight?"

"Well—"

"No, the hell she ain't!" Kaya interrupted, putting on a goofy accent as she looped an arm around Winter's neck, yanking her hard enough to make her stumble, their heads knocking together. Winter winced, but Kaya kept grinning as she declared,

"My best friend is spending the evening with me. No boys allowed. I got the heebie-jeebies from all this suicide biz, so I'm requisitioning her for the night."

"But—"

"Nope! Say goodbye."

It seemed there wasn't an argument to be had, as Winter gave an awkward smile, looking at Axel as she suggested softly, "I'll text you?"

Holding back a sigh, all Axel could do was nod. He watched the two girls walk away, unable to shake the feeling in the air. The simple, perhaps irrational, feeling that something was terribly wrong.

W: Where are you?

K: Sorry! I'm still working on the final draft. You want to just meet me here?

Winter sighed as the text popped up on her phone. *So much for girl's night.* It had been Kaya's idea to spend the night together, claiming she had been feeling creeped out since Bryce's death and wanted to hang out. Yet, shortly after school let out, Nathan Silva had called her up to ask her to come to the editor's office for the school paper, and Kaya had gone running. Winter had waited at the mall for her, but the sun had set and Kaya still wasn't done with the paper.

Sticking her phone in her bag, Winter started off towards school. The October evening air had her shivering, pulling her cardigan tighter against her body as she walked.

Clamare High was like a ghost town that night. Not a single soul was in sight as Winter trekked through the school courtyard, relieved to find the front doors unlocked as she let herself in. Walking down the empty hallway, the only sound was the soft tapping of her boots against the tiled floors. Big, block lights were built into the ceiling and covered with paneling, only half of them turned on. It cast eerie fluorescent shadows across the hall, giving everything a strange hue.

The editor's office wasn't far, but the further Winter got into the school, the more something felt... off.

It was that feeling one might get from being watched. That chill, running up your spine, that urge to turn your head and check over your shoulder. That's how Winter felt. She had thought the presence was in front of her as she continued down the empty hallway of her school, seeking it out. Something urged her to keep looking forward, to not turn her head. But she could hear it.

A faint, soft scratching— so soft that at first, she didn't believe it to be real. But it was impossible to ignore for long.

It grew closer. Her throat felt like it was closing, struggling to take a full breath as she froze in fear. This heavy feeling was coming over her, and she had the horrible feeling something was behind her.

Just look. There's nothing there— you just have to look. Just the corner of your vision, check, and then you can go find Kaya.

So, she did. Slowly, Winter turned around.

How many nights had she spent by now, laying in bed, talking to Axel? Listening to him, closing her eyes and picturing the beast he spoke about— the invisible force that held him down. To her, Axel was burdened with heavy chains. She knew the second she saw what stood in front of her now, that this was what had been conjured by her mind, her haunted imagination's worst nightmare. This was the thing she had been sketching over and over in her red book.

It was a creature made of black ink. Not faded, like shadows— but sharp, pointed, not a single curve in its jaunting figure, made of black lines and gray skin. Standing on stilted legs, it towered at least three feet over Winter's own tall form. It was even taller than the lockers that it leaned on, curling impossibly long fingers over the metal corners as it towered menacingly above her. Like a drawing coming to life— Winter briefly wondered how it would feel, to reach out and touch it. Was it real, or just a terrible vision?

But the face... Atop a thin neck, was a rounded, bald skull. It was hard to look straight at it— shifting and flickering in her vision. The jawline, which should have been sharp like the rest of its body, was non-existent, consisting of a substance like murky water— swaying and threatening to spill away at any moment. There was no contouring, nothing distinctive, except a gaping hole that must have been its mouth— fixed in a permanent, screaming expression, nothing but blackness inside. A few teeth topped it, leading to the top half of its face. Did it even have a nose? The middle of its face was so flat, Winter couldn't decipher it— and her eyes, as they drifted upwards, were immediately drawn to the eyes of the creature.

They were the only solid thing on its face. They would have been beautiful— if they weren't the stuff of her nightmares. Like sideways teardrops, distinctively shaped, lined in solid black. There was no iris— just large, solid black piercing pupils. No color in them at all. If Winter had to describe them, she would have said they were the eyes of death.

Frantic heartbeats passed as Winter stared up at the skeletal figure. It wore a loose, open collar black robe, with sharp limbs and a distinctive, boney collarbone and ribs. Winter felt frozen, until its mouth opened even wider— if that was possible— and she was met with a haunting screech. A scream, a wail, whatever horrid sound it could be called, shatteringly loud. She fell backwards, as if pushed by an invisible force, falling on her ass onto the tile. Scrambling backwards on her hands, she watched in horror as the blurry, indistinct figure moved— like a fluttering paper, its nails scratching the locker as it let go to pursue her. It flittered back and forth in front of her, each step swaying unsteadily. The only constant that didn't seem to mess with her version of reality was the thing's eyes, and its hands as those sharp fingers reached for her.

Winter's back hit a wall, and her mouth gaped open to scream, nothing coming out. The feeling of heaviness she had felt before was overwhelming now, the air thick with dread.

She never would get to find out what the beast had in store for her— because instead of screaming, she found herself gasping as a hand grabbed her by the arm. Head snapping to the side, she caught sight of wide blue eyes and the familiar glint of a silver lip ring.

"Axel!"

"What the hell are you waiting for— MOVE!"

Just like that, his yell got her going, along with a strong yank on her arm. He would have been hurting her, if she wasn't too terrified to care, scrambling to get onto her feet and run with him. The blurry-faced *thing* screeched again, as if angry they were trying to get away. She could hear it as they ran down another hallway— skittering after them, slamming into lockers with sharp metallic thuds and occasional shrieks. The lights of the hall flickered on and off, and Winter thought for sure she'd lose her balance and fall, bringing them both down and letting the monster reach them. If it wasn't for Axel's strong grip pulling her, she might have.

At last, they reached the end of the hall— to a fire escape that Axel threw himself at and managed to shove open, dragging them both into the dark night.

That was the first time Winter dared to throw her head back and look over her shoulder, through the open door, the moonlight of the evening streaming into the hallway. But the scrawny figure had stopped, just inches from the light. Its head turned, sickeningly— like its neck could bend into a broken position at will— and for the first time, she saw the hole that was its mouth close, the lower half of its face melting into a gray nothingness. Its eyes peered at her, as the door began to fall shut. Winter felt herself breathe again when the door clicked shut at last.

Was Axel's heart racing like Winter's? She could only guess— the two of them both staring in frozen, mesmerized horror at the door, catching their breath. Air had never been so important to Winter, as she bent over to grab her knees, inhaling huge gulps of oxygen, nauseated from the harrowing experience.

It seemed to click for Axel— for when Winter finally

straightened up again, his piercing blue gaze had moved from the door to her. A new fear struck her, simply from the expression on his face. She had never seen him so angry before.

"How could you?!" His tone was full of accusation and pain, as if she had betrayed his trust.

Mouth gaping open in horror, Winter began to stammer, "I-I didn't. I swear, I don't know how... I didn't make *that* on purpose."

"Bullshit! It's exactly... it's what I told you about. You're the only one who could have— you and your... your freaky powers!" Axel spat at her.

For a second, she stared at him, stunned silent. What could she say? He was right. She had no defense against it. She had no clue how that thing was here, but somehow, unconsciously, it was... and it was all her fault.

"A-Axel... I..." She tried to find the words, but her friend merely scoffed at her. His gaze studied her face for a moment, before he said the very thing that could have hurt her the most.

"I never should have trusted you."

All Winter could do was watch as he turned around and stormed off across the school courtyard. She watched him go, his head bent down, hands curled into fists at his side, until he was out of her sight.

Overwhelmed, Winter glanced back at the door to the school. Could it show up anywhere, in the dark? Would it attack anyone, or just students? It was Axel's beast— although something about it seemed more familiar than Winter would have liked.

Thoughts running wild through her head, she was left with more questions than answers.

9

UNCURED ILLNESS

"Yes, and I was thinking—" Mrs. Alessandra Dunn had been in the middle of a phone call, when the front door of the house slammed open. Looking up, she watched as Axel whipped up the stairs, calling after him, "Axel?"

Ignoring his mother, Axel fled to his room, locking the door behind him. As soon as he was alone, he threw his phone onto his bed. The damn thing had been buzzing every five minutes, spammed with texts and calls from Winter ever since he left school.

What the hell was that thing? He asked himself.

You know. You know what it was. The answer came, taunting him.

Did she really make it real? Yes. That had definitely been real.

He felt nauseous, pacing his room, running his hands through his hair. Going over to his window, he yanked the blinds down roughly, shutting himself off from seeing the house across the street.

Sinking to the ground, in the corner of his room, he found himself struggling to suck in air, breathing ragged, his heart pounding like a drum. What little breath he did receive he used to swear, cursing to the air.

Axel had never considered what his depression would have looked like before now. But with Winter having given it a face... it was shockingly accurate, and all Axel could do was feel cold dread as he remembered those soulless eyes.

It took him several minutes to calm down, curled up and shivering, his head tucked into his arms as that thing echoed in the back of his mind. When he finally lifted his head, listening to his phone buzz for the fifteenth time, Axel looked across his room, taking it in.

He wasn't a messy person. Not because that was his choice— if he had his way, his room would be a mess of posters, collectibles, and clothes. But his mother had never allowed that of her boys. So instead of posters, the faded yellow wallpaper of his room was left untouched. There was nothing on the hardwood floors, the closet door shut neatly so everything was tucked away. He didn't have a desk in his room, instead only a twin bed made up in black sheets, and a small, dark wood bookshelf lined with neat books. Most of the books were thick, leatherbound fantasy novels— the true escapism type of reads.

But the top shelf held smaller, skinny books. Pushing himself to his feet, Axel stumbled over to it, pulling out a handful of the flat yearbooks from previous school years. His mother was obsessed with buying them, having never missed a year. Axel could go all the way back to his preschool class, if he wanted to— but instead he found the book for third grade, when he would have been around eight to nine years old.

Flipping it open, Axel found his class page. Individual faces stared back at him— including his own. Ignoring his younger self, he moved to the next page— there were several group photos from the year. There, in a soccer team photo, two faces stood out to him. Once again, one was him— looking unamused at having to pose for a photo and squinting in the sun. Yet, the boy beside him was grinning brightly. An eleven year old Bryce Dibattista. Tall and lanky, tan and with bright green eyes, he leaned on Axel with a hand on his head.

They had been friends, once. Middle school, clubs, changed interests… This year, Bryce had barely spared him a glance when they passed each other in the hall. They had become strangers.

Looking at the photo made Axel nauseous, and after a few seconds, he closed it with a snap.

What has she done?

No, that's not right… I can't blame Winter. This was all me. It's my problems… my demons. I made this happen.

This is all my fault…

I killed Bryce.

"Winter. Seriously, what is your deal? Put down the damn phone."

Somehow, Winter had found the courage to go back into the school— only after joining Kaya. The beast seemed to be gone, for now, and so Winter found herself in the editor's office for the school newspaper. The whole gang seemed to be here— the president of the newspaper club, Nathan Silva, along with his vice president, Maya Burns. Then there was Kaya and Tae-Won, two of the lead writers, and the photographers, Winter's friend Oliver Blaikwood, and Catherine Winchester. It was a small group, but they never failed to have good articles with the latest school stories.

Winter never had an interest in officially joining, but she

hung out with them a lot, and Kaya was always trying to convince her to do a comic strip with her artwork.

It had been Oliver who had spoken, rolling his brown eyes as he nudged her with his elbow. Sheepishly, Winter lowered her phone. Axel wasn't answering anyway, but she had continued to try to get ahold of him.

Does he hate me now?

"Sorry, I…"

"She's trying to get ahold of Axel." Kaya interrupted Winter, giving her a sideways glance from where she sat, sipping on an energy drink. "You still haven't told us what happened, Win. You were a freaking mess when I found you."

Shortly after Axel had stormed off, Winter had gotten Kaya to come out of the school to meet her at the statue— and it had taken a full ten minutes to convince a terrified Winter to go back into the school. She was sure her face was as pale as a ghost the entire time, trying and failing to convince Kaya to leave with her. She looked around every corner until they got to the office where everyone else had been waiting— in good spirits and unaware of any sort of shadowy beast. To the rest of them, nothing out of the ordinary had happened at all. Well, besides Kaya, who agreed she had heard "something" but she just waved it off as a malfunctioning printer or nearby video playing.

"I… Well, we…" Winter hesitated, not wanting to tell them the horrific truth. Sure, Kaya knew about her gifts— but how would she feel about a real-life monster? The most she had ever made for Kaya was copying some fashionable shirt out of a magazine— which was a knockoff attempt at best. Taking a second to think of a lie, Winter looked down at her phone.

"We had an argument. A bad one."

"Geez. Don't like the sound of that. You want me to kick his ass?" Nathan spoke up, sounding distracted, never looking up from the freshly printed page he held of the Clamare Gazette.

"Ian already did that last month—"

"Kaya!" Winter sighed, frowning at her friend. "Listen, Axel isn't the bad guy here. I am. So if anyone needs their ass kicked, it's me."

"But your ass is so fiiii—" Oliver began to commend her, making a curvaceous gesture in the air with his hands— only for Catherine to smack him by the back of the head. Catherine was a small girl, but no less fierce, puffing out her cheeks in an insulted expression as she shook her head at him, red velvet hair swishing.

Winter gave a weak laugh at Oliver, shaking her head. Still, it did nothing to ease her level of concern as she eyed the wall of unanswered texts on her phone.

As they waited to finish printing the finished edition of the paper, Winter finally gave up on contacting Axel. Instead, she flipped open her sketchbook. She was going to start a new page, but she couldn't help pausing on the page that held sketch after sketch of the monster.

The dark face, with its soulless eyes, seemed to taunt her now. She had to remind herself that they had seen it for real, that it was more than just a drawing.

It really is... exactly as I drew it. She had always been so conscious of creating things. It took concentration, focus, desire... Never before had something just come into being without her wishing it.

Suddenly, Winter frowned, remembering one time in particular something had just... appeared. *But I was just a kid... And I don't know for sure if that was my fault, or if...*

"What's that?" Kaya's voice startled her out of her thoughts. Before Winter could close her sketchbook, her best friend was peering over her shoulder, frowning at the pages. "Looks like something out of *Alien.*"

Shyly, Winter pulled her book closer to her, protectively laying an arm over it. "It's nothing."

"Doesn't look like nothing. Why are you drawing such dark things?" Kaya asked, eyeing her with suspicion. "Dunn's influence?"

The mention of Axel made Winter wince, looking back down at her sketchbook. Her stomach churned, his angry tone from earlier echoing in the back of her mind. Closing the red sketchbook, Winter was quite certain she wanted to toss it in a fire and never see that horrible thing again.

"...You could say that."

That night, as they left the school, Winter tucked her sketchbook into her locker. The last thing she wanted was to take it home with her and let that hideous face haunt her further.

What the hell is going on?

All around Axel, there was a strange heaviness to the air. It was different from how he had felt before— this time, it wasn't just him. Students around him seemed grim, some even tearful. Whispers followed him down the hall, glancing towards him with mournful expressions.

Did someone die? It was sarcastic when he thought it, but then he noticed Winter waiting for him at his locker. Her eyes were bloodshot, and her shoulders shook.

Bright and early, it was a few days after the incident with the monster, and Axel had expected the day to go by without change. The thing Winter had summoned hadn't made another appearance, as far as he knew. They hadn't spoken, though Winter always seemed to be hovering near his locker, or sitting close to him in class. Her stare, filled with guilt, only made Axel more reluctant to speak to her. He was, to put it bluntly, avoiding her like the plague.

As he had been doing for the last few days, Axel stopped and pulled open his locker without a word, ignoring her. He knew it was wrong, but... he couldn't face her. Not without thinking of that creature.

If I had never talked to her, never shared...

"Axel." Her voice was pleading with him, reaching out to grab his sleeve. On instinct, Axel yanked his arm out of her grip, tugging his sleeve back down to his wrist and sparing her an annoyed glance.

His silence was stone cold, retrieving books from his locker.

"I-I need to talk to you. There's been—" Winter tried again, her lower lip quivering.

She can't hide her emotions, can she? Axel thought, bitterly. While his face remained blank, except for angry eyes, Winter's emotions were all over her face. Like a damn painting.

He couldn't stand seeing it. Not right now.

The slamming of his locker shut her up, as Winter startled and fell quiet. Her eyes followed him as he left, and Axel could hear the sigh of, "I'm sorry..."

Apologies weren't worth anything to him at this moment, as he stormed off towards his first class of the day.

English, ever since their last assignment, had actually been rather enjoyable for Axel. Mr. Poe was a funny— if not a little bit strange— teacher, and their essay assignments had been interesting so far. Axel had always been good with this class, but it had become a favorite ever since Winter sat with him.

However, today, he sat in the back next to Jovanni again. As Winter entered the classroom, she spared him a longing glance, frowned, and took a seat at the front next to Kaya.

When Mr. Poe arrived, it was clear from the look on his face that today's lesson would not be given his usual treatment of sarcastic humor. Instead, he grimly mirrored the other students.

"Morning, all... I am sure most of you by now have heard the news. It's unfortunate that we, so soon after losing one of our students, have also... lost one of the faculty."

Axel's eyes snapped forward to look at Mr. Poe. He had already figured out something was wrong that morning, but now he had begun to realize just *how* wrong it was.

"Miss Popelin was found yesterday afternoon, in her apartment, by her brother Pierre— whom many of you know personally. Understandably, Pierre has been given some time off school to attend to family affairs. The entirety of Clamare High is in mourning. I would advise you all to contact Nurse Kelp if you need any counseling or..."

Axel stopped listening, tuning out his teacher as he let out a slow, shaky breath.

"Another one bites the dust~" Jovanni darkly muttered beside him, "Heard she offed herself, too."

"Do you know how?" Axel asked.

This had to be that creature's doing. First Bryce, now Miss Popelin? What, does it hang people?

"The Chi twins were talking this morning about it. Heard from their dad that it was an insulin overdose. Painful. Seizures and shit, brain dying from lack of sugar. Bad way to go, right?" As ever, Jovanni had no tact, speaking bluntly, "Pierre called an ambulance but she'd been that way for a while. He spent the night at a friend's, and wasn't home until that afternoon."

Now Axel knew what Winter had wanted from him that morning.

Was it related to that thing?

"There is no such thing as a coincidence…" Axel sighed.

Another death I caused. He thought, though part of him still argued that it could have nothing to do with his monster.

"Well, duh." Jovanni had heard him, giving a shake of his head, "Shame, too. Miss Popelin was smoking hot."

Frowning, Axel ignored Jovi's remarks, turning back towards the front as their class began.

After class, Winter was once again waiting for him. Seeing her was enough to cause a spark of anger, Axel gritting his teeth as he tried to walk past her. It wasn't so much that he was angry at her— but rather, that he was angry with himself, and she was a reminder of that.

"Axel. Axel, wait!" She called, following him down the hall.

Once again, they went through the process of Axel grabbing his books while Winter tried to convince him to talk to her. It was clear that neither one of them wanted to talk in the busy hall, but as everyone headed to their next class, Winter's voice got more insistent.

"Axel, just let me explain—"

"No!" He finally snapped, stopping abruptly to turn and look at her. A white knuckled grip on his books, Axel glared up at the friend he thought he had. "I don't want to hear you explain. I don't want to hear from you at all."

"But, I didn't mean—"

"No. Just stop." Axel was seething, anger rolling off of him as he broke his silence. "It doesn't matter what you meant to do, or didn't mean to do. You did. Nothing is going to make this better, Winter. It's not like you can smooth everything over with sad eyes and some begging— that's not how it works. I *trusted* you, I told you things that should never have seen the light of day, and you know what? I've never regretted anything more than I regret talking to you. So just do me a favor and leave me the hell alone!"

Winter seemed to shrink in front of him, deflating visibly. She was silent, at long last. The last thing Axel saw was her eyes filling with tears before he turned and walked away.

Emotions boiled inside of him. He had been harsh, and he knew it— but nothing scared him more than the monster in his mind, and that had been made a reality. One that, honestly, he had no idea how to deal with. He had a system, a habit, a way of dealing with his issues— but this? This was something he didn't know how to fight.

Honestly, he didn't care if Winter was sorry. He couldn't care less if she was desperate for his forgiveness. There was a reason Axel didn't like people. He thought Winter was different, but at the moment he felt like she was just like everyone else. Her pleas for him to forgive her weren't going to change the way he felt.

They were nothing but empty words, falling on deaf ears.

"Winter. Come on, open up." Kaya's voice sighed through the bathroom stall door, knocking again.

She had gone looking for her when Winter had skipped their next class. Now, during lunch period, she had found her — locked away and miserable. Winter sat on the closed toilet, sniffling long after her tears had dried up. Her sobs had been reduced to whimpers, her racing mind slowing until the only thing left was Axel's words echoing. Over, and over, and over.

"Listen, you want me to kill Dunn? I'll do it. I mean, I might need your help digging the ditch but I can definitely do it without leaving any evidence, you just leave it to me." Kaya's joke normally would have made Winter laugh, but instead it just earned another sniffle. "At least tell me what he did first, though." She sounded worried.

Taking a slow, shaky breath, Winter pushed herself to her feet. She shuffled over, unlocking the stall door until she was looking at her fashionista best friend, Kaya stood before her in a slip of a dress that, no doubt, pushed the limits of their school dress code, clinging to her petite frame. Her eyes were wide, brows drawn together, and Winter had been right—concern was all over her face.

"I can't tell you that. Really, it's my fault, Kaya. Believe me. I've done something really unforgivable this time." Winter sighed.

"You always say that. You've said that since elementary school. Anytime anyone gets mad at you, you freak and think you've committed the ultimate sin, and bend over backwards to make 'things' right. And you know what?" Kaya settled a hand on her shoulder. "You always manage to."

Not always. Winter thought glumly, shrugging off her friend's hand as she slipped past her, walking to the long counter of sinks and mirrors.

"Either way… I can't make it better right now. My hands are tied. If I talk to him, he is only going to be angrier with me. And if I don't…"

Will he ever forgive me? No. I don't think he could if he wanted to… Winter, who had been staring at her reflection in a mirror, closed her eyes. All she could picture was that thing, and then— Bryce's face. Did Miss Popelin, her favorite teacher, look as pale as he had? The thought made her sick, hanging her head with a soft groan.

"Come on, don't talk like that. Things are grim enough around here. Just think of poor Pierre." Kaya remarked, joining her at the sinks, her heeled boots clattering on the tiled floors.

Pierre.

The bright, blonde boy popped into Winter's head. Miss Popelin had grown up in France, but Pierre had been in Caligo since he was little more than a toddler, and had been a familiar face most of Winter's life. He was kind, and funny, and had been on her mind all day. As bad as Winter felt about the loss of Miss Popelin, no one could feel it worse than Pierre. All they had was each other— and now, he was alone.

Gripping the edge of the sink in front of her, Winter opened her eyes at last, hazel-green staring back at her in the mirror.

"Listen, whatever it was, if Axel Dunn doesn't know that you would never do anything purposefully horrible—"

"I'm going to visit Pierre." Winter cut her friend off.

"Wha— uh... O-Okay, but..." Kaya stammered, looking confused as Winter headed for the door. "Good talk?" She called after her.

"I'll explain later!" Was the only answer Kaya got as she was left alone in the bathroom.

The Popelin siblings lived in a small, square, dark red house on Aurum Lane. It was the house of their grandfather, who had taken them in when their parents died, and then, when he passed, it had become Sophie's. As Winter approached the dark home with rose bushes in the front yard, not unlike her own, she idly wondered what would happen to it now. Pierre was only sixteen. Would it be held for him, until he came of age? Would he have to sell it? What were the housing laws for an orphaned child, anyway?

These questions had no answers, at least for the moment. Taking a deep breath, Winter walked up to the front door, ringing the doorbell. The idea of Miss Popelin committing suicide… just didn't sit right with her.

I wonder… Could it be related to Bryce? She thought. In her wildest imagination, she pictured Bryce two-timing his girl-friend Ruby in an illicit student-teacher affair. But Miss Popelin had been so proper, and Bryce…

Wait. Bryce doesn't even take French. You're being ridiculous, Winter.

Shaking her head at herself, Winter tried the doorbell again, having been waiting a good minute.

Silence.

"Pierre? Are you home? I-It's Winter. I stopped by to see if…" *If I could do anything.* That sounded so weak to her, and Winter paused before finishing, "…if you needed anything."

More silence.

Thinking he wasn't home, Winter turned to leave— when at last, the door creaked open, Pierre's pale face peeking out at her. His blue eyes were tired looking, the tip of his nose rose red.

"Hey, Winter… Come on in." He murmured, pulling the door open so she could step in. Pierre had less of an accent than his sister, but his words were still soft and lilted.

Offering him a smile, Winter entered the small home.

It was cramped, but much like Winter's home— every inch was filled with character and love. She had never been in the Popelin house, but she had seen Pierre and his sister walking home several times before, and now that she was here... She couldn't imagine it being any different. This home screamed Pierre and Sophie Popelin, exuding their bright energy. Photos on the wall featured a happy, blonde family, knick-knacks lined every shelf and tabletop. The entryway opened up into the kitchen, dining area, and a cozy living room. The far wall on the left, however, had a series of doors leading to bedrooms.

Looking down that way as she slipped off her shoes, Winter froze when she looked through an open door. It led to a bedroom, which Winter was certain had once been a very neat, pristine, lovely space.

Now, it looked like a struggle had happened. Rumpled sheets were hanging off the bed, like someone had rolled— or perhaps, tumbled— straight off the side. A fallen pillow was caught against the side of the bed. The nightstand, a small rounded table, was knocked onto its side— and a small lamp was on the floor, glass panes from the intricate top shattered and broken, spread across the hardfloor.

Winter's eyes followed the mess— spotting discarded plastic gloves in a wastebasket near the doorway, and a dried stain on a rug that looked suspiciously like vomit. Next to the stain was an empty insulin vial. Her focus was locked on that— until she saw Pierre move over and pull the door to the bedroom shut. Their eyes met, Pierre's filled with pain, Winter's reflecting regret. An awkward pause ensued between them, before Pierre gestured towards the living room,

"Please, come sit. I was just making phone calls. I could use a break."

"I'm sure... I'm so sorry about Mi- uh... S-Sophie." Winter found it strange, to use her teacher's first name, as she perched herself in a squashed up armchair.

Pierre sat across from her, crossing his legs and nervously

folding his hands over his knee. "T-Thank you. It was... unexpected."

Silence, for a moment, made the air between them heavier. What could someone say? It had been a day since the apparent suicide. Bryce's suicide had been unquestionable, he had left a note, but Winter still wasn't sure what she could have said to his family if she'd faced them like this. Pierre was a friend, but that didn't make it easier to face the pain he was going through.

"I... My mom had uh... depressed episodes. According to my grandfather, she... she had a period of life where she found it difficult to eat. She would just stop eating, and she'd sleep a lot, and... and I never would have guessed, Miss Popelin was always so cheerful. It's a shock, and if— if there's anything I can do... I just wanted to come see how you were doing." Winter finally broke the silence, opening up about her own mom— as if, somehow, that would make it seem like she understood.

I barely know my mom. I could have brought up Axel but... No. I don't really know Axel either, do I? I mean... I can listen, but I couldn't possibly understand this...

Winter had never felt the type of depression Axel had described to her over their numerous phone calls, and she certainly didn't see any of Axel's depression in Miss Popelin — but then again, it was hard to see it sometimes, wasn't it? People could be wonderful actors, when they were hiding darkness in the daylight.

Pierre looked pained for a moment before he answered her,

"They say that d-depression is common with diabetics. Soph, she was a type one. Diagnosed as a kid, long before I was even born. She's dealt with it so long, I guess it wore her down, but... I never would have thought she'd do this. It had to have been an accident. S-She must have miscalculated her dose, or…"

He sighed, rubbing a hand over his face. For a moment, the sixteen year old looked as if he was going on sixty.

"You don't have to explain—" Winter began, but he interrupted her, lowering his hand so he could look at her with weary eyes.

"No, it's okay. I just… You know, Sophie has had low sugar before. We keep juice, and snacks, and she's gone to the hospital before. I just think if I was here, if I was with her, I could have…"

Standing, Winter walked around a short oak coffee table to get to where Pierre sat.

"Don't talk like that. If you start blaming yourself, you'll never stop. It's a terrible thing to blame yourself for someone taking their life, Pierre. Sophie wouldn't have wanted that for you."

As she spoke, she wrapped her arms around his neck in a hug. It took him a moment, but Pierre slowly hugged her back, looping his arms around her. Before long, his shoulders began to shake, and Winter was certain he had begun to cry. It might have even been the first hug he'd received since losing his sister.

And although she said these comforting words to him, in the back of her mind, she couldn't stop herself from thinking:

If Axel did this… wouldn't I hold myself to blame, too? Wouldn't I drive myself crazy with all the things I didn't do?

The thought made her feel ill, guilt settling uneasily in her heart.

I have to get him to talk to me, to forgive me, somehow…

I have to fix this, before it's too late.

If this happened to Axel… Winter would never be able to forgive herself.

10

UNCLEAR VISION

W: Axel… Please answer. I'm sorry. I never meant for this
to happen.
W: Please just let me explain. Answer the phone. I'm so,
so sorry.
W: I'm going to school tonight. To face it. I'm going to fix
this.
W: If I don't come back… Forgive me.

Texts upon texts had been sent, and none had been
answered. Eventually, as the sun set on the last day
of that week, Winter had to accept that she was on
her own. Her friend was either willfully ignoring her
messages, or reading them and too angry to answer her.
There were a dozen that ran through her head that she
hadn't sent at all— *I need you. I can't do this alone. I'm scared. I
don't know what I did. I don't know if I can fix this. Don't leave me
alone. Damn it, Axel!*

Instead, she found herself sighing heavily, leaving her
phone on a shelf of her bookcase. She wouldn't be needing it

where she was going. Axel wasn't answering— and who else would ever believe her?

Winter had to wait until her grandfather went to bed for the night, and when he did, she finally crept downstairs, slipping out the back door. She was dressed for running: black sneakers, leggings, a green tank top. Her hair pulled into a short ponytail; bangs brushed out of the way as she jogged in the direction of her school.

Funny... If Papa knew I was out at night, going to fight a terrifying figment of my imagination that I don't know how to kill, he'd really be mad. She mused, a chill running down her spine at the thought. Some things weren't worth worrying about right now, though. After all, the idea of her being another one of those "suicides" was much worse than whatever her grandfather would do to her.

The school was so quiet when it was empty and dark, any noise seemed to echo off the brick walls. It wasn't hard for Winter to get in, simply envisioning the door unlocking, hearing it click with a wave of her hand.

At least sometimes that power is still useful. She thought spitefully, slipping into the front hall of the school.

The air was cold— unnaturally, like someone had turned the air conditioner on way too high, hitting her skin and causing goosebumps as she quietly made her way down the hall. After Bryce's death, Axel had told her more than once that something felt wrong in their school. She hadn't entirely known what he meant, until now.

Winter had no clue if that creature was around, but she was walking with purpose, making her way towards her locker. If she could get ahold of her notebook, with her sketches, maybe she could... erase that blurry-faced thing? She wasn't sure exactly, but she had drawn it, just like she usually did when she was daydreaming, and it was the only thing she could think of.

Reaching her locker, all was quiet, and Winter breathed a sigh of relief as she plugged in the combination— 07.29.20. — and gently pulled it open. It didn't take long for her to grab the red covered notebook, smiling triumphantly as she shut the locker.

Her face quickly morphed into sudden fear. She gasped loudly and stumbled back from the lockers. Behind the locker door stood Axel— gazing at her with blank blue eyes lined in black eyeliner. He had heavy circles beneath them.

"A-Axel. Holy hell, where did you come from? What are you doing here?" Winter breathed, holding her notebook to her chest, heart having painfully leapt into her throat at the jump scare. *Is he still angry with me?* Her eyes traced his face, looking for telltale signs. The only sign, however, was how blankly he was looking at her, and that his eyes seemed... colder. Though, she supposed that wasn't really all too surprising, considering the temperament he'd had towards her lately. He didn't have his piercings in, his face pale in the dim light of the hall. Guilt pricked at her subconscious, as she nervously spoke again,

"Did you get my messages? You didn't have to come. This is all my fault— I should be the one dealing with it." She said this, but... honestly, she was relieved to see him, offering up a small smile.

"You think I came here for you?" His words were spoken dully, but they cut through Winter like knives.

"Uh... Well... I-I thought... I mean, I texted you..." She was lost for words, eyes widening. The thing that was so strange— was that Axel was so unemotional. Everyone always said he was, but Winter always saw right through it. He had never seemed emotionless to her, not even before they were friends. Now, though... She couldn't read him at all. "Are you still upset with me? We can talk about it, when we get out of here."

"No." He answered, staring at her as a displeased look came across his face. His eyes, which she usually found beautiful, were so piercing that Winter wanted to look away. "I should have known you'd make it. You make everything up, don't you? Fantasies in your head. You snap your fingers and they just… happen. Must be pretty nice, isn't it? To bring fake things to life. You just imagine whatever you want and bam, there it is. The world is what you make it, huh?"

Her throat felt tight. Winter closed her eyes in dreadful guilt, and when she opened them again, Axel must have moved— he was standing closer now with his arms crossed. What could she say to that? *Please stop looking at me like that. That look in your eyes… It hurts.*

He was looking at her like she was a monster, no different than that thing she had made.

"You have every right to be angry, Axe. I know I've… I've betrayed your trust." Winter answered him, her voice sounding pitiful and weak in her own. She could physically feel herself trying to shrink in front of her… friend? Were they friends after this? Would he ever want to be her friend again? *It wasn't my fault,* she wanted to plead.

"Trust? I never trusted you. Not really." He scoffed, "Why would I? Didn't you ever wonder why I guard what I say around you? So you don't twist it your way, imagine something that is far from reality? You don't have any real friends — only friends you make with pretty words. Another one of your fantasies. You talk so nicely, so proper, such sweet words for the people around you. No swearing, no insults, not even a freaking joke that could be taken wrong from Miss Jozefson— No, because you're so perfect. Miss Goody, always on the right side of everything, always likable to everyone. Can't be liked by your looks— not in the "right" way, at least— so all you have is your mind and personality to offer up, and that can be softened. Because it would just…

kill you, wouldn't it? If people thought badly of you? Or… is it just that you don't want to be left behind again? For someone that is less of a burden?"

He smiled at her, and it was the first time Winter had ever thought Axel was ugly. He'd never been ugly to her before now, with that ghastly smirk on his face. "You want people to like you that badly? Pathetic. A real basket case. I should have dropped you weeks ago, it would have saved me a lot of headache."

It was like everything he had ever told her had been a lie, something to keep her calm so she wouldn't panic. Now that he was angry, now that he was done with her, it was all coming out; the way he really felt. Anxiety clawed at Winter's chest, her breathing shallow. The urge to run was coming up like bile in her throat, taking a shaky step back. But along with it was shock, wondering if this was really happening, her voice shaking as she asked, "Wh-Why are you saying this? I thought we…"

"What?!" He snapped at her— making Winter jump from his interruption. Now, he didn't sound blank at all, finally emotional as he growled, "You thought we what? We were friends? More than friends? You thought I liked you, just because I spilled a few secrets? Get out of your FUCKING head, Winter. Wake up. I told you about *it* because you were there when I felt like talking. It didn't make you special. But you were just that eager to relate to someone, weren't you? Someone that made you less of a freak?" He looked her up and down then, with those piercing blue eyes. Winter had never been looked at so critically, and she found herself glancing down at the ground as Axel continued, "You were so eager to get my attention… So eager to be my *friend*… I pitied you. I was being the nice one just by talking to you. And then you just wouldn't leave me alone, so I tolerated you until you did *this*."

Winter felt numb, shaking as she stood there, letting Axel's words cut into her. This was worse than his outburst from a few days ago. Instead of sudden raging anger, he spoke with a meticulous, practical tone that held absolute, blunt honesty. This was how he really felt about her, wasn't it? If it had been anyone else, she liked to think she would have been defending herself, or growing defiant in the face of such harsh insults. But it was Axel. Axel, who had only ever surprised her in good ways. Axel, who she had spent long hours into the early morning talking to over the phone, spilling stories and secrets, questioning and supporting. Axel, who had defended her, even saved her— who always made sure she was okay. But now... The things he said about her were nastier than Ian's attack had been. It might not have been physical, but it felt real enough to make her bleed.

That's true...

All the things I told him... He never asked to know. He wasn't interested.

He never would have paid any attention to me at school without reason to.

We don't have that much in common at all, really...

I knew that... So why does this hurt so much? It's just knowing the truth.

I was just at the right place, the right time. I tried so hard to make him like me...

And now I've brought his worst nightmare to life... so he's done pretending.

Now... He hates me...

I'm just a burden again. He's getting rid of me.

Everyone gets sick of me eventually. Even him.

The thoughts came one after the other, flooding her mind, the things that plagued her when she crawled into bed for the night and turned off all the lights— but now they were confirmed. He had just told her, hadn't he? Axel listened more than he talked, and usually, that didn't bother Winter. But every so often, she wondered what he really thought about things. She didn't have to wonder anymore. The crushing hurt of being despised by someone she loved hit her like a truck. All the words he didn't say— but she was sure he was thinking— drifted through her mind.

A soft, blurred motion caught her attention as Axel unfolded his arms, and one of his hands came up to cup her cheek. His hand was hard and cold against her skin, unlike Axel's touch had been before. The gesture was so intimate and tender, though, as if his previous words had been sweet, staring at her with those bold eyes.

Wait a second.

He was moving in front of her— and that was what betrayed *it.* The way his arms blurred with every movement. Now that his eyes weren't quite so captivating, she noticed the way his mouth looked— faded, and blurry, moving strangely when he spoke like he was only mimicking the words.

"*Winter.*" Her name sounded hollow coming from him.

Axel didn't say her name that way. Not in all the time she had known him, had he spoken to her like this. And the way she felt so cold and empty under his gaze...

This isn't Axel. The thought occurred to Winter suddenly, and once it did, everything unraveled at once.

Their eyes met again, and Winter blinked rapidly, trying to clear her vision and calm her mind from the thoughts that wouldn't stop. Every time her eyes opened, it looked less and less like Axel. His skin fading into gray, his hair melting into shadows, his clothes turning into a deep black robe that was tied around its boney waist. Aware that it was *touching* her— or was that a trick too?— Winter stumbled back with a gasping breath. Its hand slipped from her cheek, snagging on the black cord of her necklace. She didn't have time to acknowledge the cord being yanked from her neck, cut from claw-like fingers, the pendant clattering to the floor.

"WINT-AHHH~!" It tried to say her name— but it was followed by that horrible screeching howl, making the lockers in the hallway shake from the sheer force as Winter turned to run.

Wherever the real Axel was, he wasn't here to save her this time.

Winter desperately sprinted for the end of the hall as the thing screeched behind her. Her quick thinking made her run for the Principal's office— which she knew had a lock on the door. Bursting inside, she closed the door and threw her back against it, hand fumbling for the lock, dropping her notebook to the floor. Almost immediately the door jolted hard against her, rough banging like a harsh drumline.

BANG! BANG! BANG!

Winter whimpered, heart racing. All she could do was give a desperate prayer that the door would hold. She slid down against it, taking quick, panicked breaths of air.

It spoke again. But this time, it wasn't Axel's imitated voice.

"Winter! Pumpkin? It's Papa. Open up." Her grandfather's voice, as if with an echo. Not from the other side of the door — but it felt like it was coming directly into her mind, sounding off like a bad inner monologue.

Her hands went to her head, gripping at her hair. Winter didn't know whether to cry or scream. She wanted to do both, and yet all she could do was sit on the floor, pushed against the shaking door, gasping for air that refused to draw up into her lungs.

"Win, it's Kaya! I've come to pick you up!" Her best friend's cheerful tone called, another fist slamming to the door.

Not even a minute later, a third voice chimed in,

"Winter. I didn't mean to be so cold. Come on, let me walk you home, baby." Axel's voice was so sweet that it was hurtful, a poor imitation of the real thing, echoing in her mind. Having him call her baby made Winter shudder.

No you're not. You're not Axel, you're not Kaya, you're not papa. You're not even real. This is all in my head... Oh God, please let this be all in my head. It was more of a hope than anything, squeezing her eyes shut as she let out a choked sob.

She should never have come to the school alone. How would she get rid of this thing? All the hoping and wishing in the world wouldn't help her now. Her hand twitched, reaching for her pocket— until she remembered she didn't have her phone. She did have her bag, but it was filled with only school books and supplies. There were no other doors in this room either, not even a window available for escape. Getting outside the school had stopped Blurry before, but she wasn't sure there was anything stopping it from following her now.

Winter had never felt so alone in her life, nor so scared. And that was exactly what this thing fed on. She was in its element here, and she wasn't sure she'd make it out alive. So she did the one thing she could.

Whenever she had a hard night... Whenever *he* wasn't answering her messages at night, when she thought something was wrong, Winter thought his name. She said it in her mind, like a mantra.

Axel. Axel. Axel.

Part of her hoped that somewhere, he'd hear her. Feel her pleas for an answer. Even seeing what she just had seen— he was the only one who knew what this beast was. He was the only one she had to call out to. And she wasn't sure if her powers gave her such mental ability, but she hoped that *something* would make him think of her, something would make him know she needed him.

Axel couldn't sleep. He had gone to bed that night early, skipping dinner, avoiding conversations with his parents he'd rather not have to sit through. Yet, a little after the sun had set, his phone began to buzz. He read each and every message from Winter over the last few days, since they had encountered *that thing*. It wasn't hard for him to not reply— at first, out of anger and fear of what she had made, but then out of not knowing what to say. Especially after his outburst at school.

What could he say? She had made his nightmare— his depression— come to life in a physical form. It gave him chills just to picture it, the creature he had seen her sketching had stood before him. It was *real.*

He couldn't imagine anything worse. Deep down, he didn't blame Winter, but that didn't change what was now prowling their school halls. He had a hard enough time escaping it in his mind— how could he escape it in reality?

Turning onto his side in bed, he lay as stiff as a board, eyes locked on his Nokia, watching as every few minutes the screen lit up in a dull green as a new text came in, chiming loudly. Then, it began to ring, Winter's name flashing on the screen.

"Just leave me alone already..." Axel mumbled into the darkness, wishing he was as annoyed as he wanted to be. Unfortunately, he knew Winter enough to know how badly she wanted to apologize to him and after his outburst, he even had an apology of his own to give.

He just... wasn't sure an apology would be enough right now, for either of them. It didn't change what was happening, or make things better.

After the phone stopped ringing, it was several long

minutes before his phone chimed again. Axel had been idly scratching at the long, thin scars that littered his arms, fingers trailing down the older lines that didn't hurt. At last, with a soft sigh, Axel reached for his phone, pulling up his messages from Winter.

It took him a few minutes to reach the all-important last message.

Going to school... Fix this...

"What the hell, Winter?!" Axel exclaimed in irritation as he sat bolt upright in his bed. He knew all too well what *his* monster was capable of— and he was pretty sure Winter had no clue what she was getting herself into, stumbling blindly into a trap.

Leaving his phone, Axel slipped out of the house and began running in the direction of Clamare High.

He could hear the thudding pounds of the beast from all the way down the hall, echoing his worst thoughts. It wasn't hard to find them, and as he grew closer, he heard her. Winter's sobs and the screams she gave after each knock, made his heart leap into his throat, picking up his pace until that thing was in his view. Now, he got a better look at the beast. It was an exact copy of what Winter had drawn, given form.

From a twelve foot distance, the thing looked like a shadow. It was almost transparent, but that didn't stop its corporeal form from being terrifying to look at. It was insanely tall and skinny, dressed in a dark black robe that clung to it like smoke— or perhaps fog, curling around it and giving it the look of a black cloud of misery. That was new, wasn't it? It had been naked before. But it was the head that

Axel fixated on. From the back, the head was just a rounded gray orb.

"Hey, ugly! Leave her alone!" Axel hollered at it.

That horrible, distorted screech came from the monster, so loud it made Axel wince. Its head reared towards him, and Axel got sight of those distinct, ink black eyes and the strange, smoky bottom half of its face, with its gaping mouth. It only just barely acknowledged him before focusing back on the door. Even though it looked like it could pass right through the wall, its large, clawed hands were solid, shaking the door.

If Axel didn't know his own demon so well, he might not have known what would get its attention. But he knew it as well as he knew his own mind. Staring at the back of its head, he hoped its new form hadn't changed the way it operated— and he hoped even more that Winter would run when he gave her the chance.

Swallowing his nerves, Axel reached for his back pocket, pulling out a red and silver swiss army knife. It had once belonged to his brother, the initials K.D. etched into the end of the handle. *It's the only thing that'll get it's attention.* He thought, rolling up his sleeve. His little act of rebellion, of fighting back, of control. *Let's see if this still works.*

Swiss army knives were multi-purpose, but Axel had never cut with one before. He winced at the thick blade against his upper forearm, trying to use just the tip as he drew it across his skin, just enough to bleed. The pain that came was familiar, barely fazing him as his grip tightened on the handle. He only drew his eyes up when he knew he had its attention— and saw those black eyes looking back, a low growling hum coming from his demon.

Lifting the blade, he moved it half an inch down his arm and drew it down again, gritting his teeth as the new opening began to sting. For a second, he swore the monster's form darkened, solidifying and then fading again before his eyes.

Is it...? No. Axel didn't want to think about what he suspected, his hand shaking as he stopped slicing open his flesh. Thick drops of blood glistened on the edge of the knife.

The monster took a step towards him, Winter forgotten behind the door as it faced its oldest plaything. Flipping the bloodied knife shut, Axel slipped it into his pocket with one hand and dragged his sleeve down with the other, wincing at the touch of the fabric.

"Now that your attention is on me... Let me tell you what I'm going to do." Axel was surprised that his voice remained steady, but he had always wanted to tell this to his monster, and now was his chance. "I'm going to fight you. I'm going to beat you. In three years, I'll graduate. Then, I'll go on to college." He sounded more confident than he felt, spewing what, on any other day, he would have called hopeless.

The beast warbled its strange, siren-like cry, moving towards him with blurred, unsteady movements. Despite it growing closer, Axel kept talking.

"I'm going to live an average, normal, *happy* life. You'd just hate that, wouldn't you?" When Axel smiled at him, that was when it screeched in anger— and when Axel turned and bolted.

Running down the halls, he could hear it chasing him, banging off the lockers and screaming after him. Adrenaline pumping through him, Axel skidded around a corner, his heart thudding faster than his feet.

"COME AND GET ME, THEN!" Axel screamed back over his shoulder, too breathless to laugh as he kept the monster at his heels. He didn't know if that thing could read his thoughts, but if it could, it'd be flooded by what Axel wanted. The goals that the monster told him were out of reach. Not the fake home his parents painted to be picturesque, but the real deal. White picket fences, home cooked meals, children's laughter. A pretty girl waiting at the end of the walkway— waiting for him. The dream life that was so hard to achieve— the sunny blue skies that had always been unforgivingly gray in his mind's eye.

Perhaps the monster could sense his hopes growing, and that's why its angry squeals grew louder. All he needed was to keep it away from Winter just long enough. Then, Axel thought, he didn't care what happened to him.

Maybe he should have— his footing was suddenly lost, slipping and sending him sprawling forward onto the tile. Axel let out a strangled choking sound as his chin slammed into the ground, his limbs going out from under him, his injured arm painfully curled under him.

It's all over. He thought, as he rolled himself onto his back as the black robes of the creature fluttered into his vision. As he squeezed his eyes shut, the image of the life he wanted flashed before his eyelids.

It's a nice dream... for someone more deserving.

11

UNWORTHY OF A NAME

Winter forgot how afraid she was when she heard Axel in the hall, yelling at the monster. It was a momentary triumph, producing a sobbing laugh as she hugged her sketchbook to her chest. It couldn't have been another deceptive echo— or at least, that's what she wanted to believe— and she was right.

Axel seemed to have a knack for rescuing her, but Winter was more than willing to let him this time. Ian Bryars had nothing on this thing.

Minutes passed, and the pounding receded until all was silent.

Axel must have led it away, Winter thought, pushing herself up on shaky legs. She waited another minute before carefully opening the door, wary of another trap. But when she peered out, the hallway was empty and silent.

Breathless, Winter practically flew down the hall of Clamare High, not looking back for Axel— after all, he didn't cause a distraction for her just to get caught up by that monster again. Bursting out of the school's front doors, she bolted to the statue of Brendon Hendrix, falling against the bronze base as she finally came to a stop. Her hands clung to the cold metal, trying to steady herself as she gulped down the cool night air, looking back at the high school with a racing heart.

Minutes passed in the silence, the only sound being her own frantic gasps, fighting off nausea as she sank to sit on the ground.

Come on, Axel. Get out here. Winter was starting to wonder if she had to go back in after him. She didn't want to, but she would. What if he couldn't fight it alone? Did he even know how? They had run away before.

Pushing herself to her feet, she was mentally prepared herself to face that depression beast once more when, at last, the door pushed open and out stumbled her friend.

"Axel!" She cried out in relief, running toward him and throwing her arms around his neck. One of his arms curled around her, tensing up at her tight hug.

Pulling away, her eyes scanned his face. Her hand went to grab onto his arm when it touched a wet patch on his shirt sleeve, and she saw his face contort in a painful grimace. A dark red stain was creeping onto the light blue fabric. It wasn't large, but the color drained from her face when she saw it. She could smell the iron scent of blood, taking a startled step back.

"You're hurt." Winter said, as she looked down at the blood on her palm, stomach churning. "Axel... W-What did it do to you? How did you get away?"

"Not here." Axel shut down her attempt for answers, grabbing her hand to pull her away.

Winter didn't question him as they hurried away from the

monster's prowling grounds. They ended up in the small, round courtyard that sat between town hall and the sheriff's office, a little bit east of the school. Everything was quiet, not a soul in sight as Winter and Axel sunk onto a bench beneath a large ash tree. Axel kept his injured arm curled against his chest, which didn't hide the growing bloodstain.

It was pure luck that her grandfather was ex-military and had forced her to carry a first aid kit in her bag.

"Let me take a look at your arm."

As she reached for Axel, he jerked back, panic crossed his face as if her seeing the self inflicted injury was his worst nightmare.

"Axel." She said his name with a warning tone, "Let me."

"N-No." His voice shook, pulling his arm away once more. "Don't touch me. I'm fine—"

"You're not fine." Winter retorted, frowning at him.

Why are you being so difficult? She wanted to ask, but in truth... she already knew. It had been hard for Axel to even talk about his scars, much less show them or have them touched. As much as she wanted him to trust her, this wasn't an issue of trust. She could see in his eyes that this was a hard limit, and no amount of asking was going to make him agree. This was a source of pain that went far past the physical.

As they stared each other down, Winter's shoulders began to sink until finally, she held out the little medical kit. Axel opened his mouth.

"I'm not leaving, so don't ask me to." Winter spoke before he could. It might have been rude, or insensitive, but she wasn't about to leave Axel alone and bleeding. It meant the world that she knew about the scars at all, and she didn't want to push him, but... she wanted to help. Even if she could do nothing but sit beside him and make sure he properly wrapped his arm.

Axel looked at her a moment longer, his mouth still

agape, and for a second, Winter thought he'd tell her to leave regardless. After a long pause, he nodded, accepting the compromise. He took the box from her with a soft sigh. Balancing it on his lap, he slowly rolled up the sleeve of his bleeding arm.

It was the first time Winter had been shown the scars that they had talked so much about. There were three long, open cuts, bleeding fairly heavily— but as far as Winter could tell, the cuts were carefully made and not too deep. It could have been a lot worse, and she found herself letting out a sigh of relief.

"Did that thing do those?" Winter asked, nodding towards the new cuts.

"No. I did." Axel answered, frowning. "It… drew him away."

It wasn't her fault, but Winter felt a pang of guilt, knowing Axel wouldn't have had to do it at all if she hadn't gone to the school alone.

Besides the new cuts, she could make out several scars. She knew from speaking to Axel over the last month that they were made with razor blades. He had once complained to her that it took a lot of force to make the cuts deeper, so they were shallow, but the scars looked thick, raised on his skin. They went from his wrist to his inner elbow, though Winter noticed that they lessened towards his wrist, becoming thicker further up his forearm. The majority were dark in color, red and purple, still healing— though there were plenty of old, faint white ones too.

"What?" Axel broke through the sudden silence bluntly. He had seen the look on Winter's face. "Disgusted?"

Do you expect me to be? Winter thought, lifting her gaze to his. "No. Well, I don't like blood, but, no. I just… Do you mind if I ask you a question?"

"Shoot." Axel sighed, taking a roll of bandages from the kit. As he unrolled it, Winter took a breath.

"How long have you been…" Her voice faltered, hesitating, "…cutting?" She had never asked him. They had conversations on the act of it, on the purpose of it, on how it helped him cope— and a few, rare conversations on why he needed it to cope at all— but Winter had never asked about the beginning.

"'Bout a year now."

You did that much in a year? Winter wondered, her eyes dropping down to his scars again, getting one last look before he covered it completely. The white bandages were already starting to turn red. Axel's hands were shaking.

"Double wrap that." Winter murmured, "And you're going to want to disinfect it when you're home."

"Yeah, got it. Done this before." His tone earned a flinch, lowering her head.

As Axel tied off the bandage, Winter couldn't help one more question.

"Have you ever uh… t-tried… to… d-do what Bryce and Miss Popelin…"

"Attempt? Yeah. Once. Failed, obviously." Axel answered, to Winter's surprise. Still, he didn't seem at all comfortable. Hugging his arm to his chest, he added, "Enough questions, for now, Win."

"Okay, then… How about a statement? I'm so sorry, Axel. For creating that thing." She hoped that he could hear the sincerity in her voice— for the first time, he actually seemed to be willing to listen to her.

"Stop apologizing. Really, Winter, it's… I knew about your powers when I told you. You weren't hiding it from me, you weren't trying to deceive me— and I know you didn't make it come to life on purpose." Axel rubbed the back of his neck with his hand, looking up at the sky to avoid her gaze as he continued, "I thought it was pretty bad, just being in my head. Seeing it in real life is ten times worse, though. I wasn't prepared for that."

"Neither was I! I had no idea I even did it. I-I've never made something like that. I have no idea what it is, o-or how to get rid of it. I thought if I could get my sketchbook, then I could just rip the drawings up or something, but… Seeing it tonight… it's changed, Axe. From the last time."

"What do you mean?" Finally, he looked at her.

"Well… Last time it was more like a beast. All it did was screech and it moved like a monster. This time…" Winter didn't want to tell him, thinking back to her encounter.

"Go on. I want to know." Axel pushed.

Winter looked down at her feet, curling her arms across her chest, "It… had your face. For a while, I… I thought it was you. And then, when I realized it wasn't, it started to freak out. I heard different voices, like it was trying to trick me and got angry when it found out I had seen through it. But it was definitely more human. Or good at acting human. I'm not sure."

"Figures it'd be good at playing pretend." Axel scoffed. Winter shot him a confused look, but she didn't get a chance to ask what he meant, as he began, "Did it talk to you? Did it say anything?"

Winter shivered at the question. She wanted to tell him the truth, but… *I doubted him so quickly, I believed that monster.* Deep down, she knew there was more to it than that, remembering its strong influence, but it was easy to blame herself.

"No. It… wasn't particularly chatty." She lied. Axel stared at her and she was certain he would call her out on her lie, but instead, he moved to stand up.

"Let's go home. I don't want to think about it anymore."

He reached out a hand, and Winter took it, letting him

pull her to her feet. As they started off in the direction of Altum Court, she couldn't help stealing glances towards Axel.

Does he have as much on his mind as I do? She wondered, sighing.

"So… are we good?" Winter asked him.

It was a few minutes of walking before he answered her, his voice distracted and distant.

"Yeah. We're good, don't worry."

"You've been at it for hours." Axel groaned, flopping back onto his bed with a force that made Winter, who sat at the foot of it, bounce with the mattress. "I don't know why you're bothering— we both know what that thing is. It's exactly how I told you. You made it, Winter, it's not exactly a mystery." He sounded short-tempered, but his anger over the appearance of the monster had vanished the second he'd decided to rescue Winter, just two nights prior.

They were at his house since his parents didn't mind him being in his room with a girl with the door closed. His father wasn't home, nor his brothers, and his mother… Well, she was confident that her son knew better than to fool around with a girl. All it had taken was a short, "She's just a friend." to convince her to let them go upstairs undisturbed. The fact that she didn't care enough to be watchful was more telling into his upbringing than Axel wanted to get into. If they had gone to Winter's house, they would have been sitting in the living room, in view of her grandfather every second while he polished his old army service weapons. There was no privacy in her house, a special type of teenage suffocation that pissed Axel off to no end. So here they were— with Winter balancing a book on supernatural creatures on her knee, and all the time in the world after telling her grandfather she was at Kaya's for the night.

For whatever reason, she thought she could find the answer in the works of fiction and legends.

"But I've never made something like that, Axel!" Winter remarked, her voice an octave higher than normal. "I've made some wonderful and terrible things happen. But I've never made a monster. It's not possible, it has to be something else. A wendigo, a djinn, a ghost, or... I don't know." She'd been searching every variation of supernatural creature she could, but none of them matched the haunting creature that now lurked the halls of their school.

Laying on his back, Axel tossed a softball up into the air, lazily catching it over and over as he answered her, "Then how do you explain it? It's exactly like what you drew, what you imagined. Even I knew what it was when I saw it. There's nothing like it in this world."

She knew he was right. Moreso, they both knew Winter didn't want him to be right. That thing was scarier than anything in their world. Eyeing the back of her head with her brown hair tugged into a messy ponytail, Axel poked at the small of her back with his foot. He was smiling when she turned her head to look over at him, pouting.

"You know what we should do? Since there's never been one before, we should give it a name. Make it one for the history books." Axel suggested, raising an eyebrow at her. His newfound coping mechanism of joking about it was doing wonders for them staying sane when there was a literal monster in their school.

Winter laughed, pushing his foot off her back. She closed the book, setting it aside at last as she turned to face him, pulling her legs up fully onto the bed. "And what, pray tell, should we call it? Nicolas? Steve?"

She shook her head, "You know it better than I do."

Axel rolled his eyes at her, pushing himself up on his elbows as he remarked, "Nope, those are basic names. We're gonna want to make it sound creepy and unusual. Like... Sløret."

Winter's face crinkled at the suggestion, giving him a look of disapproval that made Axel laugh.

Axel's father was from Denmark, and spoke fluent Danish. Axel didn't claim to be an expert— he had picked up more Japanese from his mother than he had Danish from his father— but he knew a few words here or there.

"That sounds disgusting, whatever it is." Winter said.

"It means blurry. You know, for that thing's face, being all... faded. And the way it moves, all blurred." Axel explained, waving a hand as if it might blur, too. *That thing is a piece of me, after all.* He thought, eyes drifting to a nearby mirror on his wall, taking in his pale skin and dark circles under his eyes. *Maybe I'll start looking all faded, just like it does.* He mused, snorting softly.

"Clever. But no." Winter rejected his idea. "Maybe I'd be better off looking into a book on depression."

"No way. The quacks that write those books don't know anything about real depression." Axel retorted.

Winter eyed him a second, before tapping his knee, "Scooch."

Begrudgingly sliding over, Axel laid himself on the edge of his narrow bed, partially up against the wall. Winter moved to lay down beside him on her back, brown hair splaying out on his pillow. She took up most of the bed, but Axel wasn't about to tell her that as he lay shoulder-to-shoulder and hip-to-hip with her. One of her legs looped over his, making herself comfortable as he peered at the thoughtful expression on her face. She was in a world of her own, and he couldn't help asking,

"What are you thinking?"

"Hm?" She hummed, glancing over to meet his gaze. "Oh... Nothing important."

Liar. If it wasn't important, she wouldn't have been so quiet, she would have been talking his ear off. But Axel just reached for the small radio he kept on the shelf over his bed, turning on some tunes for them.

Winter wasn't sure how long they laid there, in the glow of Axel's blue lava lamp. Listening to soft-rock and idly discussing the monster from Axel's mind. But she was very aware she fell asleep, time slipping away in the comfort of Axel's bed.

Waking up, she felt heavy and stiff, her body aching from laying so straight and in such a small spot, pushed up against Axel.

Dreams were fading quickly from her mind as she looked up at Axel's face. At first, her eyes were watery and filmed over— *bleary*. His sleeping face was dulled in her vision, like she needed to put on glasses. Blinking several times and rubbing at her eyes, it took a second before his face was clear to her gaze, waking up and seeing him fully.

Laying there, Winter turned on her side, staring at Axel. He looked so undisturbed while he slept. It was a different kind of blankness, softer and less guarded, as his hair fell into his eyes.

That thing... It represents everything he hates about himself. It's the darkness of his mind, his depression and struggles in a physical form, meant to torment him. Winter thought, her heart aching for her friend. They hadn't known each other long, but Winter had seen so many sides to Axel, and they were all beautiful to her.

He hadn't told anyone but me, because of the way people think of depression. She could picture it in her head— the reactions, the expressions, the response they would give him. Why would anyone want to talk about their problems if they were met with judgment like that? *They don't see him. They don't really see him.*

A slow realization dawned on her,

They have bleary eyes.

Sitting up abruptly, Winter fumbled for her backpack in the dim light of the room, trying to yank her journal and a pencil out. Tossing it open, the sound of rapid fluttering pages came as she flicked hurriedly to the last page she had drawn on; a page full of drawings of the creature.

Each drawing was slightly different, but they all had the same face. Faded, gray, indistinct faces with clear, hard lined eyes that stood out dark and solid on the page.

"We see it with bleary eyes... but it sees right through us, to our deepest insecurities. Depression... bleary face, clear eyes, screeching voice, mimicking the people we trust..." She mumbled the words, writing them at the bottom of the page.

That was what Axel woke up to. Winter was curled over the edge of his bed, clinging onto her notebook, writing and drawing the creature and what she knew about depression until her hand was cramping, expanding on what Axel had told her.

"Win? How long have you been up?" Axel asked, yawning as he sat up, rubbing at his eyes.

"Axel, I've got it. I know what it is. You were right, I did make it. I just didn't remember, because it came from a dream I had. And it has a name." She looked so excited, so joyful, to be talking about something so dark. Turning towards him, she gave Axel a triumphant grin.

"Its name is Bleary."

"Winter, wait!" Why was he chasing her? Winter had never run from him before. Now, she couldn't seem to get away from him fast enough. Barefoot, she wore a long, slender white dress that contrasted her tan skin. The end of it was tattered and shredded, almost purposefully, though it was dirty and seemed to be covered in some kind of gray dust all along the bottom. Ash? Axel couldn't tell. Her hair was loose, swishing with each frantic step she bolted away from him. Every time she looked back, her hazel-green eyes were wide and full of fear. It was as if she didn't recognize him. Or worse, it was as if he were some kind of wild animal hunting down his prey.

"Hey! Stop!" His voice sounded far away, echoing down the halls. It wasn't hard to recognize that this was his home— with the white walls and cold metal picture frames. Only, the short hallways seemed to go on forever, the doors repeating themselves as Winter struggled ahead of him.

It seemed like forever until she began to slow. The hallway finally ended as she stumbled into the kitchen with Axel on her heels. She stopped in the corner, putting the island counter between them, gasping as if she couldn't catch her breath.

"S-Stay away from me!" She begged him, flinching as Axel grabbed the end of the counter. Reaching forward, Winter grabbed a knife from the block on the counter, "I'm warning you!"

Holding his hands up, Axel began to speak,

"Winter."

Wait. That wasn't him speaking. Axel's eyes tore from Winter's face to his look at what seemed to be a mirror image of himself. Except it wasn't him. It was a man dressed in his clothes, his exact height and build. But his face— his face was blurry. No distinctive features, no matter how much Axel blinked. It looked like a human version of Bleary, only less gray. Its mouth was like an empty whirlpool, and its eyes were pitch black.

Immediately, Winter's shoulders sunk as she relaxed, her face turning from fear to relief. She reached for the blurry Axel and the real Axel yelled out,

"No! Don't touch him! Winter, it's not me!" It was like the incident in the school hallway all over again. Winter had given him a few details since then, but now he got to see it for himself. This time, Winter didn't seem to recognize she was being fooled. Instead, she looked between the two of them, caught in the corner of the kitchen island. If she went down one side, she would come safely to Axel. If she went down the other, she would find herself at the mercy of the monster.

"But..." Winter's voice showed how uncertain she was. "Axel?"

"Yes!" Immediately, both of them answered, the real Axel turning to glare at the other, who merely smirked in return.

"Winter. Look. He's Bleary— I'm not." Axel pleaded with her, gripping the edge of the counter. "Just look at my face. It's me. You know me."

Her eyes met his, and for a long moment, Winter stared back at him. But then she asked,

"Do I? Do I really know you?"

Her voice echoed. In all the time they had known each other, Axel had told her so many things. Things he had never shared with another soul. Didn't that count for anything?

Somehow, in this nightmare, it wasn't enough.

"Winter, please. Just look at me."

"I can't. You don't let me. Your face is a mask, Axel Dunn... If I can't see past your mask, do I really even know you at all?"

His hand reached out for her as Winter stepped back into the arms of the pretender. Axel could only watch as Bleary's arms wrapped around her. A devilish smile crossed his face, reaching for her neck and—

SNAP!

"NO!" Axel yelled out as Winter's head lulled back, her neck jutted out at an odd angle. Like a bird, her body dangled under the grip of a monster, fragile and delicate. Axel watched in horror as the monster released her, her body sinking to the tiled floors.

His other half began to chuckle.

"I'm surprised you can even tell us apart, Axel. We're one and the same, you and I."

"No." Axel answered. "That's not true... Winter knows that."

"Does she?"

12

UNLEASHED ANGEL

S chool had become an uncomfortable place for more than just Axel. As the autumn season turned leaves orange, and winds grew colder, Clamare High only seemed more dreary. It was more than just the sudden suicides— Axel could tell that *thing*, Bleary, was affecting more than anyone knew. Winter had tried to reassure him, with her unending optimism.

"Just wait, Axe. Halloween will get everyone in a better mood! It's spooky season, what's better than that?" She had chirped in one of their latest phone calls.

"Spooky season isn't so fun when the fear is real." He had responded, glumly.

Now, wearing a black hoodie decorated with gray skulls, Axel found himself strolling across the campus lawn to where a group of girls were sitting on blankets, working on what looked to be Halloween decorations for the annual Spooky Dance the school always had.

Axel had never gone to it— but he always saw hoards of students preparing every October. The people of Caligo took their celebrations seriously.

Some of the girls were making streamers or a menu for the snack table, others were painting fake gravestones or carving pumpkins. It wasn't hard to find Winter among the carvers.

His friend was sitting in a pair of purple leggings and a big, oversized yellow sweater dress, with gray fur boots. The wacky clothing choices did nothing to distract from Winter's radiant smile, or her caramel hair in braided pigtails.

"Delilah, look! What do you think?" Winter's voice called, Axel stopped a few feet behind her. She lifted a small pumpkin that had been sitting between her knees, revealing what was the creepiest, best carved pumpkin Axel had ever seen. It was like a goblin head, with huge hollowed-out eyes, a triangular hole for a nose, and two pointed ears at either side of its head. Its mouth had strange, rectangular chunks carved out to make little pointed teeth on the top, and nothing on the lower part of the mouth. There were flames carved out all along its head, which would be perfect once a candle was placed within.

Delilah Henderson had never been that special in Axel's eyes, but she certainly acted like it. She was on the cheerleading squad, and was the type of girl who had never met a challenge she wouldn't take. She wore her cheerleader's outfit, despite the brisk air that morning, her dark hair up in two twin buns on the top of her head. Axel couldn't help but eye the gold, white, and green of her uniform, and think of Bryce.

"What a waste of a pumpkin!" Delilah sneered as soon as she saw Winter's work. "We're going for cute-creepy, not fugly-ugly. Scrap it and start over." She waved her hand dismissively towards Winter, before returning to shaking giant globs of black and orange glitter onto a cardboard sign.

Axel, temper flaring, stepped forward and grabbed the pumpkin out of Winter's hands before she could discard it.

"I'll take it." He said as her eyes met his. "It'll fit right on the porch. Mom hates Halloween."

Winter lit up, beaming at him.

"Break time!" Delilah called out to the other girls in the group.

Wiping her hands free of pumpkin pulp, Winter got up and turned to Axel. "Walk with me?"

"Uh-huh." He confirmed, tucking his new pumpkin goblin under his arm as they took off, strolling across campus.

Even while the mood had been low, Clamare High was still like a pulsing heartbeat in Caligo's center. Just walking along the lawn, Axel had to dodge a wayward frisbee from some of the jocks messing around nearby, and Winter stopped to pluck a daisy in the grass, twirling it between her fingers.

"It's been so busy! It's like being able to break the dress code for a dance has driven everyone wild." Winter groaned dramatically, bumping her shoulder into Axel's, leaning into him as they walked. "Kaya has been driving me nuts— all she talks about is the costumes she wants me to make for her. I've been doing nothing but sketching out designs. How about you, Axel? Have you decided what you're going as?"

"I'm not going." Axel's response was easy and practiced. He knew Winter was going to bring the dance up to him sooner or later.

"What?" Winter stopped in her tracks, struck speechless for a short moment. Not short enough, in Axel's opinion, as she tugged on his sleeve to get him to stop as well. "What do you mean you're not going? Everyone goes to the Halloween dance."

"Not me. Bunch of sweaty people, dressed up and jiggling to bad pop tunes? I'm good."

"Oh come on. It's not that bad! There will be snacks, and

the costumes can be really cool— I even had an idea for yours."

You were literally just complaining about it, Axel thought, amused.

"What idea is that?" he asked, quirking an eyebrow at her.

"A uh… fallen angel. Leather jacket, black wings, hair all gelled back…" Winter looked down, cheeks burning at the suggestion. He knew exactly why, grinning as he remembered a phone call a few weeks back. They had talked about his rescue from Ian, and Winter had admitted,

"I have to admit, Axe. With you being all dressed in black, and coming to my rescue, you seemed a bit like a fallen angel."

"Not a devil?"

"No, not at all. A devil wouldn't have bothered coming to the rescue."

The memory made Axel chuckle, eyeing a bashful Winter.

"And what are you going to be?"

"…A red devil."

"Oh you've got to be kidding me!" Axel scoffed in disbelief, shaking his head. "You are not a devil."

"What? Why not?" Winter whined, her head lifting so she could give him an indignant look. "I thought it was pretty neat."

"You're too nice to be a devil. Devils are supposed to be scary."

"Oh, I can be scary." Winter reassured him.

He gave her a sweeping gaze, his tone dripping with amusement as he said, "You are a terrible actor— and the least scary person I've ever met. You should have been the angel, not me. I've never met someone with a smile as bright as yours, Win."

That seemed to strike a nerve, as Winter's cheeks began to burn a bright red.

"S-Since when do Halloween costumes have to be accurate? After all, you're too alive to be an angel."

Axel snorted at her words, the two beginning to walk again, circling back towards the Brendon Hendrix statue. "Are you sure about that? I've got one foot out the door."

"Oh hush." Winter shut down his dark humor, frowning. "Really, though. How about it? Now that the camaro is running, you could even drive the three of us over so Kaya and I don't have to walk in heels."

"Ah, I see. You're just using me for my car." Axel snarked, though he knew that wasn't the case.

"No!" Winter sounded utterly horrified, shaking her head fervently. "Not at all. But I want you to come and hang out with us, and dress up. Please? A devil and a fallen angel fit right in together. We might even win the contest."

Sighing, they started back towards the group of girls, and all Axel could do was give a noncommittal shrug of his shoulders. For a second, it crossed his mind that it sounded, ever so slightly, like a date. At least, that is what some people at school may assume.

"I'll think about it."

"Axel... W-What did it do to you? How did you get away?" Winter's worried voice floated through his head. Axel sighed, squeezing his eyes shut as he rolled onto his side. He wanted nothing more than to sleep, but the events from a few weeks past kept nagging at the back of his mind. Ever since facing that *thing*— the thing Winter had started calling Bleary— he had nothing but nightmares and sleepless nights.

I'm so freaking tired. I just need a few minutes of sleep.

Yet, every time he closed his eyes and began to drift off...

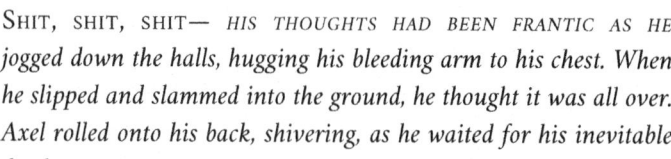

Shit, shit, shit— *his thoughts had been frantic as he jogged down the halls, hugging his bleeding arm to his chest. When he slipped and slammed into the ground, he thought it was all over. Axel rolled onto his back, shivering, as he waited for his inevitable death.*

But it never came. Axel could only hear two things; his own, shallow breathing, and the low, strange whine of a creature. It was like the sound of a dying siren as it ran out of juice, no longer screeching, but instead sounding restrained.

As he opened his eyes, he lifted his head to meet the strangest thing he had ever seen.

The monster was low to the ground, almost as low as Axel himself, his robes splayed out across the tile floor. Clawed hands and sharp, hoof-like feet hugged the ground. Its head lifted, just as Axel's did, peering back at him with those piercing black eyes. They were truly like alien eyes— glossy, almost ,in the unwavering depths of darkness. It was like looking into an inkwell.

It seemed to grimace at him, whining lowly like a caged beast. Cautiously, Axel sat up, and watched with wide eyes as the beast did the same.

'Is it... copying me?' He wondered, heart racing.

A shiver went down his spine as the thing across from him nodded its head, as if it had heard his thoughts, and had answered.

Axel's eyes drifted open, his vision blurry as he sought out the clock across the room. It felt like time was moving at a snail's pace, making out the numbers and giving a soft groan. Mentally pleading to fall back asleep, he tossed himself into a new position, squirming onto his stomach, and flipping his pillow to the cool side. Vague thoughts ran through his tired mind, but before he knew it, his awareness was slipping out of his bedroom and back into his consciousness.

Minutes passed, staring at the thing as it stared back. Even though it had been eager to go after Winter, it seemed to cower to Axel now that they were alone. It responded, slowly, as Axel moved — mirroring his movements. Salivating, black ink dribbled down its neck, spilling out of the pit that was its mouth.

'Think.' Axel urged himself. He didn't know what was happening— but if the beast decided to suddenly stop playing games and lunge at him, he wanted to have a plan. That was when he realized where they were.

Second floor. East corridor. Right by Mr. Poe's classroom. There was a janitor's closet at the end of the hall, with a door that had a sticky lock— it locked when it shut, and could only be opened from the outside. Axel knew it wouldn't stop a monster, but it just might give him enough time to get out of the school and back to Winter.

Cautiously, Axel worked his way up to standing on his feet again. Bleary's moves were jaunty and animal-like, something primal as it shambled up to stand with him. Its height was dizzying, Axel blinking up at his not-so-mental enemy. He took a step backwards— and thankfully, so did Bleary.

It moves opposite of me, like a mirror image. *Axel thought. He was trying not to think too much about his plan, but it seemed to know anyway, screeching at him as he took another step back.*

Still, it seemed powerless to stop him, as Axel strategically edged the monster towards the closet. Through the open doorway it went. Axel reached out a hand, concentrating hard— and got Bleary to wrap a clawed hand around the wooden door. With one yanking motion, the door swung shut, Winter's surprised cry of "Axel!" Coming from the great imitator.

As soon as he heard the lock click, Axel bolted down the hall—
ignoring screeching rage and banging wood as the monster burst
free again. It gave him just enough time to get out of the school, and
that was all that mattered.

HAZILY, AXEL'S EYES OPENED AGAIN, LIFTING A HAND TO RUB
at his nose as his bedroom materialized into his reality once
more. This time, as he tried to get back to sleep, it wouldn't
come. His thoughts of Bleary were too solid, dreams refusing
to surface.

Wide awake, he laid there a few more moments before
glancing at the clock again. It was late afternoon, melting
into evening— he must have gotten at least a little bit of
sleep, even though it didn't feel like it. *I might as well go see*
Winter. She'll probably call me soon anyway...

Throwing himself out of bed, Axel pulled on some clothes
and fixed his hair in the mirror of the hallway bathroom
before heading downstairs. His mother was in the kitchen,
frying something up on the stove, but she ignored him
entirely as he slipped out of the house.

Winter was sitting on the bench in front of her house,
sketchbook balanced on one knee— hard at work drawing
something. It wasn't until Axel cleared his throat and sat
beside her that she even noticed he'd been walking towards
her, startling as she lifted her head.

"Oh! Axe, hey. I was just about to come over to show you.
Check this out." Winter beamed at him as she lifted her
sketchbook— etched on the pages were intricate, beautiful

black wings. Axel could see the detail on every feather, care-fully drawn.

"Sick~" He mumbled, taking the book from her for a better look. "Are these for me?"

"For the fallen angel costume, yeah. I'll whip them up once it gets a bit darker out." Winter told him. She made things with her gift often in front of him now, but always in closed rooms or by the cover of darkness. Axel could tell that keeping her gift a secret was a big deal— though he loved watching things pop into existence.

"Sure thing." Axel mumbled, leaning back as he handed her sketchbook back to her.

There were different types of silences. If ever a person knew someone who didn't talk a lot, they came to know those silences. Winter was just that person. Often, she was a chatterbox, filling the comfortable or uncomfortable silences with her thoughts and feelings, talking about everything under the sun. It was a sign of her anxiety. But as Axel fell into a tired silence, it was like a radar went up in Winter's mind, turning to stare at him suddenly.

Tucking a lock of hair behind her ear, she closed her notebook and shifted on the bench to face Axel, giving him her full attention.

"You okay? You look exhausted, Axe."

The question wasn't a total surprise, but he frowned regardless. It took him a minute to answer.

"Just a lot on my mind, is all."

"You want to talk about it?"

She had a way of pressing without pressuring, and Axel let out a sigh.

Looking up at the sky, another moment of silence passed between them. He could feel Winter's eyes on him, waiting for his answer. As he thought it over, a bitter laugh left him.

"Bleary is my beast. You think if I die, it'll die with me?"

Almost immediately, Winter grabbed his hand, like a reflex to make sure he wasn't going to disappear spontaneously.

"Don't say that! You have no clue if that's the case. For all we know, if you died, Bleary would still be there, and would be harder to get rid of. Or maybe even impossible to get rid of— we don't know a thing about it." She sounded panicked, and as Axel's gaze turned to her, the look on her face spoke volumes. Winter really was an open book. It was easier to speak to her over the phone. Sometimes, Axel thought, she saw right through him when they were in person like this. But more so... it was easier to ignore her desire for him to live, when she wasn't right in front of him.

Suicide was a tough subject, for anyone. But for Axel, the idea of someone thinking they could "help" or "save him" was infuriating. To him, it was like prolonging the suffering of a person who didn't want to be alive any longer. Winter, with her naive, big heart, viewed it entirely differently. She had never said so, but he could see it all over her face in the way she looked at him. He knew, if he was attempting right in front of her, Winter would be reduced to tears and begging, in hysterics over him. She was the type of girl who would bend backwards to save anyone.

Even someone who didn't feel like they deserved saving.

"Yeah, I know. Still... if it was that easy, and we knew for a fact that it would work, I'd do it." Axel mumbled, looking towards the ground so he didn't have to see the look on her face any longer, as Winter squeezed his hand.

"Only as a last resort. I don't want you thinking that's the solution. I need your help to beat it, Axel. We just... need more information." She told him.

Would be my first resort if it could be. Axel thought. Still... He wouldn't leave Winter to fight it alone. She was right. They had to find out more.

"After Halloween... We go monster hunting." Axel finally said.

"Sounds like a plan to me." He could hear the relief in Winter's voice as she agreed.

As Kaya pushed pins into her hair, Winter winced and squirmed in her seat. "Careful!" She complained, not used to the beauty treatment. She had never been a girly-girl, avoiding makeup and beauty products as if they were the plague. She liked simple clothes and running a comb through her hair. Maybe the occasional braid, but not at all the intricate updo that Kaya had put her hair in now. Her fashion-obsessed best friend had really outdone herself now, taking full advantage of Winter wanting to dress up for once.

Looking in the mirror, Winter barely recognized herself. Her long, thick hair was wrapped up on her head in intricate twists and braids, held into place with strategically placed black pins. Only her bangs were loose, falling forward over her forehead, with a small black headband parting them from the rest of her hair, two red devil horns poking upwards from it.

Her skin had been painstakingly fixed with foundation, concealer, and careful contour to pronounce her cheekbones. Her eyes were done up in deep red eyeshadow that flared outwards dramatically, black eyeliner to make them pop. Moreso, she was wearing contacts for the first time in her life— she had nearly punched Kaya when those had to be put in, but now that they were, they were gorgeous, making her eyes turn a deep black. Her lips, to match, had been painted a bright red.

It was her dress that was the showstopper, however.

While most girls at Clamare High would be dressing in skimpy, neon, teeny-bopper dresses that were flashy and colorful, Winter was dressed like a mature, devilish mistress. She had on a long red gown that clung to her every curve, stopping at her ankles in flowing waves of fabric and going down her arms in sleeves so long that they fell over her hands. There was a slightly low neckline on the dress, not helped by the pushup bra that Kaya had insisted she wear, giving her a fair amount of cleavage, something Winter wasn't entirely comfortable with. But it was Halloween, and for once, she was determined to make the most out of her devil costume. She even had a pair of black pumps to wear, and a black staff with three red devil prongs to carry as a prop. Jewelry wise, she had on a gold necklace with a ruby pendant, and two gold teardrop earrings. Even her nails were done in a sleek black with little red gems in the corners.

"Oh, stop squirming, I barely touched you!" Kaya chided, stepping back with a soft sigh. "God, Winter, you're gorgeous. You're going to turn heads at the dance. Why on earth didn't you let me dress you up last year? You went as a freaking ghost— that baggy old sheet did nothing for your figure, not like this does."

Kaya herself was dressed as a zombie, with her normally straight hair all teased and puffed up, and her face powdered with pale gray and white makeup, giving her a corpse-like appearance. Her dress was black and short, and ripped in every possible spot, as if she had gone at it with a pair of scissors. She looked sexy in an entirely different way. Normally, Winter might have tried to wave away the compliment Kaya gave her, but she had to admit... looking at herself, she had to agree. For once, she felt like she was really something spectacular to look at, and all because of Kaya's expertise on bringing the devil to life.

"My heart wasn't in it last year. It's not like I was going to dance with anyone." Winter responded, giving a shrug of her shoulders.

"And this year is that different? I thought Axel was tagging along as a friend." Kaya commented, reaching for the can of hairspray.

"He is." Winter immediately answered, coughing as her hair was sprayed, a hand waving the noxious gas away from her face.

"I don't know how you've gotten so... buddy-buddy with him. Seems like you two are inseparable these days. I didn't think Axel knew how to speak at the start of this year. I don't know what you two even have in common, he's such a loner." Kaya wasn't trying to be down on Axel, Winter knew, but she couldn't stop herself from frowning at her friend.

"He's..." Winter spoke up, about to deny that Axel was a loner— but that would have been a lie. Instead, she hesitated before explaining, "There's a lot to him you just don't see. Axel is clever, and he's got this outlook on things that just... fits. He likes cars, and music, and when he talks— which isn't often, but when he does— he has some really great things to say. He's funny, too, really funny, which I don't think he realizes. And I... I just think if you knew him, you'd like him too. He doesn't make it easy to know him, but when you do, he's really great, Kaya."

Kaya raised an eyebrow at her in the mirror, "You sure you two are going to the dance as just friends?"

"Yes!" Winter exclaimed, rolling her eyes as she stood up. "It's not like that. We're just good friends."

"Yeah, yeah. Sorry, Win, I just don't know how it happened. Are you sure he's not just messing with you? Is there going to be a Carrie-level surprise at the dance tonight? Axel seems okay and all, but the dark, mysterious guys can be such jerks sometimes, you know?"

Winter gave a sigh at her friend's words.

Could Axel be messing with me? She briefly pondered it, as she crossed the room to grab the small clutch purse sitting on her bed, which was gold to match her jewelry.

"He's not messing with me, Kaya. I know he isn't, he's not like that." Winter was certain of it. "He's kind, and really sweet when he wants to be. He says things and it's like... He doesn't say it just to say it. What he says, he means— which is more than I can say for most people."

I've never met someone with a smile as bright as yours, Win.

His words echoed in her head, Winter smiling as she looked back at her friend. "Trust me. Axel isn't what he seems, I promise. Now come on, we're going to be late. He's picking us up in the Camaro any minute now." Winter said, glancing at the clock.

Sure enough, by the time they got outside, after a debate with her grandfather about the dress she was wearing and the promise to be home by ten, the Camaro was parked at the curb and Axel stood beside it. With his hands stuffed in his pockets, he looked like he usually did, dressed in black from head to toe. Except, instead of a hoodie, he wore a black leather jacket and a pair of sleek black skinny jeans, with steel-toed boots. His hair was slicked back with gel, accompanied by a silver halo resting on the top of his head and kept out of his face— which was bare except for deep black eyeliner and his signature lip piercing. The only costume part of his outfit were the wings Winter had crafted for him — strapped to his back and sticking out, covered in sleek black feathers. She was sure he couldn't drive with those on, having only put them on to show them off to the two girls—

and it worked, because Winter's face lit up the second she saw them.

"You went with the black angel costume after all!" She exclaimed as she carefully made her way down the steps.

His eyes followed her, "Course I did. Can't let the wings go to waste, can I?" He mumbled, looking grim. She knew parties weren't his favorite thing, and that made it mean all the more that he had agreed to come along.

"I know you're not big on school events but we're going to have fun, Axel, right?" Winter said, trying to sound encouraging as she offered him a smile.

"Yeah." Axel replied shortly, but they both knew he had other things to worry about than the dance. Winter could only hope that with all the activity swarming around the school, their bleary enemy wouldn't make an appearance.

"Aww, aren't you two just the cutest?" Kaya's voice interrupted. When Winter turned her head, she was frozen by the flash of Kaya's camera, her friend mischievously grinning at her from behind it. Kaya lowered the polaroid as she jumped down the steps, smiling at Axel, who looked less than pleased. But that smile vanished when she laid eyes on the car. "I thought you said he had a Camaro."

"It is a Camaro." Axel answered her, sounding bored already as he eyed Kaya with his usual blank expression.

"Yeah, from twenty years ago. It's a piece of junk. Does it even run?" Kaya shot back, eyeing the car with disdain.

"Kaya!" Winter hissed her friend's name. Her anxiety skyrocketed, stunned at the rudeness her friend was displaying. Though, she knew, Kaya probably wouldn't see it as rude, but more like being brutally honest.

"What?! I don't know if I want to risk my life in that piece-of-crap tin box." Kaya remarked, shrugging her shoulders.

Behind her, Winter could see that Axel couldn't care less

what Kaya was saying. He just shrugged his shoulders, his voice coming out with only a tenth of his usual sarcasm, "You're welcome to walk."

Even though he didn't seem too mad, Winter's heart was suddenly racing, swallowing as she said to Axel, "Don't mind her, Axe. Kaya can be a diva without a filter."

"Hey!" Kaya protested, until Winter whipped her head around and gave her a knowing look. They both knew it to be true— as fun and sassy as Kaya was, she was also incredibly difficult sometimes, particularly when it came to the finer things in life, like fancy cars. If Ian wasn't such a prick, Winter was sure Kaya would have dated him just to drive shotgun in the Supra.

Axel exhaled a sigh, eyeing Winter as if wondering how he got roped into this, before he replied nonchalantly with, "Just get in already."

It took a bit of pushing, but Winter got Kaya to slide into the back seat of the Camaro, hugging Axel's wings to her lap so he could drive. The drive to campus was short, Kaya and Axel's banter filling the car the whole drive there.

13

UNSTEADY FEET

P arking in a full parking lot, the school campus loomed in front of them, each building strewn with twinkling orange and purple lights. Every bush leading up to the high school was surrounded in fake spider webs, Halloween signs with ominous warnings shoved into the ground alongside fake tombstones. There even looked to be some fake blood on the sidewalk, causing Winter to grip Axel's arm a little tighter as they walked by.

Machine generated fog was billowing out of the large double doors of Clamare's main building, students in various costumes streaming in and out of the school. Axel had never attended one of these parties, but it did seem everyone had gone all out. Most of the costumes were elaborate, shown off by the multi-colored lights set up everywhere. During the walk to the gymnasium, he could spot multiple familiar faces. They even stopped a few times for Winter and Kaya to say hi to passing students, often being complimented on their costumes.

Finally making it into the gym, Axel stifled a groan when he saw he was right; it was *stifling* in here. Packed to the brim with students and teachers, there was a full dancefloor area and several round tables near the entrance; for girls to rest their feet after being on their heels too long, and guys to avoid having to dance. Which is exactly why Axel started towards a table, intent on sitting this party out.

Winter's hand snagged his sleeve.

"Hey, wait! Where are you going?"

"To wait until we leave."

His blunt answer brought a pout to her face. It didn't suit her, a pouting devil, staring at him with a pleading expression. The fact that her eyes were pitch black instead of hazel-green unnerved him slightly.

"Oh, come on. One dance, please?" She asked him, moving to stand in front of him as she released his sleeve.

"I don't dance, Win." Axel responded. His shoulders rolled back, stretching in a way that made his black feathered wings flutter.

"Not even one? You don't even slightly want to?" Beside them, Kaya had already dashed off towards a group of her friends on the dance floor, leaving Winter with Axel.

"No, I really don't." Axel nodded his head towards Winter's group of friends, "Why don't you go dance with them?"

He watched her head turn, and when she looked back at him, he could read the disappointment all over her face. After a pause, Winter offered up a small smile, resigning herself to leaving him, "...Alright. Well, I'll uh... bring you some punch or something, when I come back. If you change your mind, come find me. I'll save you a dance."

The smiling devil headed to dance, red dress swaying— and the angel sank into a seat, propping his chin in his hand as he leaned forward on the table. It was hard to relax when all he could think about was a monster prowling the halls.

Were they all in danger? Should he be screaming at everyone to get out of the school?

So far, Bleary has only attacked us when we've been alone. It leaves groups alone. Maybe I'm worrying for nothing, maybe it's not around tonight... Axel thought. Still, it didn't stop his eyes from constantly scanning the room, keeping a close watch on his friend in red.

"Man, Winter! You're smoking. You should wear stuff like that more often!" Matthew's boisterous voice hollered over the music.

Winter had found herself standing in a circle near the dance floor with Kaya, Matthew Thorne, and his sister Knieka. Their father was the mayor of Caligo— so Matt and Knieka were pretty popular at school, but in all the time Winter had known them, they were pretty down to earth. Matthew was on the football team; tall, broad and dark skinned with a shaved head. His sister Knieka was two years younger, a cheerleader, with the biggest head of curls Winter had ever seen, and a buoyant personality— Knieka was known for her infectious laughter and mouth full of big, white teeth.

Kaya had gushed to Winter for years about how dreamy Matthew was, and though he wasn't Winter's type at all, she could see why her friend was enamored with him. He was dressed as a helmetless stormtrooper, with big chunky white plastic panels stuck to his body, and a prop lightsaber in his hand. Knieka had decided to match him, wearing a pristine white dress and thigh high boots, accented with her hair in two puff balls on either side of her head, and a silver, circular belt around her waist.

"Me? No! You guys are stunning!" Winter retorted with a laugh, beaming at Matthew.

"Hey, aren't you forgetting someone?" Kaya asked Matthew, pointedly waving her hand to point out her own, scandalous zombie outfit.

"Well, you're so hot I didn't think it needed to be said." Matthew gave a shameless flirt back, winking at Kaya.

Kaya's giggling was interrupted by a vampire— quite literally, as a boy stepped up behind her and buried his face in her neck. Her giggles turned into a shrill shriek of surprise, leaping forward and whirling around to look at the bashfully grinning Quinn Jones. The shorter boy— dwarfed beside 6'0" Matthew— was dressed in all black with a cape, and had two pointed fangs sticking out of his mouth, with fake blood dribbled down his chin.

Before she saw who it was, Kaya's hand went flying and SMACK!

"OW!" Quinn cried out, grabbing a now red cheek.

"Quinn! You freaking bit me!" Kaya cried out, sounding indignant as she held her neck. When she pulled away her hand, Winter saw the barest red mark, like a hickey forming.

"Ah, ah, ah~ It is not Quinn. Tonight, I am Count Dracula!" He remarked, giving her a toothy grin. But he did look rather embarrassed that Kaya had hit him, "Sorry, Kaya, didn't mean to spook you."

"Bit of warning next time, would you?" Kaya grumbled, rubbing at her neck.

As his head bobbed in affirmation, Quinn asked, "Are you planning on dancing tonight?"

"Oh, fo' sure. If a certain someone asks me to dance." Kaya smirked, and Winter saw her gaze drift to Matthew.

"Well, I—" Quinn started, only to be interrupted.

"Stormtrooper TK-1912 requesting Zombie Girl's presence on the dance floor, ASAP." Matthew was grinning from ear to ear, holding out a gloved hand to Kaya.

"Zombie Girl accepts!" Kaya declared, giggling as she let Matthew pull her away. Quinn seemed to deflate, until Knieka gave a rather loud cough, making him glance her way.

"Well?" She gave him a pointed look.

"...Well, what?" Quinn asked, clueless.

"Ask Princess Leia to dance, Dracula." Winter urged him, nudging the fanged boy with her elbow.

Going wide-eyed, Quinn adjusted his glasses as he caught on, "O-Oh, right, of course. Uh... Milady, may I have this dance?" He asked, giving a gallant— if not a little dorky— bow as he offered his hand. Rolling her eyes, Knieka dragged him off, leaving Winter alone.

Looks like everyone is having a great time. She thought, with an idle smile, her eyes trailing the room. Despite the costumes, she could still recognize a lot of people. She spotted Pierre's tell-tale blonde hair as he sat beside Jae-Hwa Chi, both of them dressed in white lab coats. *Doctors, or scientists?* She wondered idly. Tae-Won was usually not far from his twin, and it took a second for Winter to spot him. He was dressed in some sort of army soldier getup, dancing beside a queen of hearts that looked like it might have been Lupita Alvarez, the principal's daughter.

Winter's gaze soon returned to where Axel was sitting— and found that he was staring at her. Giving him a smile, she lifted her hand in a wave. Her focus, however, was broken as someone grabbed her shoulder.

Gasping, Winter was startled as she turned her head— only to find familiar brown eyes, freckles, and a warm smile.

"Oliver! You scared the daylights out of me." Winter exclaimed, turning towards her childhood friend.

He was dressed in overalls and a straw hat— a farmer, no

doubt. With his tan skin and filled-to-the-brim enthusiasm for nature, Winter had to admit the costume could have fit him as an actual reality.

"Isn't that the point? Scary times, Winter. Maybe I'm a monster and you can sketch me in your red book."

"Not funny!" Winter remarked, giving an awkward laugh. *If only you knew the truth of how not funny that is...*

"Hey, humor doesn't hit all the time. Now, what's a pretty devil like you doing just standing here? Looks like you need a square dancin' partner." He put on a silly southern accent, winking at her.

"Looks like that's the case."

As he pulled her to the dance floor, Winter giggled. A slow dance came on, letting her sway to the music with Oliver— who cheesily sang the lyrics to the song, which happened to be 'Fly Me to the Moon'.

Several faster songs flew by after that, and by the time Winter pulled herself away, her cheeks were flushed and her heart was racing.

She made a beeline for the refreshment table, eyeing the spread of Halloween inspired spooky treats as she filled two red cups with smoking tropical punch. Tossing in some eyeball ice cubes, Winter took them in the direction of Axel's table, eager to get off her feet for a break.

He might have been alone when she left him, but he certainly wasn't now.

"Okay but, think about it. Everyone's here, and no one is guarding—" Jovanni's voice broke off as soon as he saw Winter approaching. Dressed as a skeleton, the gothic kid leaned back and gave her a nod. His dark hair, which Winter swore was prettier than hers, swayed with the movement. "'Sup, Winter."

"Nothing much. But I see you're plotting something, Jovi." Winter answered, setting Axel's drink in front of him.

"Thanks." He mumbled, grabbing it as Jovi answered,

"Not just me. My partner in crime, here."

"Already told you, not interested."

"Missing out, Dunn. Fine, then. I'm off to get the test sheets for history." Jovanni stood, clapping a hand on the table as he slipped away from them.

"...He's stealing test answers from your mom?" Winter asked, watching his retreating figure go out the gym doors.

"Exactly why I wasn't about to join him. Pretty sure Mom keeps them at home, though. He's not going to have much luck in her office." Axel sighed, taking another sip of his drink. He eyed Winter for a second, "You look like you're having fun."

"I'd be having more fun if you joined me." Winter said, holding her cup with both hands and gazing down at it, watching the ice cube bob up and down in the red liquid. "Sure I can't convince you to dance with me?"

Axel gave a deep sigh. Winter knew she was pushing a little hard— but honestly, why did he agree to come, just to sit and watch? She knew why, of course. Bleary was out there. He came to keep an eye out. But… Would one dance really hurt?

Peeking up at him through her lashes, their eyes met, Axel's expression stubbornly blank. A moment of silence passed between them before Winter moved to stand, grabbing her small clutch purse from the table.

"I'm going to the restroom, I'll be back."

Axel didn't say a word as she walked away.

Winter expected the bathrooms to be stuffed full, but to her surprise, they were largely empty. All except for one stall, from which she could hear the familiar sounds of crying.

"Hello?" Winter called, approaching the closed stall and giving a light tap on the door. "You okay in there?"

"Y-Yeah! I'm fine!"

I recognize that voice. A pang of sadness hit Winter.

She entered the stall beside her, doing her business— and heard when the girl left. *Maybe I can get some information.* She thought idly, finishing up and joining her at the sink with an awkward smile, moving to wash her hands alongside the other girl.

Ruby Stout was a gorgeous girl, even when tearful. She was short and petite, with a bob of honey-blonde hair and big brown eyes. True to her name, she always wore a pendant shaped like an R, accented with little rubies. Winter thought that she had a wholesome, innocently naive look to her, which was fitting since she'd moved to California from Texas and had that southern charm to her. Even the costume she now wore— she was what looked to be the good witch from the Wizard of Oz, wearing a puffy pink dress with lots of tulle, and holding onto a little, sparkly scepter.

Bryce and her were such a picturesque couple... Winter hadn't necessarily been close to either of them, but she knew of them. Ruby had moved to Caligo in middle school, and Bryce and her had been dating practically ever since. Just as Bryce got onto the football team, Ruby had gotten into the cheer-leading squad. Winter couldn't think of two people whose lives seemed more perfect.

"Hey, Ruby…" Winter greeted her quietly, unsure what to say. Reaching into her clutch, she produced some tissues, offering her one.

Ruby's lower lip quivered as she took it, giving a small, humorless laugh.

"Thanks." She murmured, dabbing at her eyes and giving

a soft groan, "I was supposed to be having fun tonight. But everything here reminds me of Bryce. I never realized how pathetically tied together we were. Now that he's gone, it's like I've forgotten how to be my own person."

"No, don't talk like that. It's understandable— that's what happens." Winter had never been in love, but she knew that loving someone meant melding together, in a sense. She could only imagine the pain of stitching yourself to another person, and then being torn apart in an irreparable sort of way. "It was unexpected, to lose Bryce like that."

Ruby gave a half laugh, half sniffle.

"You don't know the half of it. I never saw it coming. I mean..." She leaned against the sink counter, fixing Winter with her big, watery eyes as she started talking, "Bryce had a full scholarship. We talked about going to college together nearly every day. And... and he hadn't told his parents yet, but he proposed to me, end of the summer. He was saving up for a ring. S-Said he wanted to make it a ruby, and those are expensive, so I had to wait on it, but he couldn't wait to ask me. Got my daddy's permission and all."

This was news to Winter, and all she could do was watch as Ruby's body crumpled, breaking down into sobs once more.

"I-I w-w-was go-gonna b-be hi-his w-wi-wife!!" She cried out, as Winter wrapped her arms around her in a hug.

It took several minutes to calm her down again, and she found herself rubbing Ruby's back as the grieving girl scrubbed at her eyes.

"Oh God, look at me. I'm such a mess. It's just... I don't understand it, Winter. We were so happy— *he* was so happy."

Hesitantly, Winter asked,

"He didn't give any signs of depression at all?"

"No. I mean... Bryce could get real stressed, you know. His family relied on him a lot, like all ours do— that's normal, ain't it? He had a lot going on. Poor thing would come to me and just be so exhausted. But he was hopeful. He was looking forward to the future, he'd get excited about it and tell me all the work would be worth it. If anything, I was the one struggling. Bryce was the strong one."

Frowning, Winter murmured her apologies for Ruby's loss again, but her mind was far away, wondering what brought Bryce to his final moments.

"You found him, didn't you?"

"What?" Ruby's voice had snapped Winter out of her thoughts, blinking at her.

"You found my Bryce."

"Oh, uh... No. Actually, A-Axel found him. Axel Dunn. I was the second person there."

The explanation made Ruby take a shaky breath, reaching to take Winter's hand and give it a squeeze.

"Thank you. Both of you— thank Axel for me, too. I... I was on the way to meet Bryce that day. I was running late, and if I had been there... if I had found him like that, it would have done me in. I'm glad you both were there."

A pang went through Winter, studying Ruby's face as she whispered back, in what she felt was a lame response, "Y-You're welcome."

It took her quite a while to part ways with Ruby. She couldn't just leave her in such a state alone, after all— so Winter stayed with her until Delilah, her fellow cheerleader, made an appearance and took over the comforting. It had to have been at least a good twenty minutes by the time Winter slipped back into the gymnasium— and if she was honest, she was no longer in the mood for dancing.

Gotta find Axel and Kaya and get out of here. Winter thought warily, pushing her way through the crowd.

That was when a hand clapped over her shoulder,

yanking her to a stop. She turned, meeting icy blue eyes and an up-to-no-good smirk.

"Well, well. Piggy sure is pretty tonight, isn't she?"

Sitting back, Axel drained the cup of punch Winter had gotten him, sighing as he watched their classmates dance.

Maybe I just should get it over with and dance with her. He thought glumly, trying to picture himself in the sweaty crowd. *She was so disappointed... Wouldn't be the first time I've disappointed someone, but...*

The thoughts plagued him, nagging at the back of his mind.

Screw it. When she gets back, I'm gonna dance with her. He made up his mind, crumpling the now empty red cup in his hand.

Minutes passed, and Axel tugged his phone out of his pocket to check the time.

She's been gone awhile now... What the hell is with the long bathroom break?

Maybe she's not coming back. Maybe she got fed up with your bullshit and decided to walk home.

No, Winter's not that way... But everyone has their limits. When will she reach hers?

Sighing, a string of curse words ran through Axel's mind, smoothing a hand over his gelled hair.

"Hey, Axel! Are you waiting on your date?" Axel's eyes lifted as a joyful voice spoke to him. He was met with the face of Jezebel McLain. Charlie's little sister hung around the record store all the time, and she had always been kind to Axel, though, in his opinion, her music taste sucked. She liked bizarre female indie artists, whose voices sounded more like garbled talking than singing.

Jezebel's long ginger hair matched the little ginger cat ears on top of her head. She had whiskers painted over her freckled cheeks and wore a leotard-like getup that was tiger striped, along with a little black tutu.

"Nope." He answered her, giving a shrug of his shoulders.

"Oh? I thought you were here with Winter— I saw you enter together."

"Not as dates, just as friends. I drove her and Kaya here."

"Oh, that's a shame. Angel and devil make a great couple costume." She sounded truly disappointed, but soon brightened up, "Well then, can I tempt you with a dance? The DJ— Mr. Poe— let it slip that Achy Breaky Heart is playing next."

Axel had to resist cringing at the mention of the popular country song. It wasn't a bad song, but way overplayed at Clamare High. Besides, country wasn't his thing.

"You're not the first to ask, but I'm gonna have to sit that one out."

"Aww… Okay. Well—"

Jezebel began to tatter on about something, but Axel tuned her out— because his eyes had caught on two people over her shoulder. Winter was standing on the dance floor, and seemed to be in the grip of Ian-freaking-Bryars. Neither one of them looked very happy.

Shit.

"Uh— Jezebel, can you hold that thought? I um… I gotta go deal with something."

Jezebel blinked, confused, but nodded as Axel stood and slipped past her.

"Y-Yeah, no problem."

Axel barely registered her words. He walked towards Ian and Winter, trying to hear their conversation.

"Nice to see you're all dressed up for once. Being a prude doesn't suit you, Winter."

"Uh… Thank you? I guess. Listen, Ian, I have to go, I—"

"What, you got someone waiting for you? That dipshit Dunn?"

"Don't—" Winter's tone had changed from cautious to annoyed, but before she could snap at Ian, Axel decided to speak up. He stepped into the space behind Winter, glaring over her shoulder at Ian— who was dressed in a royal garb with a crown on his head. *Figures he'd think he's part of some kind of monarchy, with that inflated ego of his.*

"Yeah, as a matter of fact, she does. I owe her a dance."

Ian's face twisted from a loopy smile to pure annoyance as soon as he laid eyes on Axel, scoffing. He took a step, and stumbled, unsteady on his feet. Axel eyed him with suspicion. Something was off.

"What the hell is this, a bad love triangle? Choosing between two men, huh, Winter? You always were a greedy piggy." He gave a snort at the end of his words— but it sounded more like a hiccup.

"I don't think it's much of a choice." Axel remarked, crossing his arms. "You don't seem fond of giving girls choices."

"That's not true!" Ian snapped at Axel, "Don't make me out to be like that, man." His voice seemed full and wobbly, and that's when it struck Axel.

"Make you out to be like what? A drunken idiot? Pretty sure that's what I'm seeing." Axel wasn't much of a drinker himself, besides the occasional beer sneaked out of his dad's office, but he suspected Ian had been indulging a lot more than a single beer.

"S'not my fault if the punch is better with a kick." Ian answered. His clouded eyes settled on Winter again, still holding her by the wrist. "Well, come on then. Make your choice, pretty piggy. Me or the small fry over there."

Looking up at him, Winter frowned. "I-Ian, I um… I don't think you're f-feeling well. Maybe you should sit d-do—" She was stuttering. Though she didn't look scared, Axel suspected she was as worried as he was that this would end up like it had on Timor St. Only, she couldn't use her powers here, in this crowd full of people. Axel's eyes scanned the crowd for a teacher, but there was none to be seen.

Why are they never around to see this shit when it's happening? He thought, irritated.

"Do, do, do— Jesus Christ, get it out! What are you, f-f-four?" Ian sneered at her, releasing her wrist at long last, "Need to go to s-s-speech the-therapy, huh?"

Axel's eyes narrowed at the jock. Stepping forward, he wedged himself between Winter and Ian. He might have been shorter, but in his mind, that only meant he could kick Ian where it hurt easier. He wasn't scared, glaring up at the freakishly tall footballer.

"Really starting to get on my nerves, Bryars. Are you trying to end up on a watch-list someday?" Axel remarked.

"Watch that smart mouth of yours, Dunn, or I'll have to rearrange your face again."

"My face? At least I'm not the one shit =-faced right now."

Ian was really starting to look angry, and part of Axel was looking forward to another round— at least this time, there'd be witnesses to get Ian in trouble. But Winter's voice pleaded with him,

"Axe, come on, he's not worth it. Let's just go."

"Yeah, Axe, why don't you just go? Save your face some pain." Ian mocked her, giving that stupid grin again as Axel clenched his hands into a fist.

No way am I running from Ian-freaking-Bryars. He's nothing but a piece of—

"CLA-MA-RE HIGHHHHH~!" A loud, booming voice interrupted their spat. All three of them turned to see a grinning Mr. Poe standing on the gym stage with a microphone, "It's time for the best part of the night! Our annual *Spppoooookkkkyyyyyy* costume contest!!"

That seemed to interrupt things just enough. Ian pulled a flash from his pocket and took a swig from it. He didn't say a word, stumbling off towards the stage, along with a whole crowd of students interested in going to see the contest winners.

"Axe. Hey, Axel." Winter's voice cut through the volume of the gym, her hand grabbing his. Axel tore his gaze away from Ian's retreating, unsteady figure, to peer into her pitch black contacts.

"It's stupid to fight a drunk person. Besides, he's so far gone, a teacher will catch on soon enough and bust him."

Axel sighed, but didn't argue with her. She was right. Nodding, he spoke,

"Yeah. Can we get out of here now?"

"Definitely. Let's go find Kaya."

Following her through the crowd, it wasn't hard to find Kaya— she was slow dancing with Matthew Thorne, clinging to him like a vine and giving him goo-goo eyes.

Surprised the teachers haven't pulled them apart for an inappropriate lack of distance. Axel thought, giving a soft snort as Winter jogged over, tapping Kaya on the shoulder. He watched as Kaya, with a dreamy look on her face, said something to Winter and shook her head.

When Winter walked back, she was frowning.

"She's staying. Matt agreed to drive her home. I don't think I could separate them if I tried... Even if I had a crowbar." Winter told him, as they began to walk out of the gym together Knieka Thorne and Hayden Grant— dressed as

Princess Leia and a pharaoh, respectively— were announced the winners of the costume contest.

The ride home was much quieter than when they had left. Winter, gazing out the window, clearly had something on her mind. About what, Axel wasn't going to ask. It had been a long night, and he chose to look ahead in silence.

Pulling up to their houses, he knew he would still have to drive the Camaro back to the yard and walk home. His mom wasn't a fan of his "junker" and wouldn't let him park it in their driveway beside her Miata.

Gazing up at his porch, where Winter's flaming goblin head pumpkin was lit with a candle, Axel waited for her to get out. Instead, she spoke softly,

"Axel?"

"Hm?"

"Do you care? If... If you leave people behind when you... go?"

The question made him sigh, looking over at her. She was still looking out the window, her expression troubled, eyebrows drawn together like she was thinking too hard on something important. *Suicide isn't where your mind should be, Win.* He wanted to tell her, wondering what had brought the thought on.

"I don't think anyone would miss me if I was gone." He answered her bluntly.

Finally, she looked at him, her expression dead serious and eyes filled with concern.

"That's not true." Was all she said, before opening her door. As she closed it behind her, she leaned down to peer in through the open window. Her mouth parted, ready to say something, but Winter hesitated and Axel knew that what she said next was not what she had wanted to say.

"Happy Halloween, Axel."

Giving him a two finger salute, she turned and headed across the street to her house.

"...Yeah. Happy Halloween." He sighed, long after she was gone, kicking the camaro back into action to get it back to the junkyard.

That's not true, she says...

Isn't it, though?

14

UNCONSCIOUS WARNING

"Kaya!" Her friend's name was the first thing to leave her mouth when Winter woke up, eyes flashing open. Her heart was racing— but surely, that was just a nightmare? She had envisioned Kaya running down the halls of Clamare High, screaming with that horrifying monster at her heels. Winter and Axel had been dealing with Bleary for weeks now, it consumed almost every waking worry. Worries brought on nightmares… right?

Winter closed her eyes, wishing she could go back to sleep and dream of better things, her hand draping over her face to block the morning sunlight. She had only laid like that a few seconds when she heard the familiar buzz of her phone.

Groaning, Winter reached for her phone, blinking her eyes open once more.

Her heart sank.

Twelve missed messages from Axel… one voicemail from Kaya.

Swallowing, Winter sat up, quickly playing the voicemail.

The longer it played, the more her hands shook. On the other line was a panting, painfully familiar voice.

"Win! I-I think I'm seeing things. That thing— the creature from your sketchbook. It's here! I don't know how, but if that's a Halloween costume from Axel or something, I'm going to freaking kill him. Whoever it is, they're chasing me. I'm trying to get the hell away from it but... Shit, I think it's found me. I have to get out of here. I'm coming straight to your house. I-I..."

There was a scrambling sound, lots of interference as a horrific shriek came over the line, before it went dead.

Filled with dread, Winter checked the messages Axel had sent her. Each and every one confirmed what she already knew, warning her not to come to school. Pushing herself up, Winter wondered if she should have felt the need to rush— but her moves were sluggish, feeling numb as she pulled on clothes.

She didn't let her grandfather drive her to school, choosing to take the long walk, dragging her feet to the scene of yet another suicide. If only the police knew that it wasn't suicide at all.

"Winter..." Axel's voice was one of warning, reaching out to push a hand against her shoulder and stop her. He had been waiting for her at the edge of the crowd outside the school, knowing exactly who Bleary's victim was.

"Let me through, Axe." Her voice should have shook, but it was solid, her throat tight. Her eyes lifted to his. For once, his own eyes weren't bright, or vibrant, they were like shards of gray stone, staring her down.

"Let go." She demanded. His fingers curled into her dress

sleeve, and for a few long seconds, they stared each other down, silent. His thoughts were plain on his face: *Don't do this to yourself.*

But finally, with numb acceptance that she had to see for herself, his hand slipped from holding her in place, and Winter pushed past him, stumbling through to the front of the gathered crowd. It was hard to ignore the background noise— the whispers, the sound of crying, the shocked exclamations that pierced the air every few seconds as someone new caught sight of the scene ahead of them. The faces of her classmates seemed as gray as Bleary, pained and grief-filled... even if they barely knew the girl they grieved for.

They were pulling her body out of the building now. The front doors of the school were propped open, cops wandering around, a perimeter laid out to keep the onlookers back. But even from the barrier they had set up, Winter knew what she was seeing. A single black bag laid out on a gurney, possessing the body of her best friend. She could see blood on the tiles of the entry hall. A dark stain against the white marble floors made her stomach churn.

Watching in silence, Winter's expression remained blank, her body numb. It didn't feel real, and for once, her mind didn't race with thoughts. In fact, she wasn't sure if she was thinking anything at all, watching her nightmare come to life.

A cop car pulled silently into the parking lot, and Winter's heart contracted painfully when she saw the door open, out stepping Mr. and Mrs. Morito. Kaya's mother was a strong, loud, vibrant woman. For someone of Japanese heritage, Winter had always thought she was unusually bold, fighting any expectations the world threw at her. Her and Axel's own mother, despite both coming from the same background, could not be compared. Where Alessandra Dunn was the stereotype, Mrs. Morito was the one that broke the mold. Tattoos on both arms, short pink hair, a face that didn't look old enough to be a mother to a high school student. Her husband was just as fierce: tall and broad, a Pacific Islander with tan skin, burning black eyes, and a head full of dark chocolate curls.

But now... they looked frail. Clinging to each other for dear life, being led over to the gurney, which had been stopped outside a black van. An officer zipped it down just enough for them to see the face of their eldest child, and Winter's eyes squeezed shut. She didn't want to see Mrs. Morito as she crumpled— but she could hear her wails, filling the air with a pain unlike anything Winter had ever heard before. Gasping, wheezing, heavy sobs.

"My baby! NOOOO~!" When Winter opened her eyes again, Mrs. Morito had sunk down to the pavement, her husband crouched behind her, steady arms holding her. Despite his strength, Winter could see his shoulders shaking too. The screams of her best friend's mother chilled Winter to the bone, her body shivered at the sound.

A warm body was standing a little too close behind her. Winter took a step, twisting around to look at Axel. She saw the look on his face, and knew what he was going to say. "Don't." She mumbled, but of course, he didn't listen.

"Winter. You don't have to see this." His voice urged her. "Let's go. I'll drive you home." Surely, they wouldn't have school after this.

"Don't have to? I *caused* this. If anyone has to, it's..." Her voice cracked, and the tears were finally starting to well up, her shoulders sinking. "She didn't know, Axel. I didn't tell her about Bleary. She didn't know the truth. If she *knew* she wouldn't have—"

"The truth wouldn't have stopped this. Listen to yourself, this is what that damn thing wants— it wants you to blame yourself. I swear, Win, you couldn't have stopped-" His words might have reached her, eventually, but Axel reached his hand out for her again. It was hard not to want to comfort her, knowing Winter well enough to know how. Blame was a heavy guilt to carry, however, and she recoiled.

"Don't *you dare* touch me, Axel Dunn!" The words fell out of her mouth before she could even think about how it sounded, for once not filtering herself as her friend froze, a hand still outstretched between them. He had never heard her speak that way to him, with so much venom and warning in what was usually an upbeat voice. At that moment, Winter knew where Axel's mind went— that she must have hated him for his depression, for his monster. She didn't have the energy to tell him otherwise, not now.

Blinking as her tears began to grow heavier, Winter turned and ran. It was the only thing she could do. She needed to get away. She didn't look back to see if Axel was following, and she didn't want to see Kaya's body loaded into that van. All she could do was count the blocks of the sidewalk, her tears streaming, trying to hold onto the last shreds of control she possessed until she was far, far away.

It took two hours for Axel to see Winter again. Not because he didn't know where she was— he did. It was his first guess, and the first place he drove to. However, he could tell when someone needed time, and he was right. Winter needed to be on her own with her thoughts, even if they were dark and painful.

Sticking his hands in his pockets, he took his time walking up the hill on the far side of Evadere Park. There she sat, under the large oak tree, on the patch of dying grass. It felt like a terribly long time since the last time they were there together, and Axel didn't breathe a word as he sank down to sit beside her, crossing his legs.

Winter had her back to the tree, knees pulled up to her chest, her chin resting on her knees. Her eyes were raw and red, her face pale as a sheet, her hair wind-blown. She had been there long enough to hyperventilate, cry it out, and be left with quiet contemplation of losing her oldest friend. She was still sniffling, quiet shaking breaths leaving her as her hazel-green eyes regarded Axel's presence.

Axel hated seeing her like this.

It was a special sort of helplessness, not knowing how to make things better, short of bringing Kaya back. All he could do was stare at Winter, taking her in, waiting in the silence.

Finally, she spoke.

"Did I do this, Axel? Did I kill her?" Her voice sounded so very small, far away from him. That was always the question someone asked, when the person they loved took their own life. It was easy to take the blame, to question what she did— or didn't— do.

This time, when Axel reached for her, Winter let him, moving to bury her face in his shoulder as he wrapped an arm around her. A soft sob left her, despite her tears having run out. Axel hesitated before he smoothed a hand over her hair, trying to think of how to word what he needed to say. Gazing out at the park, which was empty in the chilly fall weather, he sighed, resting his chin on the top of her head.

"You made the thing that did. But it was an accident, Winter. You can't take the blame for the actions of a true monster." Axel's hand rubbed up and down her shoulder, trying to comfort her as she shook in his arms. "I don't think it would have prevented it, if Kaya knew. Even you and I don't know how to fight it."

Winter sniffled and found herself pulling back just enough to look up at Axel. For a moment, she was quiet, taking in his face. The round tip of his nose, the point of his chin, the gleam of his piercings. Everything except his eyes. If she looked into his eyes, she wouldn't have been able to say what she did— words she knew weren't true. Axel knew this, he could see it all over her face. Winter always had been easy to read, even before she knew his own secrets.

"And what if I'm the true monster, Axe? The freak who can create things like Bleary."

Axel smiled— the kind of smile that was usually accompanied with a scoff or a laugh, although he didn't make a sound. Looking away from Winter, he turned his gaze to the sky. He didn't need to think about his answer, he knew it by pure instinct. There was only one way to answer such a question. With a rare honesty, that only Winter ever got.

"Winter… for as long as I have known you, you've never been a cruel person. You've never been needlessly judgmental, negative, or critical. You've never done anything to bring anyone down. The only person I've ever seen you be hard on is yourself. I've met a lot of monsters, and you could never be one of them. Everything that creates Bleary in minds like mine, is nothing that you are."

Falling silent, Winter didn't seem to know what to say, stunned by Axel's analysis of her. For a long minute, they sat there in silence, Axel opening his hand and offering it to Winter, her taking it and lacing their fingers together with a soft squeeze. She had just lost her best friend, and Axel didn't know how to make that better besides just being there.

Luckily, he didn't have to make any sort of suggestion— Winter already had one.

"I need to go to the morgue." She spoke up suddenly, breaking their silence.

Axel raised an eyebrow, his eyes finally going back to her as she stared at him with a newfound determination across r her face.

"Why on earth would you want to do that?" Axel questioned her, uneasy at the thought of seeing Kaya as a corpse up close. He had seen them before, distant relatives at funerals he couldn't care less about. It was a strange thing, often feeling unnerved and yet calm while being around an empty human-shell with skin as cold as ice. He had cut through the cemetery to the junkyard a dozen times without a second thought, but he certainly wouldn't call Bonum Vale Funeral Home his favorite place to hang around.

Winter began to tell him about the nightmares she'd started having of Kaya dying. All Axel could do was listen, rubbing at his arms through his sleeves as Winter described how Kaya met her end. Guilt pricked at his conscience, not an unfamiliar feeling but it hit differently when thinking of another person doing the same thing.

"Listen, the truth is we don't know much about Bleary. We gave it a name, and we've run into it a few times, but we have no idea what it's capable of. That thing had to have put her under the same spell it put me under… the other night, when I ran into it in the hallway. I could have ended up just like Kaya if I hadn't snapped out of it and realized it wasn't you." Winter was right, and the thought made Axel sick to his stomach. *If I had found her like that, like Kaya…* He didn't want to think about it.

"Okay, so your point is?" He asked, even though he knew exactly where Winter was going with this.

"We need to see Kaya's body. I don't want to but… maybe there's a clue. Something, anything, that will tell us more about Bleary. We've been investigating this thing without any leads, Axel. Kaya, and the other victims, those are our leads." Winter sighed, giving the smallest smile as she added, "If Kaya was here, she'd be all for it. Sneaking into a morgue would be some grand adventure to her."

Winter's smile fell away, her eyes a million miles from

where they sat. Axel, in that moment, wished he could read her mind. Instead, he exhaled through his nose and gave a small nod.

"To the morgue, then. For Kaya."

Bonum Vale Funeral Home and Morgue was a short walk away from Altum Court. It was far up on Timor street, across from the local cemetery.

That very night, Winter met up with Axel in his yard, dressed in a deep red sweater and a pair of bell bottom jeans, her hair pulled into a high ponytail, bangs falling in her eyes. It was just about nine in the evening, the earliest she could slip out of her house without her grandfather knowing. When Axel appeared, he was dressed similarly— jeans and one of his signature hoodies, the hood already pulled over his head.

In silence, the two mourning teenagers trudged to his backyard and slipped through a gate to the woods that lay between their neighborhood and Bonum Vale. Winter had chills, crossing her arms tightly over her chest. They could already see the stone walls of the funeral home after only a few minutes of walking.

Glancing at Axel, Winter hoped to see his face, to find any sort of comfort in his steadfast expressions, but all she saw was his hood covering him in shadow, his head tilted down as they walked. *Is he dreading this as much as I am?* She wondered.

Winter hesitated when they reached the sidewalk, glancing across the street at the cemetery. It had never unnerved her before now. She had gone to a funeral before, but never had she lost someone truly close to her. It didn't feel real that Kaya was dead, nor that she had been killed by a monster. Ever since Bleary had appeared, in fact, life hadn't felt quite real.

"I wish we could wake up from this." Winter sighed into the cold air, shivering anew as she shuffled her boots against the pavement. "Like a bad dream."

She didn't think about the fact that for Axel, Bleary wasn't some passing phenomenon. He lived with its presence every day. That realization came when Axel, who had stopped beside her, said in a soft, hollow tone, "Me too."

Looking up at him, Winter felt immediate regret. For once, his face wasn't blank, but contorted into an anguished expression.

"I-I'm sorry." She stammered, only for him to shake his head.

"Don't be. It's fine. Come on, before they close for the night." His voice was soft, offering her a small smile that didn't reach his eyes.

Taking a deep breath, Winter followed him the few steps down the sidewalk to Bonum Vale.

THERE WAS A LITTLE BUZZER BY THE DOOR TO BE LET IN, AND when they pressed it, a familiar face met them. Quinn Jones was the son of the undertakers who owned Bonum Vale funeral home, so Winter shouldn't have been surprised to see him there. What did surprise her, however, was that his eyes, behind his rectangular glasses, were bloodshot from crying— much like her own.

It took him a second to recognize the two of them in the porch light. "Oh… Winter, Axel…" Quinn opened the door a little wider, giving Winter a sympathetic look, "I'm so sorry about Kaya. I… I didn't know she was suffering. We've had so many lost lately, it's the biggest tragedy of Caligo. Kaya was always so happy, I guess you just don't know what people are going through."

Quinn was a poetic soul, a romantic at heart. Winter and Kaya had grown up with him— and Winter still remembered him as he had been at nine years old, a Shakespearean speaker who never missed an audition for a school play. His literature quotes and fanciful view of life always made him a fun person to be around. Easy to tease, for the bullies in their school, but Winter hoped they never got him to change. The world needed more Quinns.

"I know, it's horrible. Bad start to a bad year..." Winter responded, wishing she could tell him the truth. Glancing at Axel, he must have seen the guilt on her face, because he cleared his voice and spoke up.

"Listen, Harley." *Harley? Quinn's name isn't... Harley Quinn? Oh jeez, Axel.* Winter gave a small smile at the nickname. He must have called Quinn that before, though, because their classmate didn't look phased at all. "We need to see her. Kaya. Just for ten minutes. You know, say goodbye and all. We'll be quick. Do you mind letting us in?"

Quinn eyed the two of them, his eyebrows drawing together in uncertainty. "I don't know... We're only supposed to let family in. Mr. and Mrs. Morito just left about an hour ago. My folks will be back soon to lock everything up for the night..."

Winter wasn't a pushy person, but this called for a little pushing. Stepping closer, she moved to stand in the doorway, reaching out to grab onto Quinn's arm in a desperate little tug. Her eyes implored him, gazing at him through his glasses.

"Quinn. Kaya is my sister. You *know* how much she means to me. *Please.* I feel responsible." That wasn't a lie, her voice coming out so genuinely that it cracked. Her throat felt like it had a lump in it, eyes watering at the thought of having caused Kaya's death. "I just need a few minutes alone with her, to apologize for not being there when she needed me."

She could see the resolve melt from his face, and suddenly felt herself being pulled into a hug. Quinn was shorter than her, only about 5'5", and his face buried into her shoulder as he hugged her tightly to him.

"Oh, Winter, don't ever blame yourself for another person's suicide. Of course, I'll take you both right through. I can at least give you ten minutes to make your peace before the funeral." He said when he released her, pulling a handkerchief out of his pocket and handing it to Winter, letting her dab her eyes.

Relieved, Winter glanced back at Axel with a smile as they stepped into the funeral home. The main entrance was modest, but respectful— brown and yellow striped wallpaper and brown carpet, a little counter and reception desk with a bell. There was a hallway with a sign that said "Office", and another hallway that led to a stairwell. That was where Quinn led them down into a basement with a sign for "Morgue".

There were two double doors, and a light to signal when an autopsy or embalming was taking place, but it was off now.

Winter hesitated, walking slower as Quinn held the door open for them. She felt Axel behind her, his hand touching the small of her back, pushing her gently to keep going. This had been her idea, she couldn't back out now. So, she took a deep breath, and stepped into the room full of corpses.

15

UNCOMFORTABLE TRUTH

Winter's first thought was that the morgue was freezing cold. She shivered as she took the step forward into the bright, fluorescent lighting. It was a large room, made of sterile metal cabinets, all closed and numbered, and blinding white tile floors. The lights overhead were the only source of noise, emitting a low buzz.

Axel looked as uneasy as Winter felt. Instead of his usual blank expression, he was gritting his teeth, standing in a rigid stance behind her with his arms crossed.

Quinn sent a sympathetic look their way. "Took me a while to grow comfortable down here, too. Don't worry, the deceased don't tend to bite."

"You sure about that?" Winter heard Axel mutter under his breath in response, earning the smallest of smiles from her. Was he afraid of a few corpses? That would be ironic, if true.

It didn't seem Quinn had heard him, walking forward to a row of cabinets on the farthest wall. He seemed to grow tearful once more as he settled a hand on one of the doors.

"This is Kaya. She's been cleaned up already but an

autopsy... Well, her parents opted not to, so she just has to be prepared for the funeral. Not sure when that's being done." He told them, his voice low and mournful. Nodding his head to the two next cabinets, he added, "There's Miss Popelin, and Bryce. Miss Popelin's funeral is on Saturday. Bryce's funeral should have been done by now, but his family wants to wait for relatives from Brazil, so he's being... kept, until they arrive."

It had been over three weeks since they had found Bryce. Winter still remembered the distorted color of his face, her stomach churning just thinking about it. It wasn't until Quinn's back was turned that she dared to glance Axel's way, their eyes briefly meeting. From the way he looked back at her, it seemed Bryce crossed his mind too.

A clank of metal made Winter focus on Quinn again, as he opened the cabinet and began to pull out the long metal shelf that held the body of her best friend. She was covered by a pale blue sheet, which Quinn grabbed the top of and pulled down. He stopped at the top of her chest, tucking the sheet in place with care, so they could see her from the shoulders up.

It seemed they had removed her hair extensions. All Winter could see was black hair, without a hint of green. It was the most colorless that Winter had ever seen her friend, even with the makeup from her zombie costume having been wiped clean. Her skin was pallid, and the fact that her chest didn't move with signs of breathing made Winter ache.

Quinn must have seen the look on her face, because he moved forward for another hug, "I'll leave you with her. Again, I'm so sorry for your loss, Winter. If there is anything I can do, don't hesitate to ask."

Practiced lines. Parents taught him well. Winter thought, sighing into Quinn's shoulder. She knew he meant well, but the words felt hollow.

Releasing her, Quinn turned to Axel, and his lower lip seemed to quiver with newfound sympathy. His arms unfolded,

"Bring it in, brother." The school nerd declared, taking a step towards the gothic boy.

Axel stepped back with a glare, carefully staying out of Quinn's reach.

"Touch me and die, Harley." He remarked, his voice calmer than the look on his face.

"Not a hugger, then? Okay..." Quinn dropped his arms, giving a nervous smile as he bowed his head and slipped out of the morgue, leaving them with Kaya.

"What is it with people and hugging?" Axel glowered, stepping up to Winter's side as he crossed his arms uncomfortably.

"You hugged me."

"You're not a stranger."

"Fair point."

Looking down at Kaya, Winter frowned. *Corpses are supposed to look like they're asleep,* she thought. Yet, she had dozens of sleepovers with Kaya growing up, and she knew all too well that she wasn't going to suddenly wake up. Reaching out, her fingers brushed Kaya's cheek and Winter immediately recoiled so hard that she almost tripped, bumping into Axel's chest. His hand grabbed her shoulder to steady her and he seemed to know what had startled her,

"Careful. Corpses are cold. Touching them can be... unnerving." He murmured in her ear.

That had been exactly it. Kaya must have been, at least partially, prepared already— because her skin had been the strangest thing Winter had ever touched. She could compare it to a melting ice cube, or frozen rubber— or perhaps it didn't really compare to anything at all.

"Have you got much experience with corpses?" Winter

asked dryly, gripping the edge of Kaya's table as she gave a poor attempt at humor.

"A few of my grandparents." Axel answered shortly. He looked between Kaya and Winter before saying, "I'll check Bryce and Miss Popelin."

As he moved off to pull open more drawers with corpses, Winter turned her attention to Kaya once more. She took a few shaky breaths, working her way to investigate her friend. Remembering the nightmare she'd had the night Kaya died, Winter carefully took hold of her arm, pulling it from beneath the sheet to look at her hand. Or more importantly, her wrists.

Rigor mortis had already set in, of course. Kaya's body took effort to move, her arm dead weight as Winter turned it over. Her hand had been stretched out, but there were marks on her palm from where her nails had been dug in. Then, along her wrists, were the cuts that had caused her death.

"Axel?" Winter called, unable to look up from the deep gouges. She knew, if she probed at them and pulled the skin apart, they would be deep enough to reveal bone. Even though the blood had been wiped away, the scars were no less frightening to look at. "Have you ever cut this deeply? I mean… is it possible to survive this?"

Axel, who had just pulled Miss Popelin's drawer out, stopped and turned. Even at a distance, it wasn't hard for him to spot Kaya's wrist. If he was as affected by it as Winter was, he didn't show it, his face blank as he answered her.

"It's possible to survive. People lose arms and still live, Win. But without help, cut that low on the wrist… No. I haven't cut that deeply before, but don't drive yourself crazy wondering if she could have lived after that. I suspect she bled out pretty fast."

"Mm." Winter could only give a hum in response, gently laying Kaya's arm back onto the table. Spotting a clipboard pinned to the table, Winter grabbed it and was met with the examination report, along with some signed papers refusing an autopsy. It told her basically what she already knew—death by blood loss as a result of self inflicted cuts to the wrist.

Except... It wasn't self-inflicted. Not really. That much was clear to Winter now. That Bleary beast, whatever it was, caused this. She had felt the effect it had, the sudden doubt and guilt that had come just from being in its presence. Nothing would convince her that Kaya had done this to herself, not with Bleary around.

About to put the clipboard down, Winter paused when she noticed a note near the bottom.

Deceased's eyes show discoloration.

A chill went down Winter's spine, her gaze flickering up to Kaya's face. She could still vividly remember the blackness of Bryce's eyes when his body swung towards her: dead eyes, no longer his bright green irises.

Had the same happened to Kaya?

Swallowing her fear, Winter reached once more for Kaya's face. She cupped her cold, rubbery cheek for a moment, angling her face carefully. With a shaky breath, Winter's thumbs gently pulled up on Kaya's eyelids, revealing exactly what she feared.

Kaya's beautiful brown eyes had been turned into something grotesque. It was like liquid eyeliner had leaked into them, every bit of white turning into a horrible shade of inky black. Just seeing it made Winter shudder, taking a sharp breath.

"Just like Bryce." Axel's voice came from behind her, having moved to gaze down at Kaya's blackened eyes.

"And Miss Popelin, I'm guessing." Winter responded in a heartbroken tone. Lifting her head, she looked back at Axel, "Do you think this is because of Bleary?"

"It has to be. Some kind of… lasting effect on them." Axel answered her, as Winter moved to check Miss Popelin.

It was true. She didn't want to touch Miss Popelin to check— the pale blonde woman looked so peaceful in death, like a statue laid to rest. But she did read her chart, and it said the same thing. Cause of Death: Over fifty units of fast-acting insulin injected to the inner thigh, deceased's eyes show discoloration.

Frowning, Winter left Miss Popelin alone, and moved over to Bryce.

The first victim.

Picking up his chart, the first thing that caught Winter's eye was that there was a lot more to it than Kaya or Miss Popelin's. Axel hadn't followed her to the table. Instead, he leaned back on a wall, arms crossed, eyes trained on the floor.

Mouth dry, Winter began to read from the page, a chill going down her spine with each word.

"Deceased's cause of death; self-inflicted asphyxiation. Low proximity to the ground. Markings…" Her voice shook as she rattled off the list— bruises around his neck, of course, but also, "…on the palms of the hands… rope burn… torn nails…"

Carefully, Winter set down the clipboard and rolled a bit of Bryce's sheet up, just enough to pull one of his arms free. He had the same cold, clammy skin as Kaya. While his wrists were clean of cuts, it was his hands that revealed his death had not been a pleasant one. His palms looked like they had rung the rope tightly, his nails torn. It looked like before they had been cleaned up, they had probably bled quite a bit. In the moment of finding his body, she hadn't noticed these things— but suddenly, she could picture it.

"…Axel. What happens when you hang yourself from a great height?"

The image of it was unraveling in her mind. Stepping off a high platform, the crack of the rope as it catches your body, full weight bearing down on it. She knew the answer, but she wanted to hear him say it.

"...Usually the force snaps the neck. When uh... executions are held with the trap door falling way under your feet, the height is usually greater than the body height, so you bounce down and it... well, it's quick."

"Quick how?"

"Suffocation. Most people go unconscious, and then they suffocate." Axel's voice was much calmer than Winter's, as she gripped the edge of the table holding Bryce.

"And... what if it wasn't from a great height? What if it's just being strung there? No broken neck? No falling unconscious?"

This time, he didn't answer her— and she knew why.

"You lied to me." Winter's voice betrayed her sorrow, because now, she could fully picture it. There were details she hadn't noticed. Hadn't wanted to.

Bryce's neck hadn't snapped. He hadn't gone unconscious, peacefully drifting away. He had struggled. He had been inches from the ground and had tried to get the rope from his neck. She could picture his body in her head; twisting and fighting as he hung helplessly, unable to get himself free. His death hadn't been a peaceful one, and he hadn't wanted to die. *Ruby was right. He never would have done this.*

Still, Axel said nothing, and when Winter whirled around, he wouldn't meet her gaze.

"YOU LIED TO ME!" She yelled this time, her voice echoing off the metal cabinets of the morgue.

As Winter's voice rose, Axel finally lifted his head, annoyance spreading across his face. He stared at Winter, as she frantically confronted him.

"You told me it was painless! You said he just passed out, didn't feel a thing! Why the hell would you tell me that? I thought—"

The look on her face was as if he had betrayed her, and something about that expression made Axel snap, his own voice rising,

"What, did you want to know that he died a terrible death? That he was in intense pain until his last breath? That he was probably scared?"

A little bit of Winter's anger deflated but only a little, lowering her voice.

"Yes. Yes, I did. I wanted the *truth*."

You don't know what you're asking. Axel thought, sighing.

"No, you didn't. Would it have helped anything? We had just discovered his body. That was horrifying enough."

"It helps me to know what happened, exactly what happened. I don't need you to sugar coat it, I watched Kaya —" Her voice stopped short, her lower lip beginning to quiver, "...I watched Kaya kill herself."

"You had a *dream* that Kaya—"

"It wasn't just a dream! It happened! It was *real!*" Her voice came out so sharply that Axel winced.

"Okay, it wasn't a dream. Still, I didn't think you needed to know about Bryce. It was bad enough that you had to see him." Axel sighed, rubbing his arms gently through his hoodie, "It's bad enough that we're *here*, looking at their freaking corpses."

Winter glared at him for a moment, before drawing in a long breath.

"I understand why you lied. But I don't appreciate being

lied to. I can handle uncomfortable things. I don't need to be protected."

You're so stubborn. He couldn't help but think as Winter spoke. Annoyed, he answered,

"I'm sorry, okay? But don't ask me not to protect you. Obviously, I'm going to. This dark shit— this is my world, not yours. Before you met me, you—"

"I what? Had a life of sunshine and rainbows?" Winter gestured towards the body of their classmate, "This— This is not your fault, Axel. You're not tainting everything around you just because you have issues. We didn't plan for any of this, so stop beating yourself up."

Axel opened his mouth, planning on arguing, but the words wouldn't come. This wasn't a winnable argument, at least not with Winter. They had, on occasion, butted heads when he'd be too down on himself during their late night conversations, and he knew she saw a light in him that he couldn't always see.

Instead, he walked over to join her beside Bryce's table, gazing down at his bruised, deceased former friend.

"So... Okay, you said you saw me, right? Bleary took my form, and talked to you, and tried to trick you. What was that, do you think? A vision? Or is it some sort of shapeshifter?" Axel asked. *And if it's a shapeshifter... Why did it have to be me?*

Winter had a sour expression on, clearly still annoyed with him. As he drew closer to her, she crossed her arms, glaring sideways at him. Nonetheless, she sighed and answered him.

"Not a shapeshifter— it wasn't solid when it changed, it was blurry. It left me feeling really hazy, like... waking up from a dream. I'm not even sure what got me out of it, but I just sort of blinked, and it started to look less and less like you. It was like being hypnotized, I would assume."

Axel nodded, frowning. "Alright then. Let's say that's how it hunts. It traps you into seeing what it wants you to see. And... then what?"

A dark expression passed over Winter's face, turning away from him as she responded quietly, "It... makes you feel bad." The response was lame, and it wasn't hard to see she wasn't telling the whole story.

"Makes you feel bad? How? What happened?"

"...Bleary spoke to me, and... I believed some of the stuff it said. It picked up on my biggest insecurities and, because of the form it took... it made me feel awful." Winter shook her head, "So let's say that's what it does to its victims. It gets them under its spell and convinces them of the worst thoughts they have about themselves. It literally *guilts* them to suicide... is that even possible?"

Staring at the back of Winter's head, Axel frowned. *Bleary took my form for her. What did I do? Shit-talk her?* He wanted to know more, but with her arms crossed and her form rigid, it was pretty clear she wasn't comfortable elaborating.

"With that asshole, anything is possible. Bryce had a lot going on in his life, he probably feared failing everyone. I don't know what's worse: having everyone around you expect greatness, or having people expect nothing from you because they already know you're a failure." Axel spoke from experience. How many times had his mother sneered and made a comment as if he were a failure? Some people faced the pressure of being expected to succeed, others faced the pressure of having nothing expected from them at all, because they weren't seen as a success.

"And Miss Popelin, clearly she struggled with her illness." Winter chimed in, sighing sadly as she glanced over at the blonde body.

"So what about Kaya?"

"I don't know. I mean... She was so high energy, about

everything. Maybe that got to her, maybe she was just exhausted and I didn't know it. Maybe... I mean, do you think Bleary can force it? What if there doesn't need to be a reason at all? What if it can just... make you do it?"

"No. I don't think it's that powerful. At least, not right now." Axel murmured, remembering the way he had been able to control it; something he still hadn't told Winter about. "I keep thinking... Bleary has to be gaining something from this. What if people dying makes it stronger?"

Winter turned around to look at him, her eyes widening.

"That would explain a lot. The first time we saw it, it wasn't robed— now it is. It was more beast-like, now it walks. But... that's a horrible thing to think about. It'll only get harder to get rid of— and we don't know how to do that yet anyway."

Axel nodded, silent as he stared down at Bryce's face. He could almost have laughed— his monster really was like his depression. *It just digs its claws in deeper. The habit gets easier until it's all you know, accepting your fate, not fighting it... It just gets stronger.*

He didn't have high hopes, but he wasn't about to share that with Winter.

"We'll figure it out, Win."

She opened her mouth to respond, just as there was a knock on the door, Quinn poking his head in with a sympathetic smile.

"Hey... You guys good? Mom and Dad should be back soon and I really gotta... you know, lock 'em corpses up." He attempted humor, giving a thumbs-up as he slipped into the room. He only slightly hesitated when he saw Bryce and Miss Popelin out, glancing back at Winter with an awkward smile. To his credit, Quinn didn't say a word, likely assuming they were saying their goodbyes all around.

Winter turned back to Kaya's body. Axel watched her as

she leaned down, pressing a kiss to Kaya's forehead, and whispering something he couldn't make out. When she rose again, she offered up a smile, wiping at her eyes. The two of them helped Quinn gently cover their friends and push them back into the morgue chests.

As Quinn finished locking everything up, he wrapped an arm around Winter's shoulders and gave her a one-armed squeeze.

"Bring it in, Axel." He called, holding out his other arm.

Axel, ignoring him, walked ahead of them. He heard Quinn mumble, "Guess I'll just walk you out, then."

Winter gave a light laugh as they made their way out.

Ten minutes later, Axel and Winter were trekking down the sidewalk, going the long way home. Comfortable silence passed between them, and Axel found himself going over what they knew about Bleary in his head.

So far, we know he is all about deceiving his victims and pushing them to commit suicide. Unless you snap out of it like Winter did, I doubt they have much choice. But it isn't entirely forced, either.

"Axel?" Winter's voice came out hesitantly, breaking the silence of the evening.

"Hm?"

"What's it like, when— when you're dealing with Bleary. *Your* Bleary. Do you think it's like what Kaya and the others faced?"

Axel took a breath, staring down at the sidewalk as he thought up his answer.

"It's not far off, I'm assuming. It's not really a sane place to be." He admitted, shrugging his shoulders, "The power Bleary has, to make you think the worst about yourself and your future? That's pretty much the same effect. It's just... one bad day after another, and you start to wonder why you keep going through the same things. I get kind of fed up with it. Hard to look forward to anything when every day never looks promising."

Winter nodded, falling quiet again. As Axel glanced over at her, he could see she was thinking about something. She had this look, brows furrowed, biting on her bottom lip, like she was trapped in her own head.

"What... What did you say to Kaya?" Axel asked her, causing her to look up and towards him. They were heading up Altum Court by now, not far from Winter's house.

"I told her... that I never thought she'd go first, and that I was sorry. Kaya and I... we were so close. We used to joke about living together in our old age, you know— two old ladies and a bunch of cats. I've never imagined a world without her in it."

She stopped then, turning to face him fully.

"Axel... You know, I don't imagine my life without you anymore, either. I can't picture it. For all the times we've talked about it, I can't imagine you killing yourself. I don't want to. I can't." Winter's eyes welled with tears that she quickly swept away, sniffling as she continued, "Maybe I'm naive. Maybe I'm stupid, because Bleary is a reality for you. But I can't picture losing you anymore than I thought about losing Kaya. It's not a reality in my head, I just refuse to think of it."

Axel stared at her, the grief displayed all over her face. *She just lost Kaya, she's not thinking straight.* Winter had always accepted his depression, his habits. It had never been something she'd looked down on or discouraged. But now, she looked ready to plead with him.

"Winter, I can't—" *I can't promise you anything, I don't even know, myself.*

"I know. But I just want you to know that… If Bleary ever tries to trick you, if it tells you that I don't want you around, that's a lie. You have to remember that's a lie. I don't know if — if it told Kaya anything about me, but I keep wishing she knew I loved her when she died, and I don't know if she did, because that thing makes you think horrible things and…" She was crying harder now, shoulders shaking.

Whatever Bleary said really got to her… Axel thought, a pang of guilt hitting him.

"Win. What did Bleary tell you?" He asked her, taking a step closer.

Instantly, Winter began to bawl, burying her face in her hands. Axel wasn't a hugger, by any means, but he didn't hesitate to pull her into his arms as she broke down.

All he could do, standing on the sidewalk between their houses, was hold her until she calmed down enough to say,

"It told me we're only friends because you pity me."

Of course it would say that. Bastard. Anger sparked through Axel, hatred for his monster at saying something he never would. People always thought their worst insecurities, regardless of if it was reality— and he knew Winter's issues just as well as she knew his. He could picture Bleary, in his form, saying her worst insecurities, and the idea of her believing them filled him with anger.

Resting his chin on her head, as the taller girl curled forward into him, Axel scowled, hugging her a little tighter.

"Don't listen to that bull." *If anything, it's the other way around.* His mind nagged at him, as he said softly, "I'm *grateful* for you, Winter."

Sniffling into him, Winter murmured, "Stay alive, okay? If any version of Bleary comes along. Just stay alive, Axel."

If she hadn't been grieving, he might have argued. But

how could he argue with someone when she was like this? He knew where her head was. She had just lost her best friend, she didn't want to lose another.

"...I'll try."

Do you know how difficult that is?... I won't leave while that thing is still lurking around. That much, I can promise.

"That's all I'm asking for. Just try."

16

UNQUESTIONABLE GRIEF

"Over… Under… Twist…" Axel's eyes narrowed as he focused on the movements of his hands, adjusting a black silk tie around his neck. Or trying to, at least, as he tried again for the third time. A string of swear words left him, kicking the bottom of the sink as he grumbled in front of the mirror. *Who invented these things?* He thought, sourly.

By the time I get this, it's going to be all wrinkled. Damn it.

"Hey, Sport. Having trouble?" Timothee Dunn was the type of guy who, despite not being American born, had the look of an American poster boy from one of those old war ads. He was broad shouldered and fit, with carefully combed-over blonde hair and Caribbean blue eyes that were identical to Axel's own. He was several inches taller than his son, had a jaw that was as square as a box, and was never seen without a button up shirt and tie.

In other words, Axel found it hard to believe they were related at all. Besides their eyes, he could not see a single characteristic that he shared with his father. Considering how often he saw him, it wasn't a big deal anyway. Tim, as

Axel often called him, was the local divorce lawyer for Caligo's residents, and Axel often wondered how it was that he wasn't divorced himself. Yet his mother had never complained about her solitary sleeping arrangements during Tim's late nights at the office, and didn't seem to question why his jacket always smelled like Chanel no. 5.

"No." Axel answered shortly, huffing as he turned his gaze back to the mirror.

His father leaned on the doorframe of the bathroom, watching him with a raised eyebrow and a knowing smirk. After a moment of silence, however, his smirk began to fall into a somber expression.

"Did you know her? Mr. and Mrs. Morito's daughter?"

Axel tensed, saying nothing as his father continued,

"Nice couple. Mrs. Morito was kind to your mother when we first moved here. Made her feel welcome, which is more than I can say for most. Shame about their little girl."

"Kaya." Axel interjected, "Her name was Kaya. She's… She was friends with Winter Jozefson."

"Yes. Your mother told me you made friends with Winter. Nice girl. Bit artsy, isn't she?"

All Axel did was give a terse nod, not eager to create small talk with his father. Heaving a sigh, his father continued talking, oblivious to Axel's annoyance.

"When I was your age, I had a bit of a social life. Back in Aalborg, things were quiet but kids knew how to have fun, you know? It'll do you good to have some friends, eh? High school should be the prime of your life. Some of my best years. Of course, then I started backpacking. Went from Europe to Asia, met your mother…"

This is the last thing I want to hear about.

"You know, Tim, that friend of mine is waiting for me." Axel spoke, interrupting his dad before he could get into more tales from the old days. His father looked ready to speak again, until Axel added, "We have to get to her best friend's funeral, remember?"

"Of course." His father answered, giving a half sigh. Axel thought the conversation would end at last, but instead Tim stepped closer to him. He took ahold of the tie Axel had been nervously twisting, and started to fix it. The lawyer knew exactly what to do, and in seconds, it sat perfectly, not even too tight. Looking his son square in the eyes, Tim spoke one last time.

"Truly, Axel. Keep your friends close. You should cherish the connections you make. They might still be there, twenty years from now." He looked thoughtful, clapping a hand on Axel's shoulder. He couldn't help but think of the loud, raucous laughter that echoed through his house whenever one of his dad's buddies visited from Europe or Asia. Tim worked constantly, it seemed, except when they would visit. Those were the only times he'd take off work.

His friendship with Winter wasn't like that. They didn't laugh loudly together, or yell. They laughed quietly, and whispered— like the secrets they shared.

Will Winter even want to know me in twenty years?

Will I even be alive then?

Will she remember me?

All these questions swam through his head. But of course, a parent never wants to imagine their kid dead, and Axel certainly would never share Bleary— his Bleary— with his parents. So he put a tight smile on his face, and it remained there until his father left him alone and he could jog down the stairs, rushing out of his house to get across the street to Winter's.

Mr. Jozefson drove the three of them in his Barracuda. As they cruised down the streets of their small town, there were streams of people along the way. Everyone walking the sidewalks seemed to be going the same direction, all dressed in black. Kaya's was the first proper funeral to be held for the "suicide" victims since Bryce's family was still waiting, and Miss Popelin hadn't had a funeral at all. It seemed the whole of Caligo was coming together to mourn.

I wonder how many of them even knew her. Axel thought, gazing sullenly out the window.

"Kaya was social, but I doubt she knew the whole town." Winter voiced his thoughts only a few seconds later, frowning as she glanced his way.

"Everyone's your friend once you're dead." Axel darkly uttered.

The funeral, held outdoors amongst the graves, was short and sweet. Mr. And Mrs. Morito stood at the forefront, next to Reverend Callahan. Not far from his parents stood little Ren Morito. He was twelve, liked snakes, and was quite the prankster. Axel had once seen him make Korin Cooley, one of Ian's football buddies, piss his pants from a locker full of common garden snakes and he had liked the kid ever since. Now, however, Ren was dressed in a suit that was a little too big for him, a mixture of tears and snot streaming down his face.

Axel hung out behind Winter, keeping a distance. Dead bodies didn't freak him out, but it didn't make the funeral any less uncomfortable as he listened to the sounds of the Reverend and the crying. Some people cried genuinely, out of heartbreak. Others sickened Axel with loud, obnoxious boo-hooing, crocodile tears, and comments that made them seem like they, themselves, were at death's door.

Assholes. Axel thought, glowering at the many familiar faces.

Winter didn't shed a tear. Instead, the usually emotional girl stood rigidly, hands clasped in front of her, and had a faraway look in her eyes.

"What are you thinking about?" Axel asked, as he leaned closer to her. A few more inches and his chin would have rested on her shoulder.

"...Green beans." Winter answered. Her head turned to look at him, lips twitching into a small smile. "Kaya always called me green bean, after I grew taller than her, and because I have a green thumb. She loved flowers but could never grow them. Had flower prints on everything."

Talking about the beloved memory was enough to bring tears to her eyes, but Winter stubbornly blinked them away, turning her head back to the stand that held the coffin. Kaya's coffin was made with beautiful, rich, dark wood, and had silver roses on the handles and corners. A nearby framed photo was on display, showing her with a brilliant smile and warm brown eyes.

Axel opened his mouth, searching for the words, but ultimately, said nothing. Sometimes, there were no words.

As the short ceremony wrapped up, the crowd began to disperse. Some moved to talk to the Morito family while others hung near mutual friends or walked up to the closed coffin. Not wanting to ask Winter if they could leave, Axel hovered not far from her, and kept an eye out as Matthew Thorne approached.

"Hey, Winter." His tone was sympathetic, the bulky boy squeezing Winter into a hug. "I'm so sorry for... well, for Kaya."

"It's no one's fault." Winter answered automatically, her eyes flickering briefly back towards Axel. When she looked at Matthew again, she was frowning. "You were the last to see Kaya that night, weren't you? I left her with you— at the dance."

"Uh... Yeah..." Matthew looked awkward, rubbing the back of his neck. "Well see... I um... kind of made a dumb move."

The air shifted, both Winter and Axel narrowing their eyes at Matthew. The tone of his voice had sent immediate red flags.

"What dumb move? What did you do?" Axel spoke up, stepping closer to join the conversation. Matthew glanced over at him, guilt splayed all over his face.

"Kaya... stepped off the dance floor for a bit. When she came back, I was dancing with Lacey." Matthew admitted.

"Lacey Lokken?"

"Yeah. Hayden wasn't willing to dance with her, so I stepped in. Only, I uh... had my hands a little low, if you know what I mean. Kaya got a little feisty when she got back."

Oh, so that's how it is. Axel scoffed, studying the arrogant jock. He's lucky Hayden didn't see that. Or Lucas.

Before Winter was able to respond, a shocked voice rose up.

"Feisty?! She got feisty?! You mean she liked you and got upset when you messed with her heart?!" Quinn, in a gray suit and black tie, was furious as he marched towards them.

"Oh, come on, it wasn't like that." Matthew defended himself, holding up his hands.

"It's exactly like that! You weren't worthy of her. Kaya shouldn't have wasted her precious time on an unchivalrous lout like yourself!"

Axel knew what Quinn was doing the second the short, knight in shining armor lunged forward. He followed him, looping his arms around Quinn's waist just in time to yank him back so his thrown punch missed Matthew's jaw by mere inches.

"WOAH there, hey! Hey! Not here!" Axel hissed in Quinn's ear, as the Filipino boy squirmed.

"Let go! He deserves it, that son of a—"

"Stop! Please, Quinn!" Winter's voice cut through his protests. Quite a few eyes had turned towards them. Matthew had started to back off.

"I'm sorry. But it's not like she killed herself because of me. You can't pin that on me." Matthew argued, sounding less than certain.

Luckily, Winter and Axel knew the truth. Placing her hand on his shoulder, Winter looked up at Matthew. "It's fine. Quinn is just grieving. We all are. Why don't you go and apologize to the Morito's on uh… Quinn's behalf?"

Her suggestion was a welcome one, Matthew eyeing them before he trudged off towards Kaya's parents. Axel let go of Quinn, watching him adjust his suit with a huff.

"You should have let me slug him. Kaya's dead because of him." He sniffled, lifting his glasses to wipe at wet eyes.

"No, man." Axel answered, clapping a hand on his shoulder. He studied him for a moment, watching the obvious grief splay over his face. "You knew Kaya, didn't you? You think some prick with a small dick and an oversized ego could have drove her to suicide? It wasn't Matthew, I promise you that."

Before Axel could stop him, Quinn threw his arms around his shoulders, finally getting that hug as he let out a sob, clinging to him. Looking over his shoulder, Axel grimaced towards Winter.

Yet, Winter wasn't looking at them. She had that far away look in her eyes again, holding onto the Celtic pendant hanging from her neck. Her fingers brushed over the wrought iron, over and over again as Axel tried to detach himself from Quinn.

"Winter?"

"Hm?" Even her voice was faint.

"Let's not stick around for the burial, alright?"

Most of the crowd had left by now anyway, probably going to gather at the wake. Winter seemed to snap out of it as Axel spoke to her, looking at him and Quinn as the light came back to her eyes.

"Yeah... Let's get going. Kaya wouldn't want us crying over her, right?"

"I thought Harley would never stop blubbering." Axel sighed, walking down Altum Court with Winter. Mr. Jozefson had gone to the wake, but Winter couldn't stand the thought of being in Kaya's home, eating puddings and casseroles. They had finally gotten Quinn to calm down enough to go home, though the sun was already setting, the sky a sleepy, dusk violet.

"Don't be too harsh on him. He really liked Kaya." Winter smiled down at the sidewalk, arms crossed. "Everyone liked Kaya. She always had at least one or two people crushing on her."

"And you didn't?" Axel asked. He was serious, though Winter just laughed and shook her head.

"No. I mean, I didn't really entertain it like Kaya does. She's... She was a terrible flirt. She adored people showing her interest, thrived on it. I've always rejected that sort of thing. Didn't have the time, or the interest in..." She lifted her head, meeting his gaze, and opened her mouth as if to say something. A strange expression crossed her face, cheeks burning, before she shook her head and continued, "It was more Kaya's thing to have boys fawning after her. I think she would have loved to see all the grief at the funeral. She'd be cracking jokes right about now, about how much attention she's getting."

They had reached their houses, and Winter shook her head.

"One of a kind, you know?" Suddenly, she looked exhausted, the smiles she had put on all day no longer present.

Eyeing his worn out friend, it didn't surprise him much when she spoke again before he could answer,

"I kind of want to be alone. Can I call you later?"

"Of course."

Axel watched her go, wishing there was a way to help. Instead, all he could do was give her the space she needed.

17

UNAPPRECIATED BODY

Winterberry1412: Okay, I've got one. Why did the pianist keep banging his head against the keys?
GothLight666: He was playing by ear… Gonna have to try harder than that, Win.
Winterberry1412: Okay. What about— Why is a piano so hard to open?
GothLight666: The keys are on the inside.
Winterberry1412: What the hell— am I that obvious?
GothLight666: I've taken piano lessons for six years. Trust me, I've heard it all.

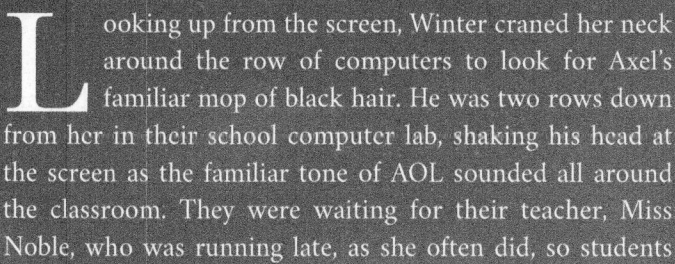

L ooking up from the screen, Winter craned her neck around the row of computers to look for Axel's familiar mop of black hair. He was two rows down from her in their school computer lab, shaking his head at the screen as the familiar tone of AOL sounded all around the classroom. They were waiting for their teacher, Miss Noble, who was running late, as she often did, so students were checking into their accounts. Chewing on her bottom lip, Winter thought for a minute, before sending another message.

> Winterberry1412: Which elf was the best singer?
> GothLight666: *GothLight666 is typing*

Watching him, Winter saw Axel type a few things, then delete them, hands hovering over the large, mechanical keys. Looking over his shoulder, their eyes met as he shot her a confused look.

"What?" He mouthed the word to her, eyebrows drawn together as he waved his hands at her. Smirking, Winter turned back to her computer.

> Winterberry1412: ELFis Presley.

A loud snort sounded from the computer two rows down, and Winter gave a triumphant grin. Axel was typing again when the door opened and in walked Miss Noble. She was a pretty little redhead who always dressed like a dame of the 1950s, despite being under the age of thirty.

"Shut down your chat rooms, little birds~ I've got an exciting coding lesson for you all today!" She declared, as the deafening tones of AOL shutting down filled the room.

After class, Winter hung by the door as Axel grabbed his bag and moved to join her, offering a small smile.

"That was the worst joke I've ever heard in my life." He informed her, shaking his head with a scoff.

"Made you laugh, though." Winter quipped, as they exited

the classroom. They walked a ways down the hall, before Axel stopped cold. It took a few steps for Winter to realize, turning around to see him staring off into the distance.

"Axel? What's wrong?" Winter asked, walking back to him.

"You don't feel that?" Axel asked, his face draining of color. He inhaled a sharp breath, taking a cursory glance around the hall of students, who were quickly disappearing into classrooms. It had been a few weeks since Kaya's funeral, and things were quiet. Almost normal, even, despite the lingering grief. Now, Axel looked shaken. He had gone from bobbing his head to music in his headphones, to standing frozen and looking like he'd seen a ghost.

"Feel... what, exactly?" Winter asked, totally oblivious.

"I'm not sure. But all the little hairs on the back of my neck just stood up and said hello." Axel mumbled. He pulled one of his sleeves up, just enough to let Winter see the goose-bumps forming on his arm.

"I don't feel anything." She answered him, frowning.

Axel's eyes seemed far away, staring past her. A heartbeat passed, then two, and then—

"Follow me." He commanded, taking off down the hall.

"Axel! What—" Baffled, Winter broke into a jog to keep up with him.

He seemed like a bloodhound, following a trail, until they ended up far from their next class. They came to a stop in the middle of a nearly empty hallway, Winter catching her breath as Axel said,

"You know where we are?" Axel asked, licking his lips, as he took a nervous glance around. "This was where I faced Bleary. After you got out. This is where I got away."

He had finally confided in her about his encounter with Bleary over one of their phone calls, not long ago.

Now, she could feel it too; a dread in the air, a heavy aura.

"...Why... did you bring us here?" She asked, as a chill spread up the backs of her arms, slithering all the way to her neck.

"Because I can hear it. That sound it makes, the freaking siren screech. You seriously can't hear that?" Axel seemed a bit horrified, staring at her now.

You're hearing things? Oh, Axel... Winter silently shook her head.

Just as she was about to say she couldn't hear it, however, there was something she did hear.

A loud, girlish scream came, followed by the sudden thud of a nearby door being thrown open. Winter and Axel both turned and watched one of the school cheerleaders run away, screaming her head off.

Axel started to march for the door, and Winter, wide-eyed, ran after him. Getting ahead of him just in time, she wedged herself between him and the door, placing a hand on his chest.

"Woah, hold up."

"What?" Axel asked, looking up at her.

Winter nodded her head back towards the door.

"That's the girl's restroom."

Axel's eyes darted to the sign above their heads, sighing out a curse as he rocked backwards onto his heels.

"Wait here." Winter remarked as she turned to slip into the bathroom.

"Win, wait!" Axel called after her, but he let the door shut behind her, and didn't follow. Some rooms, even he didn't want to go into.

Venturing around the bend, Winter cautiously moved into the restroom.

"Hello?" Her voice echoed, met by silence. That is, the silence besides her racing heart. Seeing Axel so thrown off, and knowing he heard *that thing* in his head, was enough to make her very aware of what she was walking into.

That's why it wasn't a surprise to see a body on the floor at the end of the bathroom.

"Jesus Christ!" Winter swore, rushing forward to reach the stilled body. She fell to her knees beside her, reaching for the face of Delilah Henderson. "Delilah. Hey! Delilah, come on."

There was no blood, no sign of injury. But it didn't take long for Winter to see the signs of something terribly wrong. Her dark skin had gone ashen gray, her lips tinged purple. She was already beginning to go cold, clammy to the touch. As Winter lifted her head, it was dead weight, limp in her hands.

Giving her cheek a soft slap, Winter tried to rouse her, shake her— but she got nothing. With a quivering hand, she tried to check Delilah for a pulse, finding nothing but an eerie lack of movement.

A creaking sound came from behind her, followed by Axel's worried voice,

"Winter? Everything okay?"

"No."

Her answer must have been enough for him to brave entering, as she heard footsteps announcing his arrival.

"Shit! Delilah, is she...?" Axel asked, hovering over Winter's shoulder.

"Yeah, I think so."

They both could see the scene in front of them: Delilah crumpled on the tiles, a small pile of vomit not far from her. But Axel bent down to grab something Winter hadn't seen— a small prescription pill bottle that had rolled underneath one of the sinks.

"Phentermine. Filled yesterday. She had to have downed the whole damn bottle." Axel told her, frowning.

"Phentermine?" Winter repeated him. *Why does that sound so familiar?*

Turning the bottle in his hands, Axel read the label, "It says it's for weight loss. Has a big fat warning on it. Can cause confusion, hallucinations, restlessness, nausea, vomiting, diarrhea, irregular heartbeats, weak pulse, seizure, slow breathing... Lovely way to lose weight." He looked from the bottle to the collapsed body of their classmate, face growing even more grim as he noted, "She isn't even fat. Why would she have prescription weight loss pills?"

Winter's heart sank.

"Hand me some toilet paper or something." She said, holding her hand out to Axel. He ducked into a stall and came back with a wad of paper for her, which she used to wipe vomit off the side of Delilah's mouth, gently laying her head back down before she stood up.

"Delilah was always complaining about her weight. We went to middle school together. Even back then, she would carefully count out everything she put in her mouth, and talk about wanting liposuction. I was... a little pudgier in middle school, and she was one of my worst bullies. Always had something bad to say to anyone who wasn't paper thin." Walking to the sink, Winter turned on the hot water to run over her hands, still feeling chilled from having touched yet another corpse.

Is this going to become the norm? She wondered, as she asked Axel,

"I think her mom is a doctor. What's the name of the prescriber on the bottle?"

Axel paused, checking, before he scoffed,

"Dr. L. Henderson. Think her mommy helped her, or she stole a prescription pad?"

I wouldn't put it past Delilah to sneak prescriptions behind her mom's back... Winter thought, frowning down at her body.

She opened her mouth to answer him, as the door to the bathroom opened again.

In stepped the Vice Principal Miss Prince, with the cheerleader who had run screaming now at her heels.

Another day, another death. Axel thought, gazing out the window as they watched paramedics load Delilah into an ambulance. A crowd had gathered, which meant that he and Winter, in their tiny nook of the library, were left to their own devices.

Turning from the window, he looked towards Winter instead. She had that look of concentration on her face, bent over the table as she scribbled something furiously in her notebook. From the quick, angry way she was moving the pencil, it couldn't have been one of her intricate sketches.

"What are you doing?" Axel asked, his voice revealing how drained he felt, leaning his face into the palm of his hand.

"Making notes of what we know so far." Winter answered, frowning as she looked up at him. "But not about Bleary— about myself."

"What do you mean?" Axel was puzzled, quirking an eyebrow at her.

"Well, think about it, Axel. I have never done anything like making Bleary before. I don't even know my own powers well enough to know how I did it. So here's what we know: I had a nightmare about Bleary. Did I make it in my subconscious? Is that why I was drawing it so much? It wasn't like anything I've seen before, I was just imagining it. But normally, when I make things, I have to imagine it pretty hard and... will it into being, if that makes sense. I can't just make things at random. I feel it. Look—"

She reached across the table, taking his hand. Brushing her thumb over the rings he was wearing, Winter turned Axel's hand palm up. Holding it in place, she hovered her second hand over his, so that they were palm to palm, inches apart.

A familiar warmth began to flow between them, tingling his palm with energy. He had felt it before, but the sensation still gave him the urge to pull his hand away. It felt like a strange, almost-pulling force when she was this close.

"You feel that?" Winter whispered, staring at him with wide hazel-green eyes.

Swallowing, all Axel could do was nod. As soon as he did, Winter stopped. When she pulled her hand away, it was like a magnet being nullified. Even with it gone, Axel's hands felt strangely numb.

"That's just me warming up. Unless I'm under some pretty heavy adrenaline, it takes a lot to even make simple things. Making Bleary... it doesn't make sense to me."

Reaching for her sketchbook, Winter flicked a few pages until she had a fresh two, proceeding to draw on one.

"Give me two items. One complex, one simple." She told Axel.

"Uh... okay... Give me..." His eyes trailed along the room, seeking out something to give him inspiration. "...A pen and... A typewriter." He said, as his gaze landed on an old typewriter sitting on a desk further away from them. *That's complex, right?*

Winter beamed at him, nodding eagerly.

"Okay so... A pen is not a problem. I can just think about it and—" She looked at a spot on the table between them, waved her hand, and with a fizzle of energy and a soft pop, a pen formed in the air and clattered onto the table. Axel reached out to take it, twirling the simple, black ballpoint pen in his hand. "Done, just like that. Now, the typewriter?"

For the next few minutes, Winter attempted to conjure a typewriter. Watching her struggle was an interesting sight— the aura of power coming off her was intense, as was her expression. A few times, it felt like it would appear, but then it slipped away, and Winter was left with a sweaty forehead and a sigh of frustration.

"Winter, you're bleeding!" Axel spoke up suddenly, startled by the sight of dark blood dripping from her nose.

"Huh?" Her hand went to wipe her nose, and Winter flinched when she saw the blood. She reached into her bag for some tissues, stemming it, and spoke again, "Sorry... That happens sometimes. That's the thing, Axel. I'm not strong enough to create a lot of things. Until just the last few years, I didn't even use my gift regularly. Papa forbade it, and I didn't like practicing in secret. Technology is difficult, though not impossible, but it's so much easier when I take the time to draw it. Creating something living? That's... I can't even imagine it. I..." She suddenly stopped speaking, a strange expression coming over her face, thinking hard about something.

"You...?" Axel prompted, watching her.

After a pause, Winter shook her head. "No, nevermind. I just meant to say, it's not easy to do."

Not easy? So it's not impossible then? He wanted to ask her, but she kept talking,

"That's why I don't understand Bleary. I wasn't even awake. I've made some really weird things with my powers, and I have weird dreams almost every night, but never like that."

Winter tossed the bloody tissue into a nearby trash can, and leaned back in her chair with a frown.

"How are we supposed to fight something when we don't even know the first thing about it?" She asked him.

Chewing on his bottom lip, Axel silently disagreed with her. They knew a lot about Bleary. Or at least, he did. He didn't want to compare himself to that thing, but... it was a part of him, wasn't it? He still could recall the way it mimicked his movements, and that only he seemed to hear it coming.

He didn't have to say a thing, though. Winter seemed to tune into his thoughts as she turned to look at him.

"Maybe I'm focusing too much on myself, and not enough on you." She murmured, before asking, "Axel, what is depression to you?"

"What?" The question took him by surprise.

"Well, Bleary came from your depression. However I did it, I know that. I imagined it based on you, and our conversations. So it probably plays to those rules. Your depression, your rules. The more I know about how you feel, the more I'll know about Bleary, and maybe that'll tell us how to fight it. So... let's talk."

They had only ever talked about his issues over the phone. Sometimes, not even by voice, but by text, especially AOL. Winterberry and Gothlight were less intimidating than sitting before her now, with her looking straight at him. Though Axel's heartbeat picked up, and he squirmed in his seat, he couldn't deny that she was right. This began and ended with him.

Looking down, Axel ran his hands through his dark hair, hiding his face from Winter as he took a deep breath.

"Depression is... It's..."

"Hey guys! What's crack-a-lackin'?" A buoyant voice interrupted them, instantly setting Axel on edge as he lifted his head to see their privacy being invaded by Oliver Blaikwood. Winter's chattery friend had started towards them, grinning and placing a hand on Winter's head, mussing up her hair as he fell into the chair beside her. He was unfazed by the dramatic turn of the day, but that wasn't really surprising- barely anything brought him down.

Shit. I should have looked around. Axel thought. He had been so focused on their conversation, he hadn't even realized the library was less empty than it had been before. Suddenly, he felt a bit nauseous at the thought of having been overheard.

"Ollie!" Winter gasped out his name, breathlessly laughing, "You scared us! What are you doing here?"

"Heard about Delilah. You found her?" The photographer of the school news wiggled his eyebrows at Winter, clearly looking for the gossip. Annoyance stabbed at Axel, glowering at the other boy. *Someone's suicide shouldn't be picked apart in conversations all over the school.* He thought, though he kept his mouth shut, watching the two.

"Y-Yeah. It was awful." Winter looked down awkwardly, messing with the celtic pendant around her neck. "I wasn't close to Delilah or anything, but... I wouldn't have wished that on her. Did you know she was struggling?"

"Didn't everyone? I mean, I guess not in that sense, but... She had issues. Anyone with an attitude that bad has issues, don't they?"

Oliver's words finally struck the wrong nerve. Axel spoke up,

"Isn't there a rule about speaking ill of the dead?" His voice came out just as harshly as he meant it, Oliver meeting his glare.

Oliver opened his mouth, but before he could respond, Winter's phone rang. Grabbing it, she frowned at the screen.

"It's Papa. I have to take this, I'll be right back." Rising from her seat, she left the two of them alone. Axel watched her slip out of the library, sighing quietly to himself. Now that it was just the two of them, Oliver got to respond.

"Don't get me wrong, Dunn. Actually, I relate a little bit to Delilah." He paused, before saying, "You and Winter, you were talking about her depression, right?"

Oh, great. He did overhear us, after all. Axel's lips twitched into a frown, though he was relieved Oliver didn't direct the question towards him, instead keeping the focus on Delilah. So he nodded, saying,

"Winter and I were just talking about the warning signs. Why did she do it? That kind of thing." He lied, shrugging his shoulders.

"Everyone has their own answer to that loaded question, man." Oliver rapped his hands against the table, shaking his head, "My little brother committed suicide, you know."

Eyes widening, Axel stared back at Oliver.

"No, I… didn't know." Officer Chi had told Axel when he found Bryce that there hadn't been a suicide in Caligo in ages, but the sad smile Oliver gave him now dripped with pain. There was no doubt, from the look now in his eyes, that he spoke the truth.

"That's probably because it didn't officially go down as a suicide. He was only nine… They ruled it an accident, but I was there. It wasn't an accident." Oliver shook his head, a far-away look in his eyes. "I've been thinking about it a lot lately, with everything going on. Kind of feel responsible. You know, when you're someone's brother, friend, you… feel like you should have done something. I should have done some-thing, but I didn't see it coming, not until after. Still… If I had to answer that question, why he did it, I think he probably felt pretty alone. Delilah was always surrounded by people, but how many of them do you think she was actually close to?"

Axel listened, quietly taking in Oliver's words. *Nine years old.* The thought made him angry, bitter that someone so young had to feel that way. Though he had been struggling long before he actually started cutting, and far too young by most people's standards, he couldn't speak against it, except that he could relate to the brother Oliver had lost.

"How old were you?" He asked, out of not knowing what else to say.

"Thirteen. Four years older than Aspen. It wasn't that long ago, I guess. His bedroom is still made up back home and everything." Oliver answered him. He studied Axel for a long moment, hesitating before saying, "You know... I'm glad you're hanging more with Winter and us. The paper crew and the rest. You're alright, Axel. I'm sorry we never hung out before. I'm sure it's only because Winter is a force of nature. She knows how to drag you into things, right? Did the same thing to me all the time when we were growing up. But uh... just so you know, I've got your back too, if you ever need someone that isn't Winter."

The words Oliver spoke were genuine. He hadn't been there for his brother, but people were dropping like flies lately, and he had no clue about Bleary's influence, so here he was trying to offer an olive branch. Axel could see why; he seemed even more at risk than the happy, unsuspecting people who had died so far. But the offer was a welcome one.

Nodding, Axel answered him,

"Thanks, uh... Oliver. I'll keep it in mind."

I guess the statistics are true. He thought idly. *People come together after a suicide. Especially after multiple.*

Just then, Winter came strolling back in, stuffing her phone into her back pocket.

"Hey. I gotta get home. Papa's orders." She said, reaching for her bag.

Pushing himself out of his chair, Axel spoke,

"I'll go with you."

That evening, Axel lay on his back in bed, on the phone with Winter. She was talking his ear off about an art project of hers, and his mind was wandering.

"Axe. What's up? You've gone completely quiet. You stopped mumbling in response a good ten minutes ago." Winter finally said over the line.

"Sorry." Axel answered, sitting up. Leaning against one knee, his eyes went across the room to his bookcase, thinking of the yearbook with Bryce's photo. "I think I have that answer. What depression is."

"Oh?" Winter asked, her curiosity peaked.

"It's... being alone. Not in the normal sense, not literally. But... feeling like you have no one else to turn to. Whether it's because you've given up on people, or because no one around you cares. Bleary is... It's the feeling that you're all alone. When you don't matter to anyone it's only a matter of time before you can't be bothered to matter to yourself, right? It just gets exhausting and you just want it to end. You have no one to stay for, not even yourself."

The description was bleak and he knew it, but he knew the feeling too well. When you didn't even like yourself, and no one liked you, why bother staying on this earth?

Winter was dead silent, and Axel was sure she was some sort of horrified. Until she said, with a voice that could only be described as upbeat and hopeful,

"Well... that means we know how to face Bleary. Maybe not exactly how, but we know we have to face him together, right, Axel? That's a start."

"Yeah... I guess you're right."

"Axel?"

"Yeah?"

"Do you still feel alone?"

That was a question he didn't know how to answer. It wasn't a feeling he knew how to get rid of, or something that one person could easily change. But after a long moment, he answered,

"...Not always. You've been there for me, no matter what state my mind has been in. So, I know I'm not always alone. And it's appreciated, Winter."

There was another pause of silence between them before Winter went back to the topic on hand; how to actually fight the monster. They talked about it endlessly, with no clear answer in sight. Ironically, it was like the illness itself: there was no easy fix.

They needed to know more, and Axel was afraid there would be more bodies before they did.

18

UNCONDITIONAL FRIENDSHIP

"I n tonight's news, folks are growing wary of the approaching software shutdown, dubbed the 'Y2K problem'. Government officials say that there is no cause for panic, but financial experts postulate that this tiny computer glitch could cost anywhere from four hundred million to six hundred billion dollars to rectify, as well as cause havoc among..."

Axel was only half listening to the news as he sat at his desk, trying to finish up some of the grueling history assignments his mother had given her class. His father was home for the evening— a rare occurrence— and though he had stacks of paperwork in front of him on the glass coffee table, his attention was glued to the television.

"What do you make of that, Axel?" Tim asked, reaching for the remote with a shake of his head. "Everything is going onto a screen these days. People think the world will end if screens stop displaying the right year. Ridiculous, isn't it?"

"Hmm." Axel hummed. His attention had been caught, thought not from the news.

Across the street, Winter sat on the bench in her yard. She wore a deep red knit sweater with black pants and boots.

Leaning back, her legs were crossed with a sketchbook balanced in her lap. Even at a distance, he could see her focused expression, her hair falling in her face as she traced a pencil across the page.

I wonder what she's drawing... He thought. But his memory was nagging at him. There were so many times he had seen the girl across the street, his now friend, in her yard. Gardening, sketching, hanging out with her grandfather underneath the car port. But that one time... now knowing what he knew...

Tap, tap, tap! Axel blinked as a pen rapped on his desk in his peripheral vision. He had been staring out the front window, in a daze, peering at the house across the street. The front yard had rose bushes and a little wrought iron bench. On that bench sat a pretty, brunette girl. She had a notebook balanced in her lap, a pencil in hand, and looked lost in her own world. Her head was bent down, bangs in her eyes— but every time she looked up, Axel swore she looked right at him. Sometimes, he even caught her smiling, although she was a good distance away and she never kept her head up long enough to get a good look. She had lived across the street for five years now, and Axel had never spoken a word to her, not even knowing her name, but he often saw her outside drawing, or caught glimpses of her through the windows of the green house.

Axel's gaze now lifted to see his mother standing at the edge of his desk, twirling the pen that had interrupted his train of thought. Alessandra Dunn wore a proper gray turtleneck with black slacks and had her dark brown hair twisted into a very tight bun. The demeanor of the Dunn matriarch showed that she knew exactly how to keep people in line. Her nearly-black eyes glared down at him in disapproval.

"I take my eye off you for five minutes, and you've got your head in the clouds." His mother tutted at him. Outstretching a hand, she waved her fingers. "Give it here, Axel."

He didn't have to ask what she was talking about, pulling a sour face as he tugged his headphones off his head, the sound of drums and guitar riffs fading away as he rolled the wire around his Walkman and handed it to his stern-faced mother.

"You'll get it back *after* you finish your work, not before. And you'll finish faster if you stop daydreaming."

Axel only nodded, scowling as his mother turned and left with his device. It was no use to argue that he studied better with music. His eyes turned back to the window again— but the bench was empty. He took a surveying glance around the yard of the house across the street, but a warning call from his mother made him sigh and look back down at the work-sheets he'd been given.

Ten or so minutes of studying later, he couldn't stop himself from looking up again.

There she is! His attention immediately went to the girl across the street, who had returned. And... *She's staring right at me.* It was true— she was looking straight at him, with the most curious look on her face, as if something was on her mind. Confused, Axel glanced behind him, wondering if something had her attention. When he looked back, however, the girl had lifted her hand, giving him a little wave. It took him a second to lift his hand in return, awkwardly returning the gesture through the window.

"Axel Dunn! What did I just tell you? If you can't study there, I'll close those blinds." His mother's voice made him jump, cheeks burning as he lowered his hand. They had beautiful, big front windows that flooded their home with sunlight. If Axel had his choice, he'd be studying in his room, but his mother claimed that having him sit at the desk in front of the windows would be a positive learning environment. It also happened to put him, and his entire street, on display. That's what made it so easy to get distracted by the house across the street.

"N-No! I'm almost done, Mom. I swear." He answered.

Giving him a reproachful look, his mother walked by to glance at his papers before saying, "Good. I'm going to start dinner— these *will* be done by the time I come back."

He watched her leave the room, waiting until he heard the door click to look back out the window. The girl had her head down again, sketching something in her notebook.

Guess I better finish this up, before Mom gets back. Axel thought with a sigh. Yet, as he looked down, a shiver went through him. Sitting on his schoolwork was his Walkman, headphones and all.

Did mom leave this? Setting down his pencil, Axel took hold of his cd player, glancing back at the door his mom had left through. He hadn't been paying close attention when his mom had come to check his work, but why would she have left his device with him? Sticking his headphones on, his music resumed. He glanced out the window at the girl again, unsettled.

Something felt... strange. Axel couldn't quite put his finger on it, but the hairs on the back of his neck were prickling.

An hour later, Axel was sitting with his mother at the dining room table, poking at his food. His father had called to say he wouldn't make it home in time and not to wait for him, which wasn't uncommon. His brother Kaius had chosen to eat at a friend's house that evening, and Lisden had moved out of the house years ago, so it was just Axel and his mother at the long, empty dining room table. It was after finishing most of what was on his plate in silence that his mother spoke to him.

"You can have this back." She reached into her pocket, and stopped when her hand closed around nothing, a confused expression coming across her face.

"My Walkman? You gave it back to me earlier, remember?" Axel said, as he pulled it out of his pocket, setting it on the table. It took all of two seconds for his mother to stop looking confused and start looking angry.

"I most certainly did not!" Her voice was high and sharp. Axel winced as she stood up and approached him, "Axel Dunn, I did not raise you to be a thief, no matter how much you like listening to music."

"I didn't steal it! It was left on the desk!" Axel immediately raised his voice in his own defense, as his mother snatched his CD player from the table.

"I didn't raise a liar, either. This is mine— two days. You're going to bed. Now." There was no use in arguing when she decided on a punishment, Axel left, stunned by getting in trouble for something he didn't do. Sighing, he gave a reluctant nod, watching his mother take his plate and head towards the kitchen.

Pushing out his chair with a clatter, Axel made his way to bed without dessert. A whole host of questions ran through his head, most of them were about the girl across the street.

Back to 1999

I'll be damned... Axel snorted, smiling suddenly as he stared at Winter from his desk. All these years, he hadn't known her secret... Had it been staring him in the face this whole time?

I couldn't have guessed something like that, there was no way. Still, it seems so obvious now. she'd been looking out for me back then...

"Dinner!" Axel's mother's voice cut through his thoughts, stepping into the den with a sweeping glance between her husband and her youngest son.

Axel pushed back his chair with a sigh, shaking off the memories of the past as he trudged into the kitchen to eat with his parents. It was no more talkative between them with his father present than it was when it was just himself and his mother. Though tonight, the news about Y2K gave a good conversation topic as Axel settled into eating, only half listening to his parents.

Normally, his mother made sure the TV in the living room was shut off during meals, but now, it droned on. His father was keen on keeping an ear out for more about the calendar conspiracy.

"Come on, Tim, must we really listen to that?" Alessandra chastised her husband, angrily stabbing some of the vegetables on her plate.

"Important to know what's going on in the world, dear. Our sons will be a part of this new century, after all." Timothee answered, shrugging his shoulders, "As ridiculous as it may be."

The news about Y2K didn't actually stay on long, as the reporter changed to a serious tone,

"This just in. There's been a horrific suicide attempt—"

Axel's blood ran cold.

"—on Cinis Street. Junior at local Clamare High, Oliver Blaikwood—"

His face turned as white as a sheet.

"—stepped in front of a speeding car this evening. Onlookers

say it looked to be deliberate. Blaikwood was rushed off to Salvare Vita Hospital in critical condition—"

His mother spoke past the sound of the news reporter, breaking the silence at the table,

"Oh God... Not another one of my students. I don't know what's gotten into the youth of today. It's ridiculous, these kids and their pathetic outlook on life." She said, shaking her head, "You know what it is, don't you? Kids today have it easy, so they take little problems like whether they're liked in school, and turn it into the end of the world! In my day, we had more to worry about. But today, everyone has a problem that is life-ending."

"Dear, it's probably a big problem for them. You never know. Drugs are much bigger today than they were back when we were young. For all we know, that could be causing the irrational thoughts these poor kids are having." His father intervened.

"Drugs have been around forever, Tim. I'm just saying, look at the history. The more time goes on, the weaker people get. Sixteen-year-olds fought horrific wars and died in service to their countries. Whole empires were built on the backs of babes. And today? Today, the reasons for someone killing themselves range from going up a pant size to getting a bad grade."

His mother's unforgiving argument on how weak teenagers were today hammered against Axel. It wasn't anything he hadn't heard from her before, however, and he couldn't bring himself to get into the conversation. Instead, all he could think about was the news report.

Oliver... Oliver Blaikwood. The boy that he had talked to just the day before.

Winter's second best friend, besides Kaya.

Axel couldn't excuse himself from dinner fast enough,

jogging up the stairs to get to the privacy of his bedroom. His hands fumbled for his phone, dialing Winter's number.

Pick up. Come on, Win. Pick up the damn phone. He thought, peering across the street to her dark window.

"Hi, this is Winter Jozefson, please—"

"Damn it!" Axel swore, hanging up and dialing again for another round of ringing. He had to hope she hadn't been watching the news. Finally, her bedroom light flickered on. He saw a shadow cross by the closed blinds and the sound of the phone picking up.

"Win—" He didn't even get her name out before he was met with sobbing. Hyperventilating, gasping sobs, a garbled voice trying to say his name.

"Axe—, He— I can't— it wasn't— Oliver— My f-f-fault—"

Shit. "Winter— I can't understand. Okay, okay, listen. I'm coming over. Okay? I'll be right there." He could barely speak over her sobs.

She was still gasping when he hung up, running from his room to get across the street.

Axel, upon getting to Winter's yard, moved to scale his way up to Winter's room. He had done this a few times, to hang out with Winter late at night after her grandfather had gone to bed. It wasn't a difficult climb, and was usually worth the hours of laying around, talking about nonsense.

His hand had barely touched the side of the house, when the front door opened.

"Dunn!" Mr. Jozefson's gruff tone called out.

Cold dread hit Axel, backing away from the house, his hands lifting in surrender.

"I w-was just—"

"Might as well use the door, boy." The old man settled him with a look, the two of them staring at each other for a few seconds. He had to know what state Winter was in. She had already lost one friend; how many more was she going to lose?

Giving a nod, Axel broke into a jog to get up the front steps, past Mr. Jozefson and into the house that had become increasingly familiar to him. He ran up the stairs, following the sounds of Winter's sobbing until he got to her door.

Trying the handle, it was locked.

"Win. Winter, open the door." Axel called, knocking its wooden surface, "It's me."

It only took a few seconds for the door to unlock, pulling open so Winter's tearstained face was in view, standing so close they were almost nose-to-nose.

"He's *alive,* Axe. C-C-Critical condition. H-He must be in so much pain—" She started, as Axel wrapped his arms awkwardly around her neck, pulling her into his chest as he shuffled them into her room, pushing Winter to walk backwards. Swinging his foot back, he caught the door with his ankle and tossed it shut.

"I know." He sighed into Winter's brown hair, guiding her to her bed so she could sit down.

"Oliver would never have— not after his b-brother. He wouldn't—" Winter was gasping for air as she spoke, clinging to him. If she wasn't in such a state, Axel might have been uncomfortable, but instead all he could do was rub her back and let her hug him.

"I *know.*" He repeated, frowning. "It wasn't Oliver."

19

UNSOLICITED VISITOR

T he first snowfall of the year came on the first of December. It seemed the cold weather was yet another sign of mourning. Winter was in her math class, cheek leaned into her palm as she worked through dull equations. It took hushed whispers from her classmates before she lifted her head, sweeping a lock of brown hair out of her face as she glanced out the window and saw what the sudden fuss in the classroom was about. Soft, delicate white snowflakes were falling, gathering on the cold ground outside. Just seeing it made Winter shiver. She might have been named for the season— but she was a warm weathered girl at heart.

By the time class ended, the ground outside was covered in fresh white snow. Gathering her things as the bell rang, Winter paused only when she felt her phone buzz.

A: Meet me by the statue.

It was from Axel, of course. They had been unusually lucky wth how quiet things had gotten, Thanksgiving having provided a sleepy loll over Caligo. Had the rash of suicides stopped? Was that bleary beast gone? Both Axel and Winter weren't convinced, though it had been a good two weeks since Oliver's deliberate accident. Every time it seemed to vanish, it came back twice as ugly.

As she pushed open the front doors of the school, Winter could see him waiting for her, sitting on the edge of the statue in the courtyard. He wore a heavier hoodie than usual — more like a parka than anything— and a black beanie tucked over his equally black hair. He had on black gloves as well, and the only dash of color on him was a bright red scarf around his neck. Winter blushed when she realized it was a scarf of hers that she had left at his house a few nights before, and told him to keep it because she had too many.

Winter was dressed for the cold weather as well, though a little more colorful than Axel. She looked like someone out of a classic's women fiction, inspired by Anne of Green Gables, which they had been assigned in English. She had on a tight black turtleneck with sleeves bunched at her elbows, and a black and red checkered scarf tucked around her neck. She matched it with full length black leggings and a flouncy, red cotton skirt that went all the way to her ankles and swayed easily in the cold breeze. With black boots, a small black waistline belt, and her hair pulled up on her head in a careful, intricate bun. It was more effort than she usually put into her outfits, channeling her inner Kaya. Or perhaps, her inner Axel. She nearly matched him in terms of gothic energy that day. Even her nails were painted deep, blood red.

"Enjoying the snow?" Winter asked as she reached him, her boots crunching the snow beneath her.

"It looks like cocaine." Was all Axel had to say/

It was enough to make Winter snort, shaking her head at him. Axel moved to sit on a cold bench by the statue, and she followed, sitting next to him. Rubbing her hands together,

Winter let out a sigh, white puffs of breath coming from her mouth.

"It's freaking freezing. Snow is pretty but it sure outweighs its welcome." She remarked, watching students around them as they trudged across the courtyard. Some had already started games of throwing snowballs at their friends, while others seemed to speed walk from one building to the other, not staying in the cold longer than was necessary. Winter would have been part of the latter.

Looking up at the sky, Axel closed his eyes, snowflakes falling towards his uplifted face.

"Really? You don't like it? I was going to compare it to you, Snowflake." He remarked, nicknaming her.

Winter's lips twitched into a smile. Reaching for him, she grabbed onto one of his wrists as lightly as she could, so as to not spook him or disturb his scars. She slid two cold fingers past his sleeve, touching his bare skin.

"JESUS!" Axel complained loudly, eyes flashing open as he yanked his arm away from her. "You just got out here! Why are your hands so fudging cold? Did Bleary kill and reanimate you or something?" The dark joke came with a brooding scowl, but it was hard to take his annoyance seriously because of how wide his eyes were.

"Teaches you not to compare me to snow just because my name is Winter." His best friend retorted, giving a laugh, "I really don't like cold weather. I'm naturally inclined to the warmth, Axel."

"You're in luck, then. In Caligo, we only get snow maybe a week or two out of the year." Axel said, as he started to pull his gloves off his hands. Taking her freezing hands again, he shook his head at Winter as he helped her pull them on. "You just need to invest in a good pair of gloves, Win."

Now, Winter's cheeks really were burning, and not because of the cold. The last few months had been a real whirlwind, but... *Isn't it crazy that we got to be friends?* She thought, as she gazed into his face. She used to sketch him from afar, and now, she could see him up close and personal. From the glint of his lip ring, to the details of his gorgeous Caribbean-blue eyes. *I really should ask him to do a portrait sometime...*

"Winter?" Axel murmured her name. "You're staring at me. Do I have something on my face?"

"Huh?" Snapping out of it, Winter blinked, clenching her newly gloved hands. "Oh, yeah, no. I was just thinking, I want to draw your face sometime." She said it so honestly that Axel laughed out loud, scrunching up his face.

"Why on earth would you want to do that?" He asked, drawing one of his now-bare hands along his jaw, half trying to hide his face from her.

"You make a good art subject." She answered, chuckling.

Axel rolled his eyes at her, but he knew her well enough to not argue with her desire to draw him. Just last weekend, she had sketched his entire bedroom as a location study. His only request usually ended up being that she didn't make any inanimate objects come alive.

"Fine. You want to come over tonight? We can order takeout from Damara's and hole up in my room." Axel offered.

"I—" Winter started to agree, loving the idea. Yet, she faltered. Looking down, snowflakes settled in her hair. Her nose had begun to go as rosy red as her cheeks, glowing from the cold. "Actually, can we raincheck that? I was thinking of visiting Oliver. I stopped by his house the other day, to give his parents some peanut butter cookies, and his mom said that he's out of the ICU now, and available for visitors."

"Is he conscious? Do you think you can ask him about Bleary?" Axel asked her, suddenly eager at the idea of going to the hospital. "Do you want me to come along?"

Peeking back at him, Winter gave an awkward, guilt-filled smile. "Actually, I kind of want to go alone, if that's okay. His mom said he's awake here or there, and he's been questioned by the police, so... I want to talk to him about Bleary but..."

"It's fine, Snowflake." Axel interrupted her with his new nickname, nodding. "He's your friend, I get it. Just... keep me updated? Call me?"

"Of course." She confirmed, giving him a nod. Axel reached to fix her scarf, tugging it up so that it was tucked against her face, and joked,

"Better get going before you turn into a real snowflake, Win."

Laughing, Winter stood up and bid him goodbye. She walked away, waving and watching Axel pull his headphones over his ears, chilling in the snow with his walkman as she went in the direction of Salvare Vita Hospital.

The small city of Caligo, to the south, had a robust river called the Effugere, and a single-bridged-road that led in and out of town. Right past that, as people drove into the city, were two large, fenced in compounds on either side. On the left side of the road was the old Malum Sanitarium— a mental hospital.

The place to go for physical health was right across the road, on the right side of Timor street. Salvare Vita Hospital. It had a large, square parking lot and an oddly shaped building, only able to handle about five hundred or so patients. They could only do so much there, the most serious cases being taken to the closer, bigger cities by chopper.

Winter had to wonder, not for the first time, how visitors

to Caligo felt about the two hospitals being the first buildings to see. Was that a bad omen?

Still, her mind was on more important matters— like how to fight a mental monster— as she took the elevator up to the fifth floor where Oliver was. As she climbed the floors, Winter played with her hair, which was draped over her shoulder, nervous as she thought about what she would say.

After checking in with a nurse and getting a visitor's pass, Winter slowly walked down the sterile hallway, fluorescent lights overhead bathing everyone in that hospital glow. It seemed to be busy, nurses rushing from room to room, patients being wheeled past as Winter tried to stick close to the wall and out of the way.

I wonder if Bleary is affecting more than just our friends, and we just don't know it... Maybe I should ask Papa how the news has been lately. Winter thought.

Just as she reached Oliver's door, Mr. Blaikwood stepped out. He looked like the stereotypical office worker you'd see in commercials— a tall, thin man with neatly combed brown hair and a goatee tinged with gray. His brown eyes, identical to Oliver's, were filled with exhaustion behind rectangular glasses, and his tie was undone around his neck. An empty coffee cup in his hand, he paused as Winter approached.

"Ah. W-Winter... Here to see Ollie?" He asked, his voice cracking briefly as he spoke her name.

"Yes, sir."

"Go on in. Please. He'll be... happy to see a friend." He remarked, reaching to pat her on the shoulder before he ambled off towards the cafeteria, leaving her to step into the room.

Standing at the foot of his bed was Mrs. Blaikwood. After Oliver's brother died, his family had fallen apart— his parents had divorced, and his father had moved out of Caligo, taking a job in New York, all the way across the country. He clearly still cared about Oliver— Winter knew Oliver regularly wrote and called his father, and received responses. *He must have taken the first flight back to California when he heard...* Winter thought.

Oliver's mother was similarly caring, but the woman Winter saw now didn't resemble her at all. Charlene Blaikwood was usually a jovial, giggly woman. She flirted with everyone— from the cashier at the grocery store, to the cute nurses—, giving off a silly, ditzy, somewhat tipsy persona. Even how she looked, with a short bob of reddish brown hair and big, warm brown eyes, wearing brightly colored yoga pants and shirts with big, swoopy sleeves, reflected her personality. She never lacked beads around her neck, bangles around her wrists, or incredibly high heels that she claimed "were a woman's essential, never know when you might have to boogie".

She looked crestfallen, as she lifted her head to look at Winter, her eyes blank and shining only due to the wet, unshed tears. Charlene had a reputation as the youthful mom, the fun mom, the cool mom— and now, she looked older than her ex-husband, bent over Oliver's bed. The last time Winter had seen her like this... had been after the death of her son Aspen.

"Hey, Charlene. How are you?" Winter asked in a whisper, moving to give the woman a hug.

"Oh, I'm... I'm doing." Charlene shakily responded, as they both looked towards Oliver.

Seeing him in this state made Winter start to tear up. Oliver was covered in medical supports— both his legs in casts and strung up from straps hanging from the ceiling, his pelvis in a similar contraption that kept his body laid out straight with a hospital gown and some blankets loosely laid over him. His arms were wrapped in bandages, IVs and wires snaking out from them. Looking up to his face, he seemed too small, suddenly weak and fragile. His tan skin turned ashen, and his hair, carefully combed, lay flat on his head.

Oliver was athletic, he was a daredevil with a love of nature, constantly out in the sun doing something ridiculous or practicing photography. Seeing him like this, for Winter, was torturous.

Uncertain, she hesitated, lingering at the foot of his bed.

"You can touch him, if you want. Hold his hand, or touch his hair. He's woken up a few times, but he's heavily sedated. Pretty out of it. They have to manage his pain." Charlene murmured.

Moving alongside his bed, Winter slowly reached for Oliver's hand. To her relief, it wasn't ice cold like Kaya's. It was burning hot, furnace-like, how Oliver always was.

He's okay... He's alright. Just breathe. She reminded herself, trying to take deep breaths to fight the nausea that threatened to ruin her composure.

"What... What are the doctors saying? About his... long term injuries." Winter asked, stroking a thumb across the back of Oliver's hand, counting the freckles on his face as she listened to the steady beeping of the machines at his bedside.

"He has—" Charlene's voice cracked, shaking as she recounted the result of the accident. "He has broken his legs in several places, and his hip... The doctor called it 'extraordinary lower body trauma'. His spine was damaged as well and they don't think he'll walk again." Moving to a nearby armchair, she sunk into it, holding her head as she continued, "My baby... Oliver has always been moving, ever since he was little. Climbing trees, cliff jumping, hiking. I can't imagine how he's going to take the news. I haven't been able to tell him yet. I don't want to put that on him when he's just barely holding on."

Winter, searching for something to say, felt weak in the

knees herself as she leaned on the side of Oliver's bed. That was when Charlene spoke again,

"Winter... Did you notice anything wrong with Ollie, when you saw him last? Officer Chi... he said it appears that Oliver did this to himself. There were witnesses who said he deliberately stepped in front of the car. I just don't understand, why would he do a thing like that?" The mother of Winter's friend sounded heartbroken and confused, lost in this seemingly senseless act. It was true that Oliver was as upbeat and quirky as his mother, what reason would he have for this? Was it merely Bleary's influence, or had there been a true struggle there that they hadn't seen?

Bryce, Miss Popelin, Delilah... they all had their reasons for depression, things for Bleary to feed off. But Oliver? His death makes no more sense than Kaya's. I don't understand it either. Winter thought, tearing her gaze away from Oliver to look at his mother.

"I... I really don't know..." Winter answered weakly. She wasn't a good liar, and the way Charlene Blaikwood looked at her now proved it. In a hurry to avoid giving the details she couldn't give, she changed the subject, "Mrs. Blaikwood... C-Charlene, have you had anything to eat? Or drink?"

"Oh, that's where Liam went. I haven't been able to stomach anything."

"Why don't you go join him? I can sit with Ollie."

There were few people who could convince a worried mother to leave her injured child, but Winter was one of them. After a few minutes of fussing about, Charlene gave Winter another hug and left the room, sliding the door shut behind her.

Pulling a chair up to the side of the bed, Winter sat down and took hold of Oliver's hand, settling in to talk to him.

"Ollie... I wish this hadn't happened to you. I'm so sorry...

Of all the people to get wrapped up in this, you and Kaya hurt the worst. But Axel and I, we've got a plan. Well, sort of. We're trying. We're going to face it. I don't care what Axel says. It might have come from him, but none of this would have happened if not for me."

Maybe I should tell him. Maybe I should explain, even though he's asleep.

"Would you think differently of me if I told you I have a secret? A really, really big secret?" Winter whispered, bowing her head and closing her eyes.

She remembered when Oliver and her became close friends, back when they were young kids. He had a treehouse in his backyard, and the three of them— her, him, and Kaya — would climb up there after school and spend hours together, hanging out.

"Do you remember the day we made our pinkie promise not to keep things from each other? Kaya knew then, but you didn't... I've thought about telling you a hundred times, but I just..."

I can't. It's bad enough I'm a freak, the more people who know, the worse it will be.

"...I'm just a bad friend. The worst. I should have listened to Papa. I should just keep to myself, and not say a word, and... and..."

"And stop beating yourself up. Here I am in a cast, and you have more bruises than I do." A low, husky voice interrupted her, squeezing her hand.

"Ollie!" Winter cried out, her eyes flashing open to see Oliver looking back. His eyes were drooping, heavy and tired looking, but he was alert enough to make her heart start racing, relief flooding through her.

"Hey, Win... What's with the self trial? I'm the... idiot who stepped in front of a moving car..." He sounded drowsy, wincing, he managed to give her a crooked half smile.

Does he remember it, or did his parents tell him?

"Why did you do it, Ollie? I mean… Why d-didn't you… I don't know, call me, or someone, anyone?" Winter asked, frowning at him.

Oliver's face shifted into a troubled expression, his eyes looking far away. The brown irises seemed darker than his usual warm chocolate eyes, and for a second, they swam in sadness, like he was back to standing by the side of the road. Winter, knowing he was the one-and-only Bleary survivor to date, was studying him closely as he tried to answer her.

"I… I was alone. Or I felt alone. I'm not… I don't know, Win. It just felt…" He shivered, glancing down at himself as he searched for the words. "It felt like… like I had no choice. I was just walking home, and I remember stopping and watching the road, and… and—"

Suddenly, Oliver's eyes widened, recognition coming across his face.

"What? What is it?" Winter asked urgently, clutching his hand tighter.

"Whispers. I don't know if my mind was messing with me or what, but I swear I heard— Well— it sounded like Aspen. But that's ridiculous, right?" Frowning, Oliver's face sank with exhaustion again, as he admitted, "I don't remember much past that. I just… I remember feeling a little lost, and alone, and… and missing him, more than usual. So I stepped out into the road, and then I woke up here. Mom started screaming when I woke up— the first sound I heard was her screeching for the doctor."

"Can you blame her?" Winter smiled, trying not to react to the news of his experience of whispers. It had certainly *not* been Aspen Blaikwood's ghost that urged Oliver into the road.

"No, no I can't."

"I'm just as glad you're awake. You made the news, you know."

This brought a weak grin to Oliver's face.

"I did? Did you record it? I'm going to want to watch that when I get out of here."

"I didn't, but I'm sure we can get a copy. You're going to need it for your sensational rise to fame as the boy who survived being hit by a car."

Both of them laughed, Winter's shoulders shaking, though her smile turned to a look of concern as Oliver suddenly winced and swore.

"Damn. Hurts to laugh." He moaned out pitifully, laying his head back. Flexing his fingers in her grip, he sighed, "The doctors don't have a lot of hope for me, do they? Mom won't say it, but I can tell. I won't walk again. Will I, Winter?"

Winter stared at him, her face shifting from concern to careful blankness, and then to an attempted smile. But her lips shook, quivering as tears rose to her eyes, her composure crumpling. She began to shake her head, lifting a hand to her mouth to try and hide as she broke down. Yet Oliver only, weakly, opened his arms so she could lean forward and lay her face against his chest, inhaling the scent of the hospital gown. Underneath the sterile stink was a hint of Oliver.

"...You never could hide your emotions, Win."

"I-I'm s-so-so s-s-sorry."

"Don't be... I've had nothing but lies ever since I woke up. The honesty is refreshing."

Despite him saying that, his voice shook too, holding it together only slightly better than her. Things would never be the same, Winter thought. Not for Oliver... Not for any of them.

When Winter arrived home, sniffling in the cold evening air, Axel was sitting on the bench in her front yard, by the rose bushes that were covered with snow. He offered up a smile, standing and tugging his headphones down around his neck before stuffing his hands in his hoodie's pockets.

"Hey." He spoke up, nodding towards her as his gaze looked her up and down, studying her.

"Hey…" Winter repeated the greeting, returning a smile that didn't reach her eyes, hugging herself as she shuffled towards him. "You waited for me?"

"Figured you could use some company, after. How's Oliver? Was he awake? Did you get to talk to him?" Axel asked, following her as she moved past him and trudged up the steps of the porch.

"Yeah, I got to talk to him." Winter sighed, pushing open the front door. She looked back at Axel and frowned.

"Didn't papa invite you in? Why are you sitting out here in the snow?"

"The choice between sitting by a warm fire and watching your old man polish his gun, or sitting outside in the cold… What a tough choice." His tone dripped with sarcasm, and glancing into the house, Winter spotted her grandfather sitting in the living room— fast asleep in an armchair. His rifle was sitting on the coffee table in front of him, undisturbed.

"Fair point. Well, come in now then." Winter offered.

Axel hesitated, and then nodded, following her through the house into the kitchen. He slipped into a seat at the kitchen table as Winter set about making them hot cocoa. As she set out mugs, got milk and cocoa out, and retrieved some spoons, she updated Axel on the talk with Oliver.

"So… he'll really never walk again?" Her friend asked when she had finished.

"They're not sure, but that's the grim undertone I was

picking up."

"Damn."

"And he heard Aspen."

"That's his little brother, right? The one he lost?"

"Yes." Winter heaved a heavy sigh, the very thought of the young boy sent shivers down her spine. Her back was to Axel, as she mixed their drinks, but she could feel his blue eyes boring into her. She was chewing on her bottom lip, waiting for the question she knew would come next.

"Win. How… How did Aspen commit?" There it was.

Turning around to face him, Winter gave a tight smile as she carried their cocoas over to the table, taking the seat across from Axel. She set her mug on top of a stack of old magazines, pulling her hair out of a ponytail as she told him the grim tale.

"Aspen was a-a sweet kid. But he was always a little… Well, he was a loner. A bit like you, actually. He was going places, clever and inventive, and… charming, like Oliver, but shy. Much more shy. He didn't have a very high opinion of himself, and he constantly second guessed everything he said. Couldn't even walk into a restaurant and give his own order, he was so painfully anxious."

Playing with the necklace around her neck, Winter had a faraway look in her eyes as she murmured, "He was just… struggling. Oliver saw it, and did what he could, but… sometimes you can only be there for someone so much, you know?"

Axel gave a small nod of his head. He had cupped the mug of cocoa between his hands, but didn't take a single sip, his entire focus on the sorrow drawn across Winter's face, listening as she continued.

"One day… Aspen had been pretty badly bullied. He left school early— skipped his afternoon classes, ran all the way home. Oliver thought he would just be waiting at home for him, but... when he went home, Aspen wasn't there. But there was a note. A suicide note from a nine year old— isn't that horrific?" She visibly shuddered, closing her eyes. "I was there with Oliver, and he asked me to wait at the house, call his parents' work and let them know Aspen had run off. By the time we caught up to them... Oliver was pulling Aspen's body from the Effugere river.

"During the spring, when the rains start, that river can get really high... And there's this one point, on the far side, that is real jagged and hard to navigate. Thrill seekers usually try to paddle-board it, there's injuries every year from people being idiots in the river rapids."

"Yeah, I know it. Kaius made that ride once. Came home with a broken arm." Axel answered, remembering how upset his mother had been.

"Well... Aspen had gone to the river and he... just jumped in. He couldn't swim, he knew it would drag him under. Oliver had nightmares of his blue face for months— it was rough on the whole family. He was so young, and he just hadn't found his purpose in life yet. He thought he never would, and didn't want to wait to look for it. He thought, with his speech issues, that he was really doomed, and... we just didn't know, Axel. We knew he felt bad about it, but we didn't know *how* bad."

Silence fell between the two teenagers as Winter's retelling of the story ended, staring at each other over their cocoa cups. Axel didn't know what to say, so they finished their cocoa in the quiet of Winter's kitchen. For once, she didn't add to the silence with her questions, leaving Axel to ponder until he bid her goodnight and shambled back across the street.

The Dunn house was quiet when he let himself in, already dark, signaling his parents had gone to bed. It took a few minutes for Axel to pull off his boots and jacket and start heading upstairs, commencing his night time routine. Half an hour later, he was back in his room after a hot shower, one towel around his waist as he rubbed a smaller one against his hair. The wet mop of black curls splayed across his face, as he tried to seek out his phone, having heard it chime with messages.

W: I put a candle in the window. For Kaya and Oliver.

Dropping his hair towel to his shoulder, Axel sat down on his bed and leaned against his windowsill, peering out across the street.

Winter's room was dark, except for the glow of a candle sitting in the window, flickering orange light in memory of their classmates.

But there was something else.

Axel's eyes caught it almost instantly, his heart near stopping. Standing on the sidewalk, with its black robes fluttering in the cold air, was Bleary. His monster might have been smiling, if it had a mouth. Instead, the gaping hollow seemed wider than normal, its eyes darker and glossier in the evening's moonlight. Its hood was down, the gray skin of its hollow skull gleaming.

Staring at it, Axel's mouth went dry. A cold dread shivered down his spine as the creature they called Bleary raised a hand, its long fingers seeming to wave at him.

"Her death will be your fault. Her death will be your fault. Her death will be your fault." A voice echoed in the back of his mind, as clear as day, sounding like his own voice, but reverberating, an echo that made his hands go to his ears.

"Stop it." Axel muttered, closing his eyes.

"You can't save her from herself." The voice, this time, seemed to come from behind him, like a whisper at the tip of his ear.

Startled, Axel turned around, eyes flashing open— but all there was to see was his dark room, entirely alone.

"AXEL!" The shrill scream of Winter sounded in his mind, like the shrieking of Bleary's shrieking cry.

Whirling around again, the nauseous teenage boy looked out the window once more.

Bleary was gone. And the light in Winter's window had gone dark.

Axel lunged towards his phone, dialing Winter's number in a rush.

Pick up. Pick up. FREAKING. PICK. UP.

"Axel?" Winter's voice sounded bleary, not the monstrous kind, as she answered the phone.

"Are you okay!" Axel's voice demanded, his heart racing.

"What? Yes, of course I am."

"Why did your candle go out?"

"Uh, maybe because I'm going to sleep and didn't want to burn my house down?" Axel could hear shuffling sounds as Winter sat up, stifling a yawn. "Axel, what's going on?"

"I… No. It's nothing. Sleep well, Win."

"...Yeah, you too. Sweet dreams, Axe." She sounded uncertain, like she could sense something was off, but her desire for sleep won over her need of asking questions.

The line clicked off, and Axel slowly lowered his phone, dropping it onto his bed. Looking out the window, there were no more signs of Bleary, and no mysterious sounds scratching in the back of his mind.

It was just taunting me, right? Just another way to mess with my mind. Axel thought.

Still… It took him a very long time to fall asleep that night.

20

UNCONVINCED VICTIM

"I could come up with better questions than this assignment." A bored sounding Winter said to Axel. They sat at a group table in the back of their social studies class, a ton of textbooks and worksheets laid out in front of them, along with some maps. Sitting across from them were the Chi twins, and to their right, at the end of their table, was Noelle.

This class was run by their chillest professor— Mr. Cooley. His son Korin was a senior, one of the footballers. Mr. Cooley himself was a broad, tall man with broad shoulders, big glasses, and an afro. He always dressed in impeccable formal wear, but had one of the most relaxed classes because— more often than not— he just gave them a chapter of their textbook and some questions to answer, and left them to it.

"Shoot." Axel sighed, dropping a pencil onto his textbook. "Anything is better than documenting every detail of the dismantling of Prussia."

"At least it's better than last week's lesson, tracking trade through all of the African states." Noelle piped up, picking at her nails.

"Okay, so—" Winter began, only to be interrupted,

"Hey, guys? What's going on outside?" It had been Tae-Won who had spoke, gazing out the window. His twin turned to get a good look over his head, gawking, and soon Axel and Winter were rising from the table to look as well. In fact, all the students in their class turned their attention outside, whispers and confusion filling the room.

Outside, everyone seemed to come to a halt. People walking across the courtyard were frozen, pointing upwards in horror. Mouths agape, startled cries could be heard through their class-room's partially open windows. Within seconds, more people were making their way out to the courtyard, even teachers starting to go outside. As Mr. Cooley himself ducked into the hall, excusing himself from the class, some students moved to follow him, while some were still glued to the windows.

"What's happening?" Winter asked, naive as she was. Turning her head, she looked at Axel and saw the grim look on his face.

"Someone's on the roof." He answered her. It didn't take a genius to figure that out.

Soon, they were running from the class too, making their way down the stairwell. As they jogged down the steps, they brushed by several students and teachers. But as they made their way towards the main doors of the school, a group of girls were running inside, trying to pass them. Axel's hand reached out, grabbing the elbow of Lupita Alvarez, the Prin-cipal's niece.

"Who is it?!" Axel barked at her, ignoring the shocked look on the girl's face.

"I-It looks like B-Brooks, Jovanni Brooks!" She stam-mered, as his hand slipped from her arm. Without another look, she kept going upstairs, leaving Axel frozen on the bottom step of the stairwell.

Winter's hand gripped the front of his hoodie and snapped him out of it, making him look down to meet her wide, hazel-green eyes.

"Axel. You have to go to him, he's your friend."

Friend. It wasn't a word he had used for Jovanni before, but it echoed in his mind.

"Go! Get to the roof, I'll watch from down here. If anyone can talk him down, it's you. He hasn't jumped yet, maybe he's fighting Bleary off." Her tone was urgent, pleading with him, her hands shaking against his chest, "We couldn't save anyone else. Please try!"

Axel felt sick. His skin had gathered a clammy sweat, his heartbeat racing alongside the clambering footsteps of people rushing around them. He didn't want to do this. He wanted to be anywhere but there. He didn't want to speak to Jovi, to see him in the state that he, himself, had been in so many times.

But Winter was right.

It had to be him.

"Okay." He breathed, nodding. Their eyes met, Winter's filled with the desperation to not have another death today. Axel wondered if his mirrored hers, or if he was successful in looking unafraid.

Regardless, she let him go and he turned to run up the stairwell once more, as she headed for the front door.

Clamare Highschool was four floors high, and only had one stairwell with roof access. The further Axel got, the fewer people he ran into, until he reached the roof door— where two teachers blocked the way. Neither Principal Alvarez or Mr. Poe were looking his way, both of them peeking out the door.

"Shouldn't we be trying to talk to him, Jackie?" Goddard

Poe said to Jackson Alvarez, one hand gripping his shoulder, the other holding the door open.

"No. I don't want to spook him. We wait for the police, Poe." The principal murmured in response, holding a walkie-talkie to his lips, "Latisha, what's the status on Chi?"

A static-filled response from their vice principal came, "Called it in, they should be here any minute."

Creeping closer, Axel knew he had to do something before they did. They were right, after all, if they intervened, Jovanni was more likely to jump just out of rebellion against 'the man', as he always said. Taking a deep breath, Axel bent down, eyeing the space between the two men.

If I run past fast enough, they won't stop me once I'm out there... He thought, hesitating to make his move. Reaching back, Axel yanked up his hood over his head, swearing quietly as he tried to will himself to move. *I have to do this. I have to get out there and talk him down.*

Finally, his body moved despite his fear, and he barreled underneath the arms of his two teachers, bursting right through the space between them and tossing himself out onto the roof.

"HEY! STOP!" His principal hollered after him, unable to see who it was with his hood drawn— but Axel had been right. The teachers stayed frozen in the doorway as Axel stumbled forward towards the suicidal student. Now, it was just them— at least, until the police arrived.

Jovanni Brooks was standing on the ledge at the front of the highschool, overlooking the courtyard. It was a sturdy, flat stone ledge— something that was difficult to lose your footing on, unless you were messing around or deliberately stepped off. Below them was a sea of pavement and people. Practically all of the school was looking up at him now, waiting to witness the horrifying end of his life.

"J-Jov-Jovi." Axel couldn't keep his voice from shaking as he called his name, stumbling closer with his hands out. For all his experience with suicide, it was entirely different to be on the other end. He was more used to trying to convince himself to die than he was trying to convince someone else not to.

If I can just get him off the ledge... That's all I have to do. Talk him down, Axel. He thought, looking up at Jovanni. Those words, 'talk him down', were repeating in his head like a mantra, his goal echoing in his thoughts. Axel was lucky that they were far enough from the door to prevent their teachers from listening in on their conversation.

Strangely, Jovanni looked peaceful. Despite tears rolling down his cheeks, he was smiling, a breeze fluttering his long, dark hair. He looked like a dark angel— the same description Winter had once given Axel— wearing a baggy trench coat that was flapping in the cold air. It was a cloudy day, snow on the ground below, but Axel was shivering for entirely different reasons as his friend looked back at him.

"H-Hey Dunn. Come to catch front row seats to the show?" Jovanni sarcastically greeted him. As his jaw moved, Axel could see bruises against his fair skin, etched across one side of his face and around his neck.

"Not my type of show, man. Why don't you come down and we'll go do something else instead?"

"Can't do that." Jovi sighed, a warm fog cloud billowing from his mouth, "Gotta give into it now, too late to turn back."

"Never too late. That's bull and you know it." Axel didn't entirely believe that, but his voice didn't fail him, keeping steady, "You don't have to listen to that bastard."

Where is it? Axel briefly glanced around them, but the roof was empty besides their teachers hovering at the door, watching with wide-eyes. He heard no whispers, no screeching, nothing at the back of his mind but his own thoughts, fighting to keep calm. *It was just messing with me with Winter, so... so is this Bleary's real target? Jovi?*

To his surprise, Jovanni laughed. A real, amused chuckle that shook his shoulders, scuffling his feet to scrape some snow off the ledge and watching it fall below.

"That bastard? That... bastard! I spend all my life listening to him. His... His judgement and his b-blame and his fucking complaints. No. I'm not listening to him any more, Axel. I'll see him in hell." Jovanni's voice dripped with venom and anger, grinning back at him.

"Don't you think it's too good for him to have the pleasure of seeing you? Better to let him go. You can stay right here, make your own path. That's the biggest middle-finger there is, isn't it?" Axel attempted to reason with him, swallowing his nerves. He had been talking about Bleary, but it felt like Jovi had someone else entirely on his mind.

"Now who's spewing bullshit, Dunn?" Jovanni asked, scoffing. He wasn't wrong. "There's no winning here. You know what they think of us. What they all think!" He gestured to the crowd below, "They'll gossip for a while, I'm sure. Get their kicks off the 'horror' of my death. Suiciders are weak. That's how they think of us. It doesn't matter what I do or don't do. I'm just going down as some weakling who couldn't take the heat. Why don't I just 'man up,' right? Why don't I just 'work a little harder,' huh?"

"You're preaching to the choir here, Jovi." Axel spoke, shaking his head. "Look at who I have for a mom. Don't you think she gets on my case every single day? That I'm not doing enough? I'm not living up to her expectations, either. I can't please her high standards. I can't prove her wrong when she says shit about me. It happens, but I'm still here, fighting. Same as you. Let them call us weak, we *both* know better."

Jovanni sniffled, reaching up to drag his sleeve across his dripping nose. Axel couldn't tell if it was dripping from tears or from the cold.

"Yeah, we know better. But I'm tired, Axe. It's real exhausting. I never have a break from these assholes. My very existence is an issue— an insult. I just need to be erased. Look at our classmates- dropping like flies. They've got the right idea."

"N-No, no they don't." Axel stammered. "Listen, Jovi, those suicides weren't suicides. They were murders, man. That's it, plain murder."

He meant it literally, Bleary on his mind, but Jovanni laughed,

"Hell. Of course they are! It's all murder. This world is killing us, Axel."

Behind them, Axel heard the feedback of their principal's walkie talkie, and right below, he could hear the sound of approaching sirens. He was running out of time to get Jovanni out of this without interference, and Jovanni seemed have the same realization.

"About time they got here. What line do you think they'll give me to 'save' my life?" Jovanni asked.

"The same ones I'm giving you. The good ol' 'don't do this.'" Axel answered, taking a step closer as sirens sounded in the distance. "You've got a life ahead of you. You can get away from your old man. Come stay with me for a while or something. We'll get out of highschool and leave this shit town."

"And go where? It's the same everywhere. People are people, Axel. No... This is where it ends for me."

"It doesn't have to. Jovanni, seriously, think about this. I know how it feels but—"

Just as he was speaking, a loud voice boomed over a megaphone,

"Jovanni Brooks. This is Officer Chi. I want you to do me a favor, son. Don't move. Just stay where you are, and we'll get you some help."

Jovanni snorted, shaking his head. "See? 'Do him a favor'... Even now, it's for everybody-fucking-else. They don't give a damn about me. They just want to avoid the paperwork and the messy cleanup afterwards."

"I care." Axel's voice was growing desperate now, a little higher in tone, sensing a losing battle. "Jovi, I give a damn. I don't want to see your body down there. Please, just... Let's go listen to music and get away from this crowd. Don't join the group of recent deaths. It's a bad way to go. If you get down, you can get some rest and we can work on this."

A glimmer of doubt came across Jovanni's face, dark eyes narrowing. He licked his lips, contemplating Axel's words.

"Hey Axel...?" He asked.

"Yeah?" Axel's heart was in his throat, hanging onto Jovanni's words.

"Do me a favor. Tell my old man how much I hated him." He said with a coy smile, "Tell him the best part of this is never having to listen to him again."

Axel froze, horror striking through him as he stammered out,

"J-Jovi, no. Screw that. Tell him yourself. You can *tell him yourself*. Don't you want to see the look on his face when you say your piece?"

Jovi ultimately didn't heed Axel's words. The tearstained goth looked down at the crowd of panicked students, before turning around to face his friend. For a moment, a flood of relief hit Axel, thinking that he was going to step away from the ledge and back onto the safety of the roof. Instead, Jovanni gave one of his sardonic smirks, lifting a hand. He made a pistol with his fingers, putting it to his temple.

"*Bang!* Bye, bye." Those were the last, whispered words Jovanni Brooks uttered when, with his arms stretched out, he took a step backwards.

"NO!" Axel's shriek echoed off the roof as he lunged forward. He crashed into the side of the ledge, hands clawing at the stone, but it was too late to grab his friend. Blue eyes, wide and horrified, watched him falling, the crowd scattering backwards with yells of shock.

Right before Jovanni hit the ground Axel ducked behind the ledge, squeezing his eyes shut as the sickening sound of Jovanni's body hitting the pavement filled the air, the white snow soon-to-melt with hot, red blood. For a moment, everything was deafeningly silent, before the screams and cries of the witnesses resumed.

On his hands and knees, Axel joined them, a loud scream rising out of him as he slammed his fists into the cement roof.

"DAMN YOU!" He hollered, a string of swears coming out of his mouth as he sat back against the roof ledge. His hands went to his head, gripping his hair roughly as his body curled forward.

It wasn't Jovi that he was swearing at. No. Axel could have blamed so many people at that moment— Jovanni, himself, Winter, Jovanni's pathetic excuse for a father, even their classmates. But none of them were as responsible as the monster in Axel's head.

Jovanni had always had his own version of Bleary, his own special brand of demon— but it had been Axel's, the one that came to life, that had led to this.

Hot tears rolled down Axel's cheeks, loud gasps coming from him as he finally broke down. He felt sick, hyperventilating as he sobbed harder, unable to stop the flow of emotions from slamming into him. Axel could take a lot, but this had done it, the floodgates breaking open with over-whelming force.

He had been at this very place himself. How many nights had he been ready to die? *Eager* to end it all? And still, when it came down to it, he had begged Jovanni to live— some-thing he would never do for himself— and it hadn't been enough. The feeling that ripped through Axel was indescrib-able, lowering his head to the ground. His body shook, exploding with emotions.

Anger, despair, guilt, regret... helplessness.

Why? Axel wanted to ask Bleary, even though he already knew the answer. *I'm already suffering. I'm already a goner. Why do you have to take them too? Jovi didn't deserve this shit!*

He had denied they were friends up until now, but besides Winter, Axel knew Jovanni best. He was the only one in their school that he had connected to on the same level of music, fashion, and social views. They didn't talk much about personal things, but they had a mutual understanding all the same.

Why hadn't I talked to him before now?

This question, unfortunately, also already had an answer.

Axel hadn't talked to anyone. Not for them, and certainly not for himself. He wanted to say that it was all Bleary that had caused this, but...

Some people needed less from Bleary than others. Jovanni hadn't been a mindless zombie like Kaya, caught in a vision. He hadn't been like Miss Popelin or Bryce. He hadn't needed much of a reason or a push at all. It had been all Jovanni, just on a bad, Bleary-influenced day. It wasn't a matter of some monster hypnotizing him.

It was just the truth: Jovi wanted to die, and he took action to do so.

This was what made Bleary *real,* not seeing him in a tangible form, but seeing him present in someone's mind.

A few minutes passed before the roof door was thrown open with a loud creak.

"You there!" God's— or rather Mr. Poe's— voice called out to him. He stood in the doorway, the principal behind him, both looking at Axel's hunched-over form in concern.

As the English teacher approached him in the corner of his eye, a breathless Axel pushed himself unsteadily to his feet, pulling his hood closer to his face to shield it from view as he turned. By the time Mr. Poe reached for him, Axel was running— pushing past him and Mr. Alvarez, his head ducked as he fled down the stairwell.

Axel pushed his way through the chaos of the school grounds, the distant sound of sirens, teachers trying to disperse the crowds of students. He kept his head down, attempting to hide his face, tears still freely streaming down his cheeks. He ignored everyone he could— until familiar hazel-green eyes floated into his vision.

Winter threw herself in his path, hands gripping onto his hoodie to bring him to a halt. He couldn't hide from her. She knew what hoodie he had been wearing, and had spotted him immediately as he tried to flee. As soon as she managed to, she released his hoodie and wrapped her arms around his waist instead, curling into him.

"Axel…" He could hear the pain in her voice, and to his relief, Winter didn't say anything else as he buried his face in her shoulder. Hugs were her way of comfort, and for once, Axel accepted it.

He stood there only a moment. As he tried to hold back his tears. His chest ached, lungs ready to burst as he took shallow breaths, his shoulders shaking violently in Winter's tight hold.

They had been through this before, when she had lost

Kaya. Winter knew she couldn't keep him there— no more than he could keep her there. So she let him go, peeking up into his face for a moment before she took a step back.

As soon as she did, Axel slipped away.

He couldn't be there to see the paramedics scrape Jovanni's broken body off the pavement.

Axel's eyes were closed, an arm draped over them to keep the sunlight out. A dozen things to do that day, and all he wanted was to lay in bed, letting each minute pass in silence. He was expecting his mother to barge in with a request that he be more productive— which is what he expected when his door creaked open. He heard an indrawn breath, someone preparing to speak, but it was followed by silence.

Well? What do you want? Axel thought, not wanting to move his arm and open his eyes to see the pinched scowl he was sure his mother was wearing.

Yet, instead of a lecture, he heard the soft sound of socks on the hardwood, approaching him. The creak of his bed as someone's body sat beside him. Lifting his arm above his head, he finally opened his eyes, ready to tell off whoever it was—

"Winter?" Her name dropped out of his mouth, seeing those pretty eyes staring down at him.

"You haven't been answering, so I came over." Her voice came out soft and soothing, like she was whispering to a napping child, "Your dad's home, he let me in."

Axel's phone lay untouched on the windowsill. How long had it been since he'd answered her? Friday after school? Today was... Sunday afternoon?

Closing his eyes again, Axel sighed.

"Sorry." He mumbled, guilt prickling at his conscience. It wasn't the first time, and they both knew it wouldn't be the last.

"It's okay, I don't mind." Winter answered. Was that true? At the moment, Axel was bitterly doubting it. He was sure it drove her crazy, but he felt the bed rock and shift as she lay down beside him. Her hair spread across his pillow, and he could smell her shampoo, some intoxicating fruity scent, like papaya or mango. Turning slightly onto his side, Axel wriggled to make more room for her on his twin-sized bed, already partially pressed against the wall as he let Winter hog the small space.

A long silence lulled between them, Axel not daring to open his eyes. He knew Winter would ask sooner than later, waiting for it.

"How's the fight going?" Her voice was still in a soft tone, compelling him to answer.

"What fight?" He played dumb, both of them aware of his reluctance.

"You know what fight." Finally, her tone changed, a sort of exasperation coming from Winter as her hand touched his arm, light as a feather through the sleeve of his sweater.

Axel took another few seconds of hesitation before answering her, hoping sarcasm might throw her off the topic, "With the one in my head or the one stalking our school?"

"Axel." Now he'd done it, he could tell from the way she said his name that his joke was in poor taste, and she wasn't going to let up.

Finally, he looked at her, and found her looking back, waiting on a real answer. He stared at her, and found himself beginning to talk freely.

"You should never beg a person to live. That's what I always thought. When someone wants to die… they are so tired, Winter, they want it to be over with. I always thought that there was no point in prolonging someone's suffering. It's why I don't talk about my shit. I don't need someone to beg me to stay, or give me all those lines about how it gets better and how I just need to 'hang on a bit longer.' But when it came down to it…" His lower lip quivered, bitter anger nagging at him as he continued, "…I wanted him to live. Jovi. I begged him to fight it. But he wasn't… fighting Bleary."

"What?" That got her attention, Winter's eyes widening.

"He wasn't fighting Bleary." Axel repeated himself. "I could tell. It wasn't Bleary, it was just… it was all Jovi. I wasn't telling him to fight against my monster, I was trying to convince him to fight against his own. I went against everything I've ever told myself, because I wanted to talk him out of it… and it didn't work."

"Oh, Axel…" Winter's voice dripped with sympathy, making him close his eyes to avoid the look on her face. "I'm so sorry. I'm sorry you couldn't stop him, but you did everything you could."

"I know that." Axel answered. And he did. Unlike most, who would say they could have done more, he had been there, where Jovanni had been, and he knew that you couldn't do more than that. He had tried, he had helped, and he had been there in Jovanni's final moments. Still, the sight of Jovanni stepping off the roof replayed behind his eyelids. "I know…" He repeated softly, before saying, "Do you mind leaving, Win? I just want to be alone."

"Yes, I mind." He felt her inch closer, laying up against him as she continued in a determined tone, "I don't want you to be alone."

"I won't do anything." Axel said, frowning. "There's been enough death, for now."

"I know you won't. But I want to stay beside you, Axel." She insisted.

"I don't feel like talking..." He mumbled. *Come on, just leave, Win.*

"Then we won't talk." He felt her arm curl around his own, her hand taking his and lacing their fingers together with a tight squeeze. Axel didn't stop her, listening to her whisper, "Please, Axel. I want to stay here with you."

All he did was give a slow nod, giving into her care. Before long, the only sound was their breathing, and the only feeling Axel focused on was the warmth of Winter hugging his arm. He was still lost in the aftermath of Jovanni's death. But he wasn't alone like he so often had been in the past.

21

UNWILLING PATIENT

Class sure is emptier these days... Winter couldn't help thinking. Zoning out in her math class, she unconsciously chewed on the end of a pen. For such dreary days, filled with death and monsters, the only thing Winter felt at this moment was utter boredom.

Everyone looked up when the classroom door opened and Miss Prince, the vice principal, entered. She wore a bright blue dress that hugged her figure and contrasted against her dark skin, her hair in a braided updo. Giving a smile through thickly painted lips, she scanned the classroom until her eyes landed right on Winter.

"Mrs. Chi, I'd like to borrow Miss Jozefson for a few moments, if you don't mind."

Everyone was staring at her now. Winter dropped her pen abruptly, pausing to look at Mrs. Chi. The elderly teacher glanced from their vice principal to her, and nodded.

"Of course, Miss Jozefson, go ahead."

Standing, Winter turned to grab her things. Axel looked as confused as she was. Giving him a quick smile, she moved to slip out of the class, following the vice principal in a fast walk down the hall.

Winter was led to Miss Prince's office, her eyes widening to see two familiar faces waiting for them. Leaning on the wall in the back of the office was the school nurse, Mr. Kelp — a young, fit man with emerald-green eyes and a head full of curly blonde hair— and sitting in a chair, in front of the vice principal's desk, was her grandfather.

"Papa?" Winter asked, surprised to see him. Normally, her retired grandfather would spend his days chatting with his buddies at the hardware store or the fish and tackle shop on Timor Street, or stay at home. He never came to her school— not even for family events. But here he was, wearing a pair of tan slacks and a tucked-in plaid shirt, peering at her with his dull blue-gray eyes.

Sinking into the chair beside him, Winter watched Miss Prince move around the desk to take her seat.

"A-Am I in trouble?" Winter asked, earning a snort from her grandfather.

"That's what I asked, too, when they called me to come down here." He grumbled, rubbing a hand along his jaw.

"Not in trouble, no. This is regarding Mr. Brooks." Miss Prince said, looking mournful now as she continued, "We understand you were one of the witnesses to his death."

Baffled, Winter glanced between her grandfather and the vice principal.

"One of like... a hundred other people. Not including those watching from the windows— wasn't everyone a witness to his death?" Nervous, Winter's voice came out sarcastically without meaning to, uncomfortably wringing her hands in her lap.

"Yes, we're aware. Miss Jozefson, losing a classmate— a friend— is a terrible thing. I know you were rather close with Miss Morito and Mr. Blaikwood, and now, Mr. Brooks."

"I wasn't close to Jo— erm… Mr. Brooks."

"No, but you shared several classes with him." Miss Prince frowned at her. "Miss Jozefson, you've been at the heart of a lot of tragedies recently. We're concerned about your well-being."

Winter took this to mean they thought she was a suicide risk. Or at least, they were trying to cover their bases. For some reason, this struck a sour note with her, narrowing her eyes at the vice principal in a look of disbelief. Maybe Axel was rubbing off on her, but now the biting tone she spoke with was entirely on purpose.

"Sorry, but were you concerned about Jovanni's well-being, too? Before he took a swan-dive, that is."

"Winter!" Her grandfather barked her name, and Winter knew why. She had never spoken back to an authority figure before. But she wasn't wrong.

Jovi had always been a risk. Everyone knew it. He wasn't like Axel, keeping everything to himself, playing off as just a quiet kid dressed in black. Jovanni Brooks was that kid that people whispered about behind his back. When the school shooting at Columbine happened, Jovi had been the target of some particular hazing— people pushing him around, glaring at him, whispering that he would be the next killer. It had been disgusting, but… even Winter had been wary of him after that— she couldn't deny he made her nervous. Jovi was the type of guy that liked to joke about death, and no one could ever tell if his sense of humor was really that dark, or if he just had a perverse love of scaring those around him. Winter suspected it might have been both. She also suspected that if Axel wasn't seen by his side so often, Axel himself might have had more friends.

"It's okay, Tage." Miss Prince said to him, before giving Winter a tight smile. "We were. It's unfortunate that Mr.

Brooks didn't accept our help. But there's still a chance for his friends." She slid a single business card across her desk.

Picking it up, Winter frowned.

Dr. R. Kelp, Psychiatry... Malum Sanitarium.

"You want to send me to the mental hospital?!" Winter asked in alarm, looking towards her grandfather— though it was Mr. Kelp who answered her,

"Not exactly. Dr. Kelp— my uncle— takes appointments on an out-patient level. He sees all sorts of people, and has offered his services for grief counseling for the school."

Finally, her grandfather spoke,

"I think it's a good idea, Pumpkin. Just a single afternoon session, after school." He hesitated, and then tapped two fingers on the card that Winter still held. "Your mother went to him, you know. Dr. Kelp has been around for years."

I don't like this. Winter thought, jittery as she turned the business card over and over in her hand. Despite the dread she felt, she gave the answer they were expecting— a hesitant acceptance of what they wanted her to go through. What other choice did she have?

"And Miss Jozefson?" Miss Prince's smooth voice caught her attention again a few minutes later as Winter moved to leave the office with her grandfather.

"Yes?"

"You're welcome to extend the offer to any of your friends who have been impacted by the recent losses. Mr. Dunn, perhaps?"

It took all her power not to laugh in the vice principal's face. Winter already knew the reaction he would have.

"...I'll be sure to tell him."

"No." Axel scoffed, leaning back against a bookshelf.

"Why not?" Winter asked, sitting across from him. Everyone was excited for winter break, and as a result, the library was largely empty, save a few bookworms before everything closed until January. Axel and Winter sat in the psychology section, ironically, which Winter had been idly going through while she told him all about her meeting with the vice principal.

"If I go into that place, they'll never let me out again." Like all members of Caligo, Axel had grown up hearing horrible rumors swirling around Malum Sanitarium. With his issues, he didn't want to go anywhere near it.

"So you're going to let me go?" Winter sounded offended, making him roll his eyes.

"You're sane— they won't do anything to you."

"I'm n—" Winter began to speak, her tone high and petulant, but she stopped herself. Axel looked curiously at her, wondering what had made her object, her cheeks beginning to burn. Whatever it was, she shook her head at him instead. "Listen, just come with me. Please, Axel. That place creeps me out as much as you. It isn't mandatory but Papa really wants me to go, because my mom did, and I guess he thinks it'll help me too. He's been asking way too many questions about the suicides lately— maybe he thinks I'm involved, or at risk. But he won't let it go and I... I don't want to go alone."

In any other situation, Axel would have swore and told her there was no way he was going to a mental hospital with her. But Winter's eyes were big with worry, and he squirmed underneath her gaze, rubbing the back of his neck with his hand.

Why did it have to be at the mental hospital? Couldn't the quack doctor come to the school?

Groaning, Axel hung his head. "Fine. I will drive you over.

But I'm waiting outside. I'm not having a freaking appointment."

He couldn't say if the sudden relief on Winter's face was worth it, but at least he didn't have to be the patient.

"Thanks, Axe. Really, I'll feel much better with a getaway driver." Winter sighed, stacking a pile of books by her side. The last one looked massive— at least six hundred pages or more— causing Axel to frown. For all the writing there was on people's inner demons, you would think it wouldn't have as much stigma as it did. As Axel watched her, Winter continued, "What about you? Did your mom mention grief counseling at all?"

The question earned a laugh, tossing his head back so his dark curls flopped out of his eyes. "You're kidding, right? My mom thinks therapists are scam artists and anyone who goes to them just needs to toughen up. She's not going to entertain any of her sons going to therapy. She already has done her fair share of shit talking about it."

A strange look came across Winter's face.

"What?"

"...Nothing."

"Winter."

"No, it's just... I was thinking... um... Two things. Firstly, your mom wouldn't like me very much." Winter admitted hesitantly, looking down at the books she was sorting.

"She already doesn't." Axel admitted bluntly. There was no use hiding that. His mom didn't like much of anyone. "And the second thing?"

"That you disliking therapy makes sense... besides your issues, I mean. No one would want to go if everyone around them only had bad things to say about it."

Axel couldn't argue with that. Sure, he didn't want to go and talk about his issues— it wasn't as simple for him as it was for some. People could often go on about their days, complain endlessly over their problems, and he just... couldn't. The shame of that was too high, it was pathetic in his eyes. His mother's constant negativity about it didn't help.

Maybe he was being stubborn, and he knew it. He knew therapy could help people, but he didn't trust the sanitarium on Timor street, or the infamous Dr. Kelp. Places like that, for people like him? In Axel's mind, all he could imagine was they would take one look into the darkness of his mind, where the real Bleary lurked, and throw him into a padded cell, tossing away the key and leaving him to rot.

All he could do was shrug his shoulders, and murmur a phrase his mother had ingrained in him from a young age— or at least, the English translation.

"It can't be helped."

Shikata ga nai.

Two days later, they were on their way to Malum Sanitarium. Axel was on edge, gripping the wheel of his Camaro tightly as they rumbled down Timor street. He had dressed in all black for the occasion— and in comparison, Winter sat beside him looking angelic in a big white sweater and white jeans. The only flash of color on her was her red scarf, borrowed back from Axel. Normally, it might have fit her tanned complexion and rosy cheeks, but today she looked as washed out and white as her clothes. Her face drained of blood and her expression queasy as they grew closer to the most unsettling building in Caligo. Axel couldn't help but envision the red scarf like a line of blood against her throat. He had a sense of dread he couldn't shake, and a bitter echo of the cliche line, *"It's all in your head."*

If there was one word to describe Malum Sanitarium, it was dead. Rolling up to large chain-link fences with barbed-wire on the top, the place had the look of a prison rather than a hospital. Just across the street was the cheery, bright Salvare Vita Hospital. With Salvare's beautiful garden and large parking lot, it contrasted horribly with Malum Sanitarium's red brick, black roof, gargoyle statues, and bars on every entrance. It was like a horror movie.

Strange that our town has both Heaven and Hell at its entrance, Axel thought, glowering through his windshield.

"Did you know that gargoyles are meant to ward off evil spirits?" Winter whispered, shivering beside him.

"They're doing a shitty job of it." Axel answered, eyeing the contorted, ugly statues.

Rolling through a security checkpoint, they had to provide their identification— Axel's driver's license and Winter's student ID— before the officer would open the gates. When he did, Axel didn't miss the scathing look the officer gave as he handed back his license followed by the remark of,

"Hope your visit is… helpful."

Of course he thinks I belong here and not Winter. Irritation filled him, hitting the gas a little harder than he meant to, the car jolting forward into the sanitarium parking lot.

Once they came to a stop, Winter got out and paused, turning back to look at him.

"You'll be here when I'm done?" She asked, her voice uneven.

"Yeah. I'm not going anywhere."

As soon as the promise left his lips, someone called out,

"Miss Jozefson!"

Both their gazes turned to a pristine figure crossing the parking lot towards them. She was a bigger woman— wide hips, large bust, broad shoulders— but she was dressed in a full pantsuit, with a white doctor's coat over it. She was dark-skinned, with black hair pulled into a bun, and dark burgundy lipstick. Sharp eyes regarded them behind a pair of bright red-framed glasses, extending a hand to Winter as she reached them.

"Luanne Henderson. I believe you were... one of the students to find my Delly." Her voice had a tinge of a southern accent, lilting her words.

If Winter hadn't looked pale before, she definitely was now, choking as she awkwardly shook the woman's hand.

"U-Uh-" She stammered, lost for words.

"Don't worry. I don't blame you. Delilah had... so many issues. She was a patient of Dr. Kelp as well, but I'm afraid it didn't help her in time." Dr. Henderson seemed kind, Axel noted, though it wasn't hard to see the heartache as she spoke about her daughter.

"I-I didn't know..." Winter managed to mumble as Dr. Henderson released her hand.

"I know, dear. No one did. Delly didn't like talkin' about her problems. Women like us, we need to be strong, hm?"

Both Axel and Winter could see the resemblance between Dr. Henderson and her daughter. Delilah's strength and fearless attitude reflected in her mother.

Finally noticing him, Dr. Henderson turned her focus to Axel.

"You must be one of Tim's sons, yes? He handled my divorce, Great man." It took effort to smile back at her, the mention of his father leaving a sour taste in his mouth as she continued, "You comin' in, honey? I think Dr. Kelp could make some time."

"No thanks." Axel replied dryly.

"Just us girls, then. Come on in, Winter. Ask anyone— it's never good to keep a doctor waiting. Quite hypocritical though, they don't offer their patients the same courtesy."

The attempt of humor brought on a weak smile from Winter. Yet, as Dr. Henderson placed a hand on her shoulder, steering her towards the door, Winter craned her neck to look back at Axel as she walked away.

Axel called out in what he hoped to be a reassuring tone,

"I'll be right here!"

He watched as she was led through the doors of the looney bin, waiting until they shut behind her before reaching for the dial of his car radio.

The outside of the sanitarium was foreboding, but the inside was worse. Queasy, Winter's focus followed the heavy doors as they shut behind her with a metallic thud. Low ceilings and linoleum floors. There were too-bright lights overhead that were shaped like small saucers, and Winter smelled the off-putting scent of bleach in the air. Up ahead was a security checkpoint. Dr. Henderson guided her through a metal detector and a bag search.

Easier to keep things out... or keep them in? God, I sound like Axel, don't I? Relax, Winter, it's just security measures.

"Dr. Henderson, uh... do you have high risk patients here?" Winter asked, following her down a hall.

"Oh, a few. Mostly we specialize in patients with delusions— the kind of people whose realities don't match, well, reality. They tend to try to wander. Don't let this place scare you, the patients are harmless." She took a pause before adding, "And please, call me Luanne. I'm a PharmD, you know. I take care of the balance of medications for patients, both here and Salvare Vita, split shifts. The Dr. title is nice, but unnecessary."

That makes sense. No wonder Delilah knew what medications to take and was writing her own script.

They continued down a hallway, Winter craning her neck to look for patients, but there were none to be found.

"Is um… is everyone at lunch or something?" *Or in padded cells, locked away.* There were a lot of strange rumors that floated around about this place— Clamare High's favorite spooky story.

"No, no. This floor is for outpatient processing and our personal offices, as well as the pharmacy. The patients are on the floors above us."

"How many floors are there?"

"Four, honey. Five if you count the basement, but no one ever goes down there, it's just old patient file storage."

As they came to a stop at the door at the end of the hall, a small plaque read, "Dr. Rupert Kelp, PsyD.". Luanne wasted no time in rapping her knuckles on the door.

"Come in!" A low, breathy male voice answered.

Opening the door, Luanne ushered her in, putting on a bright smile as she regarded her boss, "Good afternoon, Doctor. Here's your next Clamare High appointment, Miss Jozefson. I ran into her and a friend in the parking lot." Luanne pat Winter on the shoulder and slipped back out of the room, leaving her abruptly.

The man sitting at the desk in the middle of the room rose to greet her. He was barely Winter's height, clad in an old-fashioned three-piece suit, plaid fabric with a burgundy tie. His doctor's coat was folded neatly on the back of the chair behind him, and he was holding a silver pocket watch connected by a chain to his suit, which he promptly tucked away as he held his hand out to Winter.

Taking it, she flinched. His skin was ice-cold.

"Sorry, dear. Poor circulation." Dr. Kelp told her, giving a denture-filled grin. He had to be nearing seventy, not quite as old as her grandfather, but old enough to have a face full of markings- not only wrinkles, but freckles and moles, with a bristling mustache of sharp, little white hairs. He had eyes as green as his nephew, though darker, and a head of white and gray tinged hair that Winter thought must have once been as blonde as his handsome nephew's, the school nurse. But where the nurse gave off an athletic, arrogant vibe, his uncle was much more unnerving, his stare piercing, already examining her. "A friend, ey? Wouldn't they have liked to have come in?"

"Sorry, he... isn't a fan of hospitals." Winter apologized for Axel, both jealous and relieved that he didn't have to go through this too.

"I understand, Miss Jozefson. Not everyone can stomach seeing illness right in front of them— mental illness least of all. It *is* the ugliest of diseases." Dr. Kelp responded, dropping into his chair with a groan. It clattered as he pushed it forward, opening a leather notebook in front of him with a fluttering of pages. He reached for a pen, the click of it causing Winter's eye to twitch.

Dr. Kelp's office was, strangely, not as clinical as she had expected it to be. Rich woods and dark tiled floors made up the small room. Awards for psychology lined the walls, photos of Dr. Kelp shaking hands with his success stories— reformed patients, Winter assumed, or their families. He had a massive bookcase behind him, filled with heavy leather-bound psychology books. Someone so well read had to know what he was doing, right?

Maybe Axel is wrong to dislike this place. Maybe I can learn something useful, not just for Bleary, but for him? Would he even let me tell him if I did? Winter could tell Axel's own distrust and fear was rubbing off on her.

"Miss Jozefson?"

Dr. Kelp's voice snapped her back to attention, Winter

folding her hands in her lap as she looked up. He was poised to take notes, watching her.

"Y-Yes?"

"Would you mind me asking a few questions?"

"Isn't that the point?" Winter asked in return. Noticing the tone of her voice, she reluctantly apologized, "Sorry."

Dr. Kelp gave a strange, wheezing laugh. "Don't be. That is exactly the point. If you were a long term patient of mine, I might have a few exercises for you, but today, I just want to chat. Now... Let me start by telling you how very sorry I am for your losses. I understand you've had a few friends among the students that have taken their lives. It is tragic."

All Winter did was nod her head, peeking back up at him. She picked at her fingers, toying with the skin at the edge of her nail.

"Did you know anything about the suicides prior?"

"No."

"What about just plain odd behavior, around school maybe? Often in these situations, we wonder about a pact that may have formed. Have you ever heard of a self-harm pact?" She shook her head, and he continued, "Sometimes, students band together to perform an act together. Female students, for instance, may plan to get pregnant together. That would be a pregnancy pact. Or... Misguided students may plan to commit suicide together. A statement, you might say. In the news lately, you might have heard about that Columbine shooting. Two young men who decided to attack others, and ultimately committed suicide. They likely had a pact, a plan for their unforgivable actions. Have you heard anything like that going on?"

Winter furrowed her brows at the doctor, frowning.

"No." She said again.

"And have you ever harbored any suicidal feelings of your

own? Something that you might find shameful to talk about?"

"No."

"Have you ever considered harming yourself or others?"

"No!" This time, her voice took on an incredulous tone, the question taking her off guard.

Dr. Kelp scribbled something in his notebook, looking thoughtful.

Do my short answers give him assumptions? Winter wondered, shifting in her seat.

"What about your home life? I've met your grandfather, Mr. Jozefson. A good man— he cares so much about his family. But it can't be easy, raising his granddaughter. Is everything okay at home?"

Avoiding the question, Winter countered with a question of her own,

"Is it true you saw my mother when she was my age?"

Dr. Kelp smiled at her, leaning forward slightly, tapping his pen on his notebook.

"Yes." He gave her an equally short answer.

"What was she sick with?" Winter's grandfather talked rarely about her mother. She used to think it was to avoid hurting her, because she had been abandoned— but now, she wondered if it hurt him more.

The shrink in front of her hesitated, and the smile he pulled was not as kind as it had been before.

"I'm afraid I can't go into that. Patient confidentiality, you understand. Now, back to you, Miss Jozefson—"

"But was it genetic? Shouldn't that information be available to her next of kin?" Winter pressed, eager to know more. She knew that this was grievance counseling, but she had the rare chance to find out more about her mother.

"Are you worried because of your history with anxiety?" The question made Winter's blood run cold. Dr. Kelp stared back at her, his dark eyes gleaming, and his smile stretching. "Yes, I pulled your patient records from Dr. Morgan at the family practice."

He reached for a manila file on the corner of his desk. Winter stayed painfully silent, scratching at the corner of her right thumb nail.

"Dr. Morgan describes you as having... a rather fanciful imagination as a kid, yes? Paranoia, nightmares, panic attacks. He said you believed in monsters, is that correct?"

"When I was eight." Winter mumbled, lowering her head.

"But he prescribed you..."

"Celexa. For anxiety. Keeps me calm. School makes me panicky." She filled in his silence, fidgeting. Her fingers began to pull at the wick on the corner of her nail, trying to keep her expression blank as pain sharply tore through her finger.

"Do you take that regularly?"

"As needed."

"As needed? You refill it often."

"I need it a lot." Winter said pointedly, her breathing growing short.

The truth was that her prescription was supposed to be taken every morning, but Winter had the bad habit of playing around with it. She'd split her dose up, sometimes needing an extra kick in the late afternoon or evening. Dr. Kelp eyed her knowingly, as he surely knew that Celexa was not prescribed as needed, but he continued on,

"And you still take it today. The age of eight to... seventeen. That does seem like a necessary medication. Officially, you're diagnosed with an Acute Panic Disorder. But not from grades or stress at school— Dr. Morgan believed your fears had more to do with people and objects."

"What does this have to do with the suicide victims?" Winter asked. She felt faint, looking around the room with flighty eyes. It appeared clinical now, though it had not before— the warm colors and happy decor had stopped masking the feeling of being examined.

"Oh, it doesn't, Miss Jozefson. But you asked me about your mother." Dr. Kelp answered, his voice sickly sweet as their eyes met. He had an *'I know something you don't'* look on his face. "I can't divulge medical information about her, but I will tell you this. She was one of my *favorite* patients. Now... Are you interested in being a patient of mine, for your mental treatment? I need a new favorite— and I'd like to hear all about this 'Panic Disorder' of yours. I specialize in patients who have demons in their heads."

The wick tore, ripping up the corner of her nail and taking a chunk of skin with it. Winter bit her lip, curling her thumb into the palm of her hand as blood pooled on the sore, raw wound.

"No,. Thank you. I think I'll just continue seeing Dr. Morgan."

Dr. Kelp leaned back at her answer, offering up another smile.

"Now... Let's talk more about how these suicides have affected you personally..."

An hour later, Winter fast walked out of the building, practically breaking into a run when she got through the front doors. Her heart dropped, staring at the now empty spot where the Camaro had been.

What the HELL Axel?! Taking frantic gulps of air, Winter struggled with her purse, clawing inside of it in search of her phone, her hands shaking.

"YO! Win, I'm over here."

Her head snapped up, to a spot down and across a row—Axel had opened the window to stare at her. His inquisitive blue gaze immediately told her he knew something was up—even she knew what she must have looked like, fleeing across the parking lot towards him.

"Sorry, some annoying orderly said I was in his spot and —" Axel started, before Winter cut him off.

"D-Drive." She stuttered, sliding into the passenger-side seat. Still with her hands in her purse, she retrieved a prescription bottle, popping it open for a small orange pill.

"What the fuck happened?" Axel asked her, kicking the car into drive. He didn't have to be told twice, eyeing Winter out of the corner of his eye as she downed her anxiety medication.

Shaking her head, she couldn't find the words to tell him, at least not until later that night.

As they pulled out of the fenced-in mental hospital, all she could think about was that she had completely neglected to ask questions about depression, leaving them exactly where they had begun. Now all they knew was not to trust creepy old shrinks— and they still had no clue how to face Bleary.

22

UNFORTUNATE FIND

RING~! RING~! RING~!

"Mmm…" Winter rolled her face into her pillow, unaware of the obnoxious sound. She had just been with Kaya— at least, in her dreams. Reality hit her hard with the ringing of the phone.

Prying open her eyes, the glow of a nearby clock's figures swam in her vision.

It's almost three in the morning… What on earth— did Axel have a nightmare?

Scrambling for her phone, Winter flipped it open as fast as her numb, still-half-asleep hands could manage.

"Axel, is everything—?" Her sleepy voice started, stifling a yawn.

"Winter!"

That wasn't Axel. Instead, the panicked voice of Tae-Won Chi came over the line.

"Winter! Hey, I'm sorry for waking you— listen. J-Jae left the house, and… and we think he's going t-to hurt himself, or someone. I don't know." Grief and fear filled every word he spoke.

"W-What? Do you know where he might have gone?" Now Winter was wide awake, sitting bolt upright and reaching for the light switch.

"No clue. Dad's organizing a search party to comb the woods near our house, and he's got patrols searching the streets. I w-wanted to go right out, but he put me in charge of calling people for the search, as many students as I have the number of. He said it'd be better to have people who k-know and love Jae, you know?"

"Of course. Of course, he's right. I'll be right there. And I'll bring Axel, too. Is there anything else I can do? Or bring?" Winter asked, rising out of bed and stumbling over to her closet to find something to pull on.

"No. Just get here, Win. As fast as you can. Jae was... well, before he left the house, he was talking crazy. Said he kept— kept hearing things. I've never seen him so out of sorts."

That alone was enough to confirm Winter's fears that Bleary was involved, filling her with dread as she promised to hurry. Right before the call ended, Tae spoke again,

"Winter?"

"Yeah?"

"I didn't tell dad, but Jae... Jae has his spare gun. I know dad would call in the force if he knew— but Jae wouldn't hurt anyone. I swear he wouldn't— he's only a danger to himself. But I know... I mean... if you don't feel safe coming and joining the search—"

"No, I'm coming." Winter reassured him.

It was only after she hung up that she realized the danger of the situation. She could understand why Tae didn't say anything, she didn't think Jae would shoot anyone either... but all those searchers...

This has to be Bleary. Bleary only hurts the person it's haunting, right? She thought, stomach churning. What if this turned from suicidal to homicidal? Oliver walking in front of a car could have seriously hurt the driver, who walked away unscathed.

A dark feeling came over her, swallowing nervously at the thought of more than one person getting hurt tonight.

Dialing Axel's number, she paused to glance out the window, giving a sigh of relief when she saw the lights flicker on through his bedroom window. It only took a single ring for him to answer.

"Axel! Get dressed. It's Bleary, he's got Jae-hwa."

"I can't freaking believe this…" Axel grumbled, rubbing his hands together as they walked down the snowy sidewalk, listening to the distant sounds of sirens. "Bleary's kill-count is really racking up, but that thing doesn't want to show its face, besides taunting us. It's just getting more and more aggravating."

"We don't know that Jae is dead yet. We might get there before—" Winter started, hugging her arms in the cold of the early morning.

"Like we got there before Jovi?" Axel snapped. He couldn't help it, his miserable mood was only made worse by the recent death of his friend.

*I didn't think being dragged out of the house in the middle of the night by Winter would be for yet another person we know being killed by that thing.*He thought sourly, kicking up snow with his feet.

"I… I'm sorry." Winter stammered, her breath fogging up in the air. Axel grimaced, saying nothing as he walked a little faster. The only thing that was going to make him feel better, he thought, was beating the crap out of Bleary. If he was lucky, they would run into him again, and he'd get the chance. He still hadn't told Winter about the stalking encounter outside his window, and he didn't plan to.

It wasn't far to the twin's house on Aurum lane. They saw the flashing lights of Officer Chi's cop car long before they reached it. As they approached, more and more cars were pulling up, concerned citizens of Caligo joining the fray. Everyone had the same tired, worried expression on their face, and a rare few looked blank, like they already knew what had become of Jae-Hwa. Axel was among them. He had little hope as they got within earshot of Office Chi.

"Now listen up. He can't have gotten far, I suspect he's within a ten mile radius. He took off on foot, a little over an hour ago. He was upset, and talking like one of the recent victims— nonsense." From this distance, it was hard to tell, but Axel would have bet money on the officer's eyes being blood-shot red.

"Don't worry, Hyun-woo. We'll find your boy." The one who spoke amongst the crowd was Mr. Robert Thorne— the mayor of Caligo and father to Matthew and Knieka. They stood beside him and his wife, dressed and ready to join the search.

The father of the Chi twins nodded bleakly, calling out over the crowd to start forming groups and picking sections of the woods for everyone. Most of the highschoolers present were put together.

By the end of it, Winter had been placed to search with Tae-Won, Morgana Dorsey, and the Lokken siblings; Lacey and Lucas. Meanwhile, Axel was put with Pierre— who looked slightly terrified— Quinn, Noelle, and Nathan. He knew right away that Nathan was there to cover the story for the school paper— the smug senior had a notebook in hand, and his girlfriend looked like she was still half asleep and had been dragged along.

"I'll see you in a bit? Text me if you find him." Winter

murmured as they got ready to embark in opposite directions.

"Mhm." Axel hummed. Watching her go, he wondered how safe she was with her group on a Bleary hunt. A frantic Asian twin and three tired-looking blondes didn't give him the greatest confidence in handling a rescue mission.

He couldn't say he was all that thrilled with his group either, but when he asked about going off alone, Officer Chi wouldn't hear it. With a flashlight and boots laced up tight, Axel joined the squad of teenagers ready to trek into the woods.

"HOW YOU HOLDING UP, PIERRE?" IF THEY WERE GOING TO BE walking for a while, Axel thought, he could at least make small talk. Winter hadn't been the only one with Pierre in mind. He had wondered about the blonde boy as well after the loss of his sister. He just hadn't been sure how to approach him at school. 'Hey, I know we've never talked, but your sister just died and I feel responsible' wasn't a great opening line.

Not to Axel's surprise, Pierre looked startled he had been spoken to. They couldn't have looked more different. Axel's cold weather clothes were black and thick, where Pierre was dressed in a pristine white sweater, a puffy over-jacket, white jeans, and gray laced up boots. His blonde hair was still fluffy, as if he had just showered when he got the call and had sped-dried it. He looked like a sugar cookie if a sugar cookie had turned human, while Axel looked ready to sink into the shadows.

"I'm doing okay." Pierre murmured, ducking his head shyly.

"Well, I'm not! It was bad when Kaya got taken, but Ollie?

And now Jae? What monstrous disease is coming upon our beloved town?" Quinn crooned dramatically, a hand going to his chest and gripping at his heart.

Axel rolled his eyes, but it encouraged Pierre to speak up again,

"That is true.Of course, I was upset over Sophie, but... seeing everyone else go through this is rough." He paused, rubbing the back of his neck, "I visited Oliver the other day. He was asleep when I stopped by, so I just talked to his folks a bit, left him a poetry book by Emily Dickinson to read. I remember him talking once in English class about liking poetry..."

Axel didn't know how close Pierre and Oliver were— he didn't recall them hanging out often— but Pierre looked remorseful now.

"Yeah, I think he did." Axel lied, offering up a half smile. He had no way of knowing, though he was sure Winter would.

"Are you two with us or are you going to get lost?" Quinn hollered to Noelle and Nathan. The stoner lovebirds had fallen several feet behind them, quietly bickering with hushed voices.

The group chattered on, but it soon became white noise to Axel. He found himself entranced by the forest that night. Snow coated the ground in pure white, shimmering underneath the full moon. The voices calling for Jae-Hwa echoed through the trees, beams of flashlights occasionally cast their way. It was unusual to be disturbing an otherwise peaceful evening. Axel felt like a trespasser as twigs crackled underfoot.

Winter had warned him about the gun— and that was what he listened for, the distinct sound of a shot fired. That was, if Jae wasn't already dead. Winter was hopeful, but after Jovanni, Axel wasn't sure if a Bleary victim could be snapped out of it. He knew a suicidal person was near impossible to talk down once they had decided on it, even in normal circumstances.

"You think he would do it?" Noelle's drawling tone sounded behind him, only half catching Axel's attention.

"Do what?" Nathan asked, sounding bored.

"Off himself. This is another one of the suicides, don't you think? Jae is a total little hippie, I didn't think he'd—"

"Noelle." It was Quinn who interrupted her, his voice sharp. Axel caught the jerking motion of his head as he brought their attention to Pierre— who had teared up. The death of his sister was too fresh.

"Oh, Pierre, I didn't mean…"

As the girl tried to fix her mistake, Axel tuned out of the conversation once more. Instead, his eyes caught on something ahead of him. Maybe twenty feet away was the faintest flash of a black robe.

"Axel..." This time, Axel didn't hesitate or question it.

He followed.

If his group noticed, they didn't follow as he quietly wandered further into the forest, following his gut. The closer he got, the louder it grew, laughing in the back of his mind.

"Come. I left you a present." The voice teased him.

Axel grit his teeth, walking faster. His gloved hands reached out to grab onto the trees, wedging himself through them to get further into the thick of the forest. The snow made things slippery, as branches tugged at his jacket, holding him back as he followed the taunts of his monster.

He knew what he would find, before he saw it— before he saw *him*.

Jae-Hwa wasn't moving as Axel approached, finally moving into a small clearing. It might have been a pristine scene— like something out of a movie— if it wasn't for the red patch of snow that looked like a pillow on which his head was laying, and the neat little bullet hole on his pale forehead. The second half of the Chi twins was crumpled on the ground, like he had curled up when he had pulled the trigger. One hand still held the gun, fingers having gone stiff around it, blue at the tips. His beanie had fallen off, laying in the snow a few feet from his body.

He wasn't alone, though.

Crouched at the body with its back to Axel, was a creature in a familiar black robe, hood up. It had the huge, hulking form of Bleary— the shoulder spikes through cloth and the slightly visible hoof feet, a dead giveaway underneath a flow of pale smoke. As Axel walked a circle around it, the figure seemed to shrink— and by the time he faced it, it no longer resembled a monster. At least, not a conventional one.

Lifting its head, the face that stared back at him was his own. In perfect replication, every line of his jaw and circles under his eyes, even his hair was parted the same way. It was the empty black eyes that gave it away- the last Axel checked, he hadn't gone full demon yet.

Still, seeing his face gave him an involuntary shiver.

We've seen it grow from a beast, to a monster in a robe, to... me? It's evolving with its kills. Axel noted.

"Hello, friend." His other half crooned, grinning back at Axel's grimace.

"I'm not your friend." He answered steadily, watching Bleary pout playfully.

"Ouch— that wounds me. All the time we've spent together..."

"Go f "

Bleary began to tut at him, and Axel's voice caught in his throat, choking. His hands were shaking, curling them into fists so hard that his nails stabbed into his palms. The pain, he briefly thought, was calming, but there was no calm at the moment. Not really.

"He was struggling. They're all struggling. You think humans would learn to reveal their struggles, but the only one they reveal it to is me... sometimes, they don't even realize it themselves, until it's too late." The monster hummed. A long-fingered-hand, still holding some resemblance to his monstrous form, reached down to stroke Jae's cheek. At first, Axel thought he was transparent as usual, but he saw Jae's head turn, just slightly, from the force of Bleary's fingers against his skin. He was very much real, solid— and still, Axel knew, only visible to him.

Lurching forward with a determined step, he spat through gritted teeth,

"Leave him alone!" It wasn't right, letting that thing— his thing— defile the body of one of his... friends? Memories flashed in his head, however faint— Jae offering him a pencil in class, nodding to him in the hall, complimenting band t-shirts when he wore them. He had even, once, extended an invite to him for a party at his house, something Axel had crumpled up and tossed, of course. *Was it that they never cared — or I didn't?* He didn't know anymore, sick to his stomach as he eyed Jae-Hwa's body.

Bleary smiled at him knowingly, as if the monster could read his thoughts. "Don't worry. He's with me already, this was just his flesh-suit. I'm going to have fun playing with him."

What the fuck are you talking about? Axel wondered, biting his tongue.

"Axel!" A voice called in the distance, making him turn his head. He saw the brief flash of a flashlight through the trees. They must have noticed he had wandered off.

Turning back, his breath caught in his throat— Bleary had moved. The creature was now directly in front of him.

Not touching, but none-the-less unnerving— their noses only a few hairs away. A sour, rotting breath hotly fanned across his face, making Axel cringe but he didn't budge. He was frozen, staring into those pitch-black eyes.

"Are you going to take me next?" Axel whispered, swallowing his fear. Looking back at his own darkness, he didn't dare show any weakness. Right now, he didn't feel like giving over the control Bleary often took away.

His face— its face— smirked at him. "You'd love that, wouldn't you?"

The words made Axel shiver. He opened his mouth, ready to respond, but the words died in his throat as the face in front of him began to shift. Axel watched in frozen horror as his eyes melted away as if by acid, giving way to gaping black sockets. The features of his face began to jut out, molding into a harsher, sharper structure at the top, and sinking inwards at the bottom. His hair, shedding, fell away like molted feathers, his skin flaking off to reveal a gray, leather-like flesh beneath, pulled taut, the hood Bleary wore falling back to show his bald skull.

Perhaps it was because he stood so close, but Bleary looked more solid than he had before. As his torso and limbs stretched, growing in height, long fingers with pointed nails reached to grab Axel by the shoulders, digging into him. The strength of his hold and the fact he wasn't ghostly like he had been in past encounters,caused Axel's legs to shake. If not for Bleary keeping him in place, he might have fallen.

At last, the real face of his monster was there. As Axel looked up at him, he realized that Bleary looked slightly different. There were new spikes along the sides of his eyes and brows— if it had had brows— like that of some kind of dinosaur. Its teeth, above the gaping hole that was his mouth, were different too; more pronounced, sharper, resembling a row of rough diamond-shaped pebbles.

Axel had so much he wanted to say, but with his mouth gaping open, his voice died in his throat. Bleary's didn't though. His tall form hunched over Axel, lurching forward, a terrible shriek sounding from the monster.

The cry Axel gave was drowned out, finally struggling against Bleary's hold. His hands raised to squeeze against his ears, but it was in his head that the scream was loudest. Bleary's sharp hands released him, and Axel stumbled to the snowy ground, curling in on himself as his scream joined Bleary's.

How long he was there, he didn't know— the screech seemed to go on for an eternity— but a new hand began to shake him, and when his eyes opened, all the noise stopped.

Bleary was nowhere to be found, the eyes Axel met were wide and as blue as his own.

"Axel. Are you okay? We heard you screaming— are you hurt?" Pierre had been the one to find him, the sound of crunching leaves and thudding footsteps alerting them both to Quinn, Noelle, and Nathan not far behind.

Axel's head whirled around, bile in his throat as he looked for that thing, but all he saw were trees, and...

"Jae!" Quinn's voice cried out when he spotted the body of the boy they had been searching for. Now it was Noelle's turn to start screaming, as Nathan reached for his walkie-talkie.

All fuss over Axel was forgotten, aside from Pierre helping him to his feet. As his group chattered over what to do, Axel tuned them out, his eyes on the gun that lay beside Jae's body. He didn't pay attention to the sound of more people, or the anguished cries of Sheriff Chi.

When Winter's arms wrapped around him, the smell of her shampoo brought him back to the present, blinking as her voice sounded in his ear.

"I'm so sorry you had to find him." She murmured,

pulling back to study him. There must have been a look on his face, Winter's brows furrowing in a concerned expression. "What... What did you see?" She spoke in a low tone, so they wouldn't be overheard as they stepped back to make room for the crowd that was forming around Jae-Hwa's body. Both her hands cupped his, warming his snow-cold skin.

All Axel could do was shake his head, muttering,

"It's not going to kill me... it's going to hurt everyone else. Worst thing about depression. It doesn't affect just you."

That was the truth of it. Sometimes, Axel wondered if the guilt— the idea of burdening others— was the real trigger. He spoke up, adding,

"Jae-Hwa didn't pull that trigger."

Around them, adults were starting to try to push the search parties away, trying to create privacy for Jae-Hwa. Officer Chi was kneeling by his son, weeping, and Tae-Hyun had broken protocol to pull Jae's body into his lap and hold him, staring down at his brother with a blank horror, as if it weren't real. Nathan, insensitively, was snapping photos with his phone— no doubt for the school paper— while Pierre and Quinn had turned their backs, both with a comforting arm wrapped around Noelle, who was shaking like a leaf from the sight of their dead classmate.

Staring at Axel, Winter's hazel-green gaze had that horrible, helpless look she got when she realized the weight of Bleary's effect on him. He couldn't meet her eyes when she looked at him like that, a sickness churning in his stomach as he pulled up his hood. Shivering, he murmured,

"Let's go home, Win. Bleary won this one... he won't win the next."

Winter opened her mouth to say something, thought better of it, and gave a silent nod. She didn't let go of his hand the whole way home, and Axel didn't make her.

"Sick fuck…" Axel glowered at the last edition of the school paper before Christmas. The two teenagers sat in a window booth at Damara's, celebrating their last day of school with some pastries.

"I tried to stop him. He didn't write anything when Kaya died, not like that. Of course, everyone at school saw when Kaya died, but Jae died in the middle of the night and only the searchers knew.So Nathan… He said it was important to tell the news, even when it's personal." Winter sighed beside him, clutching a hot cup of cocoa.

"This isn't telling the news! This is glorifying people's fucking suffering! That little—!!" Axel grit his teeth, crumpling the paper in his hand. Noelle, who was waitressing, walked past them and he didn't bother stopping himself as he snarled, "Hey, Noelle! Tell your boyfriend he's a shitty journalist!"

"He's not my boyfriend anymore." Noelle sniffed, throwing her head back to look at them. "Or at least, he won't be by tonight."

She walked off, and Winter shook her head. "They've broken up before. It won't last. Noelle always gets touchy when Nathan prioritizes the paper."

Axel knew this; everyone knew this, Nathan was the lead writer of the school paper for a reason. He stepped on toes all the time to 'get the story'. Still, it left a sour taste in his mouth. Instead of the front page of the paper being about Christmas, or having any sort of festive cheer, there was a massive photo of Jae-Hwa and a two page story about the 'struggles of a small town kid' and the violent way he had taken his life. The entire thing was dramatized, as if Nathan himself had been present with front row tickets and popcorn, instead of simply being in the group that had found the body.

"He couldn't even find a smiling photo." Axel scoffed. Nathan had found the most miserable photo of Jae-Hwa possible, one from a homecoming dance a few years past where Jae-Hwa was fussing with his tie and had a painfully awkward grimace on his face, holding up two fingers in a peace sign to try and make the photo more decent—It hadn't helped.

Winter's hand reached out to cover the photo, fingers splaying out. As Axel lifted his head to look at her, she offered up a smile of her own.

"Stop torturing yourself. It's a stupid article, but we know the truth. No use fuming about it, Axe."

"I'm not fuming."

"You're totally fuming."

"I'm just—"

"Should I use a synonym? Seething? Smoldering? Ooh— Smoldering, I like that. Axel, smolder for me."

Her teasing tone managed a snort, ducking his head to avoid her triumphant grin. Successful in cutting off some of his anger, Winter thumbed through the paper and opened it to a new page.

"Look at this, though. They're holding a candlelight vigil for the victims of Bl— Suicide." She corrected herself, eyeing Noelle passing by again with a tray of drinks. Clearing her throat, Winter tilted her head as she settled her focus back on Axel. "Can you drive us?"

Axel paused, ready to say no to the idea, but...

What if I can meet Bleary again? More people are gonna be present, but it's possible... He had a real hunger to deal with that thing, only growing more eager as the victims piled up.

His hesitance must have seemed like a denial, Winter speaking again with a nervous, uncertain tone,

"W-We could go early, before the crowds get too heavy. Kaya's family will be there. Everyone will be there, really. Besides Oliver, of course, but…"

Sighing, Axel sat back, reaching for his cocoa.

"Alright. We'll go. But if I see Nathan there—"

"Yeah, yeah, I know, you'll give him the 'smolder.'"

Axel smiled into his cup so Winter wouldn't see.

23

UN-ALIVE

Kaya and Winter had spent every Christmas Eve together since Winter was eight. They had so many traditions that it was painful to go through the month of December without her. Axel, who had joined her for much of the holiday festivities, kept her distracted through it all. From stringing popcorn strands, to joining Winter in putting lights on the rose bushes. Though all the activities had been tinged with grief for her lost friend, Axel knew tonight might end up the worst night of the month. The funeral had been hard, but Kaya had been among the first. There were too many people to mourn now, and if it wasn't for supporting Winter, Axel wouldn't have gone to the memorial at all.

He was already sitting at the curb in his Camaro by the time the sun was setting, which had a new paint job: a cool electric blue, which had been his parent's Christmas gift to him. It rivaled Ian's red Supra now, and in Axel's mind, surpassed it.

Peering out the window, he watched Winter close the front door and come jogging down the porch steps towards him. She wore a navy blue, long-sleeve, form-fitting turtle-neck dress, with black boots and a silver belt. Carrying a black jacket to wear at the graveyard, and a gray scarf hanging from her neck, her hair was all curled. Axel even spotted eyeliner and a bit of plum lipstick, a rare amount of effort from his usually laid-back friend.

In comparison, Axel looked underdressed. He wore black jeans and a warm, dark blue knitted sweater, a blue beanie fit over his dark hair. As Winter slid into the passenger side, tossing her bag onto the floor, Axel gave her a small nod.

"Nice. You match my car." He greeted her, giving her one last glance before he kicking the car into gear.

"I was going to say your car matched my dress, but what-ever way you want to look at it." She quipped back, offering him a smile. As they set off, however, her smile quickly faded. "Hey uh… can we take the Prae Way?"

The Prae Way was what everyone called Praecepitus Way, a looping cliffside road that ran behind and above their neighborhood. It was out of the way, a lonely road that used to be part of the north highway of town that now was closed off. But it had the best view of Caligo, and went from the richest neighborhood of town, straight to the cemetery.

Already facing the wrong way for Prae Way, Axel came to an abrupt stop.

"You gotta give me a real good reason to take that shit road. All the potholes and ice." Axel complained, hands firmly on the wheel, reluctant to turn around.

The long pause that followed made Axel turn his head to look at her. He instantly felt his heart squeeze to see the sadness on her face, her lower lip quivering.

"Kaya and I always rode our bikes on that road to see the lights on Christmas Eve…"

Shit. Axel thought, wishing he hadn't made her give a reason. He had been trying to be extra cautious tonight, knowing the occasion, and he had already blundered into her grief.

Silently, he threw the wheel to the side and did a U-turn, going off towards Bellica Drive. Driving by Kaya's home, he realized, only made the void she left more obvious. The house was dark, devoid of any lights or decorations. In years past, it had been one of the most vibrant houses on the street.

It only took a few minutes before they were driving up Divitiae Drive, a curvy, uphill gravel road, to some of the richer houses in town. However, it was the easiest way to turn onto Prae Way. The spindly road soon morphed from gravel to asphalt, going up onto a cliff overlooking the town. There were guardrails along the cliffside, and beyond that was Caligo in full view, a gorgeous sight of snow and Christmas lights.

Axel drove slower than he normally would have.Yet, at his pace, they were still whipping along the curves of the Prae Way. As he focused on the road ahead, Winter stared past him at all the lights, the two of them were silent. A silence that Winter finally broke.

"I think Christmas might be ruined for me." She sighed, fidgeting with her hands in her lap.

"Christmas has never been good for me." Axel answered, "Nothing new there."

"In what way?" He knew what she was doing, prodding for information to make conversation. Hesitating, it took a minute for him to answer.

"My family, just... we don't do the holiday thing. The stuff you and I did. Decorations, baking, shopping for gifts. I've gotten money from my parents for Christmas since I turned ten, so... You know. We just don't make a big deal out of it." He felt awkward, stating the obvious. It was clear enough when people entered his house— the only thing remotely Christmas themed was a small artificial table tree, less than four-feet-tall, sitting on the glass coffee table. In comparison, when you went into Winter's house, you were hit in the face with a crackling fireplace, two big stockings hanging, baubles covering the rails of the stairs, bells on the door handles, mistletoe hanging on the porch, little statuettes of Santa and Reindeer all over the living room table. Her seven-foot Christmas tree was decked out in lights and tinsel, presents overflowing underneath, and her kitchen smelled like fresh baked bread every day. The difference between her upbringing and his was suffocatingly obvious.

"You miss out on the joy." Winter stated, her voice soft but matter of fact.

Briefly, he glanced her way, their eyes meeting as he nodded, "Yeah." Normally, he would have said something dark and honest, but he couldn't bring himself to make her night any darker than it already was.

Winter turned her head forward first, and her eyes went wide as she screamed out, "AXEL STOP!"

His own head turned just in time to see it. Bleary, standing in the road in front of them, with its gray face and hooded figure. On instinct, he braked hard. Instead of stopping, however, the car stalled and they must have hit black ice, as the car began to spin out of control, and all Axel could do was watch the world turn in his vision, jolting in his seat, yanking his foot off the brake and gripping the wheel as tightly as he could. Turning completely backwards as they started slowing, they hit the guardrail with a loud screech, Axel wincing as he gripped the wheel, knuckles turning white. A loud thud sounded as Winter's head hit into the passenger-side window, and he could hear her let out a gasp of pain.

Once they had completely come to a stop, Axel searched for Bleary through the windows— but it had disappeared, leaving an uneasy fear of what could be lurking in the dark.

It's never been this far from the school before. Axel thought, his heart racing as he tried to take in their crash. The driver side was facing the road, the passenger side against the guardrail. The car was silent, no hissing or mysterious clunks, no smoke coming from the engine, so that was good, at least.

Looking over at Winter, he couldn't see her face; her head was bent down and held between both hands, soft groans coming from her.

"Win. Winter, hey. You okay?" Anxiety and worry hit, Axel reaching out to touch her arm.

"Ah… N-no. I mean, y-yeah, I just hit my head." Winter's voice was shaky, sniffling quietly.

"Let me see." Axel demanded. Yanking open the middle compartment, he pulled out a flashlight, and flicked it on. As Winter lifted her head, Axel reached out to brush her hair out of the way, shining the flashlight in her face and watching her flinch back. There was a large bruise forming across the corner of her forehead, and her pupils were huge, but other than looking a little disheveled, she appeared awake and alert, her reaction to the light fairly normal as far as he could tell.

Axel's first thought was a concussion, but he had no idea how to check for one. Feeling stupid, he asked, "What's my name?"

Winter narrowed her eyes at him, lifting a hand to hide her eyes from the light.

"Punk." She answered shortly, making Axel roll his eyes.

"Yeah, you're fine." He sighed, clicking off the light.

"What about you?"

Her question made him do a double-take, checking himself over. He didn't feel any pain, and he hadn't hit anything. Besides his hands aching from the tight grip he'd had on the steering wheel, and his chest hurting from the seatbelt.

"I'm good. Come on, let's get out." Axel answered her. Seeing that Winter couldn't open her door, he threw his open and got out, doing a quick glance around. No Bleary in sight.

Leaning back into the car, he held out his hand for her, "Give me your hand." He commanded, carefully helping Winter clumsily step over the middle panel and get out. She seemed unsteady on her feet when she first stood up, gripping onto his jacket. "You good?"

"Yeah. I can stand." She answered, slowly letting go of him when she was sure she had her footing on the icy roadside.

Moving back to get a good look at his car, originally Axel thought there was little-to-no damage. But as he moved around to look at the side that had hit the guard rail, his eyes were immediately drawn to the long, silver gouges in the new paint, metal glinting in the moonlight. They went along the side of the car, through both doors, and one of his tail lights appeared to be broken.

A string of profanities left Axel's mouth, slamming a hand on the hood of his car. "You've got to be kidding me. I just shelled out $2,500 for that paint!" He exclaimed, kicking the front of his car out of anger, only to watch the front splitter he'd attached in front of his tires pop off with a metal clunk, dropping to the ground.

Throwing his arms up, Axel let out a growl, furious with Bleary for the damages to his car. It took him a minute of raging to notice that Winter had stepped away, standing further in the road and looking down from where they had come from.

"Win?" He called her name, watching her turn her head to look at him with a dazed expression. "What's up?"

"I... just can't believe we saw her." She answered, slowly

walking back towards him. Noticing she was shivering, Axel ducked into the car to retrieve her jacket, holding it up so she could slip it on.

"Her?" Axel asked, confused for a second.

"Kaya. She was just standing there, in the road. S-She was covered in blood, Axe, you didn't see that?" Winter seemed more shaken up by that than the crash, looking unusually pale.

"What? Kaya? What are you—" It took a minute for it to click. "Bleary. Winter, that wasn't Kaya, that was Bleary. I saw it. It must have been messing with your head again, because that thing that got in our way definitely wasn't Kaya."

"B-But…" Winter tried to deny it, but her expression fell as she realized he had to have been right. "It… looked so much like her." She sighed, hugging her jacket closer to herself. Glancing around, she asked, "Do you think Bleary is gone?"

"Yeah, looks like it. Bastard was just trying to scare us, I think." Axel scowled down the road. Glancing back at the car, he muttered, "What a mess…"

Winter scoffed, moving to lean against the guardrail beside the wreckage. A moment of silence passed between them, before she gave a heavy shake of her head.

"We have the worst luck, Axe."

"Luck has nothing to do with it." His blunt response earned a laugh, as Winter reached into her bag.

"I was going to wait until tomorrow, but considering our exciting car collision course, I'll give this to you now." She told him, as she held out a slip of paper.

Unfolding it, Axel looked confused. On the paper was a sketched drawing— beautifully done— of a lightbulb hanging upside-down on a chain.

"Um… Thank you?" He mumbled, glancing up at Winter's smile.

"Merry Christmas, Axel Dunn." Winter said softly, as she extended a hand over the paper he held. She had practiced this, and couldn't help but feel immensely proud as she focused on the image, her fingers tingling as the necklace began to lift right off the page. It joined the material world, solid steel forming before their eyes, the exact image from the drawing. Before long, the paper was crumpled under the weight of the necklace, laying in Axel's hand. He lifted it up as Winter pulled her own hand back, letting it dangle between them, glinting in the moonlight.

Axel shook his head, a smile on his face. "I'll never get used to your witchy powers, Winter, but they are incredible, I'll give you that."

"Witchy? I'm not witchy. I'm…" Winter started, but she didn't quite know what to call it. Magic seemed to be the only thing to explain the gifts she had been given. *What else could it be?* "…Well, I don't know what I am." The words made her a bit sad, biting her bottom lip as she reached to take the necklace from Axel. Carefully, she helped clasp it around his neck, dropping it to hang at the base of his sweater, the bright steel standing out against the dark blue fabric.

Sensing her mood shift, Axel heaved an overdramatic sigh. "Well, since we're exchanging gifts early…" He trudged back to the car, ducking through the door and reaching across to the glove box. Popping it open, he was relieved to see that the small package, wrapped in dark red wrapping paper, seemed to be unharmed. Grabbing it, Axel shuffled back to Winter, propping himself up on the edge of the guardrail as he held it out to her.

"Merry Christmas, Winter Jozefson." He mimicked her weighty use of her full name, smirking as she beamed at him.

Winter was extremely careful as she ripped away the red

paper, revealing a beautiful navy blue notebook. Designed like a door, with square, wooden panels. An intricate brass clasp and lock was on the side, and taped to the front cover was a little brass key. Unlocking it, she opened the book to reveal the lovely pages. They weren't lined, but rather left blank; perfect for sketching. The inside cover had a "property of" section in big, swoopy lettering, with a space to write her name.

"This is beautiful, Axel." Winter said in a hushed whisper, running her hand down the cover.

"I figured… the other one is tainted with drawings of that thing, so… Thought you could start fresh after we destroy it." Axel explained, shrugging his shoulders. He wasn't prepared when Winter wrapped her arms around his neck and pulled him down into a hug. She was so warm that he almost forgot it was snowy out.

"Thank you, Axel. I love it. Really."

They sat there with the ruined car for about ten minutes, Axel grumbling over the cold and the damages, before they heard the low rumble of an approaching engine. Winter turned, and saw a familiar red Supra coming around the bend. When he saw them, Ian slowed to a stop, rolling down his window with a smug grin.

"Nasty crash. Hit a deer?" He asked.

"Something like that." Winter answered, offering him a smile. The last thing she wanted to do was piss off Ian Bryars in the middle of nowhere.

He eyed her, noticing their semi-formal attire, and asked, "On your way to the memorial?" When Winter nodded, he added, "Need a ride?"

"We'd love one!" Winter immediately chimed. Axel shot her an incredulous glance, but she shook her head, adding pointedly, "You never know what could be out in these woods. Besides, it's cold, and we have no reception out here."

It would be obvious enough to Axel, she hoped, that she was referencing Bleary.

Still, Axel grit his teeth. "Do I really have to get into a car with this idiot?" He mumbled under his breath to Winter.

"Come on!" Winter urged him, hugging her new sketchbook to her chest as she gave him another reason to put up with Ian. "If we don't, we'll miss the vigil. I promised Kaya's mom I'd be there."

That seemed to do the trick, as Axel reluctantly followed her to the car. He clambered into the back while Winter took the passenger seat.

"*We* really appreciate this, Ian." She emphasized her words, glancing back at Axel, who silently sulked, looking out the window at his damaged Camaro.

"Anything for you, Winter." His words surprised her, sounding genuine as he threw the car into drive. As they set off down the road, Winter's head was still pounding, hugging onto the door handle in an attempt to feel a little more secure.

To her relief, Bleary didn't make any more ghostly appearances. After a minute, Ian flexed his hands on the steering wheel and cleared his throat.

"Listen…" He started, staring forward at the road, "I uh… owe you an apology. Both of you."

Winter startled, glanced towards Ian. Axel didn't move, though a soft snort could be heard.

Ian continued, "I was a jerk, and I know it. Losing Bryce was hard, you know? That doesn't excuse how I treated you before, but… I know you get it, having lost Kaya and all. Kaya was a cool chick, she didn't deserve to go down like that. Neither did any of the rest of them. I'm just... trying to say that we've all had enough of this shit."

"We've all lost someone lately. It's been... a bad few months." Winter managed to answer. There was a grave moment, a shared remembrance of Kaya, and Bryce, and all the others. Ian didn't say anything more, but they all knew his apology was accepted. Even by Axel, who gave Winter a knowing look when she glanced towards him.

Before long, the cemetery was in view. There were parked cars, and people were already streaming through. Lit candles in hand, they all walked towards the burial plots of the 'suicide' victims from the last three months. Everyone would be there— besides Jae-Hwa, who hadn't been buried yet, and Oliver, who was still recovering in the hospital.

Parking at the curb, the three of them clambered out of the Supra and headed to where Mr. and Mrs. Jones, Quinn's parents, were handing out candles. Tucking her new sketchbook into her purse, Winter accepted one, smiling at Quinn, who stood nearby helping his parents greet the many people of Caligo who had come to sit vigil for the loss of the students and Miss Popelin.

"What do you want to bet that none of these people ever spoke to any of the seven when they were alive?" Axel grumbled as they began walking towards the graves, earning a light elbow to the ribs from Winter.

"Don't say that. There are plenty of friends and family members here, too." Winter said. She thought Ian might have tagged along with them to Kaya and Jovanni's graves, but instead, he walked ahead of them. It took her a second to realize he was going to Bryce's, joining the Brazilian family that huddled there.

Makes sense. They were on the team together, they must have been friends. It was a sobering reminder that she and Axel weren't the only ones to lose a friend that year. In fact, looking around, she saw so many familiar faces visiting the seven victims.

With Bryce's family and Ian, were also a few other members of the football team, and, of course, it was hard to miss the honey-blonde of Bryce's girlfriend Ruby. The rest of the cheerleaders formed a sniffling squad over where Delilah was buried, along with Daniel Gold, who looked more miserable than Winter had ever seen him. Together, they walked past Miss Popelin's grave, where Pierre knelt, laying roses among the many other gifts from students. Winter didn't see Oliver's family, but she assumed they must have chosen to stay at the hospital with him. She did see the Chi family, however, standing together off to the side. She could hear them speaking Korean while Tae-Won held a small, golden urn. They were the only family of the lost who had not chosen burial.

Stopping by Jovanni's grave first, it was noticeably bare compared to the rest of the victims. Not a single member of his family was in sight as Axel knelt to put his candle down in front of the stone.

"Shitheads don't even bother with him in death." He fumed quietly, staring at the writing on the tombstone.

Jovanni Alastor Brookes
December 16th, 1983 - December 2nd, 1999

It was startling even to Winter, to see so little on his gravestone. Where other's said things like "beloved son and brother," or "Dearly missed friend," Jovanni's only had his name and birthdate. It was almost surprising he'd been given headstone at all.

"J.A.B...." Winter whispered out his initials. *He had only been days from his seventeenth birthday.* "Do you know much about his family?" She asked Axel as she crouched beside him, reaching out to brush some snow off the top of the tombstone.

"Not a lot. I know Jovi hated them though." Axel answered, frowning. "I think Jovi was an only child. He never talked about his mom, and his dad is a mean drunk. Jovi used to borrow concealer from me to hide bruises."

Reaching out, Winter touched a hand to Axel's shoulder. She expected him to pull away, but to her surprise, he didn't move. Instead he looked at her, eyes searching her face.

"I wish we could have helped him." It was the first time Winter had heard Axel say something like that. He wasn't someone who dwelled, at least not openly. For once, he was vulnerable in front of her in a way that he hadn't been even when telling his secrets.

"We're going to, Axel. We're going to avenge him. Jovi and Kaya, and all the others." Winter whispered, rubbing her hand up and down his back.

Looking at the grave, the two of them spent a few more seconds reflecting on Jovanni before they got up to move towards Kaya's.

Seeing her family filled Winter with dread, walking slower the closer they got. She had visited the grave a few times since the funeral, but today it was covered with the gifts of well-wishers: flowers, stuffed animals, photos, and a multitude of candles propped up beside her tombstone.

KAYA AIKO LUNA MORITO
MAY 12TH, 1982 - NOVEMBER 1ST, 1999
A VIBRANT SPIRIT. NEVER FORGOTTEN

"Thank you for coming, Winter. And..." Mrs Morito spoke up when she saw them reach the grave, eyeing Axel with tired eyes as she fought to recognize him. They had met before— it was a small town— but clearly, now wasn't the time to expect her to recall his name.

"Axel. I'm uh… sorry for your loss." Axel said, sounding a bit awkward but no less sincere, as he offered a bow of his head.

She gave them a weak smile before turning back to speak to her husband. Kaya's little brother, Hiro, was sitting cross-legged at the foot of her grave, making a small pile of snow.

As they stood there, small snowflakes began to fall, causing Winter to look up. She blinked wet eyes as she watched them float down, her sigh causing a puff of fog in the cold air. Leaning forward, she laid her candle down with the rest.

It wouldn't be long now until they faced Bleary. They had to— before it grew much stronger. Even though she had a good chance of joining Kaya, fear wasn't in Winter's mind at this moment. Instead, she smiled, leaning her head on Axel's shoulder and curling her arm with his. She took his hand in a tight grip. Rubbing her cheek into the fabric of his sweater, she gazed down at the candles as they cast a warm glow across the snow.

There was a certain peace in what was to come. They would face it together, for the friends they had lost— and that, to Winter, wasn't scary at all.

24

UNDER MISTLETOE

"Goodnight, Winter." Axel sighed her name into the cold air, white mist drifting from his lips. They stood in the middle of Altum Court, ready to part ways for the night. The road was blanketed in white, as Axel stomped his boots into the snow and listened to the quiet crunch underfoot.

Tonight, Winter looked more solemn than usual, and Axel couldn't blame her. Her smile had vanished, chin tucked into her scarf, cheeks rosy from the cold. She peered at him as if it was for the last time, and the dread in her eyes made it hard for Axel to look at her. She was shivering, even in warm clothing, which is why Axel had been the one to bid her goodnight. But Winter, of course, had one final thought to speak. She always did.

"Axel." The way she said his name made him shiver, too. Crossing his arms across his chest tightly, he stared at her, waiting for her to voice what she was hesitating to.

"I... I'm sorry." She said, her voice weak.

"For what?" Now, Axel was truly baffled. Out of everyone he knew, Winter was the one who had absolutely nothing to apologize for. Yet it seemed she had found something to take the blame for.

"All these years… I have lived right across the street from you almost all my life. I could have talked to you before this year. I could have…" Her lower lip quivered, and she looked at her feet, her hair falling forward like a curtain. "I should have been your friend when you needed one."

Silence fell between them, as Axel's throat closed at her words. He could see where her mind was, and he didn't like it. *Did I make her feel like this?* He asked himself.

"It wouldn't have made a difference, Win." Axel finally spoke up, unsure what else to say. He was who he was, his demons were there regardless of whether or not he had people like Winter in his life.

Still, she looked up at him with shining eyes, her expression deadly serious.

"Wouldn't it have?" She answered him, making him shiver once again. Stepping forward in the snow, Winter reached for him, wrapping her arms around Axel's neck, she pulled him into a close hug. His own arms snaked around her waist on instinct, used to Winter's warmth by now. He frowned into her shoulder. "When people fall, they need someone to catch them and pull them back up. That's how you stay out of depression— being lifted up. One hand at a time. That's how I see it, Axe."

It was a beautiful way to see it, if not perhaps naive. Winter wasn't flawless— she was a person that had been hurt too— but it was the differences in *how* and *why* that made her damage so different. Axel wanted to say that, perhaps, she was blind and her vision was unclear. The truth, however, was that she was the only one who saw him with clear eyes.

Axel, with his heart in his throat, unwilling to say the words running through his mind, stood still for the longest time and just held her. It was a flash of headlights and a slowly approaching car that made them break apart. Both of them stumbled back, away from each other. Axel stepped onto the sidewalk in front of his house, Winter now in front of hers. He watched the car drive past before he looked back at her. Silently, she offered him a smile and lifted her hand in a wave.. He held up two fingers in return, watching her turn and dash for the warmth of her house.

"Papa! I'm home!" Was the last call of her voice he heard. Taking a deep, painfully cold breath of air, Axel turned and headed inside.

His house might have been warm, but the silent halls were far from welcoming. His mother sat at the end of the kitchen table, papers neatly laid out in front of her. Her skin looked green in the fluorescent kitchen lights, eyes glowing cold, her hair loose and falling over her shoulders in dark waves.

"Axel." She said his name by way of greeting as he entered, eyes dropping to his boots. "Take those off before you track dirt everywhere."

Silently, Axel nodded and moved to do so. He didn't need to be told, but he didn't protest. His mother lifted her pen again, the sound of it scratching against paper filling the room.

Standing in socks, Axel set his boots aside, looking up again at his mother to see if she might say anything more. When she noticed him waiting, she did, frowning at him.

"What are you looking at?" She asked, sounding as annoyed as she looked. Clearly, he was disturbing her.

"Nothing." Axel sighed, heading for the cupboards. *I'll just make some tea and head upstairs.* He thought, grabbing a black teacup from the top shelf. He set about picking out a tea bag, working quietly.

"You didn't come home for dinner. Kaius left an hour ago. Were you out with Miss Jozefson again?" To Axel's surprise, his mother spoke to him again as he was setting his cup in the microwave. Normally, he'd use a kettle— they rarely used their microwave— but he'd get out of his mother's way and be headed upstairs much faster if he nuked it.

"...Yes." Axel reluctantly answered, glancing over his shoulder at her. "We went to the vigil for the suicide victims."

His mother gave a soft snort, unhappy with his answer.

"They treat kids who throw their lives away better than war veterans these days." She remarked, narrowing her dark eyes at her youngest son. Taking a pause, she looked back down at her papers and continued, "I don't care for that girl. She's a decent enough student, but her head is always in the clouds. Always romanticizes History. She needs to focus on what is real. Never will get anywhere in life otherwise. Mark my words, she'll end up working at Damara's, living on tips, like that Ritter girl." His mother didn't look up as she spoke, letting the criticisms fall thoughtlessly as she graded papers.

Biting his tongue, Axel tapped his fingers on the counter, trying to ignore his mother. But he couldn't resist the urge to rebel, and let slip,

"Didn't great things come out of history from people whose heads were in the clouds?"

The movement of her pen stopped, and Axel internally cursed. He shouldn't have said anything. Holding his breath, he stared at the timer on the microwave counting down, willing it to go faster.

"I suppose so." His mother conceded, to his surprise. He let out the breath he held, and then came the rest of what she had to say, "Though those are rare cases. It's the biggest risk, to fly without a flight path. She's more likely to plummet."

That was true, wasn't it? The higher you go, the higher you have to fall? Naive, innocent, reckless— all those words fit Winter. Axel thought, scowling.

Once again, his mother had the perfect words to demonstrate why a human being couldn't fly. Axel, this time, chose to say nothing as the microwave beeped.

He retrieved his tea and headed upstairs, eager to be alone.

Drip, drip, drip. *Axel didn't know where he was, but he knew it was dark and somewhere, the steady sound of water filled his senses. It was as if a ceiling was leaking from above. He was barefoot, able to feel the grainy texture of dry dirt and gravel beneath his feet. He couldn't see anything but blackness and pale gray smoke.*

"Hello?" He called into the darkness, inching his way forward. There was something unnerving about not being able to see where he was stepping.

A giggle sounded from behind him, making him whirl around. He briefly saw a girl lit up in the distance, as if by a spotlight, brown hair flowing as she ran by in a white dress, tan skin and long legs visible.

"Winter? Hey!" Axel yelled, trying to run after her. He stumbled as she disappeared from sight, Everything was dark again.

"Where did you go?" He called, trying to shuffle around in the dark. A soft gasp left him when he felt the ground begin to slant down. Kicking his feet, he hit something small— and heard it roll off the edge of something, clattering downwards. Was he standing on a cliff?

Confused, Axel froze as another person came into view. His older brother Kaius stood before him with a scowl on his face. Once again, it seemed like light had come out of nowhere, letting Axel get a good look at his stone-faced brother. Onyx eyes glared down at Axel, framed by dark freckles and messy black hair.

"Kai!" Axel was relieved, for once, to see him. It was better than being alone in this darkness.

Kaius scoffed at him, "Worthless freak." Without warning, he reached out and gave Axel a sharp shove to the chest, making him fall backwards.

His feet slipped off the edge of the cliff he knew to be there, and then he was falling into the abyss. Axel tried to scream, but it was lost as air whipped past him. At first, his arms flailed through the dark, trying to find something to catch onto, and coming empty. But then he began to feel hands brushing past him, able to grab him but left open, not bothering to stop his descent. He tried to grab them, but he slipped right past. Wasn't anyone going to grab him?

Panicking, Axel's mind raced at the thought of the approaching ground. He couldn't see it, but it had to be coming. Every second filled him with more fear of the potential landing.

"Help me!" He screamed, but his voice fell on deaf ears. Until, finally, a hand reached out and grabbed his own, bringing him to an abrupt stop, his body jolting upwards.

Breathing heavily, Axel looked down— where he could see the ground below, the darkness finally seeping away thanks to an unknown light source. He could tell there was still, at least, fifty-feet between him and the ground— but it looked to be a landing of swirling water, a whirlpool, roaring underneath him.

Looking up, his eyes followed the hand that had grabbed him, finding himself peering at a familiar face.

"Winter." His friend smiled at him. She wore the white dress he had seen her running around in, her hair hanging over her shoulders as she knelt on a ledge, leaning forward to keep hold of him. Her hand was cold to the touch, her grip tight, yet effortless,

keeping him from hitting rock-bottom— or in this case, water's-bottom.

"Need a hand?" She asked. Axel reached up with his other hand to grab her wrist, swinging his legs desperately to try and get up. But despite her warm eyes and bright smile, Winter didn't seem to be making any effort to pull him up, instead letting him dangle from her one arm.

"Yes! Pull me up!" Axel exclaimed, heart racing as he stared up at her.

She would save him, right? How many times had he saved her now?

Yet, instead, Winter's grip began to loosen, purposefully letting him go slowly. His own hold on her wasn't enough, horror filling him as Winter's eyes turned from hazel-green to pure inky black. The eyes of Bleary.

"Why would I want to help you?" She asked, her voice mocking as she released him completely.

Axel yelled out as he slipped, falling again into nothingness. Within seconds, he crashed into the freezing cold water of the whirlpool. He was powerless as the current dragged him down, taking one last gulp of air before he was yanked beneath the dark waters, doomed to drown. No one would be able to pull him out of that, but they didn't take the chance when he was reaching for them, either.

It was too late for him... wasn't it?

Axel was awake. He had been, ever since the nightmare. He laid on his back taking slow, shallow breaths, one arm draped over his eyes as he listened to the sounds of his house on a Thursday morning. He could have been listening to music, drowning out his thoughts, but he didn't feel like moving to grab his headphones so there he remained, motionless, recalling the vivid nightmare and trying to find reasons it wasn't true.

He could hear everything: his mother's footsteps up and down the stairs, her muffled voice through the walls, tone high and annoying as she spoke to his father— who sounded dull, meek and agreeable. He heard the thud of his mother's suitcase as it was dragged downstairs, followed by more of their voices. Not quite bickering, Axel thought, since his father rarely ever bickered. It was much more one-sided than that.

Footsteps started coming up the stairs slowly, almost in time with Axel's breathing. *Too heavy to be mom*. He thought.

There it was, the knock on the door. Axel lowered his arm from his eyes just as it opened, and his father's face peeked in.

"Morning, champ." He hummed, pursing his lips as he took a quite look around Axel's room. It was neat, as always, with the exception of a few drawings Winter had given him on his desk, and her jacket laying forgotten over his desk chair.

"Morning." Axel answered, propping himself up on his elbows. "Need something?"

"Your mom's leaving for grandma's. Come say goodbye, would you? Kaius is here, too."

He must have been out front. Axel would have heard him if he'd come into the house, he was sure of that. Kaius had never been someone subtle, his presence was *always* heard.

Stifling a sigh, Axel nodded, getting up to follow his father downstairs. This year, the Dunn family would be divided for Christmas. Not that they were usually united during the holidays, anyway.

"About time you got up, lazy-butt." Kaius was the first to speak when Axel stepped out into the morning light. His older brother flashed him an impish grin, black hair looking brown in the sun. He always looked so goddamn happy around their family, and Axel couldn't possibly say why, because happiness for Kaius was misery for him.

All Axel did was shrug his shoulders, watching as his mother shut the back door of her car— which was filled with luggage.

"I'll be back right before school starts again."Alessandra Dunn remarked, turning towards her husband and sons. She began to rattle off things to remember while she was gone, but Axel wasn't listening. Instead, he heard the vague sound of birds chirping in the distance, and the rumble of an engine across the street. His eyes watched Mr. Jozefson, get into his car and wave out the window to Winter. Axel's friend stood in the car port, arms crossed over a sweater that had bunnies on it, her hair the result of bedhead and about three times its normal size, puffed out from her head. She hadn't looked his way yet, and when she did, it was with a smile.

Axel's lips twitch into one too, watching Winter head back into her house.

"Axel? Are you listening to anything I'm saying?"

"Hm?" His eyes flickered towards his mother and the scowl she was wearing.

"I said, there's money in the tin on the fridge to get dinner at Damara's. Holiday special. I'll call when I have an update on how Obaa-chan is doing. She'll want to say hello."

"You might as well just call Lisden. We all know he's her favorite." Axel retorted, adding extra wrinkles around his mother's lips as if she had swallowed something sour and now had to pucker up.

"I'll be stopping by Lisden's apartment on the way, in fact." Of course she would. Kaius was his mother's favorite, Lisden was his grandmother's favorite, and Axel? Bottom of the totem pole.

Axel stood still as his mother approached him, wrapping her arms around him with a too-tight hug that he knew would only be worse if he tried to push her off. Sucking in a deep breath, he gave a half smile as she stepped back. The hug she shared with Kaius was twice as warm, because he actually hugged back. After kissing her husband goodbye, Axel's mother got into the car and drove off, leaving the three Dunn boys standing side-by-side.

"Welp, that does it for me. I'm off." Kaius remarked, heading towards his motorbike that was parked at the curb.

"Not sticking around for Christmas?" Axel asked.

"Nope. Got plans with a girl. A cute one." Kaius remarked, winking as he drove off.

Axel turned to look at his father. "And you?"

His father laid a hand on his shoulder, giving it a squeeze. "I'm afraid I've got to work, bud. Think I'll pull a late-night at the office. Are you going to be okay on your own?"

Axel's eyes went across the street. Winter was up in her room now— he caught a sight of her hair as she walked across her window, her back to him.

"I won't be on my own."

"Well, that does it for me." Tage Jozefson groaned as he got up from his chair, setting his empty eggnog cup on the coffee table. He had put alcohol in it when he thought Winter wasn't looking, and now rubbed his face as if the two teenagers couldn't tell he was a little tipsy. "Don't stay up all night, you two." He grumbled, nodding to Axel, "Don't let the door hit you on the way out, punk." Even though the words were rude, his voice was not, patting Axel's shoulder in an almost-agreeable manner as he moved past him.

The night had gone off perfectly. When his father had left, Axel had joined Winter in making Christmas dinner, which was ten times better than anything from Damara's. They had listened to Christmas music, and when Mr. Jozefson returned from some errands, they ate until their stomachs felt ready to burst. For the first time in a long time, Axel actually enjoyed Christmas. The Jozefson house was a little too warm for his liking, but the company was just right.

Axel glanced Winter's way, spurring her to speak.

"A-Actually, Papa. Uh…"

He turned back towards her, giving a soft, "Hm?"

"Well, uh… Lacey, from school, invited me over for a Christmas sleepover. Weird night for it, I know, but a bunch of girls are going. Axe-Axel offered to walk me over to her house, since it's so late. Didn't you, Axe?"

Winter looked over at him with imploring eyes as if he wasn't ready to lie for her. It didn't even take him a full heartbeat, bobbing his head with a p-popping,

"Yupppp." He pursed his lips, shrugging his shoulders and tossing an innocent, blue-eyed look to her grandfather.

Maybe it was the liquor, but her grandfather didn't seem to think nearly long enough about the situation, just nodding with a short, "Call me in the morning and let me know when you'll be home."

Just like that, he ambled up the stairs, leaving Winter wide-eyed.

"Was that… Did I just get a seal of approval from the old man?" Axel joked with her, offering up a smile.

"In a weird sort of way, I guess." Winter mumbled, pushing herself up with a groan similar to her grandfather. She had eaten far too much of their Christmas feast. "I'll go pack a bag."

"Sure. I'll wait for you." Axel sighed, watching her jog up

the stairs. It wasn't long before they were heading across the street together, to Axel's empty house.

"I DIDN'T EVEN NOTICE YOU HAD A FIREPLACE..." WINTER mumbled, as she dropped down onto the blanket besides Axel. It didn't entirely lessen the hard flooring of his living room, but it was enough to sit criss-crossed. Axel, on his knees, was poking the roaring flames of the fire they had started.

"That's because mom doesn't like it being used. Why we have one when she doesn't even like fires, I don't know." He glanced at her, and in the gleam of the firelight, his blue eyes glowed neon, silver jewelry glinting. "She'd kill me if she was here, so let's maybe keep the fireplace usage to ourselves, yeah?"

"Do you even need to ask?" Winter answered, giving a laugh as she stared at him, shrugging her shoulders. "Your secrets are safe with me, Axe."

Axel paused for a moment before giving a nod. Finishing stoking the fire, he sat back with her, giving a heavy sigh as he drew his legs up against his chest.

Looking into the flames, Winter didn't normally didn't mind Axel's silence. Tonight, though, she couldn't bear to be left alone with her thoughts, so she filled it with a question,

"New Years is coming up soon. Got any resolutions, Axe? Besides defeating a monster."

"No." Axel bluntly responded.

You really are difficult sometimes, you know that? Rolling her eyes, Winter pressed him for more of an answer,

"Why not? We should come up with some."

"Aren't resolutions just goals for the new year? I don't have any goals."

Reaching for the cup of cocoa she had placed on the glass coffee table behind them, Winter answered,

"Not necessarily. They could be wishes. Or dreams."

"I don't have those either." Axel mumbled, leaning his chin on his knee as he avoided looking at her.

"Axel." Winter spoke his name softly.

"What? That's what *it* does. Why bother?" She knew what he meant, but it didn't stop her from disagreeing with him. He didn't give her the chance to, instead asking, "What about you?"

"Assuming we survive? I want to learn more about my powers. I want to... to know how I made Bleary." Winter smiled, looking up at the mantle of the fireplace. She lifted her hand and gave it a small wave. With a hum of warmth that wasn't coming from the fire, they both watched leaves forming out of nothing, until mistletoe hung down between them. "I want to learn how to use it to make more than just... little things, like that."

Peering up at it, Axel smirked, and remarked, "Well, I'm not going to kiss you, if that's why you had mistletoe on your mind."

Laughing, Winter gave a shake of her head. She took another sip of her cocoa, before setting it down besides Axel's untouched mug.

"Okay, new question: What am I to you?"

"What?" The question had successfully taken Axel off guard.

"Do you remember French class, before all of this started? You couldn't call me your friend."

"You still think about that?"

"Of course I do! Axel, that was... I thought we were friends, and you didn't." Her hurt leaked into her voice, and Winter looked away as she continued, "It sticks in the mind, but things change. Look how different things are now."

She genuinely had been hurt, at the time. Maybe even determined to prove herself to him, as silly as that was. All their late night talks and it was still hard to tell sometimes if Axel cared. He was aloof, quiet, maybe even moody— and she thought the world of him.

Now, he was staring at her, silent, with a gaze that made Winter want to wilt in front of him. Nervously, she kept talking,

"I just... You know, I think we're friends, and I was w-wondering if maybe you'd agree."

For some reason, that earned a snort from her friend, and Axel finally looked away, staring down at the fire. Silent still, he seemed to be thinking, and Winter stayed quiet this time, watching the light of the flames dance across his face. He looked like a statue, unmoving, as Winter fidgeted with her fingers, waiting on him to speak. At last, he did.

"After all we've been through... I don't have friends, but I have you, so if that's what you want to call it, then yeah, we're friends, Win. I'm not good at trusting people, and you know, you've kind of... made my life a little crazy."

"I'm s—"

"But you've also made it worth it." He interrupted her quickly, not allowing the apology to slip from her lips. Glancing her way, his cheeks were flushed as he admitted softly, "You're my favorite person, Snowflake. Don't doubt that, okay?"

A breath she'd been holding finally slipped from her, relief hitting Winter like a truck. Smiling into the fireplace, she murmured,

"You know... I really wish Miss Popelin was here to hear you say that."

"Yeah. She took me off guard, you know. Stupid French class." Axel grumbled.

Laughing, Winter reached for her glass of cocoa, grabbing Axel's at the same time to hand to him.

"Let's toast. To French and friendship."

Axel pulled a face at her, "Do you have to make it so cheesy?"

"Okay, fine, what do you want to toast to?" Winter asked, amused.

Axel hesitated, studying her a moment, his loose hand going to the pendant around his neck. He looked down and smiled at it, before meeting her gaze again.

"To snowflakes and lightbulbs."

Winter's mouth popped open, and she was sure it had to be quite the expression, as Axel laughed as soon as he saw it. Recovering, she beamed from ear-to-ear, and clinked their mugs together, agreeing,

"To snow and light."

UNCERTAIN NIGHTMARES

Winter was already laying in Axel's bed by the time he came into the room. She barely heard him crack open the door and slip in.

That evening, Winter wore a pair of green shorts and a bright red shirt on that said 'Naughty'— a Christmas t-shirt that she'd had for years, now a bit tight on her, but favored so much she couldn't bare to get rid of it. It was a matching set: she had a green one that said 'Nice,' too. In her lap, she had opened the sketchbook Axel had gotten her— several little baubles drawn upon the page. One was physically made— a large plastic candy cane ornament laying next to her, nearly the size of a walking cane. She had been quite proud of the creation, though now her cheeks burned as Axel spoke,

"Neat. Another big thing to pack away in my garage all year long." His parents— more specifically his mother— didn't enjoy Christmas. They had barely decorated outside at all, besides a Christmas wreath on the front door.

Looking up at him, Axel's hair was damp and floppy, his cheeks more flushed than usual from the scalding hot showers he took. He wore a dark, long-sleeve shirt and gray sweatpants. Winter couldn't help but wonder if he was dressed so heavily to sleep because of the cool temperature of his house, or because she was here and he was hiding his scars.

I hope I'm not making him uncomfortable... She thought vaguely, giving him a weak smile as he came to sit on the bed beside her, the mattress creaking under him. If Kaya were here, she would have given a scandalized gasp that Winter was laying in Axel's bed, childishly making fun of them for their co-ed sleepover, or for being alone together. Neither Winter nor Axel found it strange at all, there was no intentions besides plotting their next encounter with Bleary and trying to sleep. There was a comfort in not being alone, and Winter now as comfortable with Axel now as she had been with Kaya.

Winter shook her head, offering Axel a smile. "Well, you don't have to keep it. I was just practicing. We have some of these over at my house, anyway." They were stabbed into the ground along the driveway, little crooked plastic candy canes.

"What are you going to do with it, then?" Axel asked, reaching to pull down his blinds.

"Just going to put it back." Winter's answer came easily, laughing at the skeptical look on Axel's face.

She sat up beside him, swinging her legs over the side of his bed. Tossing her sketchbook down onto the wooden floors of his bedroom, it fell open to the page where she had originally pulled the cane. It was still etched across the parchment. Settling the butt of the cane against the page, Winter gave her friend a sideways glance,

"Ready to see a magic trick?" She asked, grinning.

"Sureeee." Axel scoffed, though he gave a small smile.

Laying her hands over the top of the candy cane prop, Winter closed her eyes as she focused on what she wanted to do. Putting something back always felt different to her than bringing it forward, a surge of energy flowing from her hands. She didn't need to push, it was pushing for her, the cane sinking from her grip and floating down, effortlessly, into the book. When she opened her eyes, she saw the last glimpse of red and white stripes before it melted into the pages.

Leaning down, she picked up the book and snapped it shut, throwing Axel a triumphant look.

To her surprise, he wasn't smiling anymore. Instead, Axel was looking at her with an intense expression.

"What?" Winter asked, hugging her sketchbook closer.

"Win... Could you do that to Bleary?"

The question shocked her, Winter's eyes going wide. "I..."

She had gone to get her red notebook from the school, that first time she went to face Bleary, when Axel had come to save her again. It had occurred to her that she could use the sketch, but...

"I'm not sure. I tried erasing Bleary's sketch, in the red book— but it just came back. Because it's still alive, I think. I haven't touched it since." Winter admitted. Reaching into her bag, she pulled out the red sketchbook. Opening it, Bleary was on one of the pages. There wasn't even a smudge to show she had tried erasing it. The lines were clearly etched, untouched, and solid. "To do what I just did— to push an item, or push Bleary, back into the sketch... I would have to get extremely close."

"Is it possible?" Axel asked anyway, despite the cautious tone Winter had.

"...Technically. If we trapped it, somehow. If... I had the power to, if Bleary isn't too strong." The idea made her queasy just thinking about it. How could they even manage that?

"Winter, we could do that." Axel had a hopeful look in his

eyes— something she had rarely seen from him. "Think about it. Bleary is at the school, more or less. It's winter break, so no one is there for it to hunt, and the season's festivities will make it hard to find anyone, anyway. It'll be hungry for someone new to mess with. If we go, it'll come out for us. I know it will. I could distract it long enough, trap it, so you could get it back into the sketch."

"I don't know…" Winter murmured, suddenly nervous at the idea. The last time she had gone after Bleary, it hadn't ended well, and she knew it had claimed a lot more victims since then.

"I can't do it alone. Come with me tomorrow. Just try." Had their roles been reversed? Winter was the one who had been set on going after Bleary and Axel had been the reluctant one, but now he was more focused on it than she had ever seen him.

It took her a minute before she could nod her head, setting the two sketchbooks aside.

"Okay. We'll try it."

She was trying not to think about how much power it would take her— or if she could even do it at all.

Not too long later, Axel moved to turn the bedroom light off while Winter got comfortable in his bed. The silence between them as they shuffled to settle down for the night was somewhat deafening, both caught up on this new plan to go after Bleary. It was as sudden as the first time, and Winter didn't feel any more prepared.

Better to feel unprepared than to let it take anyone else, she thought.

For a few quiet seconds, Winter stared up at the popcorn

ceiling, gnawing on her bottom lip. Everything felt so normal tonight— the night before they went to fight Bleary. But at the same time, nothing really was normal. It had been so easy to lie to her grandpa, too easy. Winter had never considered herself to be a natural liar, but when it came to something so big, it had slipped out effortlessly. Now, it occurred to her that she had let him go to bed without saying goodnight or telling him she loved him. Maybe it was better that way?

"What are you thinking about?" Axel's voice broke through the dark, causing Winter to tilt her head to look at him. Even in the nearly pitch black of his room, his eyes seemed to glow like two turquoise rings, piercing right through her.

"Everything." Winter answered. She shivered, feeling goosebumps roll over her arms, though the room was not cold. "I feel like we're going to lose. Like this is a battle we can't win." She hesitated. Looking into Axel's eyes, as she whispered, "Is that how it feels for you? When Bleary is—"

She didn't have to finish, as he interrupted, "All the time."

Silence fell between them, as Winter shivered once more, and Axel's arm wrapped securely around her, hugging her into his side.

Laying there, she stared at him in the dark. His face was blank, but she had learned that it was when he looked the most absent that his mind was thinking of something important.

"What are you thinking about?" She echoed his question.

His lips twitched and Axel sighed, looking up at the ceiling.

"I know a lot about depression, not just because of my own, but through research. There was a time I thought I could make sense of it…" He murmured, his voice little more than a faint whisper. Winter waited, and he continued, "Have you ever heard of Seasonal Depression?"

"No."

"Some people are affected by the change of the seasons. I don't, I seem to be like this all the time, but I was thinking about how Bleary might be tomorrow. I looked into it once, because there's this common myth that depression and suicide gets really bad around the holidays. But that isn't true. Maybe depression is bad during the holidays, but no one wants to kill themselves then, because of family and stuff. Don't want to ruin everyone else's holiday, you know? So suicide is more common in the spring, or early summer. I wonder if it'll give us a leg up on Bleary. Maybe make it weaker, somehow?"

"Holiday cheer coming to the rescue?" Winter mumbled.

Axel gave a soft snort, smiling in the dark. "Yeah, guess so."

It sounded as if he had some bit of hope. He might not admit to it, but the thought made her hopeful, too.

She wasn't sure how long it took for sleep to take her away, but her last thoughts were of how glad she was that neither of them were alone, and how lonely it had to be, before Bleary had been given a face.

When Winter woke with her feet in snow, she felt very far away from the warmth of Axel's bed. She found herself shivering once again, hugging her bare arms and staring down at bare feet. Looking around, she saw the three schools on campus. She stood where the statue of Brendon Hendrix usually was. Instead, in its place, was a statue of Axel. She knew it was him, but his metal hands covered his eyes, and his mouth was gaping open in a scream. His expression was reminded her of Bleary.

Reaching out, she wanted to touch him, but a soft tutting noise from behind her made her.

"I wouldn't do that if I were you, Win." It was his voice, but when Winter turned, the man before her had black eyes.

"Bleary." Saying the monster's name openly made her brave, yet the fear that struck her when the anti-Axel smiled back was so overwhelming that she dropped to her knees in the snow, sitting in front of the statue.

"Is that my name now? I like it. Did sweet Axel pick it out, or did you?" His voice was so coy, so taunting of her as she sat and shivered.

Their surroundings were as eerie as Bleary made her feel. Instead of a soft white, the snow was so cold it appeared blue— the same shade as Axel's eyes. Above, the sky contrasted in a horrifying crimson, dark clouds swirling through it like smoke. For the first time, Winter's eyes caught on a rather tall fence with a barbed-wire top running the perimeter of the school.

She was in Bleary's haunting grounds. He knew it too, as he suddenly dropped to his knees in front of her. It was unnerving to peer into the face of her best friend and see only the evil that was his inner-demon. Bleary's hand reached for her, taking a lock of her hair like Axel might have done, giving it a soft tug.

"Axel has already lost, you know. He always loses. He tries and tries, but... well, his will-power crumbled a long time ago." Bleary sighed, giving her a little pout that made Winter's stomach twist. As he eyed her, she stared into the snow, sitting as still as possible. "What is a girl like you going to do?"

"I brought you here, I can send you back." Winter's voice, to her surprise, didn't shake. She was scared, but anger overcame her fear.

Bleary's laugh was a poor imitation of Axel's. "Is that so? How cute. Maybe when I'm done playing with him, I'll come play with you instead."

Releasing her hair, Axel's tormentor lifted his hand and poked the middle of Winter's forehead with an ice-cold fingertip. "Leave a door open for me in there, won't you?"

Silently flinching backwards, Winter's eyes finally looked back at Bleary, at his taunting smirk. Avoiding looking him in the eye, her gaze went to the statue of her trapped friend.

"I will... if you leave him alone." Winter found herself answering, sounding braver than she felt. But it was true, wasn't it? What she wouldn't give to take his demons as her own and let him be free from torment.

Another empty laugh came from Bleary, who rose to its feet. Taking her by the hand, the creature pulled Winter up, her legs aching from her having sat in the cold. It felt like daggers had dug into her skin, pinprickles tickling her nerves and causing that strange feeling between being in pain and being numb.

"Sure. I'll tell you what... let's play right now. If you can find your way out of the woods, I'll let Axel off easy."

"Woods?"

It was like blinking. Suddenly, Winter was no longer on the school campus. She stood by the Effugere river with the forest looming in front of her. She must have been many miles down-stream. Caligo was nowhere in sight. Just as the snow had been blue and the sky was red, this scene had equally unusual colors. The trees were pitch black, and the grass beneath her feet— though not covered with snow— was frosted with silvery ice, glinting like thousands of needles. Behind her, the river's water was gone, replaced with what looked like several pieces of harsh, mirror-like glass. It clinked and clunked as it moved, rolling like waves.

"Winter." That was Axel's voice, she could tell by the way he said her name that it wasn't Bleary. Turning on her heel, she searched the riverbank for him, but he was nowhere to be seen. His voice came from above, crackling like the school intercom.

"Axel?" Winter called for him.

"Run." His command shook with fear for her, just as Winter's gaze fell on two dark-gray wolves about twenty feet away.

She didn't need to be told twice, bolting towards the woods. Her bare feet slipped on the icy grass, toes numb and struggling for traction, but she couldn't stop with the wolves bounding after her.

It became an endless, expansive maze of trees, twisting and turning every way she ran. Her heart thudding heavily in her ears, but louder still were the voices coming overhead. The chant of, "Run! Run! Run!" Bryce. Miss Popelin. Kaya. Delilah. Oliver. Jovanni. Jae-Hwa. One after the other, pleading with her to go faster.

Run.

Run.

Run.

As she ran, Bleary laughed. Not empty as it was before— but high and gleeful. It was enjoying her panic, her suffering, her impending loss of life.

Winter wanted to find her way out, but it seemed neverending. The further she got into the forest, the closer the trees became, and the more their leaves and branches resembled barbed-wire. Suddenly, her ankles caught on the wire, which had begun to curl along the ground like quickly growing vines.

Falling forward with a panicked gasp, Winter collided with the ground, the wire snaring and curling around her like a well-placed trap. Rolling onto her back, her hands went to try and untangle herself, but it only dug into her palms and drew blood, which dripped from between her fingers.

A series of low growls alerted her to look up, peering at the two wolves. They both had familiar eyes— Axel's eyes— but the way they snarled and growled were anything but friendly. Fear rose up in her throat and Winter wanted to scream. Yet, her mouth opened and no sound came out, as the wolves lunged at her. The only sound louder than their sharp teeth was that maniacal laughter echoing from the blood-red sky.

"Winter!" Axel's voice was sharp in her ears when she came to, thrashing beside him. Her arm flung out and he just barely caught it from colliding into his nose as she pushed against him, frantically trying to get away. "Hey! Hey, stop! It was a nightmare!"

It took a few seconds for her to process his words and stop fighting him. The room was filled with a dull, early-morning light. Winter's skin was drenched in sweat, and her head was pounding. What was more, was that there was a fine layer of snow on the bed, as if it had been snowing while she had been asleep.

"Breathe, Win." Axel's voice tried to cut through her panic, and Winter realized she had been gasping. His grip on her arm was tight, and his eyes were narrow when she finally looked at him. Moreso, he had dark circles underneath them, as if while she had been in Bleary's game, he had been wide-awake.

It took a few more seconds before she was able to speak.

"I'm okay... I'm alright." Her mouth was desert-dry, heart still racing as she cautiously sat up, forcing Axel to shift on the bed to make room.

"No, you're not." He answered her, slowly easing his grip on her arm until he let go entirely. "You want to talk about it?"

"No, I want to kill that thing." As steady and serious as Winter sounded, it didn't surprise her that Axel chuckled.

"How about some breakfast first? After we clean up the snow."

As Winter nodded numbly in response, Axel moved to carefully start scooping up the layer of snow from his bed. When they had piled it all into his trash can, Axel slipped out of the room so Winter could change. She had a pair of black jeans and a long-sleeve, dark green sweater for their last stand, pulling her hair into two low pigtails. When she joined Axel in the kitchen, she noted he must have changed in the bathroom, as he wore his usual attire of all black with his dark gray hoodie, the lightbulb pendant gleaming from his neck.

He was ready with a plate of omurice— basically, an omelet with rice— to set in front of her by the time Winter sat beside him at the kitchen island.

"Thanks." Winter murmured. As they ate, she filled him in on her dream, slowly but surely telling him the more important details. Axel ate in silence, just listening, and was finished with his breakfast by the time she finished her retelling of the nightmare. Her own food, in comparison, had been poked at and barely touched. As hungry as she was, she was in no mood to eat. Her mind, however, was even more ravenous. All she could do every time she glanced at Axel was wonder what he was thinking. Of course, his face was as blank and unreadable as ever. If he had any thoughts about her nightmare, he didn't share them.

It was a morning of quiet ritual. Doing the dishes, making sure they had their bags— before they realized they wouldn't really need them and choosing to leave them behind. Today would be anything but a normal day at school.

As they walked out of Axel's house and locked the door behind themselves, he stuck his hands into his pockets and sighed heavily as he stepped down off his porch.

"You want to walk to the yard and pick up my baby?" Axel asked, peering up at the gray clouds overhead.

"Sure." Winter confirmed, trying to enjoy the walk. It was silent but not uncomfortable, and soon she was sliding into the newly fixed-up passenger side seat of Axel's Camaro.

It was on their drive to school that things grew interesting. Peering out the window, Winter was all too aware of the skies changing from a somber gray to a deep purple-red color. It almost mimicked the color in her dream, if not darker and even more terrifying. Bleary knew they were coming.

Winter was on edge, scratching her finger idly on the leather seats, until Axel reached out to take her hand and stop her, keeping one hand on the wheel. Whether that was to comfort her or to stop her from wearing out his seats, she didn't know, but she shot him a nervous smile anyway.

There were no weapons to fight Bleary with, besides the red sketchbook— and honestly, Axel didn't know if that would be any use. It had been the excuse he had given Winter — the idea of using her powers to shove it back into non-existence, but if he was honest, being here had nothing to do with that. At least, not for him.

Powers or not, Bleary was being destroyed that day. Even if Axel had to take it down himself— even if it took his life to do it. The thought had come in increasingly large waves for some time now, not that he would let Winter know that. The truth was, he wasn't sure he could stand to see another person killed and know it was his fault. Bryce had, once upon a time, been his friend. Jovanni had, whether he liked to admit it or not, also been his friend. Oliver and Jae-Hwa had been nice to him when others wouldn't. Miss Popelin and Kaya had been innocent. Delilah hadn't deserved to die alone on bathroom tiles.

He was done. This had gone on long enough. To save himself, he had to kill his own mind. He had to kill Bleary.

As they parked the Camaro, Axel couldn't help but

wonder who would have a harder time against Bleary—himself, or Winter.

Walking side-by-side towards the school, the sight of it was ghastly. The entire front half of the school had crumbled, as if it were an old war-torn building. The usually sleek columns were cracked and broken, the windows— what few remained— shattered. Looking towards Winter, he could see the horror on her face.

"What the hell happened?" She whispered, staring at the damage of the empty, ghost-town-like campus. Something was beyond wrong. It was as if they had entered an entirely different reality.

A deep shudder went through Axel. Was this even reality? Where were the cops? The teachers? Anyone, really— it was as if no one else could see what was happening. He knew why— this was it. Bleary was manipulating things now, and they were at its mercy.

The closer they got, the more the wind seemed to pick up, making Winter's pigtails flutter against her shoulders and Axel's piercings jangle against his ears.

Sensing their presence, as they knew it would, Bleary's looming figure stepped out from behind one of the many broken columns. Axel had seen it not so long ago, but beside him, Winter stopped abruptly in her tracks, seemingly surprised by the sight of Bleary. Instead of the smoking, beastly figure that they had first met, back in October, Bleary appeared as solid as they were. The ends of its long robe was no longer smoking, but solid black velvet. Its hands, as bony as they were, looked sharp and ended in spiked nails that resembled claws. Its skin, which before was like fog, now was as solid and ugly as pulled gray leather. But its eyes— they were the only part that had done the opposite. Before, they had been the only solid thing, the real part of Bleary, with those black, piercing pupils. Now, they were blurry, faded and sunken in.

Bleary Eyes truly was... well, bleary-eyed, now.

Winter was unable to look away as it lingered closer, the look on her face filled with fear. Even Axel was affected, rolling his hands into fists to try and keep from shaking. It didn't flit back and forth like it once did, but instead took solid steps forward, towering over them. When its mouth gaped open and it gave that terrible screech, it came out even louder than it had before, Axel's hands flying up to cover his ears just as he had in the woods the other night.

No one ever wanted to face their demons, and neither did Axel. But what choice did he have?

"Come to play?" A voice sounded in the back of Axel's mind, and— he assumed— in Winter's, too. He knew then that there was no chance of trapping Bleary long enough to get the sketchbook.

That was when Winter stepped in front of him, protectively putting herself in-between Axel and Bleary.

"Axel... Let me handle it. Don't look." Winter warned him.

But how could he not? It was his demon, and in the last few months he had grown accustomed to being able to see it as a physical being. It was almost euphoric, to face it down.

All or nothing, he thought.

He was able to defend himself, for the first time. It wasn't hard to lift his head and stare it right in the eyes, knowing what would happen when he did.

26

UNRAVELING THE END

A blink was all it took before Axel found himself sitting on the floor of a large shower. Water dripped from the faucet beside him, a steady sound ringing in his ears. He was clothed, but his sleeves were pulled up, the endless litter of scars on full display fresh and old. He had lost count of how many he had now, the familiar feel of cold metal alerting him to a razor blade in his hand.

But he wasn't alone.

"Screw you. That's a mean trick, turning into her." Axel automatically said when he saw Winter sitting across from him, smiling coyly at him. The difference was her eyes. Instead of her beautiful hazel-green irises, he saw only black. Bleary couldn't trick him.

"Really? I thought it would bring you comfort. You trust her. Me. Winter." Bleary's voice perfectly mimicked hers, making Axel scowl.

"Yeah, I do. But you're not her." Axel responded, idly rubbing a thumb against the blade in his hand, feeling it just barely slice into his skin.

Before his eyes, he watched the creature morph. It's hair

becoming shorter and darker, face turning more angular, clothes baggy and black. Within seconds, Axel was staring at himself, only with pitch-black eyes staring back.

World's ugliest mirror image, *Axel thought bitterly.*

"Better?" His evil half asked him.

"Hardly. Why don't you show your real face?" Axel retorted, picturing the demon that stalked the halls of their school.

At first Bleary didn't answer, merely smiling at him. Instead, he crossed his arms and sat back comfortably against the wall of the shower, drawing a leg up to his chest as he finally spoke,

"This is my real face. I'm you, at heart. Winter didn't create me. You did. We've talked before, remember? Just not so... loudly."

Axel couldn't deny it, he'd known from the start. Bleary was an old friend, something Winter hadn't entirely realized when he poured out his mind's dark thoughts to her. Maybe it hadn't been touchable, but the Bleary Winter had imagined wasn't far from the beast in Axel's mind. It didn't feel uncomfortable to sit across from the darker half of him. After all, how many nights had he laid awake going back and forth with it in his mind? Before he talked to Winter, it had always just been him in his own little mental bubble. He had never let anyone else see into what he struggled with. It was always just Bleary and him.

In truth, they were just two halves of the same coin. Bleary was a part of him, ergo he was Bleary.

As Axel refused to answer, his eyes fixated on the razorblade in his hand, Bleary continued,

"Are you really going to let her take the hit for you? The blame... The guilt. We both know this has nothing to do with your sweet little friend. This is all on you. Admit it. You let me in. You picked up that blade, desperate for a way out. The addiction, the disease, was too sweet. So you did it again, and again, and now... you don't want to stop, do you? You don't want me to leave, because you'd be alone again."

This too, was true. He could have said he had Winter, but people change and leave— People disappoint, or become disappointed. He knew that too well. There was a comfort in having Bleary to lean on. It was more than just that, he knew. He was stuck in the habit, the endless cycle. He couldn't say that Bleary was wrong. It was part of him now. He would always be someone with depression. Someone who enjoyed pain as punishment. He could have denied it, assuming Bleary was just trying to get to him, but the truth was that depression came from the way someone felt about themselves, their real emotions. There was nothing Axel could say, Bleary was speaking straight from his own mind.

Axel remembered the first time he'd put a blade to his skin. He wasn't coerced, he did exactly what he intended to do. He had brought Bleary to life, not Winter.

"What do you want me to say?" He sighed, finally looking back at the creature, "That this is my fault? It is. I have no one to blame but myself. You want me to say that I'm going to win against you? I don't care about winning. I don't care what you do to me. What I care about is that you go back in my head, where you belong, and leave everyone else alone."

Bleary chuckled at his words. "We are in your head. And while we have been safely chatting, Winter has been quite the little warrior."

A chill ran through Axel, as somewhere in the distance, he heard a loud cry.

Winter.

He opened his eyes to reality once again, snapping out of it just as he saw Winter being thrown aside. He had missed seeing her run at Bleary, only viewing the swipe of its long arm as she was tossed like a ragdoll, landing hard on the pavement in front of the Brendon Hendrix statue. The journal had been thrown aside. It— much like Winter— was insignificant to the mental demon.

Bleary had power now, real power. He didn't need to

focus on one of them at a time. Axel, cursing himself, moved to go to her— only to hear Bleary's shrill cry, causing his hands to cover his aching ears. Just as he stepped forward, the ground beneath his feet began to crumble. Axel had no choice but to stumble backwards, watching the ground disappear from where he had been standing. He must have gone back at least eight feet, watching in horror as a large ravine opened into the crust of the earth, circling the founder's statue along with Winter and Bleary.

"WINTER!" *That's Axel's voice.* It seemed so distant, so faint in Winter's ears as she knelt on the hard pavement in front of the courtyard statue. Her head felt so fuzzy, her vision wavering. Bleary's tall, dark form as it moved in front of her almost seemed normal now, after months of fighting against it.

We've lost. She thought with a chill, lifting her head to look at where Axel was. His blue eyes were the only bright thing in the dark stormy apocalypse she had brought on. The ground between them had crumbled into a large ravine, separating them so Bleary could focus its attention on her without Axel interfering again. She was alone, which is exactly what it wanted.

The sketch idea was a complete failure, just like her powers.

Pushing herself up, Winter resolved to make her final stand. *Maybe if it gets me, the one who brought it to life, it'll die, since I'm the one who brought it to life. It'll leave Caligo, and Axel, alone.* She thought as she gazed up to meet the tall beast's eyes. *I'll see Kaya again.* She thought, the last bit of joy she could find in this situation, trying to be at ease with her decision. *I'm sorry, Axel. I'm afraid you're going to have to fight without me from now on.*

It might have been dramatic, but there was this feeling she got around Bleary- this low dread that she couldn't shake. It had an effect on her, like suddenly, she couldn't find the happy vision of the future, she could only see the horrible end approaching her. She heard Axel shouting at Bleary, and at her, as she stared into pitch black pupils, and then...

"Winter." A familiar voice broke through right before reality faded— and it wasn't Axel's.

Where am I? *All it took was a blink, and Winter was standing in a yard of grass. Looking around, she caught sight of rose bushes and familiar mint green paneled walls.* Home?

Turning in a slow circle, her eyes were drawn to look across the street— The steady slate-gray panels of the Dunn residence, with its black front door and single orange tree, big paneled windows that had the curtains pulled back to allow a look into its modern interior. There was a little boy sitting on the grass. He had trucks in his hands, but he wasn't playing. His blue eyes were staring straight at her.

"Winter." Once more, her name was spoken. This voice made Winter whirl around again, meeting the warm, brown eyes of a tall, smiling, auburn-haired woman in a long yellow sundress. Winter had once struggled to see the similarities in pictures, but in person, there was no doubt. Their jawline, nose, even their bodies were built similarly. If life was in black and white and there was no difference in hair, eyes or skin color, Winter could say she was staring at an older version of herself.

"Mom?" Her voice came out in a whisper, immediate tears

pricking at her eyes. She had wanted to see her mom again for so long, but now it almost felt like a cruel trick.

"Hello, sweetheart." Janet Jozefson's voice was soft, and loving, and maybe just a little bit sad. Just as Winter remembered her sounding. But...

Winter's eyes went across the street. The boy was gone and in his place stood the full-grown Axel. His hands were in his pockets, staring at her with a blank expression. His lips moved, and Winter thought he might have been mouthing her name.

Axel... Why was her brain so fuzzy? They were... fighting? It was hard to remember. She stared at him a minute, feeling like it was important to remember, but she was drawing blanks. Looking back at her mother, however, it clicked. Bleary. Axel. The fight.

"You can't trick me, Bleary. I've been through this before. I know your tricks!" Winter said, frowning as she steadied herself, ready to fight the creature.

Only, her mother smiled and shook her head. "Ah. I forgot how strong-willed you are. I'm not that thing you brought to life, Winter. It's really me, and I'm afraid we don't have long."

It shouldn't have been so easy to believe her, but studying her surroundings, it did feel... different somehow. Winter's head throbbed just thinking about it, reaching up to touch the faded bruise on her forehead. Her eyes went back across the street to Axel, and she saw him smiling at her now— his eyes flashing black for just a brief second. They weren't alone.

"Come, sit." Her mom beckoned her, gesturing to the bench by the rose bushes.

Cautiously, Winter followed and sat down, eyeing her mom with confusion.

"I don't understand... If you're really you, then how are you here?" Winter questioned, folding her hands nervously in her lap.

"We don't have the time for questions, darling. I promise, I'll tell you everything someday, but it's too dangerous for me to stay here long. *They'll find us.*" Janet's voice was as urgent as her words, reaching out to take Winter's hands.

Questions burned in Winter's head. *They? Who's they? Who are you hiding from? Why did you run? But she stayed quiet as her mom continued.*

"I never thought you'd be so strong. I had hoped you would be weaker, like Jess. Able to live a normal life. I've kept an eye on you, but when you made that creature... I realized you're a little too much like me." Janet sighed, shaking her head at the thought.

"Jess? Aunt Jess?" Winter couldn't help but speak up now, eyes widening.

"Yes. Winter. It's called Reality Weaving." The words held weight, a shiver running through her upon finally having a name for her abilities. "The women in our family are Weavers. My mom, me, my sisters, you. Our line goes back to the beginning— the very beginning— the founding families of this world. I can't sit here and give you a history lesson, but... What people think of as scientific creation, or even Godly creation, it's more like... magic. Some call it Poesis. An ability to bring things into being, to rewrite reality. There is no such thing as coincidence."

Mind churning, Winter felt her mom squeeze her hands as she took it all in. "So... Like bringing Bleary to life? The... monster I made."

Sympathy filled Janet's eyes, and she lifted a hand to touch Winter's cheek. She was to the touch. "Yes. Dragons, unicorns, pegasi... even monsters. Anything that has made its way into modern belief, those are the results of reality weaving. It leaves echoes. We bend what is, and that leaves a mark. All the legends, they've been real. At least, in some timeline. It's complicated, and hard to teach in only a few minutes. But you need to know: You can do this. You can do whatever you set your mind to, you just have to *want it.*"

"I want it more than anything." Winter immediately answered, "I want it gone. I want to stop this. But how? Mom, I... I don't know what to do. I don't even know how I brought it here, I just had a dream."

Letting go of her, her mother reached out to the rose bushes and plucked a single bud. She held it out, dropping it into Winter's hand. Confused, Winter gazed at it until her mother waved a hand and she watched as the bud blossomed right before her eyes.

Magic.

"Everything starts with a dream. That's all I can tell you. You'll know what to do, trust in yourself. Do what feels natural, even if you don't think it'll work. Believe in the ability to make things happen." Janet advised her. She paused, studying Winter with sad eyes before she softly added, "I've missed you. I'm so sorry, Winter. I wish I could have done things differently, but leaving you was the only way. I..."

Whatever she was going to say, Winter might never know. In a matter of seconds, the idyllic, sunny outdoors changed. Clouds rolled in, darkening the sky. The air felt colder, and Janet's expression turned serious. "I have to go. You're on your own, Winter. At least for now."

"Mom, wait!" Winter cried out, reaching out to stop her— but her hand went through thin air, her mom disappearing from where she sat. Standing up, Winter turned in a circle, looking for her.

Instead, all she saw was a smirking Axel— no, Bleary— striding across the street towards her. Winter clenched her fists at her side, trying to will herself to stand still, to not show her fear. But the way it walked towards her was threatening, even as its body blurred in Winter's view— not as solid as it was in reality. The fake Axel stopped in front of her, hand reaching out to touch Winter's cheek. Its hand was ice cold and sharp against her skin, an exact opposite of her mom's hand just moments before.

This isn't him. It's another trick. It can't hurt me. She kept trying to remind herself, attempting to clear her mind enough to see Bleary for what it was. It was a lot more powerful now than it had been then, and instead of seeing Bleary, Axel's form shifted into—

"Kaya." Winter choked on her name, her courage melting away as she looked into the face of her friend. Bleary would try again, and it certainly had picked the right form to claw at Winter's guilty conscience.

Her friend was pale, so pale her skin was paper-white, lacking its natural tan. Her lips were tinged blue, eyes sporting dark purple circles underneath even darker irises. Her wrist, so close to Winter's face with the hand still on her cheek, had horrible, deep red cuts, dried blood against her skin. Her clothes were covered in blood, like they had been when she'd seen her on Praecipitus Way.

"Your mom might not have abandoned you, but you abandoned me, Winter. You didn't warn me. You led me to my death!" Kaya's voice was angry, her black eyes glaring into Winter's, gripping the side of her face harder like she was holding her in place. Even though she knew it was Bleary trying to strike guilt into her, she couldn't help the horror she felt as she stared at her dead friend.

"N-No! I... I didn't mean to. I'm so sorry, Kaya." Winter stammered out, hoping the real Kaya would hear her somewhere. Her shoulders slumped, mind beginning to feel fuzzy again, dark thoughts surfacing under Bleary's influence. "I never meant to involve you! I never meant for any of this!"

"That doesn't mean you aren't at fault. Own up to it, Winter. You killed me. And others, too. All of this is because of you."

Those words... Winter couldn't deny them. Her mouth opened, eyes widening as she tried to find the words to defend herself. Somewhere in the back of her head, she wanted to think Kaya would never blame her for an honest mistake, but it was getting so hard to believe that the longer she looked into Kaya's pale face.

She never got the chance to answer her again. A heavy force piled into her from the side, shoving her out of Bleary's grip. A soft gasp left Winter as she was pushed to the ground, onto what felt like hard, solid pavement, rather than the soft grass of her yard.

As visions faded into reality again, Winter found herself staring into Axel's frantic eyes. They were on the ground in front of the statue at school. Back to the fight with Bleary, back to reality, where it wasn't playing tricks on her mind— at least, not entirely. Axel was on top of her, holding her to him protectively. His expression was so grim, so serious... *You need to stop being so serious, Axe. I wish you smiled more.* She thought absently as her mind began to clear, feeling his hand touch her cheek where her mom and Bleary had before, his fingers rough and calloused to the touch. So many questions ran through her mind, all about why this was happening.

I brought Bleary to life because I wanted to help Axel. I wanted him to win his fight, and I thought it would be easier to have something physical to face. It was an accident when I did it but that's the reason why, isn't it? I wanted him to have more happiness. He doesn't deserve the monster his mind made. She thought, taking a shaky breath. Seconds were passing, but it seemed so slow, only vaguely aware of Bleary's screeching. Axel's face swam in her vision, the way he was looking at her so sad. He looked like he was going to say something Winter didn't want to hear.

I just want you to win, because you're incredible when you're just you, and not Bleary.

Those words echoed in her head.

Just you, not Bleary.

Just you.

Bleary didn't come from my sketches... They came from you.

Winter's hand lifted, touching her palm to Axel's forehead.

Even Winter didn't know what happened, or how exactly she did it, but the next thing she knew, Bleary was screeching louder than ever, lunging for them in the background but it was far too late. A bright light erupted between her and Axel, throwing him backwards. For her, it was like the world being turned upside-down, her mind spinning. Everything went black as she lost consciousness.

Was it over?

27

UNAWARE STUDENTS

Daylight. That's what Winter woke up to, coming in through her bedroom blinds and streaking harshly across her face. Lifting a hand, she winced and blinked her eyes open, met with Pesca's soft fur as her cat nudged into her cheek, giving an insistent meow. Yawning, she drew her face away, closing her eyes again with thoughts of not wanting to go to school.

School.

Her eyes flashed open. "Axel!"

Sitting up abruptly, horror hit Winter as she realized what she had briefly forgotten. The last thing she remembered was Axel being thrown backwards as Winter wished for everything to go back to the way it was.

In a hurry, Winter stumbled out of bed and threw herself into the hall. She could hear movement in the kitchen as she ran downstairs, grabbing onto the door frame as she caught sight of her grandpa. He was standing at the stove poking at bacon with a fork, not a care in the world.

Did the world not entirely end yesterday?

"Papa. What day is it?" Winter asked, breathless from her rush.

He stopped what he was doing and turned towards her. As soon as he did, she realized his calm demeanor was entirely an act.

"I was about to ask you that." He admitted, running a hand across his jaw. "See, I thought it was a lovely December day. I walked downstairs thinking about when we should take the lights down off the eaves, and whether I could sneak some leftover Christmas ham into my breakfast, and how bad the snow would be on the driveway."

Dread built in Winter with each slow sentence her grandfather spoke. If she could have shrunk before his stern gaze, she would have.

"But you see… None of that happened. And when I spoke to our neighbors— the Thorne's— they thought I was going senile. Because it's only September thirtieth. I have a few months of memory that no one else seems to have gone through. Especially memories of a wicked storm yesterday, around the school… and earthquakes. How I went from driving towards the school, to waking up in bed today. That there's a mystery." He clicked off the stove and crossed his arms, narrowing his eyes at her, "What did I say about no funny business?"

"I-I… I um…" Winter's mouth gaped like a fish, unsure how to answer. Her grandfather pulled out a chair at their kitchen table, gesturing for her to sit, which she did.

"I want the truth, Winter Rosemary."

The use of her middle name made her wince, hanging her head. How could she possibly explain all this to him?

"The truth… is that I was trying to help a friend. I really was, Papa. That was all I wanted, but things got out of hand. I don't really know how to explain it, except that. People got hurt, and then it wasn't about helping *him* anymore, it was about saving *them*. We didn't know what to do, or how to stop *it*, so I just... I just wanted it to go back to before. Before Bl-..." She sucked in a breath, wringing her hands in her lap.

"You're being awfully vague." Her grandfather remarked as he sat down across from her, not commenting on the stuttering word she wouldn't say.

"I have to be." Winter remarked, lifting her head to look at him, "I'm sorry, Papa, but... it's a secret. If I told you what happened, I'd be revealing a secret I promised to keep. I can't do that. All I can tell you is that everything is okay now."

He looked at her for a long, scathing moment, and Winter was imagining the worst. What would he do to get answers from her? There was so much she had to answer for, none of it good. She felt like bursting into tears, staring at her grandfather with wide, guilty, glossy eyes.

But she would keep Axel's secrets.

Tage Jozefson opened his mouth just as the doorbell rang, making Winter jump.

Oh! That must be him! She practically flew out of the kitchen, long legs throwing herself at the front door.

"Axe—"

Her voice died in her throat, gaping at the girl in front of her.

"Hey, Greenbean. Miss me?"

"Kaya!" That was what Winter had tried to say. Instead, it came out as a garbled cry of, "KAA!" As she launched forward into the arms of her oldest friend. The girl who was supposed to be dead was looking a bit peaky, but otherwise, seemed just fine. She wasn't wearing her contacts, but the green hair extensions curled from the crown of her head, and she wore her usual attire of a fashion magazine worthy outfit. It seemed that death hadn't affected her sense of style.

"Hey, Win... Mind telling me what the hell I just went through?" Kaya asked, patting her hair as Winter hugged her.

In shock, she couldn't find the words. Her grandfather spoke before she did,

"Well, I'll be damned. Kaya Morito. We attended your funeral. Well, actually, we attended a few funerals."

"I know. Or well, I would assume so— I remember dying. Kind of foggy now, actually. Like a bad dream. But it definitely happened, right?" She grabbed Winter by the shoulders and pulled her back, looking her in the eye. "Care to explain?"

Winter, in her joy, had now begun to feel a little ill. "W-What time is it? We'll be late to school." The random, awkward muttering was followed by a burning face.

"We have time." Her grandfather remarked, crossing his arms. She wasn't getting out of this, and she knew it.

Sighing, Winter spoke,

"Okay. You tell me what you remember, and I'll tell you what I can."

"Deal."

Half an hour later, they were heading to school, Kaya and Winter, walking together like they used to after a sleepover. The storytelling had been a short one. Kaya remembered being chased— she tactfully avoided the word "monster" in front of Winter's grandfather— and being upset. She remembered the pain, at first, and then described it more like falling asleep. She had bad dreams, she said, things she couldn't quite remember, but she was aware that she had died. Yet, when she woke up that morning, in bed, to the tune of her Spice Girls radio alarm clock, she was alive again. She had returned, from Bleary's world to her own. Her parents acted like she had never been gone— they didn't remember, and it was a relief to Kaya that Winter and her grandfather did.

Winter, doing all she could to spare Axel's part in the story, told what she could. There was something she brought to life— something they knew about, even if only a little. Kaya, she assumed, wasn't the only one who had survived, and the more she spoke about it, the more she wondered:

Where is Axel?

She got her answer when they reached the school. There was no mistaking those blue eyes, fixated on the two girls as they drew closer. Axel stood by the statue, where they had made their last stand, gazing at her with a focused stare.

Reaching him, Kaya looked between the two and smiled.

"Hey, Dunn."

"Hey, Morito. You good?"

"Never better." She snorted, patting Winter's shoulder. "I'll leave you two to catch up, with the uh… you know, new timeline and everything. No more monster sketching, okay, Greenbean?" She asked her best friend, winking as she drew away to head into the school.

Left alone, Winter gazed up at Axel. He stood calm, almost lazily-leaned back, hands stuffed into his pockets, but he wouldn't be looking at her like that if nothing had happened.

"I tried texting you. Would have come by, but my mom insisted on bringing me early today. If I had argued, she would have given me hell."

"I had to deal with Papa, and then Kaya showed up— alive — so, you know…"

The tension was palpable, Winter staring back at Axel as if he were an alien. Swallowing, she finally spoke— as did he, at the same time.

"Is *it* gone?" She asked.

"Are you alright?" He countered.

Laughing nervously, Winter tucked a lock of hair behind her ear, ducking her head as she answered him. "I'm fine. You?"

"Yeah. So... it happened, right? That wasn't..." Axel's voice was almost shaking, even though his face didn't show it, Winter could feel his fear coming off him in waves. Perhaps because it matched her own. She didn't even know how she did it, but here they were. As they stood there, she spotted the familiar sight of two dark heads of hair— the Chi twins— walking into school together.

Does that mean everyone is back? Winter wondered briefly.

"A bad dream? No. Definitely happened." She confirmed. Hesitating, she asked, "Do you feel any different? I mean..." Was it too much to hope that vanquishing Bleary would magically erase Axel's depression? Probably. The thought did cross her mind, as she tried to get a read on him.

"No." He answered simply, before sighing, "I don't know how I feel but, if you're asking if I'm still me, then yeah. That part isn't gone."

It was moments like this that made Winter wish she was better at hiding her emotions, as Axel was staring at her and she was sure they were all over her face. Disappointment that she hadn't solved anything.

"Hey." Axel's voice caught her attention. "Don't."

"Don't what?" She asked, not meeting his eyes.

"Don't think it was for nothing."

Wasn't it, though? We're right back where we started.

The school bell rang, interrupting their conversation before Winter could respond, and with an awkward glance, the two students moved to walk inside together.

The halls of Clamare High were bustling with the activity of a normal Tuesday morning. Winter even had to duck behind Axel to avoid a hoard of footballers— firstly Lucas Lokken, followed by Daniel Gold, Matthew Thorne, and

Korin Cooley, who were all shouting, "LOKKEN! LOKKEN! LOKKEN!". The door of the Spanish classroom opened, and Mr. Montenegro popped his head out, clapping a hand on the door as he hollered after them, "Keep it down, boys! Ay, dios mio…"

The usual cliques could be spotted all around— the cheerleaders, still in their uniforms from morning practice, the music fans, like Ella Cohen with her violin case or Jezebel McLain bobbing his head with headphones on. Even the teachers were milling about— Winter could see Headmaster Alvarez standing at the end of the hall with Lupita, and Mr. Cooley walking by with Miss Popelin, a very welcome sight. Her French teacher gave her a smile as she passed. If she had any inkling of what had happened to her, Miss Popelin didn't show it.

"Everything is back to normal." Winter mentioned, avoiding her friend's piercing gaze.

Axel let out a soft hum of agreement, before commenting, "As normal as it gets in Caligo."

Letting out a soft laugh, Winter was about to agree with him, until her eyes caught on a familiar person. She smiled, stopping dead.

"Winter?" Axel had taken notice, his eyes following her gaze until they too, landed on who had caught her attention.

Right there, leaning on Axel's locker, was Jovanni Brooks. He looked the same as he always did, dressed head to toe in baggy black clothing, occult symbolism all over, from the print on his shirt to the jewelry he was covered in. He had headphones on, head tipped forward so his long hair curtained his face, tapping one steel-toed boot against the ground.

"I think he's waiting for you." Winter murmured. When Axel gave the slightest, almost imperceptible nod of his head, she continued, "You know— your friend?"

"Yeah... Friend." Axel snorted. "Since when did I get so many friends?"

The question made her want to laugh. Instead, her eyes were fixed on Jovanni, who hadn't noticed them yet.

"He wasn't a Bleary victim... Do you think he'll do it again?"

"Yep." Axel didn't hesitate.

"You think we could stop him?"

"I don't know. That much pain... it'd be cruel to stop him." She wondered if he meant that. But Axel continued, "But he's alive now. You brought back the dead, Win. That's a start. I don't know the answers to depression, but..."

"But you're going to go hang out with him, right?"

Axel smiled, and his answer was to walk away from her. She watched him reach Jovi, the two dark haired goths greeting each other with cool nods and that weird hand-shake thing that guys always did in place of hugs. If Winter had one reason not to regret Bleary, it was that. A second chance.

The day continued on in a hazy blur, as Winter and Axel carried on in their normal routine. It was surreal to see everything back in place, everyone who had been lost returned to their normal lives. All day, Winter's mind raced, going over and over it in her mind. She had so many questions, so many things she wanted to talk about, but every class she sat in, looking over at Axel, she couldn't help but think: *What good would it do, to bring it up again? Maybe it would be better to just... pretend it had never happened?*

As the end of the day came along, Winter stood at her locker, putting away her red notebook— with all its drawings of Axel and Bleary— when she became aware of black boots in her peripheral vision, patiently waiting.

"Winter." Axel's voice hummed her name. This time, when she closed her locker, his eyes were his own and not the piercing, bold eyes of that monster.

I won't make that mistake again... I'd recognize these eyes anywhere. she thought idly, offering up a smile.

"Axel. Heading home?" She asked, leaning on her locker as he smiled back at her.

"Not yet." He answered shortly, shuffling his feet. A moment of uneasy silence came from him, but Winter waited, and after a second, "Will you come with me, first? So we can talk about... everything?"

If he felt like he needed to convince her, he was wrong. Winter immediately nodded, reaching for his hand. Lacing their fingers together, she answered,

"Lead the way."

Axel knew where he wanted to talk— and he was sure Winter did too, as they climbed the stairs up to the roof. The last time he was here, he'd watched Jovanni jump. It probably should have bothered him to be back, but Jovi was alive and well, and it was just a roof. A place he hung out often. Quiet, and away from the rest of the school, very few people chose to come out here, except maybe other outcasts like Jovanni.

Winter released his hand as he pushed open the door for them, walking past so she could go to the ledge. Leaning against it, she looked out at the parking lot, where many of their classmates were streaming out of the school and heading home for the day. With a smile, she watched Bryce wandering across the parking lot with Ruby, arm looped around her shoulders. Axel wasn't a fan of stereotypical teenage romances— high school sweethearts and all that— but he liked to think his childhood friend's love story would work out. At least, it seemed to make Bryce happy.

"Unbelievable. I can't wrap my head around it. We saw everything destroyed. It was real, and now it's back to normal." Winter was the first one to talk, filling the silence as Axel stood beside her, gazing out at the parking lot just like she was. Continuing, Winter explained, "I talked to Delilah in music. I tried to see if she remembered anything strange, but she just laughed at me, like I was crazy. Said I was being weird and asked if I was on something. Ironic, right? She doesn't seem to remember any of it. Whatever happened to her just didn't happen."

"It happened." Axel finally broke his silence, "I can't forget it happened."

His voice was quiet, and he was expecting the frown Winter gave him. She couldn't read his expression, so she hesitantly added, "It's okay if you blame me for all this. I—"

It would have been yet another time where she said it was her fault, but Axel's hand reached over to lay on hers against the ledge, and she fell silent. After a second of gathering his thoughts, he spoke,

"I don't blame you. You had no more control over bringing it to life than I had control of it being in my head. If it's anyone's fault, it's mine. Bleary is my monster, and I... I'm the one who showed it to you." Guilt riddled his voice, he could hear it even though he tried to sound neutral and keep his cool.

Turning more towards him, there was a new tone to Winter's voice as well— a determined, steady tone; confident in her words. "You showed me because I asked. We're either both at fault, or neither of us are, in that case. I'm glad you showed me, Axel."

Winter pulled her hand from the fence and stepped into Axel's personal space. Her arms wrapped around his neck, pulling him to her in a hug, her head leaning into his. He tensed up, but it was only for a second before he relaxed and returned the hug. The last time they had hugged, the world was ending, and they were certain they wouldn't make it. Now, it was beyond comforting in a completely different way.

"Bleary was always real, Axel. Even before I brought it here. And I'm so, so sorry that I brought it here. But... wherever it is, you don't have to face it alone. That's all I ever wanted you to know. Maybe that's why I brought it here, because I wanted to be able to face it with you." Winter said softly, not letting go of him. They stood like that for what seemed like ages, Axel not responding— but she had to be used to the quiet by now.

It was true, after all. Having a friend— a dear friend— who had demons was hard. Not because it was negative or annoying as some people might say, no, Winter never thought that way. He knew her well enough to know she wasn't like that. Instead, it was because Axel dealt with it on his own. Bleary put that distance there, those walls, those whispers that he had to stay alone in the dark. He knew that whatever barriers he had up were partially his fault, and partially Bleary's, though it was hard to tell him and his monster apart— at least to Axel himself.

Winter hadn't meant for this, he knew that. She just wanted to make sure he wasn't fighting alone.

"...Thank you, Winter. Bleary will be back, but... fighting it here, that was more helpful than I thought it would be." Moments later, Axel pulled back from the hug first, gently unlacing Winter's arms from his neck.

"Oh, one question, though. Why does Kaya remember? Jovanni doesn't, neither does Oliver or Jae. I tried asking around, and they seem totally oblivious." Axel asked, studying Winter's face.

"My papa remembered, too." She admitted, shaking her head. "The only thing I can guess is that it's because they knew about it before. My papa, Kaya, and you— you're the ones who remember, and you're the ones who knew about my powers. Everyone else... It's like a bad dream, I guess, for them. Might be a small mercy. I wish I could forget."

A silence lapsed between them, Axel not sure how to take Winter's wish. It didn't sound entirely honest, and she had a far-away look in her eyes— reflecting back on everything that happened. There was more she hadn't told him yet, and part of him wanted to drill her for all the dark little details of what had just happened to them. But they had gone through enough. He could wait for his answers, resolving to question her more over their nightly phone calls.

Shaking his head, Axel broke the silence,

"I have something for you." He said, reaching into his pocket. When he pulled out a familiar black cord, with a dangling celtic pendant, Winter's mouth dropped open in shock. Her hand flew to her neck, which was bare, and had been for months.

"What... How did you find that?" She asked, grabbing and pulling it over her head, her fingers turning the pendant around.

"That night we weren't talking, when you went after Bleary alone, it was in the hall, on the floor. It's how I knew you were in trouble. I figured it had to take something real nasty to pry that from your neck, so... I held onto it for you." Axel explained. He was playing it off as something simple, which they both knew that the truth was that he had fixed it himself, got a new cord for it and everything.

Winter toyed with her pendant, cheeks burning as she smiled at him, "Thanks, Axe. Really."

"Thank me by never bringing monsters to life again." He joked weakly in response.

That seemed to upset Winter, her smile instantly dropping. "About that... I can't, I don't think."

Turning around, Winter moved to sit on the floor of the roof, her back to the ledge. Hugging her knees to her chest, she watched as Axel sunk down beside her.

"What do you mean?" He asked, a little worried by how Winter was acting. She looked uneasy.

"I... I've tried making things a few times today. Willing things to be there. I know I never exactly knew how it worked, but this time, I really can't do it. Nothing happens. Not even something as simple as a pencil." Winter answered at last, sighing.

"...Do you think it's permanently gone?" Axel asked.

"No clue." Winter answered dully. Swallowing, she asked, "Do you hope it's not? I know it made me interesting, to have a power. Guess I'll be a little less exciting to have around now."

"Winter." It was the way he said her name that made her look up, where she found Axel staring at her with a fierce expression on his face, as if he were angry with her for even saying it. Maybe because he was. "It was never the powers that made you interesting. That's not why I talk to you. Don't think that way, ever."

That was what she needed to hear, the difference between Bleary's harsh words and Axel's real ones. It made every insecurity melt, lighting up a confidence that Bleary had driven away.

Winter smiled, giving a soft nod, and said, "You know how I know you're not Bleary?"

"How?" Axel asked, knowing she would tell him anyway.

"Your words are real. Bleary's never are."

They hung out on the roof until the sun set. Winter almost felt like they should have talked more about Bleary, but they didn't. Instead, they talked about anything but, until Axel spoke up, "Let me walk you home?"

The two set off, heading down and out of the school and to the main road, taking the long way. Winter walked along the edge of the curb, holding one of Axel's hands for balance.

"Why is it you always walk me home? I never get to walk you home." She teased.

Axel pulled a face, "We live across the street from each other."

"Yeah, but I could be the one walking you. Is it a gender thing? Boy walks girl home?" Winter was clearly joking with him, tugging on his hand and earning a snort.

"No."

"Not even a little? You've been saving me an awful lot, you know. Maybe you're just really chivalrous."

That earned a genuine laugh. "Maybe I wouldn't need to keep saving you if you didn't keep putting yourself in harm's way."

Giving him a sideways smile, Winter moved to walk closer to him until their hands were swinging between them, shoulders brushing.

"Maybe I just make too good a damsel in distress to pass up saving." She hummed.

"Sure." He confirmed instead of giving a full answer, looking ahead with a smile. That was how he spotted them. "Isn't that your group of dorks?"

She followed his gaze. Walking not far in front of them was a group of her friends; Kaya, Matthew, Knieka, Oliver, Grace… They all lived near Axel and Winter, heading in the same direction. Before she met Axel, she might have walked with them. Now, she hesitated. Her friends were not Axel's friends. He wasn't comfortable with them, he wasn't—

"Should we join them?" His words startled her, turning to give him a confused look.

"Should we?" She asked. *You would rather we didn't, don't you?*

"I don't mind, if you want to."

Liar. Was her first thought, but he reached out to take her hand, further showing he was willing. She didn't think Axel was a changed person— Bleary still there, behind his eyes, but something *was* different. He had friends. He had her.

His words about Jovi echoed in her head.

That's a start.

Winter didn't know if her powers would ever return, or if they were gone for good, but either way, she had made a friend for life, a person of shared trauma. What they had was unconditional, and if Bleary ever reared its ugly face again Winter and Axel would be ready to fight. She was certain of it, and she knew he was too. They were in this together.

"Hey, guys!" Winter called out, lifting her loose hand to wave, her friends looking back at them.

"Winter!" They all seemed to chorus her name, and then calls of, "Dunn!" and "Axel!" came when they saw who she was with.

Winter broke into a jog to catch up as they stopped, tugging Axel along by the hand, however even when they joined the group of high school students, she didn't let go.

At least, not so long as Axel let her hold on.

EPILOGUE

"Axel, I'm off to the store. Try not to destroy the house while I'm gone, hm?" His mother's condescending laugh echoed off the walls, shaking her head to herself as she stepped out the front door. It closed with a click, and Axel, staring at it from where he stood on the stairs, audibly sighed.

What does she expect me to do? Summon a monster that kills people and destroys the high school? Axel thought, shaking his head.

It was a strange twist of fate, to go back to normal daily life after months of dealing with Bleary. Trudging the rest of the way down the stairs, Axel made his way into the living room, wandering over to his piano. As far as he or Winter could tell, Bleary had simply never been created. Although, they both knew better.

Even so, ever since banishing the monster, something felt lighter. Axel knew it wasn't gone— his problems had not miraculously banished, but the sense of accomplishment from winning a battle was keeping it away. For now, at least.

Letting his hands drift across piano keys, Axel let himself be lost in the soft melody of Traumerei.

Maybe I should invite Winter over... She loves this song. He thought, focusing on each key. Something about it was making him sleepy, and the more he played, the heavier his eyelids got. Eventually, his hands began to stumble, and Axel got up to move over to the couch, laying back with a groan.

He should have known something was wrong when sleep came easily.

"Winter?" She was walking in front of him, holding one of his hands behind her and pulling him along. He couldn't see her face, but she wore a pale yellow sundress, and her hair was loose and wavy. He could smell her shampoo vividly, the scent of papaya and warmth, and he could hear her humming the tune of Traumerei. "Where are you taking me?"

She didn't answer him. Down a long hall they went, for what felt like ages until they came to a locked door. Winter waved her hand at the handle, but nothing happened, and she tilted her head down, stepping aside.

"Try it." She mumbled to him, nodding towards the door.

"Me?" Axel asked, confused.

"It'll work for you now." She sounded so certain, though she still wouldn't look at him.

Frowning, Axel reached out for the handle. As soon as he touched his hand to the cold metal, he felt a familiar magnetic pull against his palm. Impossible, he thought, it was a feeling he had only sensed from Winter's magic, but instead, it came from him, and the door popped open with ease.

"What...?" Questions were at the tip of his tongue, but Winter stepped past him, into the room, and he found himself following.

Inside, there was nothing, except for in one corner. There was a tall, antique-looking standing mirror. It was adorned at the top with intricate horned-shaped pieces, and was unlike anything Axel had ever seen. At a distance, the glass didn't reflect anything but black depths, but as he stepped before it, the monster stared back.

Bleary towered over him with that gaping mouth and soulless eyes. Fog gathered at the base of the mirror and its robes were fluttering. Axel jumped, trying to back away, but his feet wouldn't move.

"Don't worry. It can't hurt you now. Go on, confront it. We're safe." Winter told him.

Uncertain, Axel stared up at his monster. Winter had to be right, he was staring into its eyes, and nothing was happening.

Reaching out, his right hand traced the glass. When he felt the little vibration against his palm, his eyes widened as he heard his double chuckling.

"Bringing me back already?"

"NO!" Axel yelled, face contorting in anger. He watched as Bleary's long fingers curled along the sides of the mirror, like it was pulling itself out of a bed of water.

Axel wasn't about to let him drag his way out, so he threw his fist forward, hitting into the glass and watching the surface ripple at his touch, shattering in front of him. As the shards fell, so did blood: thick, red blood dripping down his fist as he glared at his monster's reflection. Sometime during the chaotic panic of the moment, Winter had thrown herself forward and wrapped her arms around his waist, pressing into his back and holding him steady.

Making that terrible, ear-splitting shriek, Bleary retracted its hands back into the mirror, and the surface turned black again. Winter had tucked her head into his shoulder to avoid the glass, but when she looked up, she uncurled her arms from around his waist and sighed in relief.

"See? You have the power now, Axel. It can't hurt you anymore."

"What do you mean, I have the power? Win, I don't understand."

"You will."

Her voice echoed in his head, vivid in his memory as his eyes flashed open. Back in his living room, Axel took a deep breath and ran a hand down his face.

"Just a damn dream..." He grumbled, moving to roll off the couch.

Instead of his feet touching the ground, he fell a good eight feet, slamming into the hardwood of his living room. Air knocked out of him, Axel wheezed, scrambling to roll over and look upwards.

Floating above him was his couch... and coffee table, bookshelf, desk, even his piano. Every piece of furniture was several feet off the ground, bumping along the ceiling. His mouth gaped open in awe, frozen against the ground.

You have the power now, Axel.

Could it be? Gulping down some air, Axel raised his hand above him. Winter always made this look so easy, and he had no clue what he was doing, but he knew the familiar buzz of energy against his palm.

Slowly, Axel led the furniture back to the ground with a slow wave of his hand. His living room returned to normal as he sat on the floor. Even with everything back in place, Axel was left with more questions than answers, but he knew one thing for sure.

He couldn't tell Winter about this.

ACKNOWLEDGMENTS

Dear Readers,

Thank you for reading and— hopefully— enjoying Bleary Eyes. Before you set this book down and get on with your day, I would like to say a few words, and give thanks where it's due. First, for the many, then for the few.The astute among you will see the running theme of this novel for what it is, but only a handful will truly understand it, and it is for those few that I wrote this novel.

"Bleary Eyes" is for the people in this world who have faked a smile, because they didn't want to be seen as a downer. It's for the people who are constantly juggling, who know if one thing falls, they all fall, so they keep juggling. This novel is for the people who try to voice their problems — only to have them dismissed. It's for the people who know the opinions of others, and feel like they can't speak their own. I wrote this novel for the Axels of the world, who close the door at the end of the day, and take actions they regret in the morning.

It is also for the Winters. For the ones who have friends they can't protect. For the ones who know what it's like to have someone you talk to daily suddenly disappear, and you know what happened to them, because you know their struggles. It's for the friends, who feel helpless that they can't fight another's monster.

This book is for anyone who has ever lost a friend. A father. A mother. A sibling, cousin, classmate— to the invisible demon known as Depression. It's for anyone who has seen the scars, and watched a void rip into the world when a life is taken. It's for anyone left behind, who wonders what they could have done, and for those tempted to follow, wondering if they'd be missed.

It is for the people who struggle with the very real and traumatic issues of: Depression, Anxiety, suicidal thought, cutting, choking, Diabetes, eating disorders, gun violence, and all others not mentioned here.

I am fortunate for the people I have in my life. I am a Winter with my own Axel, and Kaya. With my own Bryce, Oliver, Jae-Hwa, Delilah, Jovanni, and Sophie.

Depression is a complex monster. Sometimes, it's obvious, but it's worse when it's not. When the person that is so good at hiding it finally loses their battle, that's when you know it's not something you can face, like Axel and Winter got to do. It's a "Why?" that doesn't have a good answer. It's an ugly, personal, illness that everyone has seen, but no one wants to face. It leaves those who struggle unable to see a good outcome.

I have so many people to acknowledge, so many people to thank, but none so much as the people who can read this novel with empathy and understanding.

For the people willing to face their Bleary, and the people standing beside them, willing to see it with clear eyes. This novel is for you.

Thank you.

~

For more personal acknowledgements beyond those in the dedication, they are as follows.

To Xenøn Light, thank you for sharing your incredible mind with me while I wrote this novel. Thank you, for being the reason why I managed to write it, and for starting me off on a path with purpose. Thank you, for fighting. Thank you, for being my partner on Bleary Eyes and one of my closest confidants and dearest friends.

To Joleen Jones, thank you for getting me through this novel. For those other than Joleen reading this— this incredible woman spent long nights helping me input my manual, written down edits, into a document. She slaved over my manuscript when I had a deadline and too little time. Not only that, but there were a good number of times this manuscript made me burst into tears, being a little too personal to my heart, and she got me through them. She's my Tabitha King, rescuing my manuscript when I wanted to give up. Joleen, if you ever say, "I don't know how to help," know that you did. Thank you. Bleary Eyes would not have been published without you.

To Marci Smith, thank you for being the first person to read the first draft of Bleary Eyes in its entirety. Thank you, for being my first reader, my first reviewer, and one of my biggest fans. Your support means so much to me.

To Aditya Modak, thank you for being one of my inspirations and role-models in the world of young people writing their first novel. Thank you, also, for being patient enough with me to know that if I don't message for weeks on end, it was because of this monster of a novel.

To Andrea Dalla Bona, BountyIllustrations, Makhiyo Trish Sy, Miha Brumec, Karmen Wells, Yash Sharma— thank you all for your artistic contributions to Bleary Eyes, and for being a huge support every step of the way. I am a new author and you've all managed to treat me gently and not judge me too hard for my inexperience.

And finally;

To Katherine and Barbara McLean, Knieka Hodgson, Jamie Wijntjes, Eddie Flores, Devin Ellison, Brett Tourscher, and several other scores of family, friends, and Facebook friends. In the last two years, you have all been a huge source of support. Bleary Eyes was bolstered by your encouraging words, your attempts to give me space and time, and your excitement for the novel itself. Thank you for helping me not give up.

ABOUT THE AUTHOR

Summer Rain is a twenty-three-year-old author and resident of Las Vegas, Nevada where she finds enjoyment in exploring the city and its adventures as well as staying at home with her four cats, family, and fiance. In her free time she enjoys baking, swimming, and cuddling up with a good book.

Summer is a devoted ally to Mental Health awareness, a theme you can commonly find in her writing. Having witnessed the struggles of many around her with mental illnesses, she wishes to make an impact on those who might be struggling with the same things.

Summer is currently attending The College of Southern Nevada in pursuit of her Associate's Degree in English.

Due to her desire to support those who struggle with mental health, Summer Rain is donating 10% of the first year sales of Bleary Eyes to the AFSP (The American Foundation for Suicide Prevention.)

Newsletter

Join Summer Rain's website for updates, infrequent journal entries, updates on her latest writing endeavors, and her newsletter!

Join Summer Rain's Bookstagram for book reviews, book blog posts, and day-to-day updates on her life!

MORE TO READ

AN EXCERPT FROM THE NEXT NOVEL IN THE WORLD OF BLEARY EYES:

DEMISE SIDE STORIES

Kaya almost fell forward— thankfully catching herself as she gazed down at the gap between her hanging cage and the pathway. There was a sheer drop and some kind of inky-black water below. Kaya didn't want to find out what it was.

Taking a breath, she backed up a bit and then jogged forward to jump, landing neatly on the platform.

Thank you, kindergarten gymnastics, she thought, a surge of triumph hitting her.

Now that she was on the path, it was like a mist had been lifted from around the cages. She could see into them, and a heavy sense of horror slammed into her when she realized she recognized those within.

"B-Bryce?" Kaya's voice cracked, looking up at the once-strong jock. He was sitting in the front of his cage on his

knees, hands weakly gripping the bars. His tan skin had
turned ashen, and he looked malnourished. His cheeks and
eye sockets were sunken in and his skin stretched taut across
his skull. His once bright green eyes were faded, appearing
almost gray in the dark.

*He died. He killed himself. Oh my God, is this the afterlife? Am
I dead?* Hazy memories broke through, flickering images of a
blade crossing her wrists. Glancing down at herself, she saw
no visible injuries, but... *What if this is limbo? What if this is
hell? It sure as hell isn't heaven.*

"Bryce, hang on." Kaya urged the silent jock. He seemed
to follow her with his eyes, but otherwise didn't move. His
cage had the same padlock hers did, but unlike hers, it was
solid and locked. Tugging on it, it showed no signs of easily
dropping away. Looking at the boy, who watched her with
that dull, hopeless gaze, Kaya frowned and murmured, "I'll
come back. I'll get you out of here, okay? I promise."

"I know, Ruby... I know. I'll do better." He answered in a
shaking, near-tears voice, his lower lip quivering. A chill
went through Kaya, standing frozen for a moment.

What are you seeing? She wondered. She waved a hand in
front of him, and his eyes followed the movement, but she
knew that Bryce was looking right through her.

Having no choice but to leave him, Kaya kept going down
the path. She saw a girl with dark skin in a cheerleader's
uniform, curled up on her side on the floor of her cage, her
back to Kaya. Though she couldn't tell for sure, the name
'Delilah' ran through her mind and she was sure that was
exactly who it was. She also walked by Miss Popelin, who
had a deliriously happy smile on her pale face. Her long
blonde hair was loose for once, cascading down her
shoulders.

As she walked past, Miss Popelin grabbed the bars to her
cage and began to cry out a string of French words, loud and

frantic. Her smile never left her face as she broke into a sob, dropping to her knees.

"I-I'm sorry! I don't understand. I'll come back, I promise!" Kaya called to her, forcing herself to keep moving, away from her disheveled teacher.

She counted five cages in total that had people she knew and recognized. The worst cage was the sixth, however. There was blood all over it, and a lone tire, but no one inhabited it. Something about that one made her stomach curl.

The path felt endless, even with so few cages. But it did eventually end, with one last cage. As she approached it, however, Kaya was aware of one slight difference.

This cage had no padlock. When she reached it, she grabbed onto the bars, only to realize there was no door at all. It was a solid cage, no way in or out— a perfect prison.

Peering past the bars, her heart leapt into her throat.

"Axel!"

Axel Dunn sat in the very back of his cage, against some of the bars, legs crisscrossed and wearing a ratty pair of black jeans and his usual hoodie, along with a pair of black boots on his feet. The light from the path glinted off his lip ring, earrings, and a pendant in the shape of a lightbulb that hung from his neck, one that Kaya couldn't recall him wearing before. His appearance was somewhat off, in more ways than just his new jewelry. Like Bryce, he seemed malnourished and thin. Exhaustion covered his face in a thin veil, wary and withdrawn. Usually bright blue eyes had turned faded and dull, staring back at Kaya. His curly black hair fell into his face, unkempt. What was obvious was that he was wounded: he had a jagged cut on his forehead, and even in the dim light, Kaya spotted dark stains on his hoodie's sleeves. Blood, coming from his arms.

Again, the images of her night at the Halloween dance

popped into her head— the feeling of the blade, the sway of the ropes, the—

Oh, no. No, that wasn't real. Don't think of that. Her thoughts made her unsteady on her feet, swaying uneasily and clinging to the cage so that she wouldn't fall through the crack into the black river below.

"Kaya." His voice startled her back to the present, sucking in a deep breath as her eyes met his. "What are you doing here? You shouldn't be here."

"Neither should you. Where's Winter? Where are we?" Kaya questioned him.

"Winter… Winter is…" His eyes grew distant, and then he shook his head. "You should leave."

"Not without you!" Kaya remarked, not failing to notice he didn't answer either of her questions. "Come on, there has to be a way to bend these, or break them, or—"

"There's not." Axel interrupted her, moving to stand on his feet. He stumbled as he did so, using the bars to steady himself. He moved towards her with slow, shuffling steps. "I'm meant to be here. You're not."

"What do you mean?" Kaya wasn't getting it, the intensity of his gaze making her shrink back a little.

With his gaze drilling into her, Axel answered,

"I'm always a prisoner here. This is where I reside, permanently."

What the hell kind of gibberish—

"Don't be stupid!" Kaya snapped at him, going back to her feeble attempts of yanking on the bars. "We're going to leave, before that hideous *thing* comes back."

"That hideous thing is me." Axel said simply, in a way that made her heart skip a beat. He paused, and then added as an afterthought, "Part of me, anyway."

The two stared at each other for a moment before Kaya

decided her course of action: Not to listen or believe his bull-shit. In her mind, Axel was currently being an idiot.

"If Winter was here, she'd slap you."

That earned half a smile, albeit a little sad.

"Probably."

"Are you going to help me or not?" Kaya asked, gritting her teeth as she tried to wedge herself between the bars, hoping to brute-force them into bending.

"Not."

"Jesus. Thanks, Dunn."

"It's no use." Axel deadpanned.

Glaring at him, Kaya retorted,

"Where's your sense of rebellion? Don't be such a—"

At that moment, Kaya heard a scream in the distance.

A cacophony of sounds filled the long prison hall. Turning, she watched as a blinding white figure appeared. It looked like a girl made of pure light, burning like a lightbulb in her vision.

Winter.